MW00637301

THE SEVENTH FLOOR

Also by David McCloskey

Moscow X

Damascus Station

THE SEVENTH FLOOR

A NOVEL

DAVID McCLOSKEY

W. W. NORTON & COMPANY
Independent Publishers Since 1923

Printed in the United States of America
First Edition

For information about special discounts for bulk purchases, please contact W. W. Norton Special Sales at specialsales@wwnorton.com or 800-233-4830

Manufacturing by Lakeside Book Company
Production manager: Devon Zahn

ISBN 978-1-324-08668-0

W. W. Norton & Company, Inc., 500 Fifth Avenue, New York, N.Y. 10110
www.wwnorton.com

W. W. Norton & Company Ltd., 15 Carlisle Street, London W1D 3BS

10 9 8 7 6 5 4 3 2 1

Again for Abby, my love
And for Miles, Leo, and Mabel

The building doesn't love you back.

—CIA proverb

PART I

BREACH

1

MOSCOW
PRESENT DAY

THE RUSSIAN'S SUICIDE PEN, A MONTBLANC, WAS UPSTAIRS. Should have kept it down here, he scolded himself, even with Alyona around. If he was right about these cars, there was precious little time. He slid shut the drawer on his office desk and gently tipped Alyona from his knee.

"Up," she insisted. "Up, up, up."

Her hands were extended, fingers flapping into palms, but he was distracted by the monitors. Alyona mashed her face into his thigh with a squeal, imprinting his pant leg with sticky red stains. He looked down in panic, only to realize the stains were strawberry jam, which he himself had slathered on her breakfast toast. Normally this would have made him furious. Not now. He tickled her belly, and she laughed so hard she curled up around his feet in giggles. "Go find your mother, my sweet," he said warmly, yet with firm undertones Alyona could not miss. The toddler scampered off, running too fast, as always, nearly catching her head on the doorframe on the way out. He heard her dash out toward the kitchen, where a teakettle had begun whistling.

Back to the camera feeds: The two black cars had come to a stop in the drive. No government plates, but he knew. On the lead car he saw the telltale triangle of dirt smeared on the top right corner of the rear passenger window. The brushes at the Lubyanka's motor pool car wash did not reach that spot.

The Russian did not once consider going with them; he'd made up his mind on the matter long ago. But why had they given him this choice? They should have a rope in my mouth by now, he thought. His arms should be pinned to his sides, shirt and pants off, rough hands searching the lapel and pockets. And yet . . .

He stared at the jam Alyona had deposited on his pants leg. He dredged his finger through it and brought a sickly sweet dollop to his tongue.

Ten a.m. A slow Saturday morning at his dacha. He'd missed his ritual morning walk because he and Vera had stayed up too late, drunk too much, and, consequently, slept too late. The men outside were growing impatient since he hadn't come out, he sensed. They'd driven up to the house along the drive tracing his normal path into the woods, their cigarette smoke seeping through cracked-open windows. For a few seconds the Russian watched the cars idling outside, trying to read the energy. And what he felt, he did not like.

"Vera," he called. "I have visitors. Take Alyona into the garden to pick strawberries. We might have some with lunch."

Vera appeared in the office doorway, her gaze settling immediately on the screens. "Is this about Athens?" she said, an edge in her voice, as Alyona tumbled in behind her. "Because it would be decent of them to finally explain why they asked you to come home so quickly."

"I don't know. Take Alyona outside," he commanded.

"We'd just had Alyona all set in her school, and—"

"Outside," he snapped. On the screens, five men had emerged from the cars. She looked at him worriedly. With a small sigh, he stood up and shooed her out with a peck on the cheek, whispering, "I'll come get you when they're gone." Then he picked up Alyona and swung her around and buried his face in her sweet hair, all thick and lustrous again after the treatments, and he remembered why he had done what he had done. He took one more long sniff and kissed her head. He had no regrets. He'd make the trade again. He'd make the trade a thousand times.

He set her down. "I love you, my *klubnichka*," he said.

"I'm not a strawberry, Papa!" She giggled, wagging her finger at him with a riotous smile.

Alyona followed her mother through the kitchen and outside into the garden. His lip quivered at the slam of the door. Alyona could not shut doors any other way.

The first knocks hit the front door. He flung open the lower drawer of the office desk. Ripping out the false bottom, he found the large envelope stuffed with smaller ones. One envelope held a letter for Vera. It was a formality, loveless, but kind, even generous, he'd like to think. Twenty envelopes were addressed to Alyona, bound together with a rubber band and labeled with a note bearing the following instructions: *She is to open one on each birthday from her fourth through her eighteenth, and then when she turns twenty, thirty, forty, fifty, and sixty.* Another envelope bore the name of his grown son and contained a letter written with as much love as his disappointment could manage. Hidden inside the folds of that letter was another, smaller envelope addressed to an apartment in Athens and affixed with an abundance of postage. *Please drop the other letter in the mail for me*, he had scrawled in a postscript to his son.

The knocks, which had grown louder as he reviewed the letters, now stopped. On the monitors he saw one of the men start working on the lock.

In the bathroom, the Russian jimmied the collection into Vera's makeup bag. In his panic he worried the letters would be discovered in the inevitable and painstaking search to come. Why had he not seen to sewing them into Alyona's clothing—perhaps a jacket—as he knew he should? But time was up: the front door squeaked open as he huffed upstairs to the spare bedroom. He sat at the old dusty desk, listened to the footfalls in the foyer, the hushed murmurs, the sounds of men padding up the stairs. For a fluttering moment he wondered how he'd been made. He could not know. He doubted the Americans ever would.

The Russian threw open the desk drawer. Picked up the Montblanc. "My daughter is here, you animals," he bellowed in the direction of the stairs. "For god's sake."

A young heavy, his hair shaved close on the sides like a punk idiot, burst into the room. A second man followed close behind. Their eyes widened at the sight of the pen.

"Shame on you boys," he said. Slipping the pen into his mouth, the Russian bit down into the barrel, sinking his teeth into the cyanide capsule snuggled inside. He heard Jack's words, from long-ago Bogota: Three breaths, my friend, cup your hands over your face.

He did, taking the air in gulps: One, two. On the third they were over the desk and on him, crashing into the wall, cursing, shouting, grasping. Rolling him over, one of the men unfastened the Montblanc from his mouth. The Russian was already dead.

2

SINGAPORE

IN THE MOMENT, SAM JOSEPH DID NOT DWELL ON THE awful significance of Golikov's words, the blood that was sure to be spilled, the lives that would soon be wrecked on their account. That was all for later.

He first had to memorize them. And his recall had to be perfect, precisely as the message had crossed Golikov's lips. Sam was using his childhood bedroom as a memory palace, stashing each word, in order, into different colorful storage bins, the ones under the bed where he'd kept the Lego. But to commit the message to memory, he had to be certain he'd heard it. And even though Golikov was seated next to him at the baccarat table, he was having one hell of a time with that.

The two subminiature strontium-powered mics had—shocker—performed beautifully at Langley, only to malfunction upon arrival in Singapore. So he had no backup. The analyst's profile on Golikov had indicated that he spoke English fluently. Not true. He'd been forced into a meet on a casino floor, the type of camera-clotted surveillance environment that was precisely the opposite of where you'd like to meet a Russian. And the casino floor plans used to choreograph this bren—a brief encounter—had specified that the high-limit baccarat rooms were tucked well off the casino floor, and were therefore, in the estimation of the cable he'd written, *all but certain to be appropriately quiet.* Also false. Wildly, maddeningly false. A bank of high-limit slots just off the bacc room was jangling with the subtlety of a suit of armor pitched down the stairs. And it was Friday, two a.m., at the Sands: the tables were cheek to cheek. This was the emulsifying, brain-swirling din favored by the casinos, and, because he considered casinos to be something of a second home, by Sam Joseph himself. At least when he was gaming on his own dime. But now the racket was endangering his op, to say nothing of the cameras, and there was precious little margin to exploit.

He asked Golikov to say it once more. This time the Russian's tone was still abraded with the texture of sandpaper and broken glass, but the gruff English had thankfully slowed to an annoyed crawl. Sam smiled, as if the Russian had shared a joke, and then leaned away from Golikov to bank the message while examining his cards. He had ten thousand dollars of taxpayer money in the pot. On this matter, the warnings from DO Finance had been stern, if ultimately toothless: He was required to pay attention, and instructed to lose as little money as possible. Under the lip of the table, Sam's left hand placed his key card, labeled with his room number, in the Russian's lap. At the same moment his right hand tossed his cards to the dealer and he whispered: "Two hours."

He wouldn't have executed the pass if he'd thought he'd been made; but for a flickering moment, as the Russian deposited the card in his pocket, uncertainty overtook Sam, and he wondered if someone was watching.

Golikov bet player on the hand, and lost. He bent his cards and flung them across the felt lawn of the table and tossed back two healthy fingers of scotch. "Enough," he said, his hand slicing the air. "Done."

He tipped the dealer, patted his hands on the table, and stood. With friendly nods and good-luck wishes to Sam and the other players, he stalked off. Sam caught Golikov's eyes bouncing around the room. Appropriately afraid, Sam thought. Mark in his favor. Only the worst mental cases—the sociopaths and megalomaniacs—didn't sweat the treason.

Baccarat was not Sam's game: it was all superstition, no skill. He'd already lost fifty thousand dollars of U.S. taxpayer money in sixteen minutes. The next few hands would put his remaining twenty thousand in play. In that instant, he was far more concerned with the Finance paperwork than he was with the implications of what Boris Golikov had just shared.

Over the next ten minutes Sam worked himself back up the hole: down a mere thirty thousand dollars. Then, with a stingy tip to the dealer, one he could justify operationally to the nags in Finance, he took his leave. He exited the high-limit room onto the main casino floor, an expansive atrium swelling with tables overhung by soaring gold sculptures, and humming with energy.

Sam scanned for obvious heavies or any compatriots from the Russian's trade delegation, but it was so damn busy it was impossible to know if the opposition had him or Golikov made. And he didn't think there was a way to change that. He bought a coffee and strolled through the casino. He made a few stops: bathroom, blackjack table for a few hands, one of the bars.

Nothing amiss—he was feeling good, despite what the Russian had told him. That still hadn't sunk in, and, further, Sam was operational, ticking through a tightly scripted plan built with two goals in mind: Protect the agent, and collect the intel. Analyzing the intel was someone else's job, and his mind was already overcrowded, running hot. There was space only for the air pressure of the moment, and what it meant for the weather of the op. Gin and tonic in hand—untouched—he went upstairs to his room, where he pitched the drink into the sink. The room service tray went into the hall; DO NOT DISTURB sign on the knob; a napkin tucked under the door. In the brief seconds of indirect discussion they'd managed at the tables, Sam had proposed this as the safety signal. All clear. He shut the door, careful to keep the napkin in place, peeking out.

From a compartment hidden in the side of his suitcase, he removed a thin pouch lined with a material that resembled aluminum foil. Unzipping it, he thumbed the cash and set the pouch on the cabinet near the television. One hundred thousand dollars: the down payment authorized if the Russian's information was gold. Wellspring of another war with Finance. On the coffee table he arranged a bottle of Russian Standard, two glasses, and a spread: olives, nuts, chips, popcorn. He tossed the pens and notebooks into the desk drawer. No notes during the session, CIA had decided. Might put Golikov over the edge. And if the Russian's trying to sell us what I suspect, the Chief had said, guy's gonna be pretty spooked already.

Sam settled in to wait, and he was bad at waiting. He knew it, and so had the Performance Review Board, though they'd written it up using slightly different words (*struggles with impulse control*). His foot was tapping the carpet at a solid clip. He had nearly picked the popcorn bowl clean, then he had finished it, setting the bowl in the closet, out of sight, to avoid the appearance that he'd started the meal before his guest. He took up a sentry position at the desk, where the food was well out of reach.

AN HOUR LATER SAM STOOD UPRIGHT AT THE CLICK OF THE key card and the clack of the handle. Two men he did not recognize entered the room. They wore suits. Their eyes darted around, searching for threats: other people, weapons, items he might turn into weapons. They moved fluidly, like men who entered other people's rooms with some regularity. Sam had edged back toward the desk, with its lampstand made of marble.

"Get out of my room," Sam said, with another half step toward the lamp.

"You are Samuel Joseph," the blond-haired one said in heavily accented English.

Not a question. But it answered Sam's: They were Russians. He considered which man to start with. Both were about the same height and build. He scanned both sets of eyes, looking for weakness, and decided: the one with dark hair.

But the dark-haired man drew a pistol fitted with a suppressor and pointed it at Sam. "You move, I kill you. I no hesitate. Sit down, Samuel Joseph."

Sam did, heart in his throat. They had doubtless used the room key he'd passed the Russian at the table. If they'd made Golikov, what did they need with him?

"Much vodka for one," said the blond-haired guy, lifting the full bottle of Standard to nail the point. "For one American, I think too much." He eased into the chair across from Sam. Still standing, the dark-haired guy moved behind him. He heard the zipper of his suitcase. The heaping of clothes and shoes across the floor.

"Drinking problem," Sam said, twisting his neck for a look at what the guy was doing. He was greeted by the unfriendly end of the dark-haired guy's pistol, which jerked: *Turn around.*

The blond-haired guy snapped his fingers. "You look here. Otherwise, mess you up."

"I think you're in the wrong room," Sam said.

"Why you talk to Boris Golikov?" The second whir of a zipper meant the one with dark hair had found the money pouch. Sam watched Blondie's eyes widen slightly, then his hand beckoned for the cash, which he flopped on the table. "This for Boris?"

"This is a casino," Sam said. "It's for gambling. And who the hell is Boris?"

"What Boris say to you at tables?"

"Who is Boris?" Sam said.

"Look, we not patient guys," Blondie said. "You see us, you know. You work for CIA. Also we know this. And we know Boris wanna hava chat. Now, you sit by Boris tonight. We see this. And here's thing. We gotta know what he say. Gotta know. You tell us what he say, tell us full, and we walk out, clean and dandy." Here, hands were wiped together for emphasis. "But you play dumbass and we got some problems. Okay?"

"Boris is the Russian who was at my table?" Sam asked. "Guy who got cleaned out, that right? I've got no idea why you're in my room or who he is. Now get out."

"Samuel Joseph, now, don't play dumbass. Tell us now what Boris say to you."

"I don't know your Boris," Sam said.

Blondie glanced right through him, at his partner, and Sam knew the look—he'd seen it on agents, on security investigators, on players across a poker table. A man who'd made a call. Blondie picked up one of the snack bowls, lofting it toward the ceiling.

Humans tend to keep an eye on objects thrown into the air.

Watching the nuts spill across the floor as if in a trance, Sam sensed a flash of movement behind him. Felt a prick in his shoulder. Heat flooded his body and limbs. When the warmth reached his brain, his head began to feel quite heavy, as if his neck were unsuitable for support. Then Sam was slumping forward, crashing into the bottle of vodka.

3

LANGLEY, VIRGINIA

ARTEMIS APHRODITE PROCTER WAS SQUINTING INTO THE reflection of the rising sun shimmering orange across the surface of her beer. She slapped her card onto the bar with instructions to keep the tab open, collected her glass, and eased into her usual booth to wait for Theo. Procter was a regular at the Vienna Inn, but she was typically a night owl, and though she was also a well-known reprobate, this was her first time ordering booze during the breakfast rush, hand to God. Half the glass went down in the first gulp, the remainder at the jangle of Theo Monk pushing open the door. When her old friend reached the table, she hoisted her empty with a shake. "My tab's open."

Theo squinted into the glass and sniffed it with a wry smile. Returning with two, he wheezed into the booth, sliding one across to Procter. He thumbed the fabric on her rumpled tweed blazer, which she'd been wearing yesterday. "Walk of shame?"

"I wish. Left the office an hour ago."

Regarding the sunrise beers with disapproval, a waiter unknown to Procter deposited menus on the table. Without picking one up, Theo ordered toast, bacon, and eggs over easy. "I'm drinking my breakfast," Procter said, and shoved the menus to the table's edge.

"Still no word from Singapore?" Theo asked, after the waiter was out of earshot.

"Radio silence. Station's working their stringers at the Sands."

"Plenty of explanations."

"All bad."

Theo's silence signaled his agreement. He turned his gaze out the window and put back a good deal of his beer. She'd been drinking with Theo on and off and all around the world for about a quarter century. Drink made him a chameleon: chatty or silent, morose or joyful, kind or cruel—he might assume any combination or measure, and occasionally an anarchic blend of them all, during the same drinking session. The silence had become more pronounced in recent years. Their friendship extended back to their Farm days, and over twenty-five years they'd said most that needed saying—and an awful lot that didn't.

Theo's food arrived. He was dredging the bacon through runny yolks when Procter—empty in hand—stood, took two steps toward the bar, and stopped. She set down the glass and called for a coffee.

"Probably wise," Theo said, when she'd slid back into the booth, "not to be soused during your first briefing with the brand-spanking-new Director Finn Gosford and his Deputy Director for Operations, Deborah Sweet."

"I don't know, Theo," Procter said. "If I'm sober I might just tell the DDO how I feel, which is that it's un-fucking-believable, those two running the place. And what a hell of a first Russia briefing. I mean, they've been on the job, what, a week? A single week, and we've already got a dumpster fire."

"Doesn't take long to torch a dumpster, Artemis, you know that," he said, idly considering the blackened piece of bacon he was sluicing through the eggs.

"When was the last time you talked to either of them, anyway?" she asked.

He wiped a spot of yolk from the corner of his mouth and looked off into the middle distance, thinking about that. "Maybe six months after Afghanistan. Finn was a certified hero, of course. World was his."

"Hero," she muttered. "Fuck me."

"I've offered."

"You've tried," she snorted. "There's a difference." She looked longingly into her empty glass. "Last meaningful thing I said to either of them would've been just after Afghanistan, at the hospital in Landstuhl, when we were laid up. I didn't go to either retirement party."

"You weren't invited," Theo said, exacting his revenge. "There's a difference."

"Were you?"

"Of course not."

Procter sipped her coffee, while Theo put his toast to work as an egg mop. "Maybe Sam's on a bender," he offered, crust dangling from his lips. "Car accident. Ran off with a whore with a heart of gold. Stole the cash for his reptile fund. Coked up."

"You don't know Sam, and you're also a dumbass. He's lying low, dead, or being held by Russians. Odds on lying low drop with each passing hour."

Theo took another bite of toast, changing the subject with a grimace and a nod. "Did the new occupants of the Seventh Floor get a brief on the Singapore op this week?" he asked. "It's been so busy I can't even remember if it was covered when they were up in New York."

"They got the gist of it. Maybe not all the details."

"Well, I'm sure they'll be understanding," Theo said, a smile beginning to crease his lips. "After all, Finn and Debs are our old chums."

For the first time in nearly two days, Procter cracked a weak smile. Theo slapped his napkin onto his cleaned plate. "Let's go. We should sync up with Mac and Gus before we jump into this meat grinder."

WHEN THEY ENTERED HIS FOURTH-FLOOR OFFICE, MAC Mason, the Chief of Operations in Russia House, was in the intelligence officer's most natural position: hunched over a computer, reading the cable traffic.

Mac had tan skin and big friendly ears and hair that'd been gray as long as they'd known him. Which was as long as Procter and Theo had known each other. He'd also been in their class at the Farm, and then in Afghanistan they'd killed and nearly gotten killed together. When he swiveled around in his chair she could see that he'd been sorely tempted to put his fist through the computer screen. Unlike Procter, Mac had apparently gone home for a few hours last night. She could tell because his white shirt was starchy even if his eyes betrayed his exhaustion.

Procter and Theo took up around his table, but Mac just stayed put, glancing, in a perturbed silence, between the computer and a painting of a prowling wolf on his wall.

"What's up?" Procter finally said.

At that moment, Gus Raptis, fresh from a cut-short tour as Chief of Station in Moscow, and another comrade from their Farm class, walked into the office. "You reading this?" he asked Mac, the tunnel of his stress apparently so dim that he did not acknowledge Procter or Theo.

"Goddamn mayhem," Mac growled.

"What the hell is going on?" Procter finally barked.

Gus turned to her, his face lit by confusion veering toward rage: "BUCCANEER is dead, that's what. Scrap of SIGINT in overnight. A fragment, admittedly, but we picked up a Kremlin flunkie telling a buddy that an SVR officer recently home from Athens killed himself during his arrest."

"In the intercept," Mac said, swiveling to his computer to read the cable, "the flunkie says rumors were floating around that BUCCANEER had been brought home on suspicion of espionage."

Raptis shucked his glasses to the table. "Shit," he said. "Shit."

And that was deeply unsettling to Procter because this was only the third occasion in nearly as many decades that she'd heard Gus Raptis curse, and she remembered them all: in Afghanistan, bullet in his shoulder; in Georgetown, maybe fifteen years earlier, when he slipped on the ice last time they managed to get him drunk; and now, in Russia House's quiet recycled air, contemplating the disaster unfolding before the Bratva.

Bratva: their foursome's collective moniker inside CIA. The Russia House Mafia. Mac Mason, Chief of Operations; Theo Monk, Counterintelligence; Gus Raptis, now shuttered in a Langley holding position but until recently running the fieldwork in Moscow. And finally Procter, in Moscow X—overlord of the dirty, glorious covert action programs targeting Putin and his cronies. The Bratva's paths had zigged and zagged in the years since the Farm. Somehow they'd managed to mostly stay friends.

"Still no word from Singapore?" Procter asked.

Mac shook his head. "Station thinks the Sings will cough up the casino surveillance footage, but it may take some time. Otherwise, silence." He had joined them at the table, spreading across the chipped faux-wood surface the anodyne talking points they'd all prepared late last night for their meeting with the Director today. Mac clicked open a red pen and began to slash at the text. "Look, guys, in one hour we've got the first official Seventh Floor Russia briefing for"—he hawked something up his throat, anticipating the names—"our old friends Director Finn Gosford and his Deputy Director for Operations Deborah Sweet." Mac delivered the titles in a sarcastic singsong lilt. He swiveled over to his trash can and spat. "And, lucky us, we come bearing nothing but problems. A busted bren in Singapore, a missing case officer, and one dead asset in Moscow."

"They are going to flay us for all of it," Gus said.

"They'll flay us for just being here," said Theo.

"It'll be hard to pick just one grievance," Procter agreed. "There are so goddamn many."

4

LANGLEY

THE REUNION, IN TRUTH A BUREAUCRATIC SPANKING DISguised as an innocuous-sounding briefing ("Director's Special Update—Russia") commenced promptly at nine. The war party was thinner than the typical Russia briefings because Gosford's Chief of Staff had said he wanted only the four of them, leave the little people behind, please. Procter, Mac, Gus, and Theo wandered into the Seventh Floor anteroom outside the Director's office. The room, watched over by agents of the DPS, the Director's Protective Staff. The sitting area guarded the main hallway, cutting through the Director's suite; the furniture was new, fruits of a recent renovation, and unlike most waiting rooms at CIA, the newspapers and magazines, to Procter's great astonishment, were current.

Still, it felt alien to Proctor because it was now Finn Gosford's waiting room. It was *his* office on Langley's Seventh Floor. If you'd traveled back in time, Procter thought, and told me we'd be here waiting for Finn, I'd have said it'd be more likely that one morning I wake up with my face stapled to the carpet. Given her line of work, though, that was not impossible to imagine. No, it would have been more likely that *she* would occupy this Seventh Floor office—and hell would have to grow glaciers for anyone to give her the Director's chair.

At the moment she couldn't find a place to sit. The first week of any Director's tenure is jam-packed with background briefings, so Procter and her friends found the room and adjoining hallway gobbed with analysts. With nowhere to sit, they stood along a wall until, after twenty minutes, a group from the Near East Mission Center shuffled out of the conference room, looking shell-shocked, as if a bomb had detonated in the middle of the briefing, or, as Theo would later quip, the Director had dropped his pants. Gosford and Debs crossed the hallway from the conference room into the Director's office. "We'll do the next one in here," Finn called out to one of the Special Assistants.

And with that, Procter and her friends were told to go right on in, leaving the room full of nervous analysts, whose fidgeting and tapping and murmuring recalled the rising comprehension of steers on their way to slaughter.

Procter was often an unwelcome presence in a room. The feeling was a familiar one, but she could not remember it striking with such muscle. There were no smiles, the eye contact was reluctant drifting toward evasive, and the handshakes were stiff—not a blessed hug for an old comrade?—and fish-cold, as if Procter had shit smeared across her palms or was playing host to a fungus visible from some distance away. Greetings delivered, with everyone already exhausted, the Bratva took seats in front of Gosford and Sweet. Or, as Procter had known them back in the day, Finn and Debs.

Both of them looked pretty much the same, Procter thought. They looked good, and that was disappointing. Finn and Debs were the type of cherished enemies that you hoped, a decade on, would have slabbed on a great deal of weight, or lost their hair, or maybe a limb, to diabetes or gout or the vagaries of some exotic and excruciating infection. You wanted to stumble upon this type of rival at a reunion and find them careening downward—perhaps with a night's distance to rock-bottom, so you'd have the pleasure of watching.

But looking closer, Procter saw it was even worse. Both seemed somehow more tanned and less wrinkled. (Botox? Had to be, right?) The bags they'd once carried under their eyes had been deposited at the Bratva's side of the table. Gosford had kept his jet-black helmet of hair and Debs her frosty shoulder-length bob. The value of Gosford's watch probably exceeded his new government salary. Debs—who was sporting a tight, suffragette-white dress that stopped short of mid-thigh and seemed to have a goddamn cape attached at the shoulders—looked tauter to Procter, as if in the intervening decade her old friend had finally declared victory over about fifteen pounds of midwestern chub. There were much deeper reasons to hate them, but these were all Procter required for right now.

And then Gus, well, poor Gus made the meeting's first—but by no means only—mistake. "Finn," he said, "welcome back and congratulations."

"Director," Gosford corrected, regarding Gus behind fingers steepled in the manner of a professorial douche. Procter felt Debs's eyes boring through her. She looked up and tried to smile, and, to her surprise, Debs tried to smile back. But their bent lips were more grimace than smile, like two constipated folks in a face-off, and Procter eagerly surrendered when Gosford began speaking. "I know that we all have a shared history. But it is important that you treat me—and Deborah—as your superiors. I am the Director, and Deborah is the DDO, and it would convey crass cronyism if we did not maintain the professional hierarchy."

No one nodded or offered any recognition of this statement. Procter had the feeling that if the offer had been put on the table, a couple of them might have quit on the spot.

"That being said," Gosford said, breaking the silence to lean back and flap his tie, "this is . . . insane. Let's admit it, shall we? Say it aloud. Insane. No other word. All of us together again. Small world, small world. Has it been since Afghanistan? It must be. Over a decade. My, my. Well, we'll have time to catch up later"—*Bullshit!* Procter thought. *And thank god for that*—"but I'm afraid I'm back-to-back today. Now, to business."

Mac and Gus led the charge, describing for Gosford and Debs the facts as they had them on the mysterious death in Moscow. When they were done, Procter would cover Singapore. "It's your op, Artemis," Gus had said, with the tone of a man flinging a hot potato. "You should take that one." The briefing careened from stilted to bad to worse. Right around when Mac clarified a question from Debs about their certainty that BUCCANEER was actually dead—Pretty certain, ma'am, he'd said, belatedly choking out the ma'am part—Gosford flicked to angry, a pattern that mirrored some of his behavior when he'd run the Counterterrorism Center a decade prior. Then, he had claimed credit for operations in which he'd played a minor role, shoveled all problems to Debs, and occasionally lost his marbles on subordinates for slights, most of them minor, and quite a few of them—but not all—entirely imagined. Finn Gosford was a politician, a word that curdled in Procter's ears like vile slander.

"Good grief," Gosford said. "And how many assets are left?"

Mac turned his gaze to the ceiling, running the math. "Two more internal reporters, three outside, maybe a half dozen cases on ice, inactive for a year at least."

"And this BUCCANEER had been our best?" Gosford said.

"Far and away," Procter replied, and Gosford looked at her with shock for having taken the elaborate liberty of speaking. "Before they sent him to Athens he was our most senior asset inside SVR."

"I remember that source from last week's briefing documents," Debs said, rifling through a stack of papers. "You know this Singapore business we'll discuss in a moment recalls what REMORA told us not three days ago. Does it not?"

"Stop you right there," Gosford barked. "Stop. Stop. Who is REMORA?" He fought, had always fought, to instantly moor conversations that were drifting beyond his reach. And he didn't seem to much mind whether the boat capsized in the process.

"One of my cases," Theo said, his face blanching. "A colonel, the Deputy Chief of the SVR's Fifth Department. Their Europe guys."

"We met him a few days ago," Debs said, leafing through more of her papers. She flicked a pair of mustard-yellow frames over her face when she came to the one she sought. Licked her thumb and flipped a page. Her face was still buried in the report when she said, "REMORA offered vagaries about threats against Americans in Asia. It was not"—here Debs cleared her throat and tipped her head toward Gosford—"actionable."

A look from Debs seemed to convince Gosford that here should end that line of inquiry, so he said: "I hear we have a problem in Singapore."

Debs slid the glasses off her face and pointed them at Procter. "She'll get you up to speed on that."

And . . . I'm under the goddamn bus, Procter thought, looking up. About right. She started with a few minutes of setup, how a Kremlin insider by the name of Golikov had, through a cutout, passed a letter to Moscow Station. He was on an East Asian junket, a Russian trade delegation trawling through the region searching for partners willing to help them bust sanctions, and we know he's a degenerate gambler, so—

"I've heard you sent a Headquarters-based officer," Gosford cut in. "Why not use someone local?"

"I didn't want to risk burning someone in the Station, nor did I want the Sings involved; they are leaky as shit, goodies tend to find their way to Beijing, and—"

"Instead you thought it was safer to use a disgraced officer to handle the bump," Debs said. "One with a gambling problem. And, poof, he's gone missing. Along with well over one hundred thousand dollars of taxpayer money, not to mention a head full of our deepest secrets."

"Hey, now," Procter said. "Hey, now. Sam is, or was, a professional poker player. Not a gambling addict. He had pristine cover for travel to Singapore and a plum reason to sidle up to Golikov at the tables. Which is what happened, then—"

Debs swung in again. "Did he defect? Is he on a bender? A gambling spree? What?"

Fact was, there was no use in arguing with them. Lordy, she knew they had their reasons, mostly Debs. Procter did deserve some hell for what she'd done to the poor woman in Afghanistan, but now the shoe was decidedly on the other foot, a foot now wearing a gigantic and doubtless quite fashionable jackboot, good for squishing and stomping. They hated her, pure and simple. And probably the others, too, though with far less zeal. Gosford and Debs were politicians and Procter was a politician's nightmare: a competent extremist, inoculated against bullshit, unwilling to kowtow, even when it made damn good sense. The other three Bratva would lick some ass if required, and though her tastes were eclectic, she'd yet to work up the stomach for that. A lot of people hated

Artemis Aphrodite Procter, and each, well, each she considered marks in her favor.

"He's missing," was all Procter offered. "Right now we don't know anything else."

Debs said: "Let's recap, two options. One: you walked a disgraced, gambling-addicted officer into a Russian trap. Two: he's absconded with a small fortune in taxpayer dollars, and is likely at the tables right now frittering it away."

"The events in Moscow," Mac said, "BUCCANEER's death, would hint at the former. A trap."

Heads poked up or turned as the door cracked open and a woman appeared. It was Petra Devine, chief of what was technically termed the Special Investigations Unit, but popularly known as the Dermatology Shop: CIA's molehunters. As always and everywhere, an espionage outfit's chief molehunter was an old woman. In this case, one in a shambolic floor-length dress topped by a weird gray vest, Coke-bottle glasses, a bird's nest of curly gray hair, and jowls like a turkey wattle. Stone-cold church-lady vibes. Though in Petra's case that wattle didn't need to flap for too long before you knew that she wasn't going to be tickling organ keys or running the fall potluck. The Chief Derm was typically a woman of unquestioned loyalty, decades of service, and zero political acumen. The Derms built elaborate matrices to track anomalies in the intelligence reporting, searching for a common denominator or hidden clue to a mysterious loss. Procter had seen Petra's matrix: an elaborate map of a road to nowhere. Procter watched Debs's lip curl as Petra shambled in and took a seat.

"I thought we took you off the invite list for this meeting," Debs said.

The woman looked Debs over for a moment, then said dryly: "Oh? And why would you go and do that?"

Gosford shut one eye to stare at Petra, as if perhaps this were the sort of creature best seen through a scope—tele-, micro-, or rifle, take your pick—and Procter thought for a moment he was going to force an apology, as he had done to Gus at the meeting's kickoff. Part of her hoped he would, because that would send the meeting nuclear, a real scene, and its mushroom cloud would tower over the spat between her and Debs. Instead, Gosford cracked open his other eye, blinked, and said: "She's fine, Deborah."

Petra mumbled something, smiling at her gigantic black shoes while she took the empty seat next to Procter. Procter caught a whiff of a singular smell carried from her clothes: dog dander.

"You were talking about traps," Petra said. "And that's probably what it is. Because it never goes like this, not naturally. Sure, the shit hits the fan in this business, well and truly and often. We all know it. But we have too many problems all at once. BUCCANEER is elaborately recalled from Athens, then drops dead a few days after his inglorious return to Russia. And the same day, your boy Sam"—she'd taken Procter's shoulder into her badger grip—"goes AWOL in Singapore after a futile attempt to hear out a Russian with very important news for CIA. The business doesn't work like this. And since you are all tap-dancing around the obvious, let me articulate it for you: we have a big problem."

Amen, Procter thought.

"No one has any proof of that," Debs snapped. "There are other explanations—a commo breach, tradecraft errors, dumb luck."

Ignoring Debs, Gosford gave Petra an icy glare and said: "And what do you suggest we do about this problem?"

"Take a good hard look at things, sir"—honorific delivered like a kick in the shins. "Run a full and proper investigation to locate the breach."

"You want a witch hunt? Show trials? Am I hearing this right?" Gosford said. He had his chin propped on his hand to stare at Petra. "Turn the place inside out during my first week on the job? On what basis? We all know how awful those get. There'll be a panic, leaks, in the end we'll probably find nothing. Just burn the place down to watch the fire."

"Can't know you'll find nothing until you look," Petra said. "And I'm telling you, I think we have a problem."

"Oh lord," Debs said, "enough of these dark fantasies."

Gosford's attention had wandered off. Checking the three-by-five card holding his daily schedule, he glowered, first at the card, then over to Procter. "We need to stop this meeting here," he said. "Find the case officer. Keep the DDO's office apprised of any updates. That is all. Dismissed."

Procter had never been in a CIA meeting that concluded with a formal dismissal: she almost chalked up her second laugh of that grim morning.

They shuffled out of the office, probably with the same look as the group that preceded them, Procter thought, as if Gosford had dropped trow or ordered them up over the lip of a trench.

"Big problems," Petra was muttering to Procter. "We've got a big fucking problem inside these walls."

5

MOSCOW

REM ZHOMOV HAD THE PHONE IN ONE HAND AND PILLS IN the other. The bathroom sink was busy filling his glass. He listened to the report for a few moments until the voice on the other end, spooked by the silence, said, "Are you still there, Rem Mikhailovich?"

Rem shut off the water. "Yes. Go on."

While he did, Rem—at this hour in his bathrobe—slapped the pills from his hand onto the countertop and sorted them into two piles: on the left, those that would make him drowsy; on the right, those that would not. To the left: the orange one for sleep, the yellow for his back, the foul-smelling brown one for his blood pressure. These were swept from the counter back into the plastic case with the compartments for each day of the week. Balancing the phone between the ear and the crick of his neck, he swallowed the pink stool softener for his hemorrhoids, the green for his arthritis, lighter green for his thyroid, and the sweet-smelling little red octagon for cholesterol. The colonel's report had concluded by the stool softener: the line was silent save for Rem's gurgles and swallows, concluding with the clink of his glass on marble.

"Have a driver outside my apartment in ten minutes."

Rem hung up and went to the bedroom. Ninel, in bed, looked up from her book. "You are going out?"

"Yes."

"You look cross."

"I am."

She clapped shut the book, flung off the bedcovers. "I will pick out a suit."

HE WATCHED THE DARK CITY FLOAT BY THE WINDOWS OF his car. The jet-black suit that Ninel had selected matched the night sky and the car's paint and its leather. He was camouflaged: a faceless bureaucrat sliding into the Moscow night.

The suit was an older one, purchased in Rome when he'd been *rezident* there. Finely cut, it still clung nicely to his frame. Since that tour Rem had added cataracts, arthritis, and—thanks to his father—congenitally high blood pressure, but not a single pound. The car came to a stop under the light of a streetlamp. He caught sight of dust on his shoes and stooped down gingerly to wipe it away. Ninel had picked the shoes, too, but it had been ages since he'd worn them and she'd forgotten to polish them in the rush. It could not be helped. Ninel saw the big picture, Rem saw everything else.

And the only thing Rem could see now was the danger facing his top American asset, known inside the Forest as Dr. B; it was the reason the Director, the week prior, had permitted Rem to stay on beyond mandatory retirement.

Rem had read the ops note from that week's meeting with Dr. B no fewer than ten times. He'd quizzed his handling officer on Dr. B's body language, intonation, and facial grammar: each a plank in the emotional architecture of the SVR's most valuable penetration of CIA—ever.

The summary: Dr. B was stressed and concerned, this was obvious even from the written ops note, but not panicked. Dr. B was too cool for that, though the asset was appropriately worried—as was Rem—that the week's drama imperiled their shared mission. Rem did take some measure of pride that the chaos had not halted Dr. B's production. He'd been able to share a stack of Dr. B's reports with the Director just that morning, including a few CIA analytical pieces and minutes from the American National Security Council's deliberations on Russia. The requested China haul, Dr. B promised, would come next, perhaps by autumn.

Tremendous risks had been taken that very week to protect Dr. B, and Rem feared—no, he *knew*—that many more would be necessary in the weeks and months to come. But that was for later. Tonight, Rem had work to do. He had a damage assessment to conduct. He had leaks to plug. Soon Moscow was an orange ribbon of light behind his car. Rem was glad he'd not taken the other pills; he was already so tired.

IN HAPPIER TIMES, SAINT CATHERINE'S HAD BEEN A CONVENT. The nunnery was painted a sunflower-yellow that glowed eerily in the darkness. The buildings were fronted by rows of white columns. Rem had selected the convent because it required little of the mundane facilities work that typically accompanied the establishment of an informal prison. The most difficult part, in the end, had been relocating the nuns, who put up a more savage fight than he would have thought possible from a half dozen septuagenarians. In the end, the matter went to the Director, who called the chief of the Presidential Administration, who doubtless shook some cash at the Patriarch. The nuns were dispersed to a convent near Nizhny, and their old chapel became the holding chamber for a specially fitted box. The somber stone cellar was outfitted as an interrogation chamber. Though Rem did not like that word. These were merely conversations, he believed, even if the other person was occasionally upside down, hauled up by their arms until they lost consciousness, or locked for a spell in a dreamlike world of perpetual light and noise.

From Rem's vantage, Samuel Joseph's mouth was curled into a joyful smile, but that was merely a contortion: he was upside down, his feet were strung from the rafters. An interrogator stood beside him. For a moment Rem watched Samuel dangle from side to side, broom of hair gently sweeping the stone. The American had been spirited from Singapore on a ketamine-dribbled itinerary of vans, shipping containers, military transport planes, and helicopters. He'd been at Saint Catherine's for all of two hours. Most of it upside down, shaking things loose to get him started.

"Bring him down," Rem ordered the interrogator.

They sat at a wooden table spattered with oily stains. Here, he thought, the nuns must have prepared their food. Samuel sported a loose gray jumpsuit. His eyes were red-rimmed and hollow from the ketamine injections during transport, and his cheeks were flushed with blood from hanging upside down. Rem called for tea and they drank in silence. Samuel did not meet his eyes. When Rem had finished his tea, he spread his palms on the table and shifted his weight in the chair with a wince. Damn hemorrhoids.

"You met Boris Golikov in Singapore," Rem said.

"I met a man named Boris. Briefly. At the tables. Small talk. I did not know his name until your men kidnapped me. This detention is illegal. This—"

Rem interrupted: "What did he tell you?"

"My detention here is illegal."

"You've said that already. What did he tell you? What did he give you?"

"He asked me about my whisky."

"What were you drinking?"

"A Macallan."

"How old?"

"I don't know."

"What sort of man doesn't know the age of his whisky?"

"Ten years."

"What was Golikov drinking?"

"A Springbank. That's what we were talking about. That's *all* we talked about."

"What did he pass you?"

"I told you. Nothing."

"Why did you have one hundred thousand dollars in cash in your hotel room?"

"It's a casino."

"You did not wire money into an account at the casino?"

"I prefer cash. Feels real to me."

"You are a CIA officer."

"I am not. I am a Foreign Service officer."

Rem laughed. "Ah. Yes. But you were on a tourist passport in Singapore."

"As I've said, I was in Singapore to gamble. Not to work."

"Long way to travel for cards. Las Vegas is, what, a three-hour flight from Washington?"

"I like to visit new places."

Rem paused for a moment as he considered the man before him. "How is Artemis Aphrodite Procter doing these days?"

"Who?"

"You do not know her? What a shame," Rem said. "She is a treat. A gem of your wretched Service." Rem shifted forward in the chair. "I understand from our files that you were interrogated in Syria, however briefly. Now, we trained the Syrian security services, so perhaps you are thinking you will resist what we are going to put you through. But you cannot. And here is why: There is no clock. We can hold you forever. No one is coming. They do not know where you are, nor who took you. Oh, of course they suspect it, but they cannot prove it, and there is no trail leading from Singapore to Russia. So, we are going to hold you here, for however long it takes, until you give us what we want. You tell me why you were in Singapore and what Boris told you, and I will personally drive you to the U.S. Embassy. That can happen tonight. It can happen in this moment. You just have to tell me. We are not monsters. And you know how we operate. The spy flicks would have us Russians jerking out fingernails and electrocuting kidneys and balls and beating you senseless with leaden pipes and maybe putting a bullet in your neck for good measure. As though we were the American Mafia. And do you know what? After a few weeks of what we're going to put you through, you'll be begging me for the relatively clean experience of electrocution, or some light cutting. You will plead for a beating with a pipe. Because, unless you cooperate, you will travel into a darker and far more sinister forest. You will hear nothing, or it will be so loud you will hear nothing else. There will be no light, or so much of it you cannot see. You will be lonely, so alone, and when you are not you will wish you were. You will lose all sense of place and time and satisfaction and truth and beauty. You will beg for someone to cut you so you might feel something." Rem stood and gripped the back of the chair. "So, that was a lot. And so very dark. Samuel, I am former First Chief Directorate. An artist, not a thug. I must say I don't care for this piece of the work, but I have my reasons, distasteful though this all is. So: Out with it. Golikov. What did he tell you?"

"He told me he was drinking a Springbank."

Rem looked up at the camera above the door. "We're done for now. Put him in the box."

SAM'S BOX WAS A FRANTICALLY STILL WORLD OF BLINDING light and cloaking darkness, frozen silence and roaring noise. There were six lights set into the ceiling, behind thick plastic. Crackers, bread, and hunks of pickled fish arrived at random on a rubber plate, set on a rubber tray bearing a rubber cup filled with water. A rubber bucket toilet sat in one corner. It did not overflow and yet he could not recall anyone ever emptying it. He wore a gray jumpsuit with eighteen frayed threads coming off the pant legs. He'd counted them dozens of times.

Inside the box he could not quite fully stand. He could lie down, though. He could sit against a wall. His box was a square: Ten and a half steps, heel to toe, brought you from side to side. The sides wore a thick cloth fabric. There were no visible screws or rivets. When the lights were on, he could make out tiny red stars printed on the fabric.

Once, in the upper corner of the box to the right of the door, he'd spotted a fraying slice of fabric. When he'd pulled on it, the door opened and they told him to stop. He'd not spoken to a human in so long that he just kept on yanking—he was hoping for a fight, for a chat, for, as that old man had said, someone to make him feel something—and two men burst through the door. They jabbed his shoulder and when he woke up the fabric had been repaired. His memory, his existence, had been reduced to the box and that night in Singapore. He came to believe he'd had no life before this. CIA did not exist anymore. Neither did Procter. Neither did Natalie. Life was a busted op in Singapore and this cell, which he assumed was in Russia but of course could not know. Sometimes he wondered if his box was in a room down the hall at the Sands.

They knew who he was, of course. He'd crossed paths with the Russian services in Syria, years earlier, as the old man had said. They understood he was CIA. But to keep him like this? The only way out was to hold back the one thing they wanted. If he told them what Golikov had shared, they would never let him go. They might not anyhow, but once he'd told that old man what Golikov had said, they could never let him leave, not even in a box. The only way home was to hold it all deep inside.

When the crackers arrived, Sam would dip into the memory palace of his childhood bedroom, crouching to slide the colorful bins from beneath his bed, opening them to reveal Golikov's words, each in its precise order, spoken in that brief moment at the table. He would silently speak the truth to the cracker. He would eat it, then he would begin counting the little red stars.

6

LANGLEY

THE BUREAUCRATIC TORTURE OF ARTEMIS PROCTER WAS excruciating and, until the very end, administered at a sensible arm's length, to avoid the mess. The first prick of the knife was Procter's formal elimination, no reason offered, from the Director's Russia updates. The next was to slash her Moscow X crew to skeletons. Procter had a team of analysts and techies she'd corralled for special projects, and the Seventh Floor commandeered those, the anodyne email she received explaining that it was *critical to centralize such Enterprise Resources inside the Directorate.* On a Monday they all sat in the Moscow X spaces, by Tuesday lunch those bullpens and cubicles had been stripped down to the last stapler.

Procter wasn't due for a polygraph for another year, but Security made her sit for one anyway, pairing it with a laborious background investigation that involved calling friends and relatives and neighbors. She had tried to keep a low profile; now she had government creeps slinking around the subdevelopment asking if Artemis Procter threw ragers or snorted coke on her back patio. The investigation didn't worry her—she had nothing to hide—but she was wildly agitated, and that, well, that was precisely the point. By late spring, twenty-four Equal Employment Opportunity (EEO) complaints had been called forth from the mists of her long career, all of them focused on what the Chief considered her idiosyncratic—and brutally effective—management style, which in the complaints was described as "conduct creating a work environment that is intimidating, hostile, or offensive to reasonable people."

Procter had been up for promotion to the Senior Intelligence Service (SIS), but after the EEO complaints and the background investigation, her package was pulled from consideration. In a rather nasty gesture, the formal note explaining the panel's decision referenced a Russian blackmail attempt from a few years back that had concluded with her unceremoniously assaulting the officer making the pitch, just after he'd shown her a bunch of nudie pics snapped while she'd been drugged. "Professional lapse," was how the note described it, "one in a long string leading up to the present operational planning for Singapore." Though as yet her old friend's name and office were not associated with the torture, Procter saw the hand of Debs on all of it. Here, more than a decade on, was Deborah Sweet's revenge.

Of all the indignities she suffered in those months, the violations of her office were perhaps the most galling. Her shoestring, gutted Moscow X shop was transferred to the Ground Floor—the basement—smack across the hall from the hot dog machine. Then, Security paid a surprise visit and wrote her up in violation of Agency Regulation 32-498 (Rules and processes regarding the possession and storage of weapons on Agency property). It's just a baseball bat, she'd said to the guy, and look, it's decorative. The truth was that the bat, signed by every member of the 1997 Cleveland Indians World Series team, *had* been used as a weapon, just not recently, nor inside Headquarters. "What do you have against Cleveland?" she asked, and never did get a response. The Security officers simply impounded the bat, and a citation went into Procter's file, which was thickening rapidly during those bleak months.

The instruments of torture soon diversified, branching out from the Agency's formal mechanisms to more unofficial forms of amusement. Each morning, when Procter flicked on the lights, she would find, primly stacked on her chair, forms advertising employment opportunities elsewhere: McDonald's, Cici's Pizza Buffet, a Northern Virginia–based proctology practice, all manner of strip clubs, Goldman Sachs, a Craigslist "Casual Encounters" post seeking a submissive, Bain & Company.

During the first week of June, filthy pictures began appearing around her office: hidden in a coffee mug, in a desk drawer, stuck in folders. Visitors were sparse in those grim days, limited mostly to the occasional guest on a flyby after a hot dog run, but during a rare meeting the color drained from one guy's face and he set down his dog entirely. Procter spun to see one of the photos perched up on her empty bookshelf. She was going to explain it was a prank her friends had played—*It's not mine, I swear it*—but she could only laugh. Plus, Debs wasn't even her friend anymore. What else could she do? Word got out, though, and Security wrote her up for that one, too; a violation of Agency Regulation 16-210 (Materials prohibited on Agency premises and information systems, e.g., alcohol, tobacco, illegal drugs, adult content, etc.)

Gosford was well within his rights to fire her, ease her out with a pat on the back, or send her on a useless fiddlefuck of an assignment far from Headquarters—that happened all the time with senior officers approaching fifty with twenty years overseas in the bank—but a mercy killing was clearly not in the offing. It would have cut short the entertainment. Procter did consider quitting, not for shame but to deprive Debs of her satisfying revenge, but she would not give up while Sam was still missing.

Procter lived by two rules: Protect your agent and collect the intel. Singapore had been a total failure on both counts, the first most of all. The pain of Debs's torture aside, Procter would stick it out as long as she could be helpful in bringing Sam home. Mac, Gus, and Theo, though by no means favorites, were faring better than Procter inside Gosford's Thunderdome, and they brought their Russia House components to bear in the search for Sam. Procter spent hours on video conference with Singapore Station, sifting through every available scrap of intelligence, every lead—she went down all roads, though in the end they led nowhere. She tasked NOCs—officers under non-official cover—inbound to Russia to work their networks, rustle up any clues as to Sam's whereabouts. She hounded Moscow Station and the embassy to press the Russians for answers, and she continued to do so through back channels even after Seventh Floor mandarins decreed that she stop, pronto.

But by early summer CIA still didn't have any idea where Sam was. The trail went cold in Singapore. Was he in a gutter? Russian prison? On a spiritual journey in the Himayalas? Petra Devine and her luckless Derms continued to preach to the few who would listen that CIA had a problem. Procter tended to agree, but there was absolutely no proof, and from what she could gather, the Derm shop had been wrecked, same as Moscow X, now a backwater, with Procter in the role of chief hermit. This is the whimper of the end, Procter thought, running a team of analysts in the basement, within sniffing distance of the hot dog machine. Even Procter, whose imaginative capacity for suffering was quite developed, struggled to comprehend the rate and depth of her decline.

THERE WAS STILL THE LAST BIT TO GO, THOUGH, AND THAT ball got rolling on a Tuesday in late June, with a summons to Gosford's office. That morning, the sunlight on the march from the distant Purple Lot (her GS-15 reserved parking privileges had been forfeited amid Debs's shakedown) had been bright and pure. She was a convict in the prison yard, gazing into the blue sky, brilliant and unreachable.

She hadn't been invited up to the Seventh Floor in going on ten weeks, and the invite—extended via a phone call from one of the Director's Special Assistants—was curt and wildly nonspecific. She figured this was it. Tired at last of batting at the mouse, the cat would now sink fangs into her neck.

She waited in the anteroom outside the Director's office. *He's running behind, Ms. Procter*, the SA would pop in to say. *No, Ms. Procter, no need to leave, it'll be any minute now.* Procter wore her best jeans with a tweed blazer over a newly dry-cleaned white blouse that only sort of hid her lucky bra, the neon-yellow one with the little neon-green palm trees on it. A pair of aviators peered across the room from their perch atop Procter's nest of curly black hair. Each time she wandered into the bullpens for an update, the SA scowled at the clock and then at Procter.

"I have work to do, I can come back," Procter offered. "No sweat."

The SA tugged on his lower lip, expression souring at the mention of a scheduling change. "I'm afraid that will not work for the Director's schedule," he said dourly.

After an hour one of the caterers wheeled a picked-at spread of pastries, bagels, fruit, and muffins down the hall, parking it just outside the cramped kitchenette, presumably for later collection by the Agency Dining Room staff.

Now, Artemis Procter had been known to partake when chocolate muffins were involved, even more so when she was wildly depressed, an emotion she did not consider real or valid but was nonetheless experiencing in spades as of late. And the spread, the poor spread was sitting there all by its lonesome. Procter stood, stretched, walked over for a look-see at the muffin situation. And there was one chocolate, wouldn't you know it? In pristine condition. Procter put the muffin on a plate along with some fruit and returned to her seat.

Later she'd admit that the taste was not right. The texture was chalkier than you'd have liked or expected. But she was hungry—the low-grade, rolling anger had her famished—and the muffin vanished in about five bites. She settled in to wait.

A few minutes later the SA appeared to shepherd her into the birch-paneled office.

Debs was at the table. Gosford was writing something in a notebook at his desk, the MLP secure phone receiver pinched between his ear and shoulder. Debs's smile was strange, she thought that even then, a swirl of smugness and pure disdain. While Gosford finished his call, Debs patted a chair at the table and said: "Have a seat, Artemis."

Sitting across from Debs, Procter heard a gurgle, then felt a kick from inside her stomach, like something wanted out. Then it made another noise, almost human, a shout from inside her body. "What was that?" Debs asked.

"I'm just hungry," Procter said.

Hanging up the phone, Gosford joined them at the table. When he crossed his legs, little red roosters peeked above his shoes. Had they still been friends she would have made a comment about the cocks on his socks, but they weren't, so she looked away to avoid the temptation.

He leaned back, head supported by the heel of a hand—the Gosford cue for an imminent monologue, god help her. "You've had quite the run, Artemis," he said. "You should be proud. But, after reviewing your latest performance review and the mountain of citations and complaints, I think we can both agree that it's time for a change. Time for your next chapter. Time to move on from CIA."

She'd known it was coming, had known for months, and yet it still felt painful and raw; they were pulling her guts through her throat and had skimped on the anesthetic. "I can't agree with that. I don't think there's another chapter," she said. "I think this is the last one."

"Oh, come, now," Gosford said, "I am sure you'll figure something out. The private sector can be quite rewarding, financially and otherwise. No Beltway Bandit worth its salt would bat an eye at your colorfully checkered experience. Quite the opposite. There are surely more sordid adventures to be written in the life story of Artemis Procter. The setting, though, will not be inside these walls."

"You need a scapegoat for Singapore?" Procter said. "That it?"

"That implies innocence," Debs said. "You're just fortunate we're not sending you to the Program first, telling people you're in bumfuck Yemen while you're actually drying out in a taxpayer-funded drunk tank up in Maryland. Which, let's face it, could be helpful."

"Now, hey, now," Gosford said, with a glare at Debs. "I realize there is no value in Monday morning quarterbacking you, Artemis, and even more I understand that my disapproval will have no impact." Her stomach made that noise again, but now she couldn't be sure if it was causing the disgusted look to ripple through his face. "Plus," he continued, "you are, what, a year or so from fifty? Until then we'll send you on a long domestic temporary duty assignment, a TDY with zero responsibility. After, you'll be able to collect the full FERS Special pension, isn't that right? You've got plenty more than five years banked in the field. You're golden. Go out and travel the big wide world and have some fun."

Gosford smoothed his tie and smiled and stood, trying to end the meeting. Procter stayed in the chair. Her stomach turned over with another wet gurgle. With great effort, she swallowed. Her ass was soaked in sweat.

"Just let me keep what's left of Moscow X," Procter said, she prayed with an even tone. "Until we find Sam. Or a spot in the field where I can be useful. Most of this will get sorted in the field anyhow. I want to help. And I can be useful to you by helping bring him back."

Gosford just looked at her all piteous and glassy-eyed and said, "Put you in the field? Not after Singapore. And, at any rate, the important work takes place at Headquarters, Artemis."

"What?" Fragments of a laugh escaped after the question mark.

They looked at each other, eye to eye, with little smiles twisting on their lips, as if their obvious mutual disdain for one another were perhaps amusing. Gosford stomped back to his desk, grabbed the green line, and told his SA to patch through his next call in two minutes. He slammed the phone into its cradle and pointed at the door. "We're finished here, Artemis. Dismissed." He pretended to read a notecard plucked from his suit pocket. Procter shifted in the chair.

"Despite our differences I have a track record in the field," Procter said. "A strong one. I'm a GS-15 and overqualified for more than half our Stations. You could put me anywhere to help get him back." Her stomach yelped again. Sweat was beading on her hairline and upper lip.

"Our differences," he mused, with venom. "How rich. You planned and oversaw an operation to bump a Russian official using a disgraced case officer, resulting in the probable death of the Russian, the disappearance of our officer, and a catastrophic loss of operational funds. A shit stew served piping hot by the debauched wanderlust and all-around bugaboo, Artemis Procter!"

Gosford laughed, then looked off out the window and muttered, "You people," which Procter found odd because you're one of us fucking people, Finn, you and me, we come from the same place. His nose wrinkled in disgust, as if Procter were oozing a rancid potpourri. He was flicking around the notecard holding his schedule.

Procter was torn: sheer stubbornness kept her planted in the chair, while the sickness slithering inside her body had her frantically planning an exit. Her eyes came to rest on the Intelligence Star, framed to decorate the wall above his desk. The Star had not yet been hung on her previous visit, during Gosford's first week on the job amid the fallout from Singapore. Long ago she'd made her peace with how the Afghanistan debacle had netted out, no use reopening the wound. But now it was quite literally in front of her face. Procter never spoke of her Star; she kept it in the goddamn drawer where it belonged. Want a medal? Join the fucking Army.

This fucking guy! A grifter consultant huckster who'd been honored for shooting himself in the foot, who was now CIA Director and had promoted her Farm washout former friend Debs, a useless mop of a case officer, greedy bitch, and consummate political buttlicker, to the position of DDO, leapfrogging Procter and all her friends who'd toiled inside for years, who'd earned their spurs quietly, without getting rich. Her enemies had ridden back into town to kill her.

Procter had also just shit her pants. And, with that as perhaps the agreed-upon signal, the muffin made its second jailbreak, this time up out of her stomach to the sweet freedom of the carpet at her feet, the brazen double escapes a new low water mark for Artemis Aphrodite Procter's quarter century inside CIA.

Some of it was on her shoes. She slid off her blazer and, in a vain attempt to censor the mess, tied it around her waist. The shock on Debs's face stopped short of her knowing eyes, and Procter was back in Afghanistan, watching the Base facilities crew clean up after what she'd done to Debs. Procter figured it was ipecac in that muffin—at least that's what she'd have used.

Gosford had a hand over his mouth. He stood by his desk, having arrived, perhaps, by leaping backward like a startled cat. "Artemis, go to a doctor."

"I'll be okay," she said. "Debs poisoned me, is all." She stood, promptly keeled over to dry-heave, then swished about halfway to the door. The double-tap firing and poisoning had sapped her will to fight. She turned to them, understanding that parting thoughts from a former friend with a stain on her pants in the rough shape of the Indian sub-continent were unlikely to be well received, but she had her conscience to consider, plus she wouldn't see either of them ever again: "Someone ratted Sam out. That Derm, Petra, is a pain in the ass, but she's not wrong. We have a big problem around here."

"Are you kidding me? We should junk that useless Derm outfit," Gosford said, regaining his edge.

With Gosford and Debs, the urge to fight, to respond, was irrepressible, mechanical even. Action, reaction. "That's a stupid fucking idea, Finn," Procter said.

Someone knocked on the door.

"Excuse me?" Gosford said.

Another knock, more insistent.

Gosford yelled for one more minute. His eyes were blazing. Debs's face was a mask, but those eyes, well, damn her: they might well have been smiling.

"What would be a stupid idea, Artemis," Gosford said, "is turning this place inside out chasing phantoms. Now I would like you to apologize."

"What?" This time the whole laugh escaped. "C'mon."

"Apologize to me, right now, for being rude and insubordinate."

"I'm not going to do that," she said, "Because it *is* a stupid idea. It's a shade cunty, if you can take the heat."

PROCTER'S DEFROCKING COMMENCED PROMPTLY AFTER A cleanup session in a Seventh Floor restroom. Finn's initial offer of a breezy glide into retirement had been retracted in the wake of her mess, refusal to apologize, and choice of profanity. In an office the size of a broom closet, she signed her resignation letter under the watchful eyes of a decrepit Support officer, who then had her work through a stack of documents the thickness of a phone book, the gist of which was that Procter would receive a visit from the goon squad or—worse—government lawyers if she ran her mouth. They didn't even give her the Blue Bag, the classy thank-you present for decades of service, with the flag and the medallion and the certificate with the President's autopen signature.

Two security officers escorted her to her office, where they collected her passports (the black diplomatic in true name; the four blue tourists in aliases). They returned her impounded baseball bat. The supervised pack-out did not take long because Procter's lodgings were spartan, always and everywhere, plus there'd been a recent wave of consolidation scouring for any straggling dirty pictures that had been hidden around. Into the keeper box went a twisted scrap of metal from a Mitsubishi Pajero, a carpet from the old souk in Damascus, and a cherished picture of Vladimir Putin falling on the ice during a hockey game. Next was the sole photo on her desk: a shot of her smiling and laughing with the Queen of Jordan.

She gathered a stack of awards, Meritorious Unit Citations, and her own dusty Intelligence Star, dumping it all into blue-and red-striped burn bags for future incineration.

Then she picked up the box, flung the baseball bat over her shoulder, and rode the elevator upstairs, security officer on each flank. She walked out of CIA for the last time. Artemis Aphrodite Procter: Newly inducted member of the uncleared masses. A nobody. Because when you're out, you're out.

At the exit she handed one of the officers her blue badge, circled around the turnstiles, and strolled, box tucked under her arm, bat on the shoulder, across the prairie of Langley parking lots into the wilderness of civilian life.

7

LANGLEY

A BENDER BECKONED, BUT THE FIRING HAD OCCURRED ON a Friday, and Fridays in the summer and fall—at least since Afghanistan—meant baseball. That she had been canned technically disqualified her (it was, after all, a CIA intramural league), but if anyone questioned the participation of the Cold Warriors' center fielder, their protests were registered in silence. Procter was a known brawler; ejected, already this season, from two games for arguing calls with the umps and a third for sliding into second, spikes up, while successfully disrupting a double play.

She unceremoniously clanked her bat bag on the dugout bench. Theo, the Cold Warriors' first baseman, wrinkled his nose at her beery smell and said: "You bring me one?"

"No drinking at the ballpark, Theo. You know that."

"Right." He bent over to tie a cleat. "Just before and after."

She'd gone home for a shower and a few drinks before driving to the field. Sitting out wasn't really an option. Ten years earlier they'd jerry-rigged a park and a pickup league at the base in Shkin, Afghanistan. The initial catalyst had not been Procter or her Bratva—or even CIA—but two Marines who had played Single-A ball before enlisting. CIA participation had begun as something of a joke: Theo, for example, went one-for-forty-nine that season, and Procter wasn't much better. Her batting eye had become glaucomic since playing the game as a child. But over time, and certainly now, in the Langley intramural league, the games had become a pyre for the sacrifice of stress and grudges, of all the petty slights and useless, energy-vacuuming bullshit that defined life at CIA Headquarters.

Throughout the years it had been unspoken, though collectively and firmly agreed, that the absent were best honored if the rest of them just kept on playing. In Shkin they'd regularly thrown first pitches shortly after the conclusion of rocket barrages against the Base. One of the Marine teams took the field for a Friday night game after losing their second baseman in a Taliban ambush on that Tuesday. Sam had been the Cold Warriors' third baseman, and they had played the season opener five days after his disappearance.

Tonight, as her friends filed into the dugout, not one asked her how she was, or why she had shown up for a baseball game mere hours after concluding, in disastrous fashion, a twenty-four-year career at the Central Intelligence Agency. That would come later, over drinks at the Vienna Inn. First they had business with the Counterterrorism Center Predators.

Procter trotted out to center. The night air was bathwater on her skin; the glow of the lights was the sky torn open to heaven; the evening breeze carried the scent of popcorn and clean dirt and cut grass. She chewed a wad of gum like a maniac. She had a good buzz rolling. There was no past, no future. She was playing baseball with her friends.

Gus, the Cold Warriors' starting pitcher and the most natural athlete among them, could hurl in the low seventies and had in his quiver a reasonable, if inconsistent, curve. In an intramural league, he was nearly unhittable. The Preds' pitcher—a lanky young analyst who worked on jihadi financing networks—had also brought his stuff. By the sixth inning—league rules stipulated seven innings, no bonus play—the Cold Warriors' catcher, a reports officer, was complaining of groin pain. "I'll catch," Procter said. "I've logged a good deal of flight time on my knees." She winked at Gus, who laughed. "You won't be catching me," he said. "My arm is gassed." That left Mac to pitch the seventh.

Procter spent the bottom of the sixth in the dugout, sitting by Mac on the bench, working on a bag of sunflower seeds in a glorious and companionable silence. The third baseman, an analyst who had taken Sam's spot, sidled up and for a few moments sat quietly, though Procter could sense that he had words for her, and that she did not want to hear them. Gus grounded out to short. Two down. She spat. Oh crap, she thought. He *is* going to say something.

"Artemis," he said.

She looked up with a frown.

"I wanted to say that I heard. And I'm sorry." His voice was weak, like he was speaking into a running vacuum.

"Yeah," she said. "Okay."

"It's bullshit," the third baseman went on. "What happened."

"Save it," Mac scolded. "We're playing baseball." He kept his gaze fixed on the game, mouth churning through seeds.

Theo, as usual, struck out. This time looking. Three down. Procter began donning the catcher's gear. Theo traded bat and helmet for his glove and the plain red proletarian cap of the Cold Warriors. "Goddammit," he muttered, "I suck." Theo did suck, a feature of his life more than a bug, extending well beyond the confines of the baseball diamond to his marriages and drinking habits. Off the field, Procter was all too happy to remind him of these failings, but in the dugout she just slapped his ass as she strolled by on her way to the plate.

Mac's inning was shaky. A targeting officer called Tobin, the Preds' catcher, came to the plate with two down and runners on second and third. After a ball outside, Procter hustled to the mound for a word.

"He's too comfortable in the box," she said. "Taking an ownership stance. Soundtrack's gotta be chin music, Macintosh. You keep missing outside, he's going to poke out his bat and dribble something down the line past Theo and we're fucked." She slapped Mac's ass, too, and trotted back to the plate. Next pitch came in high and tight, nearly skinning Tobin's elbows when he lurched back and out of the box.

"Holy shit," he said, glaring at Procter. "Tell Mac to ease up. It's just a game."

"No wonder you got passed up for your 14," she said, smacking her glove and easing into her crouch. "You're an idiot, Tobin."

She signaled for a fastball in. This time Tobin swung and missed and his exaggerated (intentional! the bastard) backswing clocked her in the helmet, rocketed off her mask, and sent her plug of gum into the dirt. "Lord almighty," she said, and spat.

"Oops," said Tobin, "sorry. And you've already had one spanking today. My bad."

She picked up the mask, shouldering past him on her way out to the mound. "He's still crowding the plate," Procter said. "He's been warned and now we've got to deliver. And first base, well, first base is open, Mac."

"Ribs?" Mac whispered into his glove.

"If you can manage."

She slapped Mac's ass with her mitt and took up behind home. Tobin's elbows were luxuriously draped over the plate, taunting them, an affront not only to her and her friends personally but to all pitchers and catchers everywhere, for all time. She punched her mitt, rearranged the mask. "Scoot the fuck off the plate," she said. "You own the box, not the plate. You are an infringer, Tobin. You are line-stepping. And you have been warned."

"Why are you here, running your damn mouth, after what happened today?" Tobin said, unmoved, check-swinging as he waited for the delivery. "You should be out somewhere, drunk."

To his credit Mac put some sauce on it; the fastball scored a direct hit on Tobin's left kidney and he bent like a hinge at the waist and dropped the bat with a grunt that made Procter grin. He just stood there in the box, hands on his knees. Procter picked the ball from the dirt and threw it back to Mac. "Take your base, Tobin. Move along." She slapped his ass, too. "Go on."

It spoke volumes about the spirit of the league that the Cold Warriors had thought nothing of beaning a coworker, that both benches were beginning to spill onto the field, and that Tobin was quite obviously keen to rush the mound and fight a fellow officer who was, in fact, his superior. Procter took a measure of pride in this. Because if you couldn't lather yourself into a murderous rage over a game of baseball, then what were you, really?

Tobin righted himself, and charged the mound. And the cords of her rage—drawn frighteningly tight since Sam's disappearance, the hopscotch of workplace humiliations, and, at last, today's firing—twanged inside her and she was on Tobin's heels, sprinting to protect Mac, who had his fists up, bobbing, waiting.

Procter overtook Tobin before he got to Mac, jumping onto his back to ride him into the dust of the mound. She figured she had about two seconds before the teams collided in the infield and they pulled her off. The only sound was the ringing noise in her skull. Mashed into the dirt, her nose excavated smells of dust and leather and blood. She climbed on Tobin, wrestled his hands from his face, and punched him square in the nose.

AFTER THE BRAWL, THE GAME SPUTTERED TO A MADDENING conclusion: a scoreless tie. No one apologized or tried to smooth things over—which Procter did appreciate—the umps abandoned them, and the two teams melted back to their dugouts to pack up. "Feels like a ten-drink night," Theo said, zipping up his bag with a flourish, holding an undershirt against the skin of his clawed-up cheek.

They went to the Vienna Inn, the four of them, and for the first round, in their usual booth, spoke only of the game and the fight. Well into the second, Mac at last nudged her to tell the full story of her meeting with Gosford and Debs. She spared no detail, up to and including the impromptu cleanup session in the Seventh Floor restroom and her ignominious final trot out the door. She finished her beer, on to the third—tonight Mac was buying—and Gus, god bless him, he always said this like his teetotaling wasn't assumed: Gus said he would drive tonight. "Have as many as you like."

"We gonna fit in your Corolla, Gus?" Mac asked. "Last time you had the twins' sweaty lacrosse stuff in there. Bit tight. Bit smelly."

"I've got the minivan this time," Gus said. "We'll have enough room to lay Artemis in the back."

Procter raised her drink, removing a few inches with a long thirsty pull. She set down the glass, trading it for her ice pack, which she returned to her red-raw left ear.

"I thought Tobin was going to yank that off," Gus said, flicking his own.

"You got there just in time," Procter told Gus. "Turns out it's tricky to remove an ear while somebody's smacking you with a batting helmet."

"What do you figure was in the muffin?" Theo asked. "Ipecac, or what?"

"Probably. Never turned down a chocolate muffin in my life," Procter said. "Debs knows this. Mac, your nose is bleeding again."

"Oh shit," he said, and cradled it in the rag he'd set aside on the table.

"We knew about the yogurt," Theo said, rotating his ice pack from the cheek that had been clawed to the one that had been punched.

"It's just brutal," Mac said through the bloody rag. "And the symmetry? Unreal. Deborah Sweet holds a grudge. Bad case officer, exceptional grudge-holder. Credit where credit's due."

Procter looked around at her friends. She had tried to convince herself she might repeat her familiar work pattern, well worn over a quarter century at CIA: Survive, lie low, somehow return to the field. There was a finality here that she could not get her arms around. All your life you're CIA, then you're not. Something is dead, she thought. Yesterday it was dying, and now it's dead.

Even as these thoughts cartwheeled through her mind, Procter did appreciate that her old friends did not offer useless, sugary condolences, nor ask her that most vile of questions: *How are you feeling?*

Instead, they swapped stories from the brawl, the Farm, Shkin, the decades of life they'd shared together. They laughed about Theo's second wife and the legendary destruction of his prized fish tanks; about the glorious prank with the filthy pictures that they'd all pulled together at the Farm, when they were undaunted and young. They laughed about Debs and the yogurt and mulled again the baggage she'd so clearly carried all these years, to pull a stunt like today's fiasco on a subordinate and a former friend.

Soon Procter was quite drunk. Gus and Theo, on the other side of the booth, were laughing, having drifted into their own discussion, the snippets of which, to Procter's ear, struck her as fabulously raunchy. One of Theo's signature stories, she presumed, heard it a dozen times: his wild night at the Kabul Station Talibar, for her money the most debauched place she'd ever set foot in, and that included a club near Lakeland, called Physt.

But Mac, next to her, seemed contemplative, lost in thought. She leaned in close. "Do you think," she said, "that the place really is rotten? That Petra's right and we've got a problem?"

"It's possible," Mac said. "It's also possible the Russians made a mistake in Singapore, I just don't know."

"Timing's certainly odd," Procter said. "Fiasco happens once Gosford and his people are installed, after they've been read in and gotten all the intro briefings. How many Goslings did he bring inside with him?"

Mac thought about that. "Maybe ten, fifteen newbies to the Seventh Floor. At least half of them couldn't pass a polygraph if they'd had to apply."

"Long list of suspects," she said, and let it drop.

He turned to stare at her dead-on. "Look, Artemis, it goes without saying we will do whatever we can to bring Sam back," he said. "I won't say another word about this mess, but I want you to hear that from me."

His words were conjured from the depths of rusted layers of trust and shame, guilt and powerlessness. If they'd asked her how she felt—and, again, they were too close for such callous treatment—she would not have known what to say. But, without saying anything, Mac had known what she needed to hear. She tipped back her drink. "Thanks," she said. "Thanks for saying that."

Mac tilted his head toward her, and they looked across the table for invitation to Theo's story, because theirs had run to its end. Gus was in tears of laughter, Theo now arriving at the punch line: the case officer had come to, chained to a fountain, short seventy-five grand in operational funds.

When Gus had stopped laughing, Procter raised her glass to her friends. There was everything to say, so there was nothing, and in a solemn and wordless clink of their glasses, they toasted the end.

"It's not how I thought it would go," Theo said, "for any of us. I pictured speeches, gratitude, a sense of conquest. Of having run the race and finished well."

"You're drunk," Mac said.

"Well, so what?" Theo said. "Am I wrong, too?"

"Mostly you're drunk," Gus said. "You're always mostly drunk, Theo."

"I'm just saying," Theo continued, "that I saw a different ending, you know? A better ending. For all of us, I mean."

Down went the last of Procter's drink, glass clattering on the table. "Me, too," she said. "I mean, a scoreless tie? Hell's that about? I pictured us winning."

8

McLEAN, VIRGINIA

PROCTER WAS MOWING HER LAWN, A LITTLE DRUNK, when the package arrived. A Thursday afternoon, two weeks after the canning: she'd met Mac for a beer at the Vienna Inn, made it two, then shuffled home for another over yard work in the broiling heat. After mowing, she edged, weed-whacked, and then blew the cuttings into the flower beds, bare and rocky save for a plastic hummingbird with spinning wings, left behind by the previous owners.

Parking the mower alongside her new RAV4 in the garage, she collected the mail from the box and the package from the porch. She dumped it across the mail pile, which, by this point in her skid, was consuming most of her kitchen countertop. Not that the loss of the countertop mattered: the real estate required for meal prep was on a slide as well. She nuked a Party Pizza, placed the whole thing on a sturdy paper plate, popped open another beer, and shambled into the living room. She'd sunk into the recliner before she realized that the remote was on top of the television, plumb out of reach. She ate in a silent stupor, her mind powering down until her phone chirped in her pocket.

"Cummings," she said, "thanks for the ring back."

"I listened to your message, Arty," he said. "I don't get it."

"Don't get what?"

"All of it. You want a job? What the hell?"

"Might need a spot."

"You in the States?"

"Yeah."

"When'll you come down for a visit?"

"Not sure. Maybe soon."

"You done being a spy?"

"Not a spy."

"Right. Whatever. You retiring?"

"Something like that." She was bent over the trash can. In went the Party Pizza box, the plate, and the two beer cans, forming a fresh geologic layer atop last night's: a plate, four cans of Coors, and another Party Pizza box.

"Something like they finally fired your ass?" Cummings said.

"You're getting warmer. Look, if I give you a few weeks' notice can I have a job?"

"At the park?"

"Where the fuck else? You own any other businesses? If so, I'm all ears."

Cummings was making a weird noise, a cross between a wheeze and a chuckle. "Fine, fine. Sure. We'll find something."

After the call she stood alone in her kitchen. She'd bought the house from another CIA officer after she'd been pushed out of the field to land in the Penalty Box—two years of riding a desk at Langley under adult supervision. She'd served her sentence, but many of the moving boxes from back then were still unpacked, standing in as tables and footstools in her living room. In those first months her motive had been nothing but sheer sloth, but in the intervening years she'd arrived at the firm conviction that unpacking would signal defeat, an acknowledgment that she *belonged* in the Penalty Box. There was no furniture in the first-floor sitting room, which she crossed on her way upstairs. The second bedroom held a weight rack and a collection of dumbbells, bands, and free weights that had probably been manufactured during the Nixon administration. The equipment had been her primary contribution to the home's décor.

She turned the volume on her EDM playlist up far as it would go. The menu: thrusters, push-ups, bench presses, sit-ups, band work, cleans, snatches, dead lifts. There was no structure to it. Suffering was the only goal. Around the middle of the workout there was some suggestive business with the bands that got pretty close to snapping off her legs. By the dead lifts she couldn't hear her own thoughts, and the pressure building inside her stomach from the pizza and beer was becoming so volcanic that she had to take a short breather.

After a shower, Procter slumped back into the recliner, this time flipping between QVC and a baseball game. On her return trip to the kitchen, from the corner of her eye she caught a glimpse of the package on the countertop. The shipping label made her frown. The package had been through customs. She bent down for a look.

Return address: Helsinki. "Well, well, well. What the shit," she said.

As a general rule, in the field she had worried about bombs, but Artemis Procter thought you were a pussy if you didn't do things yourself: fixing cars, mowing lawns, and, yes, opening your own goddamn mail. Plus, on the Greek isle of Hydra, an old fortune-teller had shown then nine-year-old Artemis Aphrodite Procter her own death, and this, well . . . her eyes swung to the layered garbage heap, to the still-packed box living its second life as a footstool, over to the slush pile of mail threatening to submerge her toaster. This, she thought, is not it. And if it was, that'd be okay. Merciful. She slit open the box. Inside was another box. She cut that one open.

Looking inside, Procter at first wondered if this was a parting taunt from Debs, but the Helsinki mailing address made no sense, and her stomach dropped from the sudden, certain knowledge of the entity that had mailed it. The box was crammed with nude photos of Artemis Procter. All had been snapped two years prior during a failed pitch in Dushanbe, and all were already out there on the interwebs for all to see. This was not a threat—at least not yet—this was a Russian signature. Inside that box was a CD and another box, small and felt. Russkies apparently still burning CDs, the asshats. She put that aside. Set her jaw at the felt box. Exhaled deeply. Flicked it open. A tuft of hair. A vial of blood. Two squares of cardstock smudged with fingerprints. A siren was ringing through her skull.

This should be taken to Langley, some distant voice said. The CD should not be inserted into a personal computer. Get in your car right now and drive to Headquarters, it said. But she was rifling through a closet. She was tossing aside dusty unread books and dustier unopened boxes. She was ripping through a container of old power cords and batteries. There, the old laptop. The damn annoying voice shouting about obligations to CIA had faded, and she could now only hear the baying siren. She was responsible for her friend. Plus, they'd sent her the goddamn box anyhow. Plus plus: she'd been drinking. Plus plus plus: she no longer worked for CIA.

She powered up the laptop and inserted the disc and clicked play—and waited. Old slow computer. Procter was sorely tempted to smash it to crumbs, but she needed this ancient machine. She took some comfort, watching the wait-wheel turn, in the knowledge she would smash it later.

Procter made it all the way through the video once, propelled by duty to her friend. The first four minutes were a slew of edited, stitched-together table-setting: shots of him seated at a table, saying his name, denying he was CIA, then offering what seemed to be a winding confession. He was in a darkened room in front of a brick wall. Lefortovo? Impossible to tell. He looked progressively thinner as the videos went on, as if before each new recording they'd scooped out more of him. Minutes four through ten were a series of quiet shots: an overhead of him emerging from a room; seated, bound, in a chair; two men—their faces off-camera—holding him up so his toes dangled on the ground and his shoulders were elevated almost above his head. For one full minute she watched him swing upside down. The swinging was rhythmic, almost peaceful. His dangling hair lapped against a concrete floor. His eyes bulged. There were a few shots of Sam lying naked alongside a skeleton of a woman, wrapped in her track-marked arms. Minutes ten through fourteen were the most difficult to watch. Once or twice she desperately wanted to shut it off. But she could not.

She forced herself to watch those four minutes in which Sam Joseph was spread on the floor, face shoved into the wall. He was murmuring, but she could not make out a single word. Sometimes he would seem to smile, and it was so eerie she'd have to look away. At minute fourteen, a cheerful voice, in Russian, said: "Samuel has doctors. He has visitors. He is being fed. He is not sleeping so well but otherwise he is fine. He is counting. He counts to pass the time!"

She only shut off the ringing in her skull by picking up a stool and hurling it into the wall across the living room. She barely heard the thud. The video concluded with a shot of Sam giving the wall that dead smile and the narrator saying again: CIA Officer Samuel Joseph counts to pass the time!

9

MOSCOW

"IT WOULD BE BEST, I THINK, TO TELL THEM THE TRUTH."

Curtis had his back to the wall of the box, knees pulled into his chest. Sam's new cellmate spoke English with an unplaceable lilt that Curtis insisted was Pennsylvania Dutch, but nevertheless sounded foreign. When pressed, Curtis would drag them into a thicket of stories about a childhood in a small town near Lancaster, the name of which Sam could not remember and even Curtis seemed occasionally to fumble. If not for all his lies, Curtis could have been a priest. He had a confessional air, and a dogged ability to shepherd even the most wandering conversations home to his favorite topic: the truth.

"And why is that?" Sam asked.

"Because then they will let us go."

Sam had counted his meals since Curtis's arrival. He could not be certain of hours, much less days or weeks or months, but he knew he had shared fifteen meals with Curtis.

"They are not going to let us go, Curtis," Sam said.

Curtis masked his face with his hands and let out a desperate sigh. "How can you be sure?"

"I've been telling them the truth. And here I am."

TWO MEALS LATER, SAM AND CURTIS SAT ON OPPOSITE SIDES of the cell, staring through each other. He felt Curtis trying to read his thoughts. Sam, on the other hand, had been counting the fiftieth line of stars on the wall, and had maddeningly lost track while trying to remember how many stars were blocked by his cellmate's head. "I do not think," Curtis started in, "that Procter would approve of how you are handling this."

"Who?" Sam said, his eyes coming into focus to rest on Curtis.

Curtis hung his head and snagged another cracker from his tray. "Do you want to die here? What about your parents? Natalie?"

"How did you say you knew about Singapore?" Sam asked.

Curtis sighed theatrically, then offered his convoluted tale: How he'd been a deep cover officer for Moscow Station. How the Russians had snatched him off the Moscow streets on day one and brought him here. How he knew all about Golikov. He miraculously knew, for example, that Golikov had shared a secret with Sam, and pleaded that if Sam would only tell them what it was, they might both go free. "I have a wife and two little boys," he would say, and then he would sob. Curtis was an exceptional sobber; he could draw it out for what felt like hours; the mewls and heaving and, eventually, shrieking would reach such a pitch that Sam would have gladly traded it for the thumping sounds they piped through the unseen speakers, the ones that were only screams.

Curtis's performance must have sent the Russian listeners up the wall, because one meal after that, two men flung open the door and dragged him out. The shrieking, Sam thought, by then had deflated. His captors did try to feign a disastrously bloody and high-volume torture session for Curtis immediately outside the door of the box, complete with a cacophony of screams, grunts, plaintive cries, gurgles, and the whir of an unseen drill. It went on for what could have been hours. And then it stopped just as soon as it had begun. Eventually, they brought Sam to a room with a monitor showing Curtis kneeling in front of a wall. A nameless interrogator sat across from Sam. Together, they watched Curtis on the screen for a few significant seconds.

"What did Golikov tell you?" barked the interrogator.

"He asked me about my whisky."

"If you do not tell us, we will kill Mr. Hasp."

"Curtis?"

"Yes. Curtis Hasp. A fellow CIA officer."

A man walked into the frame; he held a pistol at his side. They all hung there for a moment. Through the speakers Sam heard Curtis whimpering.

"What," the man repeated to Sam, "did Boris Golikov tell you?"

"He asked me about my whisky."

The interrogator sighed and then made a short phone call. A gunshot blared through the speakers on the monitor. Curtis lurched forward. The video went black before Sam could see how well the man could mimic a lifeless body slumping into concrete.

"Thank god," Sam said.

HE WAS ROUSTED FROM SLEEP BY THE SCRATCH OF FINGERnails across his face and forehead, and above him in the darkness settled the outline of a face. He could not feel his legs. He could not move his arms. He could not draw breath. A tongue slithered in his mouth, long and snaky, tickling his gums and the backsides of his teeth. Hands cradled his head and he felt the pressure of someone sitting atop his chest. When the tongue retreated, he heard, as if from a great distance, a raspy female voice that he could not understand. Her hands brushed him: hair, cheeks, shoulders. Then her fingernails went back to work: a few clawing strikes that raked skin off his face. He tried to shout but found he could not make a sound. Her tongue again plunged into his mouth, this time drilling for his throat, trying to draw breath from his lungs. When her lips unclamped from his, the wetness of her tongue began to slide along his neck.

HE OPENED HIS EYES TO BLINDING LIGHT AND PEACEFUL quiet. A skeletal woman with exhausted, visionary eyes sat cross-legged in front of him. Her gossamer hair was pale gold and hung lifelessly down to her shoulders. Her face was emptied of life; track marks covered her arms. She wore bright red lipstick and a dead smile that seemed to slide into his chest.

"When you sleep, Samuel," she said in perfectly intoned English. "I visit when you sleep."

Sometimes when he woke, she wore a starchy blue jumpsuit. Sometimes she was naked.

Her hair smelled clean and fresh, like flowers. Her skin was white and dirty, the color of milk swirled with ash.

Anarchically crooked teeth bristled through her dead smile. But her lipstick was never smudged. It was the brightest red he had ever seen.

She does not have a name, he decided. She never had a name.

HER SPINE WAS A STRING OF PEARLS. SHE WAS SPRAWLED ON the floor beside him. She was the little spoon and this time she was naked. It was quiet. The lights were on. He'd no memory of his last meal. He could not remember the number of little red stars on the walls, much less where he'd left off. Since the woman had arrived, he'd managed so little counting. She sensed his stirring and said, "You should not have done that to me. I am very sick. You will be sick, too."

He rolled away from her. He fixed his gaze on the little red stars and began counting.

ELEVEN THOUSAND FOUR HUNDRED AND TWENTY-SEVEN.

Eleven thousand four hundred and twenty-eight.

Eleven thousand four hundred and twenty-nine.

Eleven thousand four hundred and thirty.

Eleven thousand four hundred and thirty-one.

Eleven thousand four hundred and thirty-two.

The fog was rolling in.

He had the strength to mark the star where he had stopped. A victory. He had notched a victory. He fell asleep.

HE WOKE TO THE SMELL OF WHAT SHE HAD LEFT IN THE bucket. She sat cross-legged on the far side of the room curling her hair around her fingers like ribbons. He could taste her lipstick on his tongue. This time he was naked. She wore her blue jumpsuit. "I hear you have a secret," she said. "Will you tell me? I will go away if you tell me."

He rolled toward the wall. Squinted. Aimed. Found it.

Eleven thousand four hundred and thirty-three.

Eleven thousand four hundred and thirty-four.

Eleven thousand four hundred and thirty-five.

Eleven thousand four hundred and thirty-six . . .

REM SHUT THE FOLDER AND EXTINGUISHED THE VIDEO OF Samuel Joseph and his companion, the ghoulish girl they'd plucked from a Moscow street corner with promises of endless smack. He checked his watch: He had reservations tonight at the White Rabbit. The restaurant was a splurge on his bureaucrat's salary, the luxurious date a peace offering to Ninel because lately he had done nothing but work. He was tempted to cancel—he had the Director first thing tomorrow and there was still more tape to review—but he would not. Rem had been married since he was twenty-three, most of that time to Ninel. He knew where the lines were drawn. He shrugged on his suit coat, clicked off the lights in his office, and left for dinner with his wife.

"YOU ARE QUIET TONIGHT," NINEL SAID, SPEAKING OVER A forkful of peas held suspended in front of her mouth. She wore a dark blue dress and the pearls he had brought her from Tokyo. Her gray hair was pinned up. He had always liked that she did not dye it, as a few of his mistresses had. Ninel's beauty was regal and timeless; why ruin it with gimcrack youth?

Their table sat by a window facing the Moskva and the lights of the Arbat. The bustling dining room was shaped like a half cylinder: long, with art deco half-moon windows at the ends, a screen of cloth stretched across the ceiling like the skin of a dirigible. The wing seats were poorly cushioned and he had to shift his weight constantly. He was working on an asparagus-and-nettle soup and a sinking feeling about his meeting tomorrow with the Director. He was still quite hungry.

"Work," he grumbled. He did not elaborate. With Ninel, there was no need.

"How is your soup?" she asked, signaling for the waiter.

"Fine," he said. "Quite good." He slurped at a spoonful to make the point and readied a glower for the approaching pickpocket of a waiter.

"I wish you would order more food," Ninel said. "The beef ribs, maybe? Your favorite. It's a special night." The waiter had arrived. "Another glass, please," she said.

Sixteen hundred rubles, he thought. Added to the damage inflicted by Ninel so far made the total . . . 12,830. And she was going to order dessert, probably with the ice wine to boot.

"I am not so hungry," Rem said, frustrated that the waiter had not even met his glower.

"Is that so? Or do you have another of your exhausting math exercises running?"

With a harrumph he took a sip of his mineral water and dredged his spoon back into the soup. "Don't be ridiculous. We've talked about this."

"Yes," she said. "We have." The waiter returned with her wineglass. This time Rem landed his glower, which shooed off the waiter before the man could sell them something else.

"Well, since it is casting quite the pall, why don't you tell me about this problem at work?" she said, taking a sip. "What's bothering you?"

"Oh, it's fine," he said, slicing the air with his spoon. "Let's not gum up dinner with shop talk. Tell me about what you're reading. I saw *Norwegian Wood* out on your nightstand. Are you dipping back into it?"

Ninel was clicking a fingernail on the base of her glass. Her right eye had shuttered slightly—she was careful, though, to track him steadily with both—and she leaned back in her chair, a posture she adopted while taking a minute to sprinkle cut glass through her tone of voice. "Six months before your already delayed retirement," she said, "and you are sweating work. Allowing it to ruin delightful dinners! I'll give you a choice, Rem. Two options. The first is that we have a chat about your impending retirement. You could answer basic questions, all so far deflected or ignored. These might include: How do you feel about retiring? What do you plan to do with your free time? Are you going to schedule a trip for us to celebrate, as we've discussed? Correction: As I have alternately begged and demanded? Other questions might arise, as conversation warrants."

He now aimed the glower at an asparagus spear breaking the surface of his soup. "What's the other option?"

"You talk about this problem at work, of course."

"That one, then."

Staff arrived to clear away their plates. Before the waiter could offer dessert, Rem waved him off. "The check."

"Well, then"—she patted a napkin to her lips, which she did when she was holding her tongue—"go on."

"I'm responsible for someone's security," he said. "Someone quite important to us. And I am worried they are in danger. Or soon will be. It is difficult to explain without going into details."

"What can you do about it?" Her hand went up. "Apart from ruining our dinner?"

Oh god, he thought. His back was turned, but he could easily picture the smug look on the waiter's face. It was, in fact, all he could picture.

"I think I know how to protect this person, this source," he said. "But to do so . . . well, I would have to do something quite nasty, Ninel. No other way to put it. And I am not certain the Director would back my decision, though he may want me to do this thing anyhow, because it eliminates a potential problem and places all future blame squarely at my feet. I am not even sure this nasty thing is necessary. As usual, it's all confusing. And it's all on my shoulders." He clanked his spoon into the bowl. Thoughts of Samuel Joseph had washed away his appetite.

"You are a fanatic," Ninel said. "A good soldier. A workaholic, whatever. Take your pick. You need to go easier on yourself. You are done in six months, Rem."

"Bah," he said, and shifted his ass around, searching for relief. He looked out the window, beyond Ninel. An image flashed through his mind: The American spread in the box, the heroin-dripped girl sucking on his face. What the hell had that been about? "He's Pyotr's age. Kind of looks like him. Not sure I can do it. Not sure if I need to and not sure if I can. We had rules once, Ninel. Once upon a time we had the goddamn rules. Now to get ahead you've got to break them. It's a damnable thing."

"Who are you talking about? Who looks like Pyotr?"

He treated her to his usual imploring look. It said: *Right here, Ninel, here you've found the line.*

"Fine," she said, turning to the window. "But who cares about getting ahead? You're *ahead*, Rem. You're so far ahead, you're six months away from being done."

The waiter arrived. "We will have dessert after all," Ninel said.

"Delightful. I will bring the menus." He took one step away before Ninel's voice stopped him.

"No need," she said. "I know what we want. I will have the rhubarb pie"—new total: 13,420—"and he will have . . . Rem, dear, what do you want?"

"I am not hungry."

"He will have the honey cake. We will also have two glasses of the ice wine with dessert. And coffees for each of us after. Thank you." The waiter hustled off, joyful bounce to his stride.

"What is the damage now?" she said.

He pounced on his water to dodge her eyes. For about ten seconds no one spoke. Ninel fixed him with an unkind smile. He sighed. "I don't know."

"Which price did you forget?"

"I didn't forget. You need to know something to forget it."

"*Which*"—Ninel could skillfully compress paragraphs of tension into single words—"did you forget?"

"The ice wine."

"Twelve hundred per glass."

He thought for a moment. Refolded the napkin in his lap. "Seventeen thousand five hundred and seventy."

She leaned into the table to take his hand. "My dear, this little quirk of yours is going to be insufferable on our vacation after you retire."

"I agree," he said, squeezing her palm. "Let's skip the trip, then."

PART II

DEAR FRIENDS AND CHERISHED ENEMIES

10

KISSIMMEE, FLORIDA
THREE MONTHS LATER

SLEEPY PETE WASN'T ACTUALLY SLEEPY. HE SHOULD'VE been called Spunky Pete or Mean Pete. He was a known biter, after all. Hell, he'd bit her twice.

First time right near the elbow when she was learning the ropes. Spent an afternoon at the hospital up in Hunters Creek. Happened to everybody. It was a when, not if, kind of a thing, Cummings would say. Second time on her left hand. A smidge embarrassing.

She was grabbing at Pete now, but her hands were butter in the wet heat. She pulled Pete up from the muddy lagoon. He was working a creepy half smile and his limp feet left scars in the sand. She dug in her Birks and yanked him across the beach. The crowd was screaming, louder than usual, primal vibes were building: there was blood coming. She'd seen this movie before, lord she had. The kids would plaster the video up on social media and that night it would hit FOX 35 and the other Orlando stations. There was a certain notoriety to violence, but it was mostly bad for business—Gatorville's customers figured out pretty quick that they could be next.

She paused for a moment to catch her breath, and Sleepy Pete set to crawling back toward the lagoon. She waddled through the sand after him and got her hands on his hind legs and then she was on his back trying to cover his eyes so she could clasp shut his jaw. Her Cleveland Indians ball cap slipped off into the wet sand and her frazzled black hair tumbled down to cover her eyes. Sleepy Pete was pissed. She couldn't blame him. There was a human chick on his back slapping hands on his face and dragging him by the tail out of his sweet lagoon. Tail whipping around, he started twisting and writhing to sink his teeth into her arm. She was focused now, muscling his snout into the sand, covering the eyes.

With one hand she snagged the hat from the sand and put it on the gator bastard. Here's one hell of a photo op, folks, she gritted into the mic pinned to her shirt. The cap fell off pretty quick, but she figured it was a bit embarrassing for the gator and she was all for embarrassing Sleepy Pete on account of the two bitings. Once she had his snout mashed into the sand she slid her hand down to his gator lips or whatever the fuck and pinned the jaws shut. She was straddling his shoulders. She lifted Sleepy Pete's head into the air so his under snout was pointing right at the crowd. A murmur went up from the bleachers, and she whispered into his little gator ears that she owned him, that this was her swamp.

Then the gator whipped his tail and she lost purchase and was in the sand, muttering holy hell, ah fuck, into the hot mic with the gator pouncing at her and the crowd wild, parents shielding young eyes, this being the type of crisis that could trigger therapy down the road, the exotic varieties not covered by insurance. She hurdled a fence, the gator's jaws snapping shut a few inches behind her shorts, and she rolled into a thicket of palms, curses filling the mic and booming over the loudspeakers. Cummings was dashing into the ring after Sleepy Pete.

"Artemis!" he was yelling. "Artemis, dammit. Dammitall, Artemis, get back in here. Artemis!"

ONCE THEY'D SAFELY RETURNED SLEEPY PETE TO HIS lagoon, after they'd distributed apologies and refunds and all manner of gift certificates, after they'd warned the lawyers in Kissimmee of the deluge of lawsuits that was surely coming, after Procter had smoked three Virginia Slims on the emptied bleachers, Cummings sat her down in his office to scream at her. Within a few months' time, she thought, canned from CIA and now maybe Gatorville. A twofer that hadn't happened to anybody before, and probably wouldn't again. But Cummings didn't want to fire her, he just wanted to yell. Labor was always short around Gatorville. He couldn't afford to go looking for someone else.

"You still want me to cover the Jumparoo tomorrow?" she asked Cummings when he'd finished shouting.

He pointed at the door: "Get the hell out."

Her trailer sat on a few acres off Boggy Creek that Cummings had rented her on the cheap, a sandy patch thick with palmetto and oak neighboring a swamp that bubbled in the heat. Procter's Sunshine State domain boasted a galley kitchen with a banquette, a bedroom, bathroom, and a cramped living room doubling as a storage facility. The sofa was sagging and turquoise and floral-printed. Most of the curtains were beads.

Procter parked her RAV4 next to the rusty weight rack. The swamp bristled with the whine of insects. The air was wet, the sky thick with unfallen rain. Inside she dialed the EDM up so loud that the trailer's windows shivered and the bead curtains shimmied.

To distract herself from the day's agitations, she tended to the small armory snuggled under her bed. First, she lapped bore oil through her dear friend, a twelve-gauge Mossberg shotgun. Next, she cleaned the handle of her cherished bat and then applied pine tar, working it a ways up the barrel for good measure. The M4 was in fine shape. She debated disassembling and cleaning the Mk 48 belt-fed machine gun but could not summon the energy. The cases went back under the bed.

She took a shot of gin and flopped across the sheets. By and by, with the first jets of rain drowning the croaks and bonks of the frogs, Procter fell asleep.

NEXT DAY CUMMINGS METED OUT PROCTER'S PUNISHMENT for the Sleepy Pete fiasco: for three weeks she would cover the eleven-thirty and the two-thirty Gator-Mania shows, then string up the whole chickens and pig carcass for the four o'clock Jumparoo. "And, Artemis, you are gonna manage tear-down," he said, folding his chubby hands in front of his mouth and leaning back in his chair, which he did when he was pleased with himself.

Jumparoos brought solid coin for Cummings, but Procter couldn't stand them: her end—teardown, aka cleanup—was a pain in the ass, like mopping up after a long day at the Colosseum. Pig and chicken giblets went airborne across sections of boardwalk, where they would be trampled, mashed into the slats by tourists hustling for cover. By late afternoon the flies were rolling, the air was ripe, and Procter had to use the Meat Stick to floss the gore from the boards. The stick was, in fact, a broom handle filed down to floss the slats. And sometimes it got stuck.

She was yanking at the thing when she caught sight of him standing at the far end of the boardwalk. He looked the same. What had she expected? Bent back? Hollow eyes? Bald? Prison beard? He stood tall, half smile on his face at the sight of the Meat Stick. Bags around the eyes were flabbier, but unless you knew where he'd spent the summer you'd think nothing amiss, other than perhaps that wiry handsome guys were rare around Gatorville, and when they did appear they tended to be draped with kids.

The stick popped free, and she tossed it aside. When she'd reached him, she drew him in for a hug. For a few moments they hung there. She did not want to let him go. And she had no idea what to say.

She knew Sam was out, of course. Mac had called with the news the day of the swap, when Sam returned stateside. And Theo had visited Gatorville weeks earlier, while they were debriefing Sam at the Farm. Mostly she and Theo drank, and he'd spilled a few details: There'd been a trade. Mac and Gus had done something vaguely heroic. Bodily, Sam was fine. "And mentally?" she'd asked. "Too soon," Theo had said. "Too soon to say on that one."

Her mouth was opening when he said, "You know you've got a good deal of blood on this shirt, Chief." A half step back, and he tugged at it, a blue-black number stenciled with an albino gator submerged in the swamp, eyes peeking above the surface.

"Pig's blood," she said. "Occupational hazard."

Sam looked down. A few gators were thrashing in the brackish water below.

She pulled him in for one more hug, her version of being overcome with emotion, and said, "Look, I'm no good at these types of speeches. So how about you assume I said exactly what I should have in a moment such as this?"

"You just did."

"I appreciate that. And it's good to see you. Well and truly. I confess I am surprised Gatorville is on your USA return tour." This was surprise, not self-loathing—that would have been a decidedly off-brand emotion for Procter. Even though she and Sam went back more than a decade, she'd figured that he wouldn't be too keen to trek down to Central Florida's third largest alligator-themed amusement park to make breezy chitchat with the woman responsible for the op that sent him to a Moscow prison camp for the summer.

"With a new lease on life, how could I miss this?" he said, nudging his chin in the direction of the discarded Meat Stick. "When do you get off work?"

She checked her watch. "Near enough to now." She scanned around the boardwalk. "Looks like I got most of it."

"Got a place we can talk?"

"This isn't a social call?"

He tried to force a smile, but the skin of his face seemed to fasten tighter to his skull as his jaw clamped shut and the humor drained from his eyes. "Needs to be private," Sam muttered, dropping his voice to a harsh whisper. "We have a problem, Chief. A big problem."

THE SUN HAD VANISHED, AND THE BOG BRISTLED WITH frogs and crickets when she turned onto the sandy drive leading to her trailer. Sam rode in the passenger seat. After they had left Gatorville—separately—she had picked him up from a restaurant in Kissimmee; he did not want his rental traveling to her home. She stepped into the sand, arched her back to stretch. "Let me sparkle back up," she said, "rinse off the blood and such, and then we can get down to business. Meantime, make yourself comfortable."

After she'd showered, Procter made two gin and tonics in plastic Gatorville souvenir cups. She gathered a pack of Slims and a lighter, and for an ashtray she selected a Gatorville mug, the one with the gold rim and the handle shaped like a gator tail. They slid into the banquette.

Sam Joseph had been a rising-star case officer who made a bad decision: he'd fallen for an asset, a Syrian, during their tour in Damascus, Procter's first tour as a Chief. The CIA's Performance Review Board had sent him to the Penalty Box—two years riding a desk under adult supervision—but he had recovered, clawing his way back to the field for a few tours until he'd been directed to Headquarters, where Procter, on a trip through the Box herself, had snagged him for Moscow X.

"Jaggers," she said, fixing herself a smoke. "Welcome to paradise."

Burt O. GOLDJAGGER was Sam's "funnyname," the alias used in written cable traffic to avoid printing his true name on documents. Procter often went with "Jaggers" over his Christian name.

She shoved the Slims and lighter his way, but he waved them off.

"Quite the place," he said, giving the bead curtain a smack. "Your cousin owns it?"

"Nah, I bought it straight-out. Picked it up on the way down."

"I meant the gator park," Sam said.

"Ah," she said. "Right. Yes. Cummings. Mom's big brother's kid. Land's been in the family since the forties." She puffed out clouds of smoke while she spoke, cigarette pinned in her teeth. "Pay's not so great, but I've got my pension, and the perks are swell"—at this Sam made a face, and Procter put a solemn hand to her heart. "Plus, I eat and drink on the Gatorville tab. And there's thirty percent off at the gift shop," she said, raising her souvenir cup approvingly. "Only ten percent at the emporium, though."

"There's a difference between the gift shop and the emporium?"

With a long last drag of her cigarette, she crushed the butt in the mug and gave the gator-tail handle a flick. "Emporium's fancier."

"Quite the setup here," he said, jerking his head around the trailer, with the tone of a man commenting on a mysterious skin rash.

"It's a single wide, Jaggers. And I'm single as hell, so it works for me. She lit up another and screwed the ball cap backward so Chief Wahoo faced the wall.

"You know, Chief," Sam said, "they're not called the Indians anymore and you shouldn't be wearing that offensive hat."

"Oh dear," she said. "My bad. The guy who got caught banging his asset is offended. I'm so sorry." She twisted the hat back around and smiled all big and white. Then it evaporated.

He was chuckling. "You're such a dick, Chief."

"I'm not a Chief anymore," she said. "Just a dick. What've they got you doing now, by the way?"

"Back in Moscow X desk-riding," he said. "Working for Gus. When I got home they stashed me at the Farm for a bit, let the family and Natalie come see me, spend some time together but in the nursery, you know how it goes. Then it got rolling: security and Counterintelligence debriefings, writing it all down, a roto-rooting from the docs and the shrinks. The capstone was a month of mandatory leave. Gus called me toward the end, asked if I wanted my old job back."

"And here you are," she said.

"And here I am." His phone shivered in his pocket. He looked at the name, wrinkled his nose, and typed out a reply. The phone chirped with a response and he thrust it back into his pocket.

"Natalie?" Procter inquired.

"Yeah."

"What's she have to say?"

"That she misses me."

"Well, of course she does, you're the tits. Remind me: How long have you two been together?"

"Little over a year."

"And does Natalie know you're here?"

"No."

"Where does she think you are?"

"Vegas."

She laughed. "You know, Jaggers, most guys would lie to their girlfriend about where they're going *in order to get to Vegas.* Instead, you're using Vegas as the alibi for a trip to the swamps outside Kissimmee, and you, presumably, are not even here for sex or some other vice. To cap it all off, you're lying to the woman who waited faithfully for you to emerge from a Russian prison and who, if memory serves, is a gem sparkling from all angles, and a Levantine, to boot. Said differently: Sam Joseph's kryptonite. Now, look, you've come a long way and told lies to get here, so I imagine some heavy shit's coming. You should feel free to dish it to me whenever you're ready."

Sam picked up the pack of cigarettes and fixed himself a smoke. He blew ragged clouds through the bead curtains for a moment, thinking, she figured, about how to begin.

"I need to go through it from the start," he said. "I've had to tell the Russians one story, the Agency another, and Natalie and my folks a third, and it'll help me to give you the clean version, front to back."

"You start where you want," she said, with a quick sip. "I've got oodles of time."

"The dates are a little fuzzy," Sam said, "on account of the obvious. But the cable comes in from Moscow on the morning of . . ." He stopped talking and just stared past her. His brain seemed to have misfired.

Bad start, she thought. This might be rough.

"That cable arrived from Moscow Station on the morning of the fifteenth," she said, "March fifteenth. Hard for me to forget that day now."

"Right. By next afternoon I've made my arrangements for Singapore—room, surface transport, pocket money. I wire money into my account and take the hundred grand of cash for the down payment to Golikov. You approve the final cable and I sign the receipts for the money."

"You signed them 'Daffy Duck,' I heard," Procter said. "The receipts."

"Heard?" he said, chuckling, "You didn't look?"

"No one looks at the fucking receipts except for the Finance smurfs, which is who complained to me. But keep going."

"Next morning I'm wheels up from Dulles. Wheels down in Singapore next afternoon and straight to the high-limit bacc tables to scout for Golikov. No sign of him. I mean, hell, the guy's given us a hotel and a two-day window, but the place is not small. Upstairs for a shower and Red Bulls, and then I stroll through the hotel for the lay of the land: the exits, the flow, where security has the fixed points, and how they're moving. I scout the sight lines into the high-limit bacc rooms. Back to the tables for a bit, then I cool it. No sign of the guy, it's seven a.m., and we know the delegation is in meetings all day. I go upstairs, sleep. I'm up by noon, and I try to sweat out the jet lag in the gym."

While he spoke, Sam rolled the bead curtains in his fingers as if praying the Rosary. "That night I'm at the bacc tables again. High-limit room. Not the ones for whales. The tier below. Every seat is taken. And I see Golikov. He's playing and looking around like he's creeped. I cash out, toss down a sparkling water at a bar, and return for a seat at his table. And I'm lucky. There is a seat open, right next to him. I order whisky, a Macallan, and I casually mention that during a recent run in Vegas I'd sampled the forty-year. Guy fumbles the cards at the signal, but recovers, says he's drinking a Springbank. We drink and play a few more hands, and then he leans in close to say something. I've blocked it from the Russians. And from the Agency . . ."

Waiting for him to go on, Procter again wondered if Sam's mind had wandered off the path. The silence lingered, and Sam seemed to vanish inside his own thoughts, which Procter sensed danced between a reluctance to put words to what had happened next or, perhaps, an inability to remember the events at all. For a while he pecked at his drink. "Take your time, man, don't rush on my account," she said, easing out of her own chair to get some more ice from the kitchenette.

When she'd settled back into her seat, Sam looked at her with a face that was somehow both resolved and afraid. "Golikov," Sam began, his speech slowing, "told me this"—he cleared his throat, and for a brief moment paused, then stiffened, as if readying for a dive off a cliff, or bracing for the impact of a car wreck—"*I have a name to sell you. An SVR penetration of CIA. Very senior. You have a mole at Langley.*"

Procter was staring straight at Sam, her fingers tracing idly along the rim of her glass. "Those are Golikov's words?" she asked.

"Every last one of them."

11

KISSIMMEE

PROCTER COULD NOT HELP BUT WONDER IF HER OLD friend was misremembering things. Nearly four months in a Russian dungeon, and who could blame a cat for fever dreams? Certainly not Artemis Procter. If anything, she'd take some of the heat herself, seeing as she'd midwifed the busted op. But she knew better than to question him in that moment, and what's more—this part arrived on a swell of nausea—it made too much goddamn sense. "That would explain a few things," Procter said, and swatted the bead curtains. "They got Golikov's key, didn't they? The one you passed him."

"I've assumed so," Sam said. "They came into my room, asked what Golikov told me, and when they didn't like my answer they jabbed me with something. World went dark." From there he recounted a few dim memories of waking in darkness, sometimes in bone-chilling silence, sometimes to the roar of engines, once or twice to the crash of waves and the smell of the sea. He assumed a leg of the journey had passed inside a shipping container. Each time he woke he would hear voices, feel a jab in the arm, and the darkness would return. The interrogations kicked off after he'd been hung upside down for a few hours and visited by an older man who spoke English fluently, with only the faintest hint of an accent. No one ever told him he was in Russia, but he couldn't figure where else he might be. "Agency thinks they had me in a facility outside Moscow," Sam said. "I was never formally on the rolls anywhere, far as Russia House knows. Or would tell me."

"But it wasn't Lefortovo?" Procter asked.

"No. I am sure of that."

"This old guy who visited you," Procter said. "You know who it was?"

"Debriefers showed me pictures at the Farm. It was a guy named Rem Zhomov."

"And what did he want to know?"

"The name means something to you?"

"It might."

"He wanted to know the same things they all did, in the end." Sam explained that while he would eventually have conversations—some even civil—on the subject of his past Agency experience, his network of contacts, and his time in Syria, Golikov and Singapore occupied the vast majority of his interrogator's interest, including Zhomov's. Specifically: Had Golikov given Sam anything while they'd been at the tables? Paper? Names? Information? Thumb drives? "I knew they would kill me," Sam concluded, "if I told them what Golikov had said. They put people in the cell with me, they tried to convince me to talk. A guy they claimed was CIA. A woman . . ."

And for an entire dreadful minute, sixty seconds flat, he simply stared off into space, presumably reliving whatever hellish fragments of that experience remained lodged in his memory. When at last he resumed his story, it was to tell her that the woman did not have a name. Then he went silent, his eyes staring at the beads, his head bobbing slightly, as though he were counting, as she had seen in the videos they'd sent. "Even now," Sam said, whispering to the beads, "I am not certain the woman was real."

Two-minute pause: a very long time to sit quietly, one-on-one, across a banquette.

Procter listened to the din of the swamp, growing louder in their silence, and let the anger wash over her. She'd already set down her glass out of respect to Sam, and she now sat there with him until he could shake himself loose from wherever he'd been, or whatever this woman had done to him. He picked up the story again, without warning: "Finally it all stopped. They put me in a hood, marched me into the light, then into a van, then a plane—I heard engines—and when we landed it was raining and an Agency delegation was there to greet me. They tell me it's Vienna, and my first thought should have been relief, but it was panic. I was in a pinch."

Procter said, "The mole could be debriefing you."

"Right."

"Who was on the flight?"

"Deborah Sweet, Mac Mason, Theo Monk, Gus Raptis, and a few other hangers-on."

"You're sure about that?" she asked. "No harm in not being sure, after what you'd been through."

"I am completely sure. I paid close attention."

The part of her that had wanted to believe him all along, that was presently kneecapping doubts about Sam's mental well-being because a traitor busting up Singapore meant it wasn't her fault, much less his; well, the mention of those names made Procter sick, no bones about it. That list made her want to stop right here and tell Sam he should cut his losses, retire to Vegas with Natalie, and move on. She would keep up the drinking, and soon they would both forget all about it. But buried behind Sam's eyes she saw fanaticism: to root out the traitor that had put him in a box, to expunge memories of the woman who had haunted him there, to get even, an impulse that resonated with Artemis Aphrodite Procter, always and everywhere. She lit another cigarette.

"Who ran the debriefings when you got home?"

"A team from Security led the charge. Russia House and Seventh Floor folks made the rounds, of course, all the usuals. The Director even showed up for a how-are-you-doing-sport, I'm-proud-of-you sit-down."

"Anyone pay unusually close attention to what you said?"

"Not really."

"Anyone conspicuously absent?"

"No."

"So what did you tell the Agency?" she said. "In the end."

"Everything except for Golikov's words about the mole."

"You told anyone else what he said?"

"Who else could I tell?"

"Jaggers, you are breaking a thicket of Agency regs and federal laws talking to me about this. Not to mention withholding it during your official Agency debriefings."

"You think I don't know that? What was I supposed to do? The list of people who knew about Golikov was small. It includes the DDO and a few people inside Russia House. I don't even think Gosford was aware of it."

"And most of them are my friends," she said. "Is that why you came to me?"

"I came to you because you're my friend, and you're out. And, what do you mean, 'most of them'?"

"I go way back with Debs, Mac, Gus, and Theo. We were all in the same Farm class. Used to be close with Debs, but not anymore. Those guys were—are—my best friends, I suppose."

"I thought I was your best friend." He was smiling, thank god. She'd never been happier to see a smile.

"Once we've killed a bunch of people together and then nearly gotten our own asses killed right after a suicide bombing, well, after we live through something like that you are welcome to the number one slot on the list. Gotta do more than get imprisoned for me, Jaggers."

She tried a wink and wondered—in a thought most foreign to her reptilian brain—if she'd crossed a line.

But he said: "I'll hold you to that," and shot her a wry smile, and it was like they were joking again in Damascus Station. Jaggers was a rising-star case officer and she had her first Chief gig and the world was on the table in front of them, not a meal fighting you on its way up or down.

She shoved aside her drink, almost knocking it off the table.

He was looking at her very closely. "Do you buy it, Chief?" It was almost a whisper. Had he sensed her earlier skepticism? Was he uncertain himself?

"I wish I didn't. But BUCCANEER's death, Golikov's compromise, your kidnapping"—she wiggled three fingers in the air—"all occurred in a span of two days. Now, I guess we could call that a coincidence. Shit happens. But your imprisonment . . . well, that's a tickler, isn't it? It makes more sense if they were worried Golikov had something valuable to sell."

"Who was BUCCANEER?" Sam asked. She'd forgotten: Sam wouldn't have had access to that case, and upon his return the Bratva and his debriefers would have had no reason to tell him.

"SVR colonel we'd been running for about five years," Procter said. "He was recalled from Athens. Killed himself during the arrest at his dacha outside Moscow."

"And this happened the same week as Singapore?"

"Same day," Procter said.

"So we start there," Sam said. "Compare the two BIGOT lists. Singapore and BUCCANEER. See who had access to both, who overlaps. That, at least, should be fairly easy."

"Molehunts are absolutely not easy," she said flatly. "You run one—hell, you *find* a mole—it's like tossing your cookies on a Tilt-A-Whirl. Flies right back and slimes you in the face."

"Look, I get it, I just . . . Oh shit!"

A bat, bird, or some other goddamn swamp creature had slammed into the trailer. Outside came a muffled squeak and the flutter of wings. Sam had almost spilled from the banquette onto the floor.

"Gets weird out there at night," Procter said.

12

KISSIMMEE / I-95 NORTH

THE HOURS TO COME WERE MARKED BY THE SATISFYING crescendo of operational planning and preparation. A return to form, really, for a woman who had spent a quarter century playing the Game, and who, mere months removed, had forgotten none of its charms. The prospect of running an op that was not gator-related had her pacing the trailer while she spoke; it had her making smile-like things—nothing excessive, mind you, just once or twice—and it had her garaging the gin to park coffee cups across the banquette, an unheard-of switch in the predawn hours, at least since her arrival in Florida three months prior.

The discussion of which documents Sam might reasonably access, and how he might go about it, had her nearly giddy. And this was even before the coffee had begun to bite—the machine was still gurgling away on the counter. Procter, never one for paperwork, even found herself enthralled while completing an excruciatingly detailed write-up of Sam's experience in Singapore, in Russia, and what he had told his Agency debriefers upon his return. Time pleasurably vanished as they made plans for the Northern Virginia piece of the operation: safe house, commo plan, document storage, petty cash, her alibi for travel.

As had often been true on the inside, it was more fun to focus on the *what* and the *how* and the details of the op than the wider picture, god forbid. The vistas got pretty disturbing the more you zoomed out, sprawling as they did across two threatening horizons, one with Procter and Sam as jailbirds and the second with a good friend a traitor, perhaps both, if things were to go sideways, as they usually did. Ignoring this made the exercise far more enjoyable, but right around dawn Sam ruined it, asking what she thought about the fact that this extracurricular return to the field wasn't merely frowned upon or difficult, but mildly felonious.

"What of it?" she retorted after she'd heard enough. "You have any better ideas?" She was up at the counter, the overworked coffee machine having grown uncooperative by first light.

"I go to Gosford," he said, without conviction.

"And he goes to Sweet. Shovels it onto her plate." She was maniacally flicking the buttons. "He says handle it, Debs. Then what?" Rough shake of the pot. "We've got a key suspect running the investigation. Fox in the henhouse." She gave the coffeepot a smack right on the lid, and the light clicked on. She returned to the banquette and stared at Sam while the machine bubbled to life. "Are your feet getting cold from conviction," she asked, "or are you just uselessly fiddlefucking around with the possibilities?"

"The latter," he said after a moment. "Fiddlefucking. But the idea of taking documents from the building? It does give me the creeps."

Procter was up for another cup. The machine was not even half done, and the warming plate filled with coffee when she lifted the pot to fill her mug. Hisses and gurgles accompanied its return. "The whole place exists to steal secrets," she said. "Remember that."

BY MIDMORNING SAM WAS GONE. WHEN SHE DROVE TO Gatorville it was not to prep for the Jumparoo, but instead to tell Cummings she needed a few weeks off. When he pressed for details, none came. "Godfather shit," he muttered, swiveling his chair away to review the schedules taped on the wall. "You were out, now they're pulling you back in, that it? You're leaving me with a hell of a mess, Artemis."

"I don't follow the reference, but yes, I understand I am leaving you in the lurch."

"Can you cover the Jumparoos tomorrow, at least?"

"I cannot. And I'm real sorry about that."

"You don't look real sorry. You look goddamn happy, and sober, to boot. And what's with that creepy half smile? What the hell is so important you just up and leave your job for?"

"I wish I could say."

He laughed, and with a red pen and a dose of theatrics began crossing her name off the schedules. "You know, Artemis, for a spook, you are a god-awful liar."

FOR REASONS MORE PERSONAL THAN OPERATIONAL, Procter drove to Northern Virginia. She had always felt free on the road, at peace with the world when it was unrolling through her windshield. And on this drive that mostly held true; though the route was I-95 and traffic snarls did tip her into the occasional rage blackout. Most of all, Procter drew out the journey because, in a retirement that had put everything in the rearview, here now was a chance to savor the feeling of having it all in front of her again. Procter was an old pro, and she knew instinctively that the arc of an operation bent toward disappointment and chaos. But on the drive she could bask in the delusion that this op would break the mold. In a week's time, such fantasies would not be possible. But on the road? All was fair game. By Jacksonville she'd convinced herself the ending would be different. By Savannah, she thought it might even be a happy one.

13

CRYSTAL CITY, VIRGINIA / LANGLEY

FOR THE UNOFFICIAL NORTHERN VIRGINIA OPERATION Procter chose a dumpy three-bedroom house a few blocks off Twenty-Third Street in Crystal City. It might have once been public housing: the crumbling red-brick box boasted walls the color of stained teeth, moldering carpet, and the soulless void that lingers in abused rental properties. Upon arrival she found beer cans piled on the deck and a spray of mustard across the back window. The only neighbor who ventured outdoors was a geriatric Vietnamese man who wore candy-cane-striped pajamas, emerging at regular intervals for smoke breaks. She booked the property for two months with cash from the reptile fund.

The house was within walking distance of the room she had booked at the Crowne Plaza Hotel. Her cell phone and RAV4 could never go to the home—not with the stolen documents she planned to review and store there. Procter had few moral or ethical qualms about the investigation, but she was keen to avoid prison time on the back end. She and Sam had designed the tradecraft accordingly.

First afternoon was a grocery run for food (all of it frozen) and then a hopscotch through Northern Virginia for a rapid printer/scanner combo, external hard drives, a Jackery portable power station, stacks of legal pads and pens, rubber mats, a set of precision screwdrivers, and a laptop. At an electronics store run by Albanians she purchased, in cash, two BLU View 2 smartphones with TracFone prepaid plans. On each she downloaded Roblox, an online game platform she'd come to know thanks to Cummings's kids. Procter had become intrigued by the little monsters' addiction after her nephew explained—never once looking away from the screen, mind you—that, yes, you could send messages to anyone in the game, see, you just have your little character write one on a board, they hold it up, and no, Aunt Artemis, come on, you don't need a phone number or credit card or email or anything to sign up. How do you think I got on here anyhow?

Holy shit, Procter had said to her ten-year-old nephew, this is a game-changer.

As a rule, Procter despised video games, but she was intrigued, always and everywhere, by novel ways of communicating anonymously, and instantly recognized that the system could make an effective plank in an asset's commo setup. At the tail end of their Florida all-nighter, she and Sam had built a simple shoot-and-scoot plan, a preset schedule for when they would log in to Roblox to check for messages. Her last stop of the shopping spree was a dingy convenience store for a carton of Virginia Slims and a pack of fluorescent lighters festooned with chameleons and what were maybe geckos. In the good old days, she thought, the tech for this operation would have required five or so years of Directorate of Science &Technology nerd time and millions of dollars of taxpayer money. Now all she required was Best Buy.

By nine p.m. she was idling in a parking garage beneath Inova Fairfax Hospital, where, since returning from Russia, Sam had conducted his regular meetings with a CIA-contracted shrink. Not far from the junction of Route 50 and I-495, the sprawling campus offered reasonable anonymity and, in addition to Sam possessing clear reasons for frequent visits, it had the added advantage of bordering the headquarters of a defense contractor, DynCoTel, which would feature prominently in the cover story she would use with her friends. The box with the phone was in her trunk. His Acura pulled into the spot next to hers. She popped the trunk. The box quickly disappeared into his backpack. Sam shut the trunk and walked off.

IN THE FRONT YARD OF THE CRYSTAL CITY HOUSE, INSECTS dive-bombing the porchlights, Procter christened the new carton of cigs with the Vietnamese neighbor watching from his front stoop. They sat in the knowing silence of two people who understand, at once and on instinct, that they will share a space but not words.

Inside, Procter blasted EDM while she physically removed the laptop and printer/scanner's wireless hardware to air-gap the devices, ensuring they could never be connected to the internet. She downloaded an operating system on a thumb drive for use on the laptop. Procter microwaved a Party Pizza and watched it swivel, the bubbles rising and falling with each turn. Raindrops big as marbles slapped the kitchen window; they were mesmerizing, and she fell into a kind of trance. Smoke was pouring out of the microwave, the burnt husk of her pizza still riding the carousel inside. The smoke detector wailed. She scraped over a chair so she could reach it to mash the button. She threw open the window to the rain.

SAM STEPPED FROM HIS CAR INTO THE LANGLEY PARKING lot on an unusually warm October morning. He had a designated space. And thank god, because the lot behind him was already full, the cars stretching dozens of rows back to the A-12 Oxcart spy plane on display at the lot's far end. The Langley hordes shuffled past: heads down, toting lunch boxes, every man, woman, and child (the damn interns) sweating on this forced march over asphalt radiating an enervating heat from the morning sun. Sam did not have problems with most of them individually. But, like any good field man, he despised them collectively. He slid on a sport coat to cover the pit stains blossoming on his shirt. He pulled a gym bag from the trunk and melted into the crowd marching inside.

The theft would mark the first occasion on which Sam might spin the role of bureaucratic leper to his advantage. He'd done a stretch in the Penalty Box after Syria, much of it hoping someone, someday, might sidle up behind his desk and garotte him out of his misery. Langley managed to be dull and smug, tribal and bureaucratic, a nerve center and totally removed from where the espionage actually happened: the field. He did not like the morning trudge through the parking lots. He did not like the antiseptic smell of the hallways. He did not like the gulch between him and the ops. And most of all he hated himself when he felt the pull to meddle in the field, as he'd hated the Headquarters flunkies who'd done the same to him during his foreign tours. In Istanbul and Baghdad and Cairo and Damascus they'd called Headquarters the ten-thousand-mile screwdriver, turning the crank from the comfortable refuge of Langley's donut-scented recycled air. The Seventh Floor's intramural baseball team was even named the Screwdrivers.

His irrelevance, now, was a godsend. The wide berth granted him on account of the spell in Russia meant his days were marked by very few managerial interruptions. And he was learning that the bureaucratic gutting of Moscow X prior to Procter's firing further offered him tremendous leeway in his comings and goings. Gus Raptis was Chief of Moscow X now, but Sam rarely saw him in Procter's old office down near his cubicle in the basement. Gus had taken a temporary desk upstairs in the main Russia House vaults, away from the Moscow X lepers he now oversaw.

This would be the first real step. With Procter there had been only conversation. Now there would be physicality. There would be paper. His CIA job was—and always had been—stealing, but normally he'd taken secrets belonging to foreign governments, not his own, and the risk had always been brief stints in foreign jail, not a lockup alongside Rick Ames in Terre Haute. Political hacks could purloin all the classified material they wanted. But workaday intelligence officers had the book tossed at them. All morning a battle had raged inside Sam Joseph about the wisdom of this path. And he'd arrived, over and over, at the same place: in his box, counting little red stars, praying that the nameless woman would not visit him in his sleep, unable to figure why he was there at all, if not for some rot in his own Service. Onward.

With no sign of Gus and no more than a handful of others in bullpens across the vault, he got to work. The first tranche of documents would be straightforward: the entirety of the Singapore compartment, the Golikov cables, and the BIGOT list for BUCCANEER's reporting, which would specify who inside CIA had access to his information. Thankfully, by dint of his role in Moscow X and Procter's recollection of her Agency ID and password, Sam could access this haul digitally. For two hours, he printed the cables and emails. When colleagues strolled by, he flipped to baseball highlights on the unclassified machine. The printed documents went into the gym bag. Logging off, he collected his lunch from the fridge, slung the bag over his shoulder, and went to the gym for a brief, unfocused workout. After, he showered, bought a bag of pretzels from a vending machine, and went upstairs to commit a felony.

IT IS A SIMPLE MATTER TO REMOVE DOCUMENTS FROM CIA Headquarters.

There are no checks at all.

Sam merely strolled through the badge readers with the gym bag at his hip. No interruptions, no complications. He threw the emptied bag of pretzels away in the trash bin near the door. He drove the twenty minutes to Dr. Portnoy's practice on the Inova Fairfax campus, where he parked in a stretch of the blue garage that he did not believe held cameras. He'd spotted Procter's RAV4 on the way in. She was in the driver's seat. The trunk was cracked open. He flung it wide. The setup was precisely as Procter's Roblox character (which bore a striking resemblance to the actual Procter) had explained: the printer/scanner, plugged into the portable power station, was ready to accept the documents. He removed the stack from his gym bag, set them in the tray, and punched scan. He shut the trunk at the sound of the agreeable beep and whir. He would return for the originals after his appointment with Portnoy. He caught sight of a spray of her curly black hair through the glass. The rest of her was shrouded in shadow.

THAT EVENING, IN THE CRYSTAL CITY SAFE HOUSE, WITH the scanned files sprawled across the apartment floor, Procter set to work reconstructing the frenetic timeline leading up to Singapore. She built a chicken-scratch chronology, flipping through the yellow legal pads, cross-referencing dates, tidying events to see if names might be eliminated or punted down the list. The op had been planned with such haste, and her friends had been so geographically scattered, that she could not clearly remember when each of them had first learned of Golikov's outreach and Sam's travel to Singapore for the meet.

Procter reread Golikov's letter, which was appended to the cable. A Mexican American businessman, a contact of Golikov's working in Moscow, had initially passed it to the ambassador, who followed instructions on the envelope inside and passed it to the Acting Chief of Station, Gus's former Deputy. The money line, which had appeared in the cable: *I have information critical to safeguarding the security of CIA.* To establish his bona fides, Golikov had included the meeting minutes from a Russian Security Council deliberation on Ukraine. He'd written that Langley should figure out how to make contact securely—he would be traveling in Asia in the coming weeks. Golikov proposed the brevity code regarding whisky, which Sam had used at the tables in Singapore.

The cable and the transcribed letter had arrived in Russia House on the morning of March 15, she saw. Here Procter's memory took over: The cable had been flagged as high priority well before the daily meetings, but Mac and Theo had been out of the office. Debs and Gosford, too—still up in New York, though they were taking briefings. She remembered that because Gus—at that point fresh from Moscow, still awaiting a more long-term role at Langley, and also judged the Bratva member least likely to send either Gosford or Debs into a murderous rage—had been dispatched to New York Station to be sure the new regime felt Russia House had played a positive role in the transition. Gus, she remembered, had been the first to flag the cable. He was an early riser, typically working through the cable traffic no later than seven-thirty. That morning, she remembered, a note from him had been waiting on her machine, requesting that she give him a call, and leaving a number for his temporary desk in New York.

Had Debs read the cable? Had it been briefed to Gosford? There was no reply, no traffic from either on the matter. Sorting through the cables, she saw that Theo had first formally weighed in on the morning of the seventeenth; Mac by midafternoon. Both had returned early from separate vacations. Mac had been with Loulou in Upstate New York, Theo was off drinking on a boat and calling it fishing. By the morning of the eighteenth, she remembered, they had both been pulled into a dumpster fire emerging on one of Theo's cases—Procter had vague memories of Debs's involvement here—and Singapore had been left to her. She made her notes in the legal pad, working between her memory, the cables, and the Golikov delegation's travel itinerary. Procter sketched a small star next to the dates of March 19 and 20. To dispatch heavies to Singapore, Moscow would have been required to know Golikov's name and the basic outlines of his message by then. The timing worked, she thought, just barely.

Procter tore two sheets of paper from her legal pad. At the top of each she wrote the name of a compromise. The first: Golikov. The second: BUCCANEER, the poor soul who had committed suicide before his arrest. Reviewing her reconstruction of Singapore and the BIGOT list for BUCCANEER's reporting, she wrote the names of the officers with access to each, assuming the widest net possible for Singapore. Outside, thunder rumbled, and the first spits of rain slapped the windows. Procter crossed out names if they did not appear on both. She wondered if the BUCCANEER compromise, the attempted arrest and eventual suicide, had been a mistake on Moscow's part, if someone outside Zhomov's shop had gotten a tad overzealous, because it eliminated Moscow Station from the list; BUCCANEER had been handled in Athens, his reporting sent directly to Russia House and the Seventh Floor.

When it was done, she sat for a long while reviewing the names that appeared on both lists. Most were friends, current or former. Could she buy this list? No, she thought, not really. Easier to think Sam had lost his marbles. And yet . . .

We've got a big problem, Petra had said. Procter could accept the theory—she was not insane. But to accept this list? Stomach-turning. There were other names on it, but four stood out: Mac, Gus, Theo, and

Debs. It was time to talk to her friends, she decided. Have a word, lord knew she had reasons for words with all of them. The two papers she tore into ribbons. The ribbons she flushed down the toilet.

The microwave clock's red block letters warned of approaching dawn, her stomach that she'd neglected her dinner. Procter tramped into the kitchen and downed two sleeves of Ritz crackers in a compulsive, agitated frenzy, watching the storm wash the parking lot into an oily puddle.

14

GREAT FALLS, VIRGINIA

ESPIONAGE HAD BEEN THE MASON FAMILY BUSINESS SINCE his paternal grandfather had served with Angleton in Italy during the war. Mac's father had gotten his wars, too: fighting in Vietnam and then joining CIA, where he became a legendary runner of Afghan muj in the halcyon days at Cold War's end. As with most dynasties, by the third generation things got a little wobbly, and for a spell prior to joining CIA, Mac had tried to abdicate his responsibilities. He wanted to try his hand as a painter. He would not often speak of that season, but Procter had surmised that at some point in the years after college, the combination of artistic failure and a cuff on the ear from his old man had driven Mac back to the family business.

And Mac got his wars, too. When 9/11 rocketed him into the counterterrorism game, and now, when a second Cold War had him occupied with Russia, as his old man had been. Mac's first decade at CIA had been entirely mediocre; if anything, he was behind the curve, trading on his family name with little genuine accomplishment. Gus, after all, had been running their Base in Afghanistan even though they'd all been in the same Farm class. But Afghanistan had changed Mac. He'd been rightly made a hero, and from there on out had decided to knuckle down and play the game he had so long resisted. Procter had been in his debt since Afghanistan, and had chosen to repay him by refusing to resent his success, though resentment—for more than a few reasons—would have been more than a little satisfying and damn well within her rights.

Of all her friends' homes, Mac and Loulou's was the lightest, the most unburdened. The spirit here was one of parties, and even if you arrived, as she had, before the socially acceptable drinking hour, the place always seemed on the cusp of a celebration. Why was that? The Masons' breezy, semi-open marriage? The midcentury modern design, which Procter couldn't really describe save to say it had always felt to her that the house had hosted swingers' parties well before the Masons' arrival? Loulou shuffled in with a tray bearing bowls of popcorn, pretzels, and nuts. Mac poured the scotch. For two hours they drank and laughed and told old stories until, with a gentle nudge of his wife's knee, Mac said that he and Artemis did have some shop talk on the agenda. Loulou, an old pro at receiving polite ejections from her husband's conversations, left them with smiles and pecks on the cheek.

Procter and Mac ducked into the back house, where he'd parked all the paintings he refused to work on and Loulou refused to let him destroy. Crossing the tile floor of a room that smelled of dust and old paper, they went upstairs to the box-clotted study, where the air grew even more stale. In Mac's hands rode the bottle of scotch and two fresh glasses. Phones had been left in the main house. Guiding them toward two easy chairs set under the window, he sloshed scotch into the glasses and, handing her one, said, "I really wish I'd had more notice before you came up here. We could have arranged something." They clinked glasses and sat.

"Came together at the last minute," she said. "And I'm not up here for long."

"And you're interviewing where?"

"DynCoTel," she said. "Beltway Bandit, I know, I know. Save it, I could use the cash. Insider threat role."

"Let me know if I can help," he said. "Though I don't think I know anyone over there."

"I will. And thanks. You and Lou are solid? Things good?"

"Good, good. All good. Lou's been busy with a few contracts. I've been stapled to the office."

"Oh come on."

"What?"

"Don't be a modest shit. You're a hero now, least I hear."

"Good lord. Who's your source on that?"

"People talk, Mac, people talk."

He smiled his easy, friendly smile, the one he used to chat up assets, to survive in the jungle of Finn Gosford's CIA. Vanity, she thought. With Mac you play to vanity.

She continued, "I mean, the papers covered some of it, but I want details. The scoop, man. Tell me how the swap went down. I only got bits from Theo when he came to see me. I've still got my clearance, even if they ran me out."

THIS IS HOW CIA GOT SAM BACK.

The version Procter heard from Theo came with the caveat that he was on a drinking junket advertised as a fishing trip. *Expedition* had been the term he'd used, and he'd been close enough to venture into Central Florida for a stopover at Gatorville. He showed up with four bottles of Seagram's, more or less setting the agenda for his visit, which was a blur. Brief snatches of clarity subsumed into the muck of drink and friendly banter. But one morning they did sober up sufficiently to hold a human-style conversation about the matter. Theo was helping her pin a whole chicken on the Jumparoo line; straining upward, his shirt riding up to expose his chalky white belly, he asked if she'd heard the whole story about Vienna. About what Mac and Gus had done.

Theo pretended to spank one of the chickens. Bad little bird, he said. Bad little thing. He jerked on the pulley to send it across the water and reached into the cooler for another. "You wrestle these goddamn lizards, Artemis?"

"I do," she said. "I sure do."

He gazed thoughtfully into the water as he sipped his beer and, for the second time that day, asked: "What kind of fish you have in there?"

CIA case officers are an obsessive lot. Attention to detail, the sorting of facts and information, are fundamental to the trade. Procter had known quite a few who indulged this talent outside the building as fanatical hobbyists. Many of the diversions could be useful, even practical: Sam Joseph had his poker; she knew a guy in the old Latin America Division who'd run a professional woodworking business from his garage. Others, though, tilted pathological, hobbies and interests of the sort favored by autistic children. Memorizing historical baseball standings, in one case Procter knew. And in Theo's: an encyclopedic knowledge regarding the husbandry of exotic fish.

"Theo, like I told you earlier, I have no clue."

"Maybe peacock bass?"

"A what?"

"I saw some full-grown unicorn tangs in the tanks in the shop where we snagged this." He thumbed the shoulder of his T-shirt. Stenciled atop a picture of a gator leaping from the water, jaws clamped around a strung-up pig, were the red block letters: BONECRUSHER BENNY BRINGS IT BIGLY. And below: GATORVILLE, FLORIDA, USA.

"That's the emporium shop," Procter said.

"I think I also saw a sunshine pleco. And there was a tank all set up to be an Amazonian biotope—"

"Theo," she cut in, fixing herself a smoke and blowing a cloud of it toward the brackish lagoon, "I know you traded in your wife for an aquarium, but me, I don't know shit about the fish, and I don't care to. So, as I explained this morning, stop asking. Tell me what happened with Sam."

"Well," Theo said with disappointment, "all summer we were getting our shit kicked in. Gosford and Debs were preparing to purge Russia House, I swear it, looking for more scapegoats because the White House was pissed. They weren't angry he was missing per se—they couldn't have given a shit about Sam. It was more that they were worried about the possibility of a scandal if it came to light, and with those awful tapes the Russians sent you floating around out there, plus the risk they might mail them elsewhere to increase Sam's negotiating value, or to just create chaos and problems for us, well, a blow-up seemed fairly likely. Honestly I think Gosford would have preferred the Russians kill Sam, put his head on a pike outside the Kremlin, and be done with it.

But the Russians are not that merciful. At some point the Seventh Floor geniuses realize they might want to solve the fucking problem and bring him home, go fucking figure." With a grunt, Theo sent another chicken out over the water. Why aren't they jumping, Artemis?"

She peered into the water. "Only gator in there right now is one of the juvies who already ate today and isn't much interested in these chickens—or us, apparently. The real fun starts when we open the other gate." She pointed her cigarette out into the lagoon, where the outlines of the gators had clumped around the submerged gate. Thirty minutes until the next Jumparoo: bloodlust was in the air. "Keep going," she said.

"More chickens?"

"Yeah, 'bout ten more. And also with the story."

"Well," Theo said, squatting down for another bird, "we come up with an idea to solve the problem. A White House flunkie drove out to Langley for a conclave and said, right to our faces, figure it out. I want options, nothing off the table." He strung up the bird, regarding it with pride.

"Who's there for the meeting?" Procter had asked. For no reason, then, other than context.

"Me, Mac, Gus, Debs. The brain trust," Theo said, with a filthy and anatomically questionable gesture of his fists. The chicken rattled across the water on a squeaky pulley.

"And we're shooting the shit in this meeting," Theo said. "It all has a very informal feel, and Mac throws out an idea: We kidnap one of theirs. Not rocket science, of course, we've thought about it before. But it's pretty damn aggressive. Mac says we need to kick 'em in the nuts so they'll stop pinching ours. Helluva meeting. One of the best ever."

"Snatching a Russian," Procter said. "Kind of a big deal, right? What was—Oh shit! Theo!"

He'd slipped off the dock, and was now shouting and splashing around down there like crazy. Procter saw the juvenile headed toward the racket, and with that she had plunged in to drag him over to the ladder, kicking back a few times at the gator, whose interest, she would later reassure him, sprouted more from curiosity than hunger.

Once they'd clambered back up to the boardwalk, the dreary quotidian things that so often derail important discussions forcefully took command: Procter and Theo had to change clothes. Cummings, who had seen the tail end of the splashdown, had to be assured that, no, she was not pawning work off to her degenerate friend. No, Theo was not feeling litigious. Yes, she would get her ass sparkling clean to run the Jumparoo. By the time the show was done, Theo was thoroughly drunk, and she was not far behind. "I'm not much of a swimmer, Artemis," he had slurred that night, raising his glass to her. "Not so aquatic." And this, given his love for fish, was simply incredible. The next morning, he'd been up early to catch a flight. He'd stolen one of her work hats, she discovered later, the bastard.

PROCTOR WAS SURPRISED TO FIND THAT MAC—A FAR MORE reliable narrator than Theo—told the same story. It picked up speed exactly where Theo left off, which was that the White House had indicated they were open to the CIA proposing a Russian intelligence officer as the target. If Langley could wrap its arms around it, the White House would iron out the legal side, ensure the ongoing covert action work with respect to Russia was molded for such an op. They required a country in which there were Russians of value to Moscow, and preferably where the local service was some combination of friendly, ambivalent, and incompetent. "Any guesses?" Mac said.

"Has to be Vienna."

"Spy City," he said. "And REMORA," Mac went on, with a long pull of scotch, "was the critical node here."

Procter remembered REMORA, of course, though she hadn't developed, recruited, or handled him. He was one of the CIA's top Russian assets. A high-flying colonel, Deputy Chief of the SVR's Fifth Department (Europe), REMORA had been recruited by Mac and Theo two years earlier in Morocco. He was handled internally by Gus in Moscow. Gosford and Debs, Procter recalled, had developed a particular interest in REMORA upon taking the reins, though here her memories were fuzz; she could not recall precisely why they'd been so hot on the case.

"Theo and I snagged the first breakthrough from REMORA. Which is"—thinking for a moment, another peck of scotch, a little light pouring through his eyes—"mid-July. Second week or so. REMORA's privy to a discussion at SVR about what the Russians are doing with Sam. He's heard that Sam was smuggled from Singapore to an unofficial prison outside Moscow. Not sure precisely how, but a shipping container was involved. We of course wanted to know why in the hell they'd taken him. And REMORA said he'd asked and been treated to hell-if-I-know shrugs from everyone. SVR goons had been the heavies in Singapore. Running theory in his circles was that they'd gotten a little excited about dishing it out to an American, and went overboard."

Procter cut in: "What did REMORA say had happened to Golikov?"

Mac made a face. "Butchered him in his hotel room like Khashoggi. Russian gorillas had intercepted him, but he tried to run, there was a fight, and he died. They cut him up, allegedly, and smuggled the body out in the morning. Apparently the parts were stuffed into a bunch of suitcases."

"And how . . ." Procter asked, selecting her words with care, "how did REMORA explain the interest in Golikov to begin with? How did they know he was meeting with Sam?"

Mac's eyes narrowed in the direction of one of the boxed paintings, then shifted fixedly toward Procter. "I've had some doubts," he said, "about the chain of custody on this intel, I must say. I don't think REMORA was lying, I merely wonder if the telephone game had become so muddled he was shoveling us gibberish picked up in the halls. But, in any case, REMORA said that a fellow member of the trade delegation had reported Golikov to one of the security minders during the Asia trip. Said Golikov had apparently been spotted filching classified documents from the embassy during the leg in Bangkok. Golikov's a well-known gambler and, according to REMORA, rumor had it he was in serious debt. Anyhow, the gorillas see him talking to Sam in the casino. They go upstairs to ask him questions and search his room, and then, boom, sideways. REMORA also claimed the gorillas snagged Golikov with documents on a few thumb drives upstairs, a tangle of Security Council minutes, various budgets, internal Presidential Administration memos, and a bag of content lifted from Bangkok. Golikov was there to do a deal, gorillas snipped it midstream."

"So it was a mistake to grab Sam?" Procter asked.

"According to REMORA."

"So why not just hand him back in Singapore? Turn him loose?"

"Well, and I'm speculating here, Artemis, I'd imagine that by the time they had him, that team felt they had to bring him to Moscow, and by the time they'd drugged him and smuggled him out of Singapore, beaten him, and doubtless had a very rough conversation about whether Golikov had passed him anything, by then there'd have been a debate inside the Kremlin over whether a price might be extracted for his return. Once he was in Russia, what could the Russians do, really? Admit to their mistake? That'd be off brand. Look at Ukraine. Look at the Cold War. Look at five hundred years of Russian history. Not going to happen."

"So that's the Russian motivation to send me the tapes, advertise that they had Sam?" Procter said. "Marketing? Shake the bars so we sit up and take note?"

"I think so," Mac said. "Kindling a four-alarm intelligence fiasco in Washington, well, that's all gravy for them. Sure, they look brutal for kidnapping our guy, but, hey, Ukraine and all, the barbarism is old news, and it skyrockets Sam's value as a negotiation chit because now they know that we know, and so on."

"But we have nothing to trade," Procter said. "Viktor Bout's gone. Hanssen's dead. Ames is off the table. No Illegals in the pen."

Mac's scotch was still going—Procter's was not—so Mac downed his and stood to refill their glasses. Finger to his nose, Mac eased back in his chair and searched the room, scanning across the boxes of paintings as if taking some unspoken inventory. "Precisely," he said. "We've got nothing to trade for him. We had to change that. And we had an opening from the White House to be aggressive. Europe is REMORA's stomping grounds, so we asked him for the roster in Vienna and his assessment of the political stature of each officer there. Found an adviser to the *rezident*, a general with family connections in the Kremlin. REMORA said he'd been in Vienna for a few months. Some boondoggle, he imagined, passing a pleasant summer in Austria. REMORA knew where they'd put the guy up because it had been so damn expensive. From there, it wasn't so tricky. Gus was out there with me."

"We just bagged him up?"

"Guy walked from the rented mansion to the embassy every morning. Roughly the same time. Special Activities Center led a snatch-and-grab out of a van; we took him into the mountains outside Salzburg, nice little private house, very comfortable. Kept him there until we could make the trade."

"I heard you were rough on him," Procter said. "That it wasn't so comfortable for the Russian."

Mac's smile was all proud schoolboy. "You heard that, did you? From whom?"

"People talk."

He smiled again—this time with far less mirth. He wiggled his knuckles. "There were aspects of that trip that I enjoyed more than I should have."

"I'm sure the bastard deserved whatever he got." She paused, taking a sip of her drink. "And you—you deserve the Intelligence Commendation. I should have already said it. But congrats."

"You want applause?" Mac said, smiling.

"Join the State Department," she finished. "And you want a medal? Join the Army."

He clinked his glass to hers. "We think the same way about these goddamn things. I'm not in this business for accolades."

"Well, it's gold for job security. Makes it harder for Debs or Gosford to push you out. Gus, too."

"That it does. For good, and for ill."

There was a silence, then Mac said: "Sam, by the way, seems to be doing fine, given the circumstances."

"That's good to hear," she said. "If I have time I'll see if I can drop in and say hello."

"He'd like that, I'm sure."

They settled into another friendly silence. She remembered now that the op that had distracted Mac and Theo that week had been preparation for a meeting with REMORA. Vaguely disturbing warnings, she recalled. "REMORA," she said. "Did he also tell us something in the run-up to Singapore? Or am I nuts?"

"No, that's right," Mac said. "Theo and I were getting ready for a face-to-face with REMORA, in France. Even Debs made the trip to Lacoste to join the meeting."

"Debs?" Procter said, sitting up. "That's bizarre."

"Tell me about it," he grumbled. "She insisted. Said she wanted to get into the field, roll up her sleeves."

"And what, exactly, did dear old Debs contribute to the discussion?"

"Very little. I met Theo there for the fireside chat with REMORA, who made the two of us wait a bit, naturally. Theo thankfully had the place all set by the time I showed. REMORA can be picky about the hospitality. Debs joined at the end. Wanted to shake REMORA's hand, I suppose, get a few stories she could bring to the Oval with Gosford."

"When was the meeting?" Procter asked, imagining the chronology she'd scrawled the night before, on her legal pads.

"It was within a few days of Singapore. Maybe two days before? Three? I don't remember the exact dates. REMORA had a rumor he wanted to sell us. Vagaries about Russians targeting Americans in Asia."

"That," Procter said, "gives me hives. Could we have done something with that?"

"Not a chance," Mac said. "It was all too vague, even Debs agreed. I recall she said as much during that rough meeting on the Seventh Floor the morning after Singapore. I was in the Adirondacks with Lou when I heard that REMORA had signaled for a meeting. I scurried back to Washington, prepped with Theo, then flew to France. In the end I wound up cutting short my vacation for a useless tidbit."

As if summoned by mention of her name, the motion-sensing light outside clacked on, and downstairs the door creaked open. "Mon amour," purred Loulou, "t'es là?"

"Oui, ma chérie," Mac said, "nous avons finis. Prenons un verre? Artemis va rester ici ce soir, avec nous."

"Goddammit," Procter snapped, "please, in English. It's been twenty years since my tour in France, and my frog talk was never so sparkly to begin with."

15

McLEAN

NEXT EVENING, THROUGH THE WINDOWS OF THE RESTAURANT, Procter watched Gus's sparkling minivan pull into the parking lot. Washed it weekly, she was sure, probably on the way home from church. Two things that mattered most to Gus Konstantinos Raptis: Greek Orthodoxy and the Central Intelligence Agency. If there was any room left, he had a wife, Connie—a former Agency hand, she had done something with the analysts before the kids were born. Old man Raptis—like old man Mason—had been an Agency man, earning his spurs running the muj in the eighties.

Gus had been the top man in their Farm class. He was steely and athletic; played lacrosse at Cornell, and Procter heard he'd been something of a top man there, too. Gus had *it*, the right stuff, the father's stuff. This was not the loser son who piddles away the family glory, this was the heir, the successor to the legendary runner of muj and killer of Reds.

The winning seemed to carry over into the home. Raptises were churchy, and monogamous—never a visit to the Penalty Box, in work or in marriage. Until he'd cut short his tour in Moscow, Procter had always gotten the sense that Gus and Connie were deeply in love, having gobs of sex, and generally upbeat about the future. In other words: aliens.

Gus took a seat in the booth across from Procter. Dark hair, neatly combed, crisp suit, and white shirt—always the white shirts—but probably from Jos A. Bank or some other mall provenance. There wasn't much money; no family reptile fund. Connie didn't work anymore, and for three years their eldest, Nico, had been bleeding them dry. That Nico had driven a stake through the family was that most tortured brand of Agency knowledge: the secret known by all. There were rumors Gus had dipped into his retirement to fund the latest trip to rehab, at some new place out in California.

Gus looked her over with those stern eyes. A minister's gaze, Theo would say when they were drinking and the conversation rolled to their friend. "He sees our sins, Artemis."

"He wouldn't be friends with us if he could," she would reply.

Procter ordered a burger and a beer, Gus a sparkling water. The guy managed judgment even in his ordering habits. When the waiter had left, Gus said he had thirty minutes, tops. "Why didn't you tell us you were coming?" he said. "This is no notice. Where are you interviewing, anyway?"

"DynCoTel," she said, and gave him the same speech she'd given Mac. She asked after Connie and the kids—he answered with polite evasions—and then she gave up and steamrolled him: "I've been thinking more about Singapore," she said, "and I could really use your help on a few things."

He said, with a kind smile: "Why in the world would you think about *that*?"

"Guilty conscience, I guess."

"That's a new one for you."

"You'd be surprised at the dark thoughts that pop into your mind when you're alone and wasted in a trailer. It's a challenge to wrestle your demons and gators at the same time. More of an either-or situation, turns out."

"Good grief, Artemis." His eyes softened, and he said, his tone sympathetic: "Tell me how I can help."

"I'm just wondering if I screwed up," she said. "If I missed something and sent Sam into the pit. It's been eating me alive."

The food and drinks arrived. Gus asked for a lime and they sat twiddling silverware until the waiter brought it. A gas fireplace punched on. Gus watched the flames for a moment, sniffing the carbonation sparkling up from his drink. She'd never seen him take a sip of booze, perhaps the only non-Mormon employee of the Central Intelligence Agency about whom she could make the claim. Theo's sins were on display, front and center, primo shelf space, much as Procter's. Gus's sins were the hidden varietal: pride, greed, envy, things that only priests cared about, not the shit that left you with a trail of marriages, in a gutter, or stringing up chickens at Gatorville. Only Mac had managed to tie the knot so elegantly: he'd re-cast his sins as virtues.

Gus was stabbing the ice in his drink. He raised his eyes when he saw the waiter bearing down and rudely waved him off. Gus Raptis, a waiter's nightmare: unsmiling and cheap. Were those sins? she wondered.

"Well, let's put that insane notion to rest, Artemis. It's absurd. Much as I applaud the sudden and long-overdue flickering of any moral compass inside you, I don't think it's pointing the right direction here. You're suggesting Golikov was a dangle? That it was a trap?"

"You don't think it was?" Procter said, placing the ball on the tee of their conversation.

"Golikov," Gus said, taking the swing, "was the real deal. The outreach was too elaborate. It was the right mix of paranoid sophistication and civilian inexperience. That letter, his offer, was genuine."

"You called me that morning," Procter said. "After the cable came in."

"Right . . . I was up in New York, briefing Deborah and Gosford. Had to be less than a week after Gosford's confirmation."

"You remember briefing the details on Singapore to Debs and Gosford?" she asked. "Did it wind up in their read books up in New York?"

"Now, Artemis, why are you—"

"Please, Gus, just asking. Please."

He sighed. "There was a briefing, yes. For Deborah. I was there to get her up to speed on our Moscow operations. She was keen for the lay of the land."

"She got the scoop on Golikov? The letter? All that? Same day?"

"She did," he said, tone bristling like sandpaper. "I told her what we knew about Golikov, that the trade samples were solid, and that we wanted to know more. We hadn't made any plans to bump him for a chat yet, of course, but I said that as a matter of course we would put something together and see if we could see what he had to say. I called Mac that morning; he came down from the Adirondacks, briefed Deborah with me. We covered the waterfront on Russia, of course, lots going on, but the Golikov outreach was on the agenda. Right at the top."

And here Procter logged an anomaly: when Mac had explained the chronology around Singapore, he had not told her about the stopover in New York, the briefing with Gus and Debs. Had he forgotten?

"How'd Debs take that?" she asked.

"Now, Artemis, really," he said, his voice rising. "What exactly are you driving at here? Care to explain?"

Put it out there, she thought. Advance a theory and see how it plays. "We started having big problems soon as our old friend Debs took over. Odd, isn't it? Week one on the job, the Russia compromises start." She took a bite of her burger and watched his nostrils flare as she chewed.

Procter had often wondered if, in the black weeks after Singapore, Gus Raptis had quietly suggested to Debs that he might take the helm of Moscow X. He was homeless in those months, having cut his Moscow tour short to sit stateside while Russia House tried to find a spot for him. Moscow X in its glory was primo real estate, and Gus required a foothold. Had he schlepped to the Seventh Floor with a coup in mind? Gus would never admit to it, though. He was a political animal, and in this jungle you had to be careful whom you ate, especially if they were your friend. Those who in the past had tried to eat Procter had found her to be poison going down; all had coughed her up. And Gus knew it.

Rather than venture his own theory, though, he licked his lips, checked his watch, and looked outside toward his minivan. "Satisfying as that notion might be," he said, "there's about a hundred explanations for what happened that week, and only one of them involves a mole."

"Bullshit," she said, poking around for a response. "Give me a break."

But Gus just shrugged, yawned, and stood. "Suit yourself, but it's the truth. Now, Connie's expecting me, Artemis."

"Just one more thing." She gently took his wrist. "I've been on a bit of a tour, Gus, as of late. Patching a few holes, hammering out the dents in my life, that sort of thing. You're a hero now, you and Mac. And I should have said congratulations to you when we sat down. For Vienna and for leading the charge to bring Sam home. But I didn't know what to say, you know? I got steamrolled and fired and you two got accolades and promoted."

His eyes softened again, and he did not try to tear his arm away from her. "Just a few more minutes," she pleaded.

Checking the time on his phone, scanning plaintively into the darkness, Gus sighed. He eased back into the booth.

"Did we ever get anything on why they went after Golikov and Sam?" she asked, repeating the question she'd put to Mac, for comparison.

"REMORA gave us a tip," Gus said. "A month or so after you left. He told us that Golikov was apprehended with thumb drives of looted documents, that snagging Sam was a mistake. Working assumption has been he was going to sell the tranche to us and request to defect."

"REMORA," she said, rolling the name over her tongue. "If memory serves, he gave us that little warning before Singapore."

"Ah yes," Gus said. "The meeting Deborah famously wedged into."

"Why do you think she went?" Procter asked.

"A story for the Oval," Gus said. "What else? Deborah just joined at the end, after Mac and Theo did their dance: Mac primed REMORA, Theo joined to reset the energy and initiate the deep stuff: the heart-to-heart or, if necessary, give him little slap to get things back on track. All the work was done by the time Deborah arrived. Might as well have been a photo op."

"I forgot they have that little two-step," Procter said, though in truth she hadn't heard of it in the first place. "What'd you make of the intel REMORA had for us? The warning?"

Gus sniffed at the bottle of sparkling water; his eyes were bright and lively, as if behind them his thoughts were hustling to keep up with her. Gus wasn't a politician—leave that for Gosford and Debs—but he was that species' closest relative at CIA, wielding effortlessly the potent blend of mirth and menace so necessary to thrive in the Langley jungle.

"That slice of REMORA's information was . . . vague," Gus said.

"You think he's full of shit?"

"Only sometimes. He is a mercenary. He tries to sell us things. At heart, he's a snake."

"One of our snakes."

"There you have it," Gus said. "Much of his stuff is solid; much of it leaves us desiring . . . specifics. I was a skeptic when he first came on our radar. But I've generally been won over. I handled him for a time inside Moscow, of course. One sec . . ." Gus, scowling, began typing on his phone.

In the silence Procter began harvesting stalks of relevant information from the dim fields of her mind. A year earlier Gus was fresh in Moscow, a bachelor tour for a married case officer, his loving wife at home, spotted once, Procter remembered now—and never again—by Loulou while working a shift at the Nordstrom in Pentagon City. Connie Raptis hadn't worked in going on a quarter century, but there she'd been, bored and lonely with Gus in Moscow. There were, Procter recalled, two squirrelly rumors that she'd picked up around that time, the type that lives in about five Security computers and nowhere else. One: That Gus had traveled stateside for an early polygraph. Two: Wicked whispers about a Foreign Intelligence Surveillance Act—FISA—warrant on a senior CIA officer in Moscow, permitting the Feebs to monitor phones and email traffic. For a few months Gus had been on a loose leash, meeting Russians in Russia, and while CIA trusted its people, sometimes the Feebs didn't, and god knew what turds they'd dug up about poor Gus's journeys inside Russia. The rumors went away, Gus remained in Moscow until the dawn of the Gosford era, and Procter had forgotten all about it. But now she shone a new light: simplest place for the Russians to recruit a senior CIA officer was in Moscow.

She took another bite of her burger and, finding it chewy, spit it into her napkin. She shoved aside her plate and took a drink of her beer.

Gus slid the phone in his pocket, smiled, and sighed. "Never knew you to be a picky eater, Artemis. Florida's made you soft."

"Speaking of, when's the Raptis clan coming down? Free tickets, I'll hook you up. There's gator jerky."

"Connie's more of an Epcot girl."

"I don't know Gus, that Mickey Mouse shit's pretty expensive," Procter said, and left the subtle barb, like her grin, hanging. There'd been a time, back in the Farm days, when he'd been buoyantly fun. That Gus had been taken outside and shot, only to be replaced by an austere, graying guy chained to a host of family problems, a man who drove both legendary ops and a minivan through the Northern Virginia suburbs. Whatever Raptis had touched during his career had turned to gold, but now Procter saw only unmet potential. Gus would've been a fantastic WASP if he hadn't been so goddamn Greek, a great lay if he hadn't been so happily married, an exceptional drinker if not for the teetotaling.

So instead of swinging right back after her shot at the Raptis family bank account—and lord knew Gus had buckets of material—he simply scowled, his face darkened, and he checked his watch, though by this point he knew damn well what time it was: "Here is my view: REMORA may sometimes bring us garbage. Rumors, mumbo-jumbo, telephone games. I think some of that may have happened with respect to his messages regarding Sam's incarceration. REMORA's intel was collected thirdhand—how could something *not* be a garbled mess?" Each of Gus's words were files sharpening the next. "But here's the deal, Artemis. REMORA, for all his flaws and his mercantilism, well, he has passed us gold. In person in France, in moving-car pickups with me in Moscow, in his drop sites. It wasn't all gold, but enough was. It shined well enough. And you know what? He gave us intel the Russians simply would never willingly part with. A network of French Illegals, a ring of American servicemen run by SVR in Germany. That is why I believed, and believe, his information about Singapore, and about that officer in Vienna that we snatched up. Now perhaps you'd like to tell me why we're having this discussion in the first place? Your curiosity is very pointed for someone seeking absolution from vaguely defined sins, especially since you commit so many with admirable specificity. My advice? Start with those. The road to redemption will be straighter."

"You used to be more fun, Gus."

He cracked a smile at that. "Time's up, Artemis. Good to see you. Next time, in Florida."

He stood, slipped three ones on the table for his sparkling water, and walked out into the night. Procter shoved away her burger. When she paid the bill, she saw that, though he'd finished the entire bottle of Perrier, his money had only covered half.

16

MOSCOW

JON TARRMAN UNBUCKLED HIS SEAT BELT AT THE TURN. Molls slowed their Lada and mouthed a silent, *I love you.* Tarrman mouthed, *I love you, too,* and, clicking open the door, rolled from the car into a grassy bank.

He'd rehearsed the roll dozens of times at the Farm, on the streets of Washington, and even inside the tight corridors of Moscow Station, somersaulting between the cubicles at the tail end of a dead sprint. One constant: it always hurt. Tarrman made a noise upon impact, rolling into a crouch in time to watch Molls inflate the JIB, the Jack-in-the-Box, an inflatable copy of Tarrman now standing in for him in the passenger seat. He shuffled into the trees as Molls turned the corner out of sight.

He wondered if it would be their last night in Moscow. In this environment you really could not get aggressively black and expect to stay in-country. Things were bound to get ugly. He just hoped the Russians wouldn't kill their cats. Or Molls, or him—though even under the newer, nastier rules of the Game, he did expect more lenient treatment than his old friend Sam had received earlier that year, when the Russians had nabbed him in Singapore and sweated him here in Moscow. Tarrman had diplomatic status, after all.

Tarrman slid his fingers over the water-filled vodka bottle in his pack. Unbroken, thank god. He flipped his jacket around, red to a weather-beaten black, and put on a gray knitted cap. To complete the look of a peripatetic drunk, he tugged the bottle from the bag, sliding it into a paper sack. He took a brief inventory of the pack: a six-month supply of Lexapro for CLAW's wife, a thumb drive bearing the CIA's intelligence requirements inside a hidden partition, and seventy-five thousand euros. There was also an ops note, handwritten by Tarrman for his prized asset.

Tarrman trudged through the trees, emerging in the courtyard of an old Soviet-era apartment block that smelled of wet concrete and dog feces. He marched through the courtyard, reaching the street on the far side. He felt black and noted that the tenement, the courtyard, and now the street appeared as advertised in the casing report he'd memorized over the past week. On the far side of the street, he noted the presence of CLAW's parked BMW. Tarrman might well have had the license number branded behind his eyelids. The car was the safety signal for the meeting. All clear. Up the road he saw a graffiti-flocked trailer, its hitch resting on a pile of concrete blocks. The trailer had not been in the report, he was sure of it, but Molls had cased the place four days prior, and it was not so unusual for vehicles to come and go.

He was sixteen minutes early. He made a brisk tour of the street, walking with a slight wobble, advertising the vodka bottle, and plopped onto a bench just outside the tenement, careful to avoid the patches of grime and bird droppings. He took a long slug of water and rehearsed, yet again, the flow and script for this brief encounter with CLAW, an FSB colonel and prolific thief of Russian state secrets. Tarrman listened to the reassuring rhythm of his own heartbeat. Moscow was his.

TWENTY MINUTES LATER, AND TARRMAN WAS GROWING impatient, and worried. A woman had emerged from the apartment building; she was now pacing the street, smoking, yammering on her phone with someone about a television show. Tarrman's Russian was near-fluent, but even he struggled to understand her machine-gun, gutter dialect. He fixed his eyes toward the alley up the street, where

CLAW would hopefully appear any minute. Tarrman would walk to meet him, and they would stroll to another wooded area for five or so minutes. Brief encounter complete, he would wind back home.

But instead the world exploded around him. Shouts. Footfalls. The slam of metal on concrete. The bystander was shrieking. Tarrman stood, his instinct to run suffocated by the feel of rough hands taking hold of him from behind. Two men, rushing out from an alcove across the street, snatched his bag. He was on the filthy ground, dirt and mud and god knew what else thick on his tongue. A hand pinned down his head. He was trying to explain that he was an American diplomat, a Second Secretary at the U.S. Embassy, when the men behind him lifted his arms high above his head. The chicken-wing seizure, a KGB trademark from the Cold War's twilight, an era somehow more civilized than the present. Tarrman glimpsed another herd of black-clad men hustling toward the parked trailer. They were frog-marching a man who looked like CLAW.

"I'm a Second Secretary at the U.S. Embassy," Tarrman said again. But the pain in his raised arms had become white-hot, blinding. He blacked out.

REM'S CAR CLOPPED THROUGH GATE 3A AT LEFORTOVO, toward the newer wing of the prison where the "cousins" of the Federal'naya sluzhba bezopasnosti, the FSB, the Federal Security Service, would hold the American. Rem's aide was there already; he stood smoking near the door, under a lamp casting a pool of eerie light onto the ocher building. Rem stepped out of the car. "Bortnikov is already here," the aide said.

"How is the American?" Rem asked.

"He's in one piece," the aide said, stamping the cigarette into the ground. "For now."

REM WAITED FOR BORTNIKOV IN AN EMPTY SECOND-FLOOR interrogation room. Interrogators sat in the chair nearest the door, the supplicant facing, so Rem took the interrogator's seat and folded his hands on the table. The room grew warm as the minutes ticked along. Sweat trickled down Rem's ankles; it beaded along his white hairline. Was spying a young man's game? He did not think so. It was waiting, more than anything. And Rem had again thoughtfully sorted his evening pills. He could wait a long time.

REM HAD BEEN ALONE WITH THE BLINKING CAMERA IN THE room for forty-eight minutes when the door squealed open and Bortnikov strode in. Rem did not turn his head; he waited. Bortnikov stood behind him. The man did not want the prisoner's chair. They hung there for a moment, Bortnikov facing the back of Rem's head, Rem facing the empty seat.

Rem spoke: "This is the second arrest you've made based on my agent's information in six months. And it is the second to end in violence, in a manner guaranteed to make Langley ponder whether a mole is responsible. You are putting the best agent Russia has ever had in tremendous danger."

"We have had this conversation so many times, Rem Mikhailovich," Bortnikov snapped. "We have had it in your office, in my office, in the President's office. Why are we having it here?"

Rem shifted his weight in the wooden seat; he wanted to stand, but he felt that standing would be some sort of concession to Bortnikov and he tried to ignore the discomfort. "Each arrest puts my agent at greater risk, so each arrest merits the conversation anew. I agree that these traitors should be sidelined, perhaps even arrested. But the implementation of these arrests by your men has been boorish. The Athens *rezident* killed himself this spring. Now am I to understand your men jumped the American before you were fully certain he saw the look-alike for their asset? If action is required, why could they not merely fall from windows or collapse into oncoming traffic, like normal traitors? We already have so many problems, Alexander Vasilievich."

"We think Tarrman saw the look-alike."

"You think. The whole point of the charade was to be certain, to *know*. If Tarrman didn't see the look-alike, the American will go home and tell Langley their asset, our FSB colonel—whom they know as CLAW—was rolled up before the meet, when we want CIA to believe your men followed the traitor to the site. Do you understand this? We want them to believe that an error of tradecraft compromised their asset, not a mole. If Tarrman missed the look-alike, CIA will presume, correctly, that we arrested their CLAW weeks ago. That CLAW was compromised by an insider at Langley."

"I choreographed the op, Rem," Bortnikov said. "Spare me the lecture."

Rem wanted to turn back for a read of Bortnikov's face, but he resisted the temptation. A light above began flickering, buzzing like the wings of a heavy bee. And, like an insect, Rem gazed toward it as he spoke. "I wonder, though, if you do require the lecture, Alexander Vasilievich."

In two steps Bortnikov closed the distance and banged his fist on the wooden table. He stood over Rem and put a finger so near his face that he could smell the man's fish dinner. Then, gathering himself, Bortnikov stood straight, wiped his nose, and spat. "If your agent is such a hotshot, why have they provided only two names? Give me more to work with."

"If I fed you more names, you would arrest them, and my agent would be in even hotter water. Soon we wouldn't have an agent anymore. Everything is a nail to you, Alexander. Your brutish nature will be your downfall."

"Pride will be yours, Rem. And come, now. Me, brutal? Look at your treatment of Samuel Joseph earlier this year. Torture would have been merciful compared to what you put him through. I'll have to be far more restrained tonight with this Tarrman. He's under diplomatic cover and my masters are telling me I've only got tonight with him. We'll give him a scare, deliver a message before we send him packing to Washington."

"I hear he has cats," Rem said.

"Three of them. Quite large. Like raccoons. The Tarrman woman, Molly, was apparently quite fond of them. Gave us a hell of a time. Got in our way, so we couldn't deal with them cleanly." He rolled up his sleeve to expose a clawed right forearm.

"Is that from the cats?"

Bortnikov grimaced. "I'm afraid I don't know."

Foreign Intelligence Service Review Board:
Director's Case 24-6 (DOCTOR B), Annual Evaluation, Module E (Outlook: Objectives and Collection Requirements)

Special Investigator: *Check, check. Yes? All good? Okay. This is the final module of the annual case review for 24-6. Let's—*

Gen. Rem Mikhailovich Zhomov: *Enough. It has been . . . [checks watch] eighty-three minutes. I gave you ninety. My back is tired.*

Special Investigator: *The Director has been very clear, Rem, he—*

Gen. Rem Mikhailovich Zhomov: *I know that. I wouldn't be here unless he'd twisted my arm with painful clarity. Finish your questions so we can both get back to work.*

Special Investigator: *The last module of the review is the most contentious, as you know.*

Gen. Rem Mikhailovich Zhomov: *It always is.*

Special Investigator: *And it obviously concerns the . . . how should I put this . . . restrained approach you've taken to managing this case. There are those in the security apparatus who believe Dr. B is not being pushed in the right direction, who say that opportunities are being missed. We've received the name of only two Russian assets of the CIA, for example, the* rezident *in Athens, the one known by CIA as BUCCANEER, whom we recalled from Greece and who killed himself in that horribly managed arrest. And the FSB colonel known as CLAW. And there is a certain . . . uh . . . eh. . . . how would I put it . . .*

Gen. Rem Mikhailovich Zhomov: *Good god. I understand there's no real value in shooting the messenger, but even so, it can be fun. So be clear and do not tempt me. Ask your goddamn question. And just read it from the paper. If any nameless figures among the cousins—perhaps ones with names such as Bortnikov—wish to challenge my perspective, they know precisely where to find me. Or they can lobby the Director, who has so far seen fit to trust my judgment on this case.*

Special Investigator: *[rustling of paper, clink of glass on table] Fine, Rem. Fine. You're not making this easy on me, you know, I'm only doing my—*

Gen. Rem Mikhailovich Zhomov: *Just read the question for the module.*

Special Investigator: *[coughs, inaudible mumbling] Please describe your objectives for the case in the coming year.*

Gen. Rem Mikhailovich Zhomov: *A wonderful question, thank you for asking. Dr. B is the most valuable penetration we have ever run inside any Western special service. Ames and Hanssen don't hold a candle. We're talking about an asset who might function similarly to Philby, if he'd hung on. So the order of the day is source protection. Keeping Dr. B in harness and in the game. There you have it, the objective: survival. The architecture of the case—the commo plan, the collection requirements, the unique mechanism through which we engage the good Doctor—well, it has all been designed for longevity, hasn't it? If we'd run this case through the normal processes and departments, Dr. B would already be in prison. It would be 1985 all over again, the damn Year of the Spy, with a dozen or more arrests and disappearances. Every two weeks Bortnikov would have a new captive and a few more chances to punch CIA officers in the head during interrogations. The CIA's Dermatologists would know something was rotten. Dr. B would eventually be cooked.*

Special Investigator: *What, then, is the longer-term objective, Rem? If the priorities in the coming year are not collection so much as preservation?*

Gen. Rem Mikhailovich Zhomov: *The success of Russian culture and civilization depends on American weakness and division. And the Americans are destroying themselves, are they not? American politics are dysfunctional and polarized. Their economic life is fundamentally twisted and unjust. The culture is sick. There is no unity, no shared sense of purpose. Americans are increasingly soulless and decadent and self-referential. This rot is happening both bottom-up and top-down. And it's happening independent of us, but we can help speed things along, can't we? Hasten the decline. Our information operations, for example, help feed the rot from the bottom up. The top-down approach is where Dr. B comes in. It has become fashionable to predict the death of human intelligence, but it has its value, does it not, in a world where we still have humans? We can wreak all manner of digital havoc, but we cannot turn an enemy institution inside out unless we've got hold of some of its humans, preferably those damn near the top. Dr. B is our Trojan horse to wreck CIA. There are destructive mechanisms that will be available to the Doctor in the not-so-distant future: budgets can be slashed or frivolously redirected; competent officers may be fired en masse; any number of intelligence-sharing agreements with allies might be shredded; lunatics, sadists, and incompetents might be placed in key posts; selective leaks of CIA misdeeds and rumors and crimes might undermine its credibility and weaken its political footing; reforms kneecapping Langley might be proposed sub rosa; and yes, of course, dozens and dozens of assets might be compromised. None of it will be possible if Dr. B is pushed too hard, or in the wrong directions, or too quickly. The good Doctor is the rare case in this damnable business where future value exceeds that at present. Now, do you have what you need?*

Special Investigator: *I need the one-line answer, Rem. For the summary. How do you want it to read?*

Gen. Rem Mikhailovich Zhomov: *Repeat the question.*

Special Investigator: *[flapping of paper] Please describe your long-term objective for the case.*

Gen. Rem Mikhailovich Zhomov: *To destroy the CIA. Now, time's up.*

17

CLARENDON, VIRGINIA / LANGLEY

SAM AWOKE A FEW HOURS BEFORE DAWN, GRIPPED BY FEAR that the nameless woman was snuggled beside him in bed. Her distinctly sweet smell flooded him before he could even open his eyes. The taste of her lipstick was muscular, overpowering the sour dryness left by sleep, and he thought his tongue could feel a few chalky flakes deposited along his bottom teeth. Light-headed, with the sheets around him churned and dampened by sweat, he sat up and looked around for the little red stars, but it was too dark to see the walls. He listened to her breathing and, as always, pawed frantically across his skin for evidence of her nocturnal blandishments: sores and scratches and exposed flesh and sticky stripes where her tongue had been. He did not feel pain. His underwear was on. His skin was dry and smooth. Sam's heart began the slow climb down from his throat.

He could only be certain he was not in the box when his eyes came to rest upon the dim glow of his bedroom windows: there hadn't been a single window in Russia, but here, here in his home in Clarendon was a window. This could not be Russia. This could not be his box. There had been a time when he'd had blackout shades—no longer, and never again, as long as he lived. Natalie was sleeping peacefully next to him. For the most part he did not like sharing a bed with her, but he was grateful for it on mornings when the woman haunted him. Unlike most ghosts, she was at her most terrifying around first light.

He swung his legs out of bed and sat there for a few moments with his head in his hands. Natalie rolled over. "How did you sleep *habibti*?" she murmured.

"Fantastic," he said, leaning over to plant a kiss on her forehead. "Really great."

IN THE SHOWER SAM MOVED THROUGH THE MEMORY PALace of his childhood bedroom, but this time the Lego bins held numbers that he had reviewed with Procter on Roblox the night before. He did not like to think about what would happen if he forgot them, or put them in the wrong order. And if he got them right? Well, he did not like to think about that, either.

He and Natalie ate breakfast at the dining room table. He had met her at a grocery store a few blocks down the road, in Clarendon, a year before Singapore. Two or so sideways glances between them, she had smiled, and Sam—who as a matter of principle took his shots when they concerned the attentions of well-made Levantine women—walked right up to her in the bakery and asked if they might have dinner.

"I have a boyfriend," Natalie had said, with a tone of regret.

"That's too bad," he replied. "But what do you think about dinner?"

Now they sometimes shared a bed and she was scooping out a cup of yogurt at his table. "What do you have going on today at work?"

"Not much," he lied. "Normal day. You?"

"Nothing. The usual chaos."

"Those kids are lucky to have you."

"Do you want to have dinner tonight?"

"Sure," he lied, a night alone smashed on the rocks of her love. "I can pick up salmon."

She made a face. "Maybe a rain check on your salmon? I'll swing by Kazan's on the way home. The usual?"

"Perfect," he said. "Sounds like a plan. I should be home by six." He took his cup and bowl into the kitchen. Natalie followed.

"You really slept well last night?" she asked. "No . . . uh . . ."

"None," he lied, opening the dishwasher.

"I'm so glad, Sam," she said. "That feels like . . . like progress."

"Totally," he said, loading their dishes.

"What did Dr. Portnoy tell you? A month without nightmares and you're on your way."

"Something like that." He slid shut the dishwasher.

"And how many days does that make without one?"

"Seven," he said, and this time felt a little sick about the lie.

AT HIS BASEMENT DESK SAM SPENT AN HOUR PRETENDING to read the overnight traffic. His calendar, visible to the entirety of Moscow X, was blocked out from one to three p.m. The red box said: "Doctor's Appointment." That was a stand-in for appointments with his Office of Medical Services–mandated psychologist. Though the readouts of those sessions, written up by Dr. Portnoy, were submitted to Sam's personnel records and, he knew, his Russia House superiors and a few up on the Seventh Floor, no one had once asked about these chats, much less pointed out if he left early or returned late.

Russia House has many rooms. One of them is known as the Backroom. The door is green-painted and unmarked. Behind it is a honeycomb of cubicles staffed by the small team of officers managing the Agency's most sensitive Russia cases, many of which, even today, are documented in hard copy. At nine-thirty he called Lanzasta, one of the Backroom analysts, on the green line phone on his desk. "James," he said, "how's it hanging?" But before Lanzasta could misread this salutation as an earnest question and respond, Sam barreled ahead: "Awesome. Look, we've got a potential inbound from a Russian financier who's living in the Gulf. Thought I could put a few questions to you about Moscow? Guy's a rambler, and some of his stuff on the city doesn't add up. I'll pay you back with lunch. Pick your poison." The offer was dead on arrival, and intentionally so: Lanzasta always brought his own lunch, typically lugged in a cooler large enough to transport a decent batch of organs. And like many analysts, Lanzasta preferred to eat from the relative peace and security of his high-partitioned cubicle.

Lanzasta declined the offer of food, accepted the invite, and Sam said, “I can come up your way. Eleven-thirty too early? I’ve got to make a doctor’s appointment out in Fairfax by one.”

The Backroom crowd usually thinned out over the lunch hour, decamping to read newspapers over silent lunches in the cafeteria, yet another awful feature of this place that made Sam wonder if, by osmosis, he was becoming all he had ever hated.

Sam did not have access to the vault, so he punched the buzzer and waited for the click. Once inside, he cheerfully greeted the few reports officers and then Lanzasta, squatting in the first bullpen of cubicles inside the door. The far back wall of the Backroom held a bank of safes, each for the material produced by a single human asset.

“The number is 132-1,” Procter’s Roblox character had scrawled on its message board, “over on the left.” From his current vantage he couldn’t make out any numbers. He noticed sweat sticking to his pants and shirt. He set the gym bag down in an empty desk in the bullpen next to Lanzasta, who joined him at the circular table in the center. He and Lanzasta had worked on Syria together back in the day, when Procter had been Chief in Damascus, and he had expected that they would fall into a conversation that was completely natural, even casual. But immediately upon sitting down, Sam could tell something was wrong.

“James,” he said. “What’s up?”

“Something happened in Moscow last night,” he whispered. “Asset didn’t show for a meet. You know Tarrman, one of the case officers out there?”

“Yeah.”

“Well, they arrested him. Brought him to Lefortovo. PNGed him and his wife. Killed all his cats.”

Sam made a face. “The Tarrmans are okay, though?”

“Yes, bodily. They’re out of Russia and on their way home.”

“What happened to the asset?” Sam wanted to ask which one, but he would not; he didn’t have access, and Lanzasta was oversharing as it was.

“We don’t know.”

“Well, shit.”

"Anyway," Lanzasta said, tossing his lunch bag toward a trash can, and missing horribly, "crap day up here. What did you want to talk about?"

Sam, reeling from the news but refocusing on the task at hand, put to the analyst a few questions about the atmospherics in Moscow. A volunteer in Dubai claiming access to a variety of Russian oil tycoons had provided his debriefer with a ream of information on his life and times in Moscow. Sam, at Raptis's direction, had been tasked with the evaluation. It was a softball, a way to keep him busy, make him feel included. And it was a microcosm of the Langley self-licking ice-cream cone: Sam knew of at least four others across the alphabet soup of Agency components who were evaluating the case.

When Lanzasta had finished answering, Sam thanked him and proposed the first essential lie: "I've got about a half hour. Gonna log in to one of these machines until I head out." This was not technically permitted, but practically it happened with sufficient frequency that Lanzasta did not bat an eye. "Cool—good to catch up," was all he said before returning to his desk on the other side of the high-partitioned cubicle.

Sam logged in, pulled up the cable database, and for about five straight minutes simply stared into the screen. Sweat was pouring through his shirt. Hearing the murmur of Lanzasta and his teammates, Sam typed out a few senseless paragraphs so they might hear the clack of keys. He checked his watch.

Standing, peering over the top of the cubicle's partition—stretching, for good measure—he wiped his hands once more and made friendly eye contact with Lanzasta. Sam's ears felt like they'd been put in an oven; this was a regular tic during surveillance detection runs in the field, and in this moment it was reassuring, making him feel dialed in, ready to cross the line, to commit the act.

"Safe 132-1," Procter had written, "will be three, maybe four to the left from the one at center."

"How many up or down?" he had asked.

"No clue," Procter had written.

Ten steps, and Sam was looking up at the wall of safes as if it were a hill he might climb. A ball of saliva crowded his throat, his ears were aflame, but he could rise above it to remind himself he appeared casual, normal. This was simply the rush of stealing. He wasn't dead to it, thankfully—they didn't want you dead to it. They worried what you'd do if you got dead to it.

And here, it was here he made his first and only mistake—later, he'd chalk it up to the rust one collects in the Penalty Box. Rather than pounce on the opening granted by the room, at that moment populated by Lanzasta and two disinterested analysts, Sam instead went to a safe to which he had once had formal access: the case file of an executive for Russia's state-owned arms exporter.

Sam unlocked the safe and took a stack of papers back to his workstation. His vision watery, he stared uselessly at the reports, silently counting to one hundred and eighty, randomly turning pages and doing so quite loudly, almost jerking the staples out, as if Lanzasta simply had to know how feverishly he was working over here, on business that was critical and, clearly, entirely legitimate. He flipped more pages. Felt beads of water tickling his legs, sliding into his socks. His hands were steady, though. And bone-dry.

He mentally ticked through the combination he'd committed to memory, sliding each Lego bin from beneath his bed to memorize the numbers. Maybe he would forget it. But when had he forgotten numbers in his life? He wouldn't be so lucky. His heart was drumming his ribs.

Sam was up. He left half the stack of papers at the workstation and returned the other half to the safe. He stood there, fingers on the dial, watching the sweat evaporate from the handle. Move.

Three steps to the left, same row, and he saw the safe's number: 132-1. REMORA's trove. Sam turned the dial, swishing and clicking, swishing and clicking. Click. The bolt released. First try. The safe swung open. The creaky hinges might well have been a gunshot. Bam. Violation of Agency Regulation 2353-5 (*Procedures regarding handling of Sensitive Reporting material in Agency safes*); specifically the lines stipulating that if you mishandled said material they would *submit your file to the Performance Review Board and/or consider termination or prosecution pending Security inves-*

tigation. Bam. Bam. Now the vulnerable part. As the Chief had said, the stack was healthy. There was no reason to lift an entire case file out of a Backroom safe in a single haul, but he'd have no guarantee of operational cover in a fucking minute's time and so he fished it all out and shuttled it to the workstation and began sorting, rifling to be sure he had it all. The structure inside these safes varied wildly by case. And Theo Monk, REMORA's current handler, was a notorious slob. First folder. Copies of the finished product. Into the gym bag. Next: the personality file, the background material, photos. Into the gym bag. Six folders, labeled chronologically, with the entirety of the ops cables and notes. Gym bag. The GQ/OATH documents: the Finance Smurfs' accounting. Gym bag. Next up: asset validation and assessments. Drop of sweat from his nose, goddammit. Into the bag. Then: thick reams of the operational traffic. He set the papers down and wiped his face with his sleeve. Next: logistics. Buff-colored folder. Commo might be in there. Had to be, right? What else was there? Move.

Fingers still and serene, Sam reassembled the remaining folders and documents into the sandwiched order in which he'd found them, and stuffed them back into the safe. He spun it off, then peered around to see if anyone had taken an interest in him. Lanzasta's head was tipped down over a binder. He wiped the safe with his dry sleeve—no use leaving prints on there—and returned to the workstation for a breather.

The Backroom door buzzed, then clicked open. He snatched a look at the entryway, and watched as Mac Mason, Gus Raptis, Theo Monk, and the DDO, Deborah Sweet herself, walked into the vault. Sam felt his stomach slingshot into his head.

Sam gripped one of the arms exporters' reports and pretended to read. The words were squiggly black lines.

"Just Singapore," Deborah was saying, cocking an eye his way. "Damn committee." They were walking toward him.

He looked up as they passed, each shooting him curious glances. Mac nodded as he went by, so did Theo. Gus offered a grunt. Deborah Sweet stood outside an empty office. At his eye contact she gave a thin smile. Mac had wandered in front of REMORA's safe. Hands on the dial,

Sam saw now, in pure bright terror. Mac was turning the dial, tongue on his lips in concentration, and the door—oh god, the door—was cracked open when Gus called out. "Never mind, Mac. Theo's already got a copy in here."

Sam's breathing slowed at the *clunk* of the safe closing. Footsteps. They went into the empty office and shut the door. He wondered if he should stay put until they left, just to be sure, but his window was closing. It was either bolt or put it all back. From the gym bag he removed a folder of medical questionnaires from Dr. Portnoy, along with copies of *Foreign Affairs* and the *Economist.* These were left on the desk, reasons for a return visit this afternoon to replace the documents, after Procter had made copies. He returned the arms exporter's material to the safe, logged off, and called—his tone steady and calm—goodbye to Lanzasta, who said, *Later Sam*, and did not once look up.

Out the door, gym bag slumping along his waist, he marched and weaved down the Headquarters hallways, basking in the curious realization that, for the first time since Singapore, he felt in control. That he was the one making things happen. The consequences, the risks, were no less real—they were merely less relevant. The run of sweat had thinned to a remnant trace along his lower back. He reveled in the weight of the stolen documents on his shoulder, swishing in the bag, and the smack of adrenaline pumping through him. He smiled at friends and acquaintances and strangers on the way out. About time, he thought, some proper spying got done around Headquarters.

18

CRYSTAL CITY

PROCTER WAS IN THE SELF-PARK GARAGE AT THE CROWNE Plaza, staring at a dirty handprint on the rear passenger side door of her RAV4. Maybe the driver of a neighboring car had bumped into her? But had anyone even parked nearby? She looked up and down the rows of the sparsely occupied garage and wondered about that. Maybe someone at the hospital? Had Sam shimmied around to that side when he'd fed the REMORA documents into the trunk-housed scanner earlier that afternoon? Had someone tampered with it?

She could not *know*. They called it seeing ghosts—believing hostiles have you made when in fact you're free and clear of ticks. Throughout her career, Procter hadn't been one to see ghosts. That she was wondering about them now made her feel washed up and pathetic, like a retiree loser past her prime, a slander all the more galling for being inconveniently true. An eerie feeling took hold in her mind.

She made a patrol around the car, checking the doors, handles, and hood for any signs of entry: scrapes, more prints, missing flecks of paint. Flicking on the flashlight she kept in her glove box, Procter searched for evidence of a rushed beacon install: the telltale small box stuck on by magnets, typically under bumpers or inside wheel wells. She found nothing, but the commercially available beacons were now so small that she could not be sure that she would. After a mental recap of her stops since arriving in Northern Virginia, Procter concluded that any watchers would have probably conducted the beaconing here—the deep install jobs demanded too much time and privacy for even a skillful surveillant to have pulled one off anywhere else. Plus, by now her hotel was common knowledge. They knew where to find her car. "Goddammit," she muttered. She did not want to review the camera footage now; there was so much to read tonight as it was. She lit a Slim and puffed a lungful of smoke over the creepy handprint.

WITH THE CIGARETTE PINNED IN HER TEETH, PROCTER wandered to the soiled concrete wall behind the RAV4. She got on her tiptoes and grasped for the metal electrical enclosure. She'd used magnets to stick it on the electrical box beneath one of the lights, where it had a clean view of her car. She plucked it off, tucked it into her bag, stamped out her Slim, and went up to her room. On her hotel room desk, she opened the box and removed the Arlo camera she'd purchased at Best Buy. She'd forked over an additional eighty bucks from the reptile fund for the upscale model with a two-month battery life. That was more than enough—and if it was not, by that point someone watching her car would be the least of her problems.

After two grueling hours reviewing the footage on fast-forward, Procter had convinced herself no one had done an install, quick, deep, or otherwise, in the Crowne Plaza garage. Anticipating a long night, Procter packed toiletries and a change of clothes in her duffel. Sliding the camera into the electrical enclosure, double-checking that the lens had a clean view out the hole she'd drilled, Procter gathered everything up and returned to the parking garage. After remounting the camera, Procter removed the gym bag with the scanned REMORA material from the trunk. With the documents slung over one shoulder and her duffel the other, Procter set off on foot, on a carefully planned and zigzagging route, toward the Crystal City safe house.

IN THE MAKESHIFT SAFE HOUSE SHE HAULED HER RATTY legal pads and the box of printed REMORA documents to the living room. She arranged the papers in piles, each stack a square on the chessboard of the floor: biographic trove; another for the ops traffic; yet another for the validation cables; a heap of the finished reports. She sat down with the documents stacked in a circle, like friends around a campfire, terror and ghost stories assuredly to come.

To recruit assets, case officers must possess the delusional optimism of the well-below-average male hitting on the perfect woman, the energy to eagerly face rejection ninety-nine times out of a hundred, fueled throughout, each and every time, by the fervent belief that success undoubtedly awaits. And so it began with REMORA: Mac and Theo, eying the Russian in Paris, believed him recruitable. "Significant potential," Theo wrote in the one of the cables, "by dint of his ego and greed." That was two years ago, Procter saw. One-in-a-hundred shot—and they'd hit the mark.

She skimmed the REMORA biography: raised in Nizhny; father had been KGB First Chief Directorate. Now a colonel, he had done a run of tours in Europe, first attracting CIA's attention while stationed in Paris.

Theo and Mac's dance with REMORA in the City of Light had been one of mutual interest. "He's trying to recruit us," Mac wrote in one missive back to Langley, "and he's not hiding it." The meets happened in public, in restaurants, and sometimes with the French in tow. Everyone knew who everyone was; the courtship unrolled in the pure bright light of day.

There was camaraderie, yet there would be no consummation. REMORA's Paris tour was winding down. Theo made the formal pitch, which REMORA politely rejected. Two weeks later he was back in Russia, and a few months after that, CIA heard of a new crop of promotions. REMORA was on the list: Deputy Chief of the Fifth Department (Europe).

For a full year out from Paris, the REMORA file was empty. Then, last autumn, CIA learned REMORA was traveling to Morocco. The recruitment went down in Marrakesh, yet again a dance between Mac and Theo. The reams of cables from that week sat in their own pile, which Procter now leafed through. Dawn neared, but she paid the morning no mind.

Procter snagged a red pen and slid over to the stack of finished intelligence reports sourced from REMORA's information. She thumbed through eight from the Morocco conversation alone, all graded by the analysts as either Outstanding or Excellent, a trend that would continue for several months.

By midwinter, though, REMORA's information was becoming fluffier. And here, Procter sat up with a frown. A case assessment, written by Petra Devine, argued that REMORA's most recent intelligence could have been written by a U.S. think tank. "And its primary points and messages have indeed already been included in such reports," she wrote. But the White House was hooked. "Unique insight into Moscow's strategic thinking," said one of the feedback notes appended to the file.

When the Gosford regime took power, Debs had carted reams of REMORA's intel into the Oval, Procter now saw. In fact, from the write-ups alone one could be forgiven for believing Debs had played a leading, and possibly heroic, role in REMORA's development.

Procter's journey through the files now slammed into the France meeting at which REMORA had issued his vague warning, in March, days before Singapore. It was here that Debs, the DDO, had most unusually traveled alongside Mac and Theo. She considered that meeting in France, playing through the sequence of arrivals, the batting order, comparing what she'd so far heard from her friends to what she saw in the cable. Five or so minutes alone with a Russian, she thought. Plenty of time to pass a note, offer a warning. Procter read and reread the ops cables and meeting readouts; she studied the commo plan; she reviewed the finished reports and compared these to the prior fluff.

She soon came to a July cable sent to Mac and Theo by Petra Devine: "Can you detail the chain of custody of REMORA's information with respect to our captive case officer? Please clarify."

Theo had basically told her to screw off. "REMORA heard it from the Chief of the American Department on the squash courts. Russia House stands ready for more good questions from our friends in Dermatology."

Thirty thousand each month, Petra Devine wrote, is an exorbitant sum to pay for think tank reports with SVR blue stripes painted on them, but by summer this tack found no purchase. REMORA had policymaker attention—the good kind, for a change. He'd provided penetrations—"selectively, carefully," Petra wrote, "the stream's still too constipated for my liking"—and his access, when coupled with the blessings from Mac, Theo, Gus, and Debs, cemented institutional faith in his information. Petra again: "I have yet to obtain reasons from Russia House for the rapid fluctuations in the specificity of REMORA's intelligence, particularly given source's consistent access."

Procter was lounging on the sofa like a drunk leopard, bars of morning's first light rippling through the slats of the soiled blinds. In the anodyne language of her Dermatologists, Petra was calling bullshit on REMORA. About a month after drafting that note, Procter recalled, scribbling the dates in her chronology, and Petra Devine would be fired.

19

RESTON, VIRGINIA

THEO MONK WOULD HAVE RISEN FAR HIGHER INSIDE CIA IF not for a hungry cock and thirsty liver. Not that either disqualified you from the Seventh Floor pantheon; such appetites could well be marks in your favor. But overindulgence did travel with certain risks, chief among them the prospect of domestic bedlam. Case officers were expected to tolerate a certain amount of personal chaos to excel in the job, but there was a limit, and somewhere around the time he finally achieved his GS-14, in his pursuit of ladies and booze, he had found it.

Theo had been in her Farm class, and one of her favorites. He hadn't been attractive, really, but he was charming. He'd talked his way into the Agency during a recruiter's visit to the University of Michigan, where he was drinking and, when he found the time, studying international politics and journalism. In those days, the meager late Clinton years of the post–Cold War peace dividend, before 9/11 and the bureaucratic fattening to come, Farm classes were small, hiring a trickle. How Theo had cleared the bar was apparent to Procter on day one: this was a guy who, through his spirit and charm, encouraged the spilling of secrets.

Gus had been the teacher's pet because he put in more work than the rest of them combined. Theo was your B student: cleverer than the top man, with none of the drive. If Mac had been pressed into CIA service by his father, and Gus had joined eagerly to fill the father's shoes, Theo had signed his papers because he didn't want to while away his days in the Rust Belt. His family owned a plastic-extrusion manufacturing business in Grand Rapids. He seemed to love them, but he loved adventure more, and he'd told Procter in the early days of the Farm that if he'd stayed in Grand Rapids he'd have drunk himself to death out of boredom. Turned out he would damn near accomplish the feat at CIA.

Theo was also a pussy hound. Sometimes lovable, often deplorable, always a good time, if you were in the mood for one. "The man's a sex addict," Gus had said once, she forgot when. Procter herself had shared with Theo a few drunken make-outs while at the Farm, usually after he'd appeared outside her room with a bottle of something awful, on the heels of one of her phone battles with her soon-to-be-ex-husband, Tom, which Theo could hear through the walls.

He'd married a chick named Diana, a Statie, before his first tour in Ankara. At the wedding Procter bet Mac a hundred bucks the marriage wouldn't make its second birthday. As it happened, it barely made its first, and Procter used the winnings to treat Theo to chili dogs at the Vienna Inn, during one of his return trips from Ankara to finalize the divorce.

The second wife, acquired not long after he lost the first, was a hippie lady called Fayla. "That her Christian name, Theo?" Procter had asked, and never did get a reply. He'd admitted to marrying Fayla because the heat in the sack was solar and, footnote, she was also pregnant with his first and only child. Fayla named the daughter Milangela, though to Theo she was always and only Millie.

By the time Fayla had packed up and moved out West with Millie, she'd stolen most of Theo's furniture, drained a portion of his retirement, and, in a fit that would grow to legend among those in the know inside Russia House, taken a hammer—literally—to what at the time, as now, was Theo's primary extracurricular interest beyond, in order, liquor, sex, and espionage: exotic fish.

Procter was in his living room now, bathed in the rippling glow of the tanks. She had completed a quick circuit in search of the work hat he'd stolen from Gatorville during his visit a few months earlier. No dice, and she wasn't going to ask, because he probably didn't remember. Theo was making martinis with Seagram's. He pressed a dangerously full drink into her hands. She watched a few fish disappear behind a large plant.

"Did insurance cover it, when you had to replace the whole setup?"

"Hard to insure fifty-four grand worth of exotic fish, Artemis."

"If J.Lo can get insurance for her butt, you could've managed. But I meant the water damage, Theo."

"Oh no. God, no. That was almost as expensive as replacing the fish."

"How's Millie doing, anyway? You told her I was sorry I didn't take her to the zoo this summer, right?"

"I did. She knows you like her more than me. And she's good. Fifth grade this fall, can you believe it? Getting big. Knows a bunch of bad words. Makes me feel old. It's nice when she comes in June, and nice when she leaves in July."

Theo's living room, she thought, looking around, was doing the noble work of preventing a third marriage. Two huge fish tanks, each must've been three hundred or more gallons, consumed an entire wall. Smaller tanks were scattered throughout the rest of the home. Opposite the large tanks was a shimmering bar stocked with dozens of liquor bottles Theo seemed to collect but never use, and the rail stuff he drank like water. Between the bar and the fish tanks were two couches, where they took their drinks.

"What fish is this?" With her martini glass Procter gestured at a rainbowy shape emerging from the rocks.

Theo perked up immediately. "*Gramma dejongi*," he said.

"Its name is Gramma?"

Theo looked as if he'd been stricken with sudden nerve damage. "No. Moron. *Gramma dejongi* is the species. It's also known as the Cuban basslet. Tough to find, damn sanctions." Excruciatingly long slurp of his drink. "They are endemic to the waters off Cuba. So you gotta get them from dealers who'll do business with Cubans. Black spot on the dorsal fin, gold with purple patches on the fins. Fascinating fish. There's a platinum type, too, which I'd like to acquire." Tip of the glass, and the rest of his martini was gone.

The fish had flitted back into the rocks, and Theo trotted to the bar to shake out another drink.

"How much did that fucker set you back?" Procter called out.

"About six hundred, but that one wasn't so bad. In one of the tanks upstairs, I've got a soapfish I dropped ten grand on." He started shaking another martini. "How's the drink?"

"You could afford better booze if you bought cheaper fish."

"I meant, do you need a refresh?"

She shook her head, though with Theo's drinking habits, ten grand would not go very far if he was buying top-shelf booze.

Theo refilled his to the brim and fell back onto the couch, somehow without spilling. "If you're here for sex, we should start now, before my blood's run to gin."

"That's thoughtful, Theo, really is, but I'm gonna pass tonight. Not the sexiest vibes in here these days. I've also heard rumors about your medical issues and I don't need the rash."

At this he laughed and took down half the martini, then set to foraging for the olives at the bottom with his tongue, like a lizard. "I got pills after Budapest," he said. "Cleared everything up real quick."

They both laughed. His smile was mischievous and cheerful, but Procter, who hadn't intended to veer this direction, immediately regretted her playful comment. Because it wasn't a joke, not really. Theo had gotten an STD in Budapest—which one, she did not know or care to know. And his pecker might have recovered, but his career had not. The circumstances surrounding its acquisition had meant that he was doomed to ride out his days inside Russia House, never to rise to the coveted Seventh Floor jobs beyond.

Two years earlier, Theo had traveled to Budapest to bump a visiting Russian businessman. A nickel magnate, Procter recalled. Guy hadn't said no to the pitch but he also hadn't shown up at the bar Theo had picked for the follow-up, so Theo hung out for a few more days to see if he'd get another shot.

And at some point, a woman named Katya intersected his drinking, and they drank, and went dancing, and Theo woke up in a hotel room, his member the color of a fire engine, a minefield of bite marks across his neck, the lithe Katya replaced by a man who called himself Daniil, who had a pack of incriminating pictures of Mr. Theo. Daniil said that these were reminders of his sins. And Theo had said, in his effortless Russian, "Seriously, Daniil, who ran your traces on me, who thought any of this would be compelling grist? I'm a well-known sinner, inside Langley and out. This is like trying to blackmail the village drunk inside the tavern. Facts are well known, Danny. Come, now, fuck off."

Bluster aside—and the fact that Theo, to his credit, had reported the pitch—he'd gotten his foot and other things snagged in a Russian honey trap and couldn't *really* remember critical details, such as when he'd been drugged by the delightful yet diseased Katya, or what, if anything, he had told her. Procter and Theo had swapped stories because the same Russian blackmail shoe dropped on her in Dushanbe about a year later, and Theo was good company for commiseration as long as you were clear, up front, that it wasn't going to end in bed.

But in the glow of the aquariums Procter regretted tickling that slice of his memory, because she wondered now if he'd made other, similar mistakes, which he had perhaps not reported.

"Look, Theo," she said, snatching a few quick sips of courage, "I need your help. Singapore is scratching at the old memory. I've been trying to piece together a few things that are still grinding my gears."

"Sure," Theo replied distractedly. His attention was directed toward a school of fish in the aquarium. "What's eating you?"

"Your meeting with REMORA," she said—at mention of the asset his head swiveled to face her—"right before the Russians snatched Sam. I've been thinking about whether we had the clues then to prevent it from happening."

Theo, back at the bar, this time to pick at the olives: "I don't follow."

"REMORA said the Russians were aiming to kidnap an American in Asia. He'd flown the emergency signal and moved personal travel around to deliver the message to you and Mac in France. I've been beating myself up about it. Wonder if we should have yanked Sam back. If we plowed ahead blindly."

"You're asking if we should have been able to determine, among all the Americans at that moment across Asia—the continent of fucking Asia—that the one officer we were sending to Singapore was the target?"

"Yes."

Theo laughed with a mouthful of olives, the chuckle still running when he fastened back into the couch. "Come on, Artemis."

For a moment they watched the fish, the throaty hum of the filters filling the silence. "Debs went to the meet," Procter said, aware she was sliding a rock to the conversation's edge. "I always found that strange."

Theo licked his lips, then the rim of the glass, and shrugged. "She wasn't interested in running the meeting. But she did want credit, a story for Gosford and probably the White House. You know how it goes. The Seventh Floor toadies want to hop into the field and look the agent in the eye, who cares if it's hell on the handler?"

"I recall that you and Mac took the meeting and then Debs joined later. Pitched it as a sort of fireside chat with you two, make sure everything was square, then open the cage, let in the political animal. That about right?"

"That's . . ." Long sip, doleful glance almost through her, toward the fireplace. "Shit. Gimme a sec. Goddammit."

He returned a few moments later with a purple net on a telescopic pole and the same mournful expression on his face. Theo cracked open a larger aquarium on the floor by the fireplace and dipped in the net to scoop out a black mass, at rest on the pebbly bottom.

"That fish shit?" she asked over her martini, twisting for a view.

"That," he said sharply, "is a wrought-iron butterflyfish. Deceased. Very rare. And just purchased yesterday. For two thousand bucks. Makes me wonder . . ." He just stopped talking, his attention consumed by the dead animal. The fish went into a Styrofoam coffin—he had a stack of them handy—which he marked with a Sharpie before collecting a water sample and heading into the kitchen. She heard the freezer door clack open, then shut. Theo was mumbling sadly when he shuffled back into the living room.

"You freeze them for dinner?"

"Forensics." The delivery was entirely humorless. "Autopsy at the store tomorrow, for a refund. Where were we?"

"I was asking how you and Mac and Debs set the batting order for the REMORA meet. You and Mac did the fireside chat, that right? Then Debs swooped in."

"Right," he said, and pounced at his remaining drink. This time she held out her glass, which he dutifully collected on his way to the bar. "Mac and I did the fireside."

"And that was where REMORA said his piece about the Russians looking to hunt Americans in Asia?"

"Yes."

"Was there any extra color, beyond the cable? Anything at all."

"We wrote up what was said, Artemis, come on." *Shake-shake-shake.* He slid her the martini and started on his own, his third of the evening. "What're you after here?"

"How was his mood?"

"Mac's?"

"Theo, focus. REMORA's. He'd moved his calendar around to make the meet, to give us that intel. He thought there was value, right? Was he excited? Nervous? Sniffing for your approval?"

"He was calm, Artemis. As usual. He's a pro. He had solid cover for the meet and its associated operational acts. Again, as usual. He was a mercenary, believed he had something of value and wanted payment. Simple."

"REMORA talk much about whether SVR frowned at him moving around his vacay? Jetting to Europe two weeks early?"

"Not much. Some. Not much."

"REMORA arrives first." She delivered the falsehood evenly, casually, without fanfare or the hint of a question.

"Right," he said. "REMORA was there first. He almost always arrives first. Mac and I meet him, do the grunt work. Debs takes her victory lap."

Her heart sank. Was he lying or did he not remember? Because she remembered the cable word for word: *C/O Mason and C/O Monk arrived early. REMORA was twenty minutes late for the meeting, in good spirits. DDO Sweet joined after the fireside chat.*

"Why'd you want Mac to go? You're the handler."

"Artemis," he said—pause, *shake-shake-shake*, the metal furring with condensation—"I love you, but I am finding this conversation frustrating."

"That's a good tool, labeling the emotion," she said. "Therapist helping you with that?"

"Dr. Seagram manages my mental health, and he tends to recommend that I bury it all down deep and drink for sport while I'm at it." He smiled into the glass, then, for effect, tipped back a long sip. When he came up for air he was sporting a Cheshire smile.

"Why'd Mac go?"

The question erased his smile. "It's simple, Artemis, and I think you know the answer, don't you? So I wonder why you're asking me? The dynamic between REMORA and myself is fine, it is workable, but it is not as productive as the trio. And, if you recall, when I took over the case, that bag Petra Devine and her Derms were hounding me to step it up. Quality of the output was dropping. And Mac wanted to help. He wanted the handover executed perfectly so REMORA would keep producing. Me, Mac, and REMORA: the best intelligence arrives when the three of us are present. To REMORA the whole thing is a financial arrangement, a negotiation, so we're looking for advantages. And it's an advantage to have a partner when engaging with him. That work?"

"Works."

"Want to tell me why you're poking like this?" Theo said.

"Want to tell me why you aren't sure who arrived first to the meet?" Procter asked. This was her sharpest foray yet into the fray. She wasn't sure she had it right, but she knew something was off, and she'd socked Theo across the face for a reaction.

Theo set his jaw and stretched out his arms, bringing the heel of his hands to rest on the bar top, his eyes downcast, glued to his feet and the floor. She'd known Theo for twenty-five years. Knew him well enough to know that he was hiding something.

"Mind your own fucking business, Artemis," Theo said, slowly raising his head. "You want to answer mine?"

"My conscience," she said. "As I noted earlier."

"Well, cut that crap out, will you? It's pointless and it's making me furious."

Procter met a stare from Theo blending frustration and fear. "You're right," she said. "I'm sorry. I got carried away. I should go. I've gotta be up early for interviews and you have a fish to bury. Thanks for the breezy chitchat and the shitty martinis."

They hugged goodbye without enthusiasm or warmth, Theo's eyes still shining with anxiety, and the front door clapped shut behind her, and she was out, walking briskly into the night, hearing the rattle of the shaker pouring through an open window, and her heartbeat, keeping frenetic time inside her head.

20

WASHINGTON, D.C.

PROCTER AND DEBS HAD COME TO THE BAR TWICE, SHE recalled, before Afghanistan. Basement karaoke joint off Dupont. Then, as now, it was a shadowed warren of low-slung tables separated by half-height dividers. Neon lights played along the walls, the strobe twirled above, the air was thick with the funk of salty socks and a crooning Korean guy belting out Beyoncé. A smoke machine, rolling from behind the stage, enveloped the singer. Procter pressed through the crowd toward a table in back, where Deborah Sweet sat sipping something that had an umbrella poking out of it. Even from a distance, and through a considerable amount of smoke, Procter could tell that this getup was a doozy. At some point after leaving CIA, Debs had shed the dreary pantsuits and sensible shoes for a wardrobe that functioned as a massive neon sign, directing everyone's attention her way. Tonight her old friend wore a pouf of a fur vest, chunky pink eyeglasses, white snow boots, and skintight black pants. The vest recalled a Highland sheep, or perhaps a bath mat. Procter's purse went onto the floor—the snow boots, she saw leaning over, were pearly white and pristine. She took the seat next to Debs, facing the smoky stage.

"Still no waiters?" Procter asked.

Debs pointed off through the smoke in the direction of the bar. "Still got to make the hike."

Procter flicked the umbrella of Debs's drink.

"They're out of pineapple," Debs said, gathering the drink closer.

At the bar Procter ordered a Clipper-Tini and listened to the Korean guy while the bartender worked. From her vantage she couldn't see Debs; she could barely make out the stage. The bartender draped Procter's drink with a pineapple wedge, then tipped in an orange paper umbrella.

"They told me they were out of pineapple," Debs said angrily, when Procter eased back into her seat.

Procter shrugged, took a sip. "Pleased to see the place still in business."

"Are you?" Debs said, eyeing the now-empty stage, momentarily visible between curtains of smoke. The din of conversation floated all around. They sat close, each speaking, at times, directly into the other's ear.

"When I got your email, Artemis, I had to fight the urge to delete it. But I realized I was more curious than angry, and these days you're not really . . . formidable."

"That an olive branch? Your small talk could use some help, Debs. Don't they have people to help with that sort of thing up on the Seventh Floor? You might consider hiring someone with good communication skills. Just a thought."

"They could have helped you, too, Artemis. Kept you from committing dire errors such as calling the new Director a cunt."

"For some strange reason I wasn't feeling so tip-top that day," Procter said. "Plus, I said his idea was a shade cunty. Not that he was one."

"Oh right, forgive me." Debs snatched a drink and took a breath through her teeth. "Anyway, I was trying to remember the last time we really talked. I'm a glutton for pain, what can I say? When was it?"

"I recall a breakfast or something before Afghanistan. Foggy memories of bacon and stilted conversation. So north of a decade."

From behind a wall of smoke the Korean guy had returned for an encore. This time: Sinatra, and mangled horribly, even by the handicap of a Sparkle Karaoke Thursday night.

"North of a decade," Debs repeated. "So what's up Artemis? Is this a clumsy stroll down memory lane? A plea for your old job? Do we have business to conduct?"

"You weren't always such a grumpy buttlicker, Debs," Procter said. "I liked you better back then."

DEBS'S DAD MANAGED AN UNSUCCESSFUL GROCERY STORE outside Cleveland, her mom hadn't been around. Debs had come to CIA through the kind of banal corporate pathway that probably had Langley's Skull and Bones forebears twisting in their coffins: a job fair. All it took was four years of Division I volleyball and a 3.4 GPA at Ohio State, and the six-foot-one-inch Debs was towering over an Agency recruiter explaining that she wanted to change the world.

They'd been the only two women in their Farm class, and the shared gauntlet of joining a boys' club had drawn them together, as had Procter's valiant attempt at playing setter in the pickup volleyball games Debs had organized.

At the end of the Farm, one of the instructors sat Debs down and told her flatly: She'd flunked. Debs wasn't fired from CIA—there were plenty of other, lesser jobs to be done—but a stone wall now blocked the path to the summit, the only way to join the jocks that ran the place.

What had done her in? Oh sure, there had been rumors, all terrible: the most popular had it that the long-legged and comely Deborah Fraser Sweet had been flunked by the species of crusty Farm graybeard who still considered vaginal ownership a straight line to secretarial work or, depending on brain size, perhaps to do whatever it was the analysts did over in the New Headquarters Building.

But Procter knew better, and it was not merely that she'd passed the Farm while in possession of a vagina all her own. No, Procter had spent six months watching Debs plan and run ops, and the plain fact was that the woman had committed two fatal sins.

One: She'd cracked under pressure running her surveillance detection routes, always thought she was clean when she obviously was not.

Two: She couldn't write. And spying is writing. Procter had once walked into the lead instructor's office and found him hunched over his computer. He didn't look up at her. "I'm spying now," he'd said. "Watch and learn. I'm spying very hard." *Tap-tap-tap* on the keyboard. And it turned out the grocer's daughter from Grafton could not write so good.

Debs's washout opened a gulf between the two women that grew and grew and never did close. But what, precisely *had* happened between them? There'd been Afghanistan, of course, but by then things were already bad. Procter's prank had laid bare the disdain, not caused it. The best she could figure, Debs had come to see Procter as a traitor to their cause. Whatever that had been.

But if Procter was a traitor, Debs had become something far simpler: a bully. Less than a year after washing out of the Farm, 9/11 happened, the Agency ballooned, and CIA began to grow fat on its success finding and killing terrorists. It was in those waters that Debs honed her skills at Seventh Floor Trapdoor, the Langley tradition of officers playacting something akin to Stalin's Politburo during the Terror: meetings—lots of them—and yanking the rug out from beneath colleagues and friends.

When Gosford left for a consulting gig with Bain in New York, he took Debs with him, and together they cashed out. Of all breeds, Debs was, to Procter's tribal mind, among the worst: a washout case officer, all politics and no talent, who'd returned, like spurned royalty (with the wild wardrobe, to boot) on the backs of a foreign army, conquering and burning her ancestral home in exchange for a throne.

"AND YOU . . ." DEBS SAID, SMIRKING TOWARD THE STAGE, "well, you were unfortunately always just like this. Some things never change." She flicked the paper parasol in Procter's drink.

Procter stuck it in her own curly hair. "You want me to get you another?"

"No. I'm here out of some measure of curiosity and because we were once friends. The tank will be empty in about five more minutes."

"Fine. Look, Debs." She'd rehearsed the pitch a dozen times that afternoon, but now had to fight the swell of exhaustion rising at the thought of groveling before this wretched woman. "I'm up here doing a spot of interviewing and seeing old friends. I've heard dribs and drabs about what Sam went through over there, and, well, I've been wondering if I should have—could have—done more to keep him safe. And I thought about you. About how we were close and then we weren't. And I honestly thought we might bury the hatchet. Put the muffin and yogurt aside for good."

"It's a good thing the Russians didn't know about your weakness for chocolate chip muffins. Why *do* you love them so much, Artemis?" Debs laughed, and her mouth parted into a cruel smile.

Now, here—even as she savored the delightful fantasy of smashing Debs's face into the table—Procter began to feel a bit queasy about the next bit. As a matter both of deeply held principle and her suspicion of tactics advertising the power to end conflicts without bloodshed, Procter did not engage in apologies. But she'd gamed this out. With Mac, play to his vanity. With Gus, his sense of duty. With Theo, his spirit of camaraderie. With Debs, you had to grovel. There really was no other way.

The karaoke had stopped, replaced by blaring house music. The fog machine rolled and the strobes turned and twisted, throwing a smattering of blue-green light pinwheeling across Debs's face. Both had their arms folded on the table, elbows nearly touching.

"Debs," she said, working the words up and out, "I'm sorry about Afghanistan. I got a skosh out of control. And I'm sorry we fell out before that. I wish we hadn't."

A silence spun open. Procter began toying with her hair. She had wondered if Debs might also apologize for conjuring sadistic mischief to run Procter out of the Service. Instead, Debs brought her hands together in front of her mouth and treated Procter to an absolutely sickening display: a curt nod of acceptance. With it, twenty-five years of chaotic history were suddenly decided in favor of Deborah Sweet. Procter was now jerking her hair around her fingers. She snagged the parasol, which snapped. She pulled the pieces from her hair and set them on the table.

But the whole point of groveling through a fucking apology was not to receive one from her old friend; the point was to throw Debs off-kilter. And in that moment of imbalance, Procter struck: "Look, those few months after Sam disappeared, I blamed myself. Still do. You know this shit inside and out, Debs, and I need your perspective. I screwed up. Where did I go wrong?"

A scrim of confusion—wonder?—pulled through Debs at this display of prostration. "What do you mean?"

"The warning we had from REMORA. It's eating me alive."

Her forehead's Botox-smooth parchment creased ever so slightly. "The meet in France before Sam was kidnapped? The one during my first week back in the building?"

"Right," Procter said. "REMORA had a warning for us. I've wondered if we could have saved Sam. I've had some time away to think on this, to reflect on my mistakes, and I can't figure this one out. Where did I go wrong? Could I have done something with it?"

Debs sat back, thinking. "Unlikely," she said. "We pushed him—hard—for specifics. He didn't have them."

"You think the warning was even about Singapore?"

"How do you mean?"

"Well, first REMORA tells us the Russians are looking at snatching an American in Asia. Then, a couple months later, he tells us snatching Sam was an accident. A snafu." She let the tension, the apparent contradiction, hang there without resolution. She hoped Debs would not ask how Procter knew of the July meeting.

"I'll get the next round," Debs said. She smacked the table and disappeared into a wall of smoke on her way to the bar. A Korean duo had taken the stage. Procter watched them break into a heated argument over their song selection.

When Debs returned—this time only her drink had pineapple—they snatched a few sips and watched the couple onstage decide that, no, the creative gap simply could not be bridged. The girl shoved a microphone into the guy's chest and huffed offstage before they'd even started the song.

Debs dipped back in. "I've spent a lot of time with the REMORA case," she said. "It plays well downtown. And his product can be quite solid. But sometimes it's not. Sometimes it's the dregs, but he tries to sell it to us anyway. In that case, I think he heard rumors about something going down in Asia, an American's involved, and he got excited, over his skis, as it were. I was there with Mac and Theo. He never had the details we would have needed to keep Sam at home. Much as I might enjoy blaming you for it, I don't think you could have stopped it."

A middle-aged man in a rumpled suit filled the onstage void to a chorus of applause and boos and drunken hoots. His untucked shirt, wind sock of a tie knot, and cowlicked hair gave the impression that his journey to Sparkle Karaoke had been perilous, perhaps terminating with a leg strapped atop a bullet train. "K-pop," Procter murmured. "It's going to be goddamn K-pop." It was, and they both set to hastily sipping their second Clipper-Tini, rushing on account of both the chalkboard-clawing acoustics and the reality that a frost was yet again settling over them.

And it was here, with Procter's ears under assault, sensing that this rare spot of grace from Debs would run maybe a moment longer, that she cast out from shore for a trip further into the deep. Procter pressed her mouth close to Debs's ear. "There was a debate this spring about REMORA. Whether he was providing intel in line with his access. I thought I recalled Mac or Theo proposing a fireside chat with him. That happen during the March meet?"

"Mac and Theo did it."

"Both of them?"

"I think so. They had the place all set up. REMORA is usually late, so I planned accordingly: showed up after Mac and Theo had warmed REMORA up."

Procter logged the order as she put back the last of her drink.

The cable had this order of arrival: Mac and Theo, then REMORA, then Debs.

Her friends had provided jumbles of that same roster.

Could be a series of innocent mistakes, she thought. Could be, could be, could be.

Debs checked her watch, said she really had to go.

"Hey, one more thing, call it a crazy idea," Procter said. Debs wasn't looking at her, was instead rifling through her purse. "Petra Devine was a crazy old Derm before she got canned, but she was competent, and as you recall she had a theory running during my last months." The skin twitched where Debs's crow's-feet would have been, if not for the filler. "And I wasn't sure then what I thought of it and am even less sure now, but it came up at our busted-up meeting on the Seventh Floor, as you probably remember. The basic gist was that the cleanest explanation for the losses that weekend was that we had a penetration inside CIA"—Debs's face was lit by some dark wonder—"and I'm curious what you think about that idea. If someone on the inside screwed us. Burned Golikov and Sam and BUCCANEER." She refrained from mention of CLAW—that hadn't yet made the papers.

There was a long sigh, and Debs blew a stream of breath from the corner of her mouth across Procter's hair before wrapping a tuft of it around her fingers. "They have serums that could make this less psychotic." Debs let Procter's hair fall and put down the last sips of her Clipper-Tini, watching the stage.

"The untamed vibes," Procter said, tying her hair back up, "work for me."

"Makes you look like a mop," Debs said. "A pissed-off little mop." Then, after a snort of laughter and a glance at her watch and another sad sigh, she said: "This past summer REMORA laid his hands on solid intel explaining what happened in Singapore, Artemis. Snatching Sam was an accident. Golikov was there to sell us a trove of documents. Seems more likely, does it not?"

"And BUCCANEER?"

"He was recalled from Athens. The breach could have happened there, for all we know."

"Are we looking?"

"Artemis, I cannot discuss this with you," Debs said, with some measure of satisfaction. "You know this. Shame on you. Now I've got to run."

Shame being a foreign emotion, Procter let that one wash right over and went back to it, scanning intently across Debs's body for some sign, some tell: but all she saw were the red-bruise cheeks and lips curling in anger and the back straightening as she marched her way through the maze of tables and smoke toward the door. Procter snagged her wrist before she got there, and Debs shot her a look like she might clock her, but Procter was desperate, and said, "Why is the Derm shop shuttered? Who had Petra Devine pulled from the REMORA case assessment?"

Debs now took a single step toward Procter, pulling her ear nearly into her mouth. Shouting over the house music, she said, "You think poisoned muffins are bad, just wait until you see what I'll do next if you keep trying to dredge shit up."

"Unfortunately for you, Debs," Procter said, "I escaped your Langley labor camp."

"You may have crawled back to the swamp hole you came from, but you still receive a pension. And I imagine that pension's a load-bearing beam for your drinking problem. So, if I hear of you digging where you shouldn't, I will sic the Feebs on you. Maybe have the lawyers take another hard look at all that shoddy paperwork you filed before sending Sam off to lose his wits in a Russian prison along with about a quarter million of taxpayer money. The Game is much harder now than it was when we were in diapers at the Farm. And you won't have a clue how to play against me, much less win."

Debs jerked loose her wrist and zigzagged through the crowd until she was lost to the smoke and the door. The karaoke had started again, a crew of twentysomethings belting out more K-pop. Procter reclaimed the table with her purse and went to the bar. The bartender pointed to her empty. "Another?" he asked.

"Gin this time," she said. "Huh? Can't hear. Say again. No, straight'll be fine, thanks."

21

LANGLEY / CRYSTAL CITY

THE CALL ORIGINATED IN MOSCOW. ON THAT, AT LEAST, CIA would have no doubt. It was quite short, thirty-six seconds to be exact, but that was expected. Anyone listening—and there were more than a few possibilities on that score—would have heard a middle-aged male speaking French with a Slavic accent, phoning a Parisian number inquiring about cigars.

Cornelia Huggins had served in Russia House for thirty-eight years. Her vault was small, the size of two or three broom closets jammed together, and visitors could be forgiven for assuming Cornelia was, in fact, a loyal and unrepentant Communist. The wallpaper was midcentury Socialist realism: bright-red chugging tractors, belching factories, rough-cut collective farmers clutching stalks of wheat in patriotic ecstasy. On her desk sat busts of Marx and Lenin. A portrait of Stalin hung above the door.

Since Cornelia's maiden days in the Cold War twilight, her room, known as the Parole Bank, had held twentyish odd phones that would ring when internal agents signaled, through elaborate verbal messages, their imminent departure from Russia and availability for a chat with CIA. The room was often lifeless: many agents could not leave Russia more than once in a blue moon.

But today one of the phones was blinking when Cornelia completed her morning ritual of opening the vault, flicking on the lights, kissing her fingers, and pressing them to Lenin's bronze pate. "Oh my, my, my," she said to herself, logging in to the database with the voice mail. Was one of her boys ready for a chat? Ready to emerge from the deep freeze? The thought stretched Cornelia's heart.

The small group cleared for the traffic inside Russia House and the Seventh Floor received an urgent cable from Cornelia with the collateral. Matching the coded parole to the layered mazework of the case's global commo plan yielded the agent's request: a meeting, at ten p.m. local time, three days out, at a property near Lacoste, France. An old Luberon farmhouse rented by CIA solely for the use of one of its most productive Russian agents.

To be fully certain, the techies ran a voice match, comparing the clipped phone call to the hours of recordings hoovered up from microphones worn by Gus Raptis during brief encounters on the streets of Moscow, and by Mac and Theo during those early visits in Paris and Marrakesh. It was him.

REMORA.

A tear welled in her left eye, and she nearly wept for joy.

LANGLEY WAS A SOCIAL HIVE, A WATERING HOLE, AND today, even in the basement, the animals working on Russia had their noses up, sniffing at the wind. Something was happening. When Sam Joseph reached the Moscow X spaces the buzz in the air was so thick it might well have been humidity. Murmurs of conversation seeped through the crack at the bottom of Gus's office door, and Sam logged the oddity that today the boss had chosen to actually sit down here. Did it have anything to do with the Tarrman debacle in Moscow? A few minutes later the door swung open. Gus ambled over to Sam's desk. "Gotta head upstairs for a few minutes, walk with me."

Moscow X was still sequestered in the basement near the hot dog machine, so on the walk through the zigzagging Ground Floor corridors, past the loading docks, the desks manned by the green-jacketed minders, and into the elevator bank, Gus pressed Sam about an inconsequential report he'd requested two days prior. Upstairs, when they'd crossed through the Russia House Front Office and reached the green door of the Backroom, Gus said—tersely, Sam thought later—"This is where you get off." He punched the code and went inside, careful to shut the door behind him.

Across the room, Sam saw Mac's office door open. Mac was examining the three-by-five card holding his schedule. Theo shambled out from behind him and began chatting up his EA, arms folded across the top of the cubicle partition rising above her desk. The EA's phone trilled; she answered it, said yes, yes, of course (a few times), and hung up. She looked at Theo with a smile and said, with a cheerfulness that could only be explained by ignorance or malice: "The DDO's on her way down now."

"Now?"—Mac, from across the room, in disbelief. He'd looked up from his schedule, shock congealing to frustration.

"Now," the EA confirmed. Toothy smile. Malice, Sam thought. Gleeful anticipation of delivering bad news to Theo.

"She's going to crash it again," Theo growled. "Ramrod us."

Mac said, "She's tweaked because of Tarrman. Because CLAW's gone missing. She wants answers. We should just let her run the damn meeting. Take the weekend off. Or send poor Gus."

At that moment, standing stock-still outside the Backroom, lacking operational cover for his stillness, Sam instinctively began collecting every bit of sensory information. He logged Theo's facial hair: wispy and overgrown, sprouting in uneven thickets from the chalky pallor of his cheeks and neck. Sam thought the guy looked like he might be ill. He was standing still, clutching the EA's cubicle partition, swaying as if he were light-headed or so slight as to be wrecked by the breeze of recycled air fluttering through the vents. What he looked like, Sam thought, was a man nursing a crushing hangover.

If Theo was sick and tweaked about some mysterious slight, Mac appeared to be weighing something, lost deep in thought. His eyes met Sam's, then filled with recognition—maybe amusement?—and he smiled broadly. "Sam. What brings you aboveground?"

"Gus and I were discussing something. He left me here."

At that moment Gus swung open the Backroom door. He eyed Sam curiously—right where he had left him—then beckoned to Mac and Theo. "I've pulled what she asked for. Let's—"

Then Deborah Sweet stamped into the Russia House Front Office. Mac began by saying they were just getting things ready, but her hand went up, glacially slow.

Sweet, as always, was dressed for the spotlight. And this day provocatively so: in a too-tight blouse covered by a jean jacket. Sam knew the gossip, of course, of this group's shared history, much of it nasty, and it came through now, in the little twitches of her mouth, in the glaze of her eyes as she stared them all down, which he interpreted as a pure malice countering the Bratva's contempt.

"I told you three," she said. "I was explicit that I was to be added to REMORA's distro list. So why do my EAs hand me cables sent to you three alone? I'm to be in the loop. I am the Deputy Director for Operations. POTUS has taken a personal interest in this case and the Director has asked me to be involved. To run point. I was clear on this. I am to be told immediately when he sends word or signals; and that's even more critical when it occurs mere days after another Russian asset goes missing. My office has communicated all of this to the woman in the Parole Bank." Sweet slid her bright red frames to the crown of her head. She marched past Mac and Theo, toward the Backroom door, blowing past a seething Gus. Mac and Theo followed, sidling past Sam.

Gus shot Sam a look of disgust. "If I'm not back in my office in thirty minutes, send help," he said under his breath. "Until then, scram." He shut the door.

22

ALEXANDRIA, VIRGINIA

AS AGREED WITH SAM ON ROBLOX, PROCTER FOUND A parking spot in the Hoffman Town Center garages, bought a movie ticket with her credit card, watched half of a flick whose title she'd forgotten by the end of the previews, and then returned to the car. In an era of ubiquitous technical surveillance, movie theaters were helpful places to convince digital watchers that her pattern was boring, unworthy of any further analysis or interest. Her alibi for the day—visit to DynCoTel, nap in the room, soaking in a mindless movie—was entirely consistent with the movement of her phone and car. And yet the reality was very different: reviewing countersurveillance footage, clandestine commo with Sam, and now an urgent face-to-face meet outside the theater. She waited.

AT PRECISELY NINE P.M. SAM SLID INTO THE CAR. THE TOP level of the parking garage was nearly empty, and it was quiet except for the buzz of the lights overhead.

"REMORA signaled for a meeting or sent a message," Sam said, shutting the door. "And an officer in Moscow, guy named Tarrman, got picked up by the Russians last week while trying to meet CLAW. You remember CLAW?"

"I do."

"Well, he's missing. Another Russian asset disappeared."

"That makes two in about six months. Plus Golikov. Plus your kidnapping."

"Not a normal trendline for the business," Sam said.

"Not so much. How'd you find all this out?"

"Gus asked me to follow him upstairs for a chat. We parted ways outside the Backroom. Mac and Theo materialize. I'm standing there and I hear maybe a few seconds of bitching about the DDO. Then Sweet shows up, snarling about not being included on all the REMORA traffic, griping about Tarrman and CLAW, and—"

"Debs was pissed?" Procter asked.

"Yeah. Furious. Her office flagged the cable. She wasn't included on the distro."

"And she said 'REMORA'?"

"She did. She said the crypt aloud. Mentioned that it was all the more important she be involved, given CLAW's disappearance earlier in the week. Then they all disappeared into the Backroom."

"Who?"

"Gus, Mac, Theo, and Sweet herself."

"I assume you've got no clue what came out of that?"

"You assume correctly."

"Well, goddammit, Jaggers." And then from nowhere, for a vanishing second, the image of the Chief's younger self crashed into him, and upon fading it left him with a hollow feeling of loss. Procter sighed. "It's hard to figure REMORA signaling for a meet, isn't it?" she said. "Quite the fantastic coincidence after my conversations this week. It feels like we've rubbed someone the wrong way."

"You go way back with these four," Sam said. As soon as the words were out he could feel a silence split open between them; they hung there for a moment. Procter grunted.

"Back then Farm classes were small," she said. "You knew everyone."

"But they were your friends."

"They were. Are, in most cases. Remind me: What class were you in, Jaggers?"

"Twenty-nine. Late '11."

"I was class seven, 2000. Heady fucking times." She was staring out the windshield as if watching her mind drift elsewhere.

"What was the DDO like back then?" Sam asked. "Hard to picture her as a trainee."

"Deborah Sweet," Procter murmured wistfully. "Lot of the instructors figured Debs would only be good for laying or typing. Turned out she was also good for ringleading savage pranks."

"The DDO was a prankster?" Sam asked. "Come on."

"Hand to God. We all were. See, back then, CIA hadn't gone soft, and the pranks were unchained. When someone left for a few days, they might come back and the door would be bricked shut, or for the truly ambitious, we might brick people in their dorm rooms overnight, without waking them up. Eyebrows were shaved, of course. A few instructors got their boats painted bright purple. You might be driving up to D.C. unaware that stuck on your car there is a magnetic bumper sticker embossed with a huge schlong and you're wondering why people are honking and rolling their tongues into their cheeks and giving you two thumbs up when they pass."

Procter smiled for a moment. "State trooper pulled me over for that one."

Sam laughed, shook his head. "In my class the worst that happened was we filled an instructor's shower with leaves."

"That's because your generation has no goddamn fun," Procter said.

"I've always wondered," Sam asked, "when did she get the nickname? Was that at the Farm, or did it predate the Agency?"

"That was a gift from Theo at the Farm," Procter said, "Lil Debbie." She laughed. "Six-foot-one without shoes, and the makings of a colossal bitch. So neither little nor sweet, as it were. I usually just called her Debs to both sides of her, but what can I say, I'm polite. A thoughtful lady."

"So what was the best prank you guys pulled?" Sam asked.

Procter again looked out the windshield; he could see that her eyes were shining.

"There was an instructor, a graybeard named Ganston. He had one of the houses down on the river. One night I'm hanging with Debs in the bar and Ganston's name comes up, and suddenly Debs is smiling. And I know that smile. She's got an idea, a way to practice our recent breaking-and-entering training. It's solid, a few rough spots but nothing we can't smooth out. And, look, for any breaking-and-entering op you want to limit your time on the X, don't you?"

"You do," Sam said, smiling. "You certainly do."

"So we needed more hands. I recruit Mac and Theo. Debs pulls in Gus. Operational conclave begins around midnight, all of us hunched around in a circle, gaming it out, building the shopping list. Next day's Saturday. Debs and I head to a bunch of dirty bookstores in the city. Gus and Theo go out for crafting supplies. Mac preps to handle the lock-picking."

"Ganston locked his door?" Sam cut in. "No one locks their doors at the Farm."

"Ganston was a locker," Procter said. "You spend a good bit of the eighties in Moscow, and you lock doors when given the chance. Anyhow, all of us spend Saturday night in Mac's room cutting out pictures. Everyone's got their own scissors and collection of magazines and we're all telling jokes and laughing and drinking."

The Chief shut her eyes and took in a long breath through her nose. "Even now, Jaggers, I can travel to that room. Beery smell and friends laughing and the thrill of a crime lumping in your throat. I stay in that room, and I can make a dozen mistakes and it'll be fine because I've got time to fix them all, to walk down other paths. Book's not yet written."

Procter opened her eyes. "Instead, I'm here with you. Committing felonies in a parking garage."

"Could be much worse," Sam said. "Somehow it could be worse."

She laughed. "Well, Sunday afternoon at one p.m. sharp we're outside Ganston's house, because they're out on the boat. Mac picks the lock in about two minutes, tip of the hat to the B&E guys who'd given us the demo just that week. We're in. Theo's lugging a box that looks like we're here for some illicit crafting work, which, in a way, I guess we were. And we get to work."

"Where'd you hide the pictures?" Sam asked.

"Where *didn't* we hide them? They went everywhere. Books. Mugs. Drawers. Into picture frames. Tucked under carpets. Taped beneath clocks. Slipped into pill bottles. Into pillowcases. Where else? Ah yes, into boxes of breakfast cereal. Between slices of bread. Inside the toaster oven, but we fished those out because we didn't want to start a fire. We're not lunatics."

"Clearly," Sam said. "Obviously. But hold on. The pictures. What did you guys end up choosing?"

"Oh, a little bit of this, little bit of that. They ran the gamut of sexual expression, I'd say. It was a real collage of humanity's erotic experiences, least as of the turn of the millennium. We did hit a snag, though."

"What was that?"

"Ganston came back early. Found out later that Priscilla got sick. Pickup rolls into the driveway an hour early. Gus, who is downstairs, hears the car doors. He calls to Theo, who's in the kitchen. Theo tramps to the foot of the stairs and calls up to us. Says it's time to boogie. I'm up there sliding a meaty stack of photos into the sheets of the Ganston marriage bed, Debs is working in the bathroom along with Mac, and you know what we all hear upstairs? I'll give you a guess."

"No clue."

"Nothing. Nothing is the answer. Because Theo's not speaking so loudly. None of us upstairs heard the warning. Theo and Gus have already bolted out the back door, expecting we'll follow. And about ten seconds later I hear Priscilla Ganston coming up the stairs, talking about pills and a nap. And there's only one place to hide: the closet. Me, Mac, and Debs squeeze inside—barely. And we hold our breath. It's one of those closets with slatted sliding doors, so we can peek through into the room. Priscilla marches in, opens a drawer in the bathroom. Screams. And, lordy, Jaggers, I can still hear it now. A laugh almost burst right out of me. Mac's got his hand over his mouth and also over Debs's mouth. Everyone's shuddering in the closet. By this point Ganston's up there asking what the hell's going on. And I can't quite see everything that's happening, but I can tell that Priscilla's holding up a picture like a badge, and if memory serves Debs had handled that bathroom, and I wouldn't say the selection was so heterosexually oriented. And Priscilla is of course wondering about this. Her tone's accusatory, I'd say. And there's an argument, Jaggers, a rather bleak marital argument which drags on in that bedroom for about ten, maybe fifteen minutes. And me, Mac, and Debs are in that closet, holding each other up, dying of laughter on the inside. I couldn't see much in there, but I could see Debs's eyes, I could see Mac's, and we're all feeling it. We're in communion, folded into Ganston's pants and shirts. That kind of thing just doesn't happen very often, does it? Life is mostly fights. Rare to have a moment of pure joy. It was a very nice afternoon."

"How did you three get out?"

"Well, the Ganstons discovered other pictures. And once you've found a few mixed in with the tea bags, and maybe another in the mug itself, well, you've got a pattern. You've been pranked. They eventually flipped on the television in their front room, and we tiptoed downstairs and sneaked out the back door. Reunited for beers with Gus and Theo that night and spent the rest of the Farm reliving every minute of it, as one does."

"Ganston never caught you?"

"Not officially. But he knew. He figured Theo was involved, and probably Debs, and it wasn't a stretch to cast the net out wider to me and Mac and Gus. Though Mac was sly about that stuff. He was the ideas man who could stay under the radar, slink off when the heat got cranked up. Only time it ever really came up, though, was with Priscilla. There was a Christmas party a few months later, and I'm standing in line for a drink. Priscilla sidles up to chat: The weather, plans for the holiday, books she's reading. And toward the end she gets this freaky gleam in her eyes. She grips my shoulder, leans in close, mouth basically on my ear, and says: 'Next time leave a few more like you did in the sheets.' Then she gives me a little wink and melts into the party. Holy hell."

"What pictures did you tuck into the sheets?" Sam asked.

"I have absolutely no clue," Procter said. "Then and now. I probably should have asked." She laughed and smacked the dash.

"Makes more sense," Sam said, "why Debs did what she did when she ran you out."

"Yeah. It was direct payback for when I poisoned her yogurt in Afghanistan."

"It was yogurt?" he said.

"A strawberry yogurt," she replied, "if memory serves. There was a particular brand Debs favored, name escapes me now. Fast forward almost a decade from the Farm, and we're in Afghanistan. Debs is working for Gosford and they're paying our Base a visit. I found a Marine, kid from New Mexico, who kept a ghost pepper hot sauce handy, mailed to him monthly by his abuela. There was a Mexican place in the city we liked when we were at the Farm, and Debs wouldn't touch anything spicy. 'Makes me queasy, Artemis,' she'd said once. I didn't actually see it, though. When I came into the dining area for breakfast there was a facilities guy working a mop across the floor and another using towels to shovel the mess painted on the counter and the side of the fridge. Two or so others milling around like it was a crime scene. 'What happened?' I said, and the one polishing the side of the fridge just said that crazy boss lady in from Headquarters must be equal parts lactose intolerant and stupid, because one spoonful of yogurt and we're on the set of *The Exorcist* here."

"But she knew," Sam said. "That it was you."

"Sure, sure," the Chief said. "But just like Ganston, she couldn't prove it. The events of that evening overtook everything, in the end. Not the prank, of course. What happened later. Not many nights mark the eras of your life, but that one in Afghanistan was clear as it gets. There was a before, and an after."

He knew the stories about Afghanistan, the blood and the scars and the rumors. He'd just not heard them from her. But he knew that good friends don't ask just because they are curious, or have an opening. On her face he could see that the reminiscing was done, the door to her memory was closing.

The Chief started the car. "When you showed up at Gatorville after the swap," she said, "there was a part of me that thought: Better not to know. Even Christ put off confronting Judas until the Last Supper. The Good Lord was God, but he was human, too. He knew that uncovering a double is pure anguish, turns everything inside out."

"What convinced you?" Sam asked. "To dig."

"Well," she said, "they fucked with you. On my watch. For one."

"Sure. And two?"

"I'd wager this traitor played a role in running me out of the Service. And not being the goat is something of a North Star for me, Jaggers. I'd intended to commit career suicide on my own terms, in spectacular fashion, not for a quarter century of work to fizzle out with a dull murder that's easily forgotten."

He turned to her, pained look in his face. "Speaking of murder. Whatever we've rustled up has one of your friends bothered. I've been thinking: You might want to split for a bit. Get out of D.C. Lie low."

She put her finger to her nose. "I am going to have one conversation I've been putting off. I'll touch base after that, maybe in a few days."

He stepped outside, shut the door.

She rolled down the window. "Hey, Jaggers. One more thing, seeing as we're getting all fucking nosey and sentimental tonight. How'd you manage to keep the secret all those months? Color me curious."

"I knew that if I told them they'd kill me. They couldn't send me back home if I knew about their mole. The only way out was to hold it back."

"I'd have thought that after a while death would've held a certain appeal."

"Sure. Plenty of days I thought maybe just tell them. Be done with it."

"Well?"

Sam began to chew his gum as if otherwise he might grind his teeth down to dust. "My cell had fabric-lined walls stenciled with tiny red stars. I needed a job. A project. I could count those stars. That's what kept me going. Didn't matter what happened, or who was in my cell. I just had to count."

"No fantasies of revenge, that sort of thing?"

"Revenge seemed pretty abstract in that cell. The stars were real. The mole was not."

"Still feel that way?"

"Less and less each day."

She put it in drive but kept her foot on the brake. "Jaggers," she said. "How many stars were there?"

He leaned closer. "Over sixty thousand."

"Come on."

A spurt of air escaped his nostrils. "Sixty-six thousand five hundred and twenty-eight. Bit of time required to cycle through, it turns out, even if you do manage to stay on track. Things slow down when you get to the higher numbers. They take a while to say aloud."

23

MOSCOW

IN AN UNMARKED AND WINDOWLESS ROOM ON THE ground floor of the Forest's second, and newer, tower, Rem Zhomov sat at a chipped table sifting through the latest haul from Dr. B, freshly arrived in that morning's dip pouch from Paris. There were the usual goodies, including a thumb drive that would keep his analysts busy for months, and a run of images from the subminiature digital camera Dr. B used to photograph documents inside Langley. "The contents," Dr. B wrote in an appended ops note, "should answer questions six through thirty-one on the list of intelligence requirements" recently passed by SVR, "excepting questions twelve, eighteen, and twenty-seven." These stragglers would be addressed in the next tranche, assuming continued cooperation from a raft of unwitting subagents inside the CIA's China Mission Center.

Dr. B's intelligence was typically greeted by a celebration inside Rem's Special Section. And this tranche should have been doubly so: Dr. B had sent reams of information on the Agency's China operations: political assessments, technical programs, the names of officers enrolled in Mandarin language courses, those in the pipeline for Beijing Station or NOC assignments in China. Here, as Rem had promised the Director, was one of the near-term promises of Dr. B's platform: the collection of information Russia might trade to Beijing for a windfall, including higher prices on exported oil, drawings and plans for stolen technologies, and political assistance for Russia's agenda in the broader Russkiy mir, the Russian world. But he could not celebrate now. In fact, the first page of Dr. B's twenty-two-page ops note made Rem wonder if the dosage on his blood pressure medication was up to snuff.

The first paragraphs detailed how Artemis Procter, a personage well known to Rem, had ventured up to Northern Virginia, in part, it seemed, for conversations about the debacle in Singapore and the circumstances surrounding the kidnapping and eventual swap for Samuel Joseph. This, Dr. B wrote, was not worrisome on its own: Procter had been run out of CIA in Singapore's wake, she was emotionally distraught at the kidnapping and interrogation of a good friend. The conversation, wrote Dr. B, was "fine," but had been "too specific for my liking, particularly with respect to the peculiarities of our case." Dr. B knew of at least one other similar conversation Procter had pursued with an Agency colleague while visiting Virginia. The summary: "Procter is pursuing the line of thinking that required us to force her out in the spring, her pet theory; namely the existence of a penetration inside CIA (me)." Dr. B explained that, "because of the nature of her questioning, and the use of a few specifics with respect to Singapore and our case, I began to wonder if Procter had access to our documents. I brought the light inside for a look."

Blood pressure now seemed a quaint concern: Rem could feel his heart plunging into his stomach. The "light" was a reference to a small black light, concealed inside a watch, fashioned by the SVR techs for Dr. B. At the beginning of the case, Dr. B had outlined the procedures CIA would use to safeguard the documents, and the Doctor had suggested spreading *metka*, spy dust, across the case files. The compound, nitrophenyl pentadienal, was a tagging agent, a colorless and odorless powder that could be applied almost anywhere: doorknobs, car handles, computer keys, papers. "There is a risk to bringing the compound inside the building," Dr. B had argued then, "but if we are to run the case in this way, we require a failsafe, a backstop to track at all times who has accessed the documents."

Dr. B had immediately noticed something amiss: *metka* lingered on a table inside the Russia House Backroom, one that Dr. B understood had been occupied, in recent weeks, for a brief spell by one Samuel Joseph. A subsequent visit with the light to Samuel's spaces in Moscow X revealed yet more *metka*. "And Samuel Joseph," Dr. B wrote, "does not have formal access to our files."

"*Blyad*," Rem muttered. Bloody hell. He did not know it, but he was sitting so far forward, stooped over the ops note, with only his toes remaining on the floor, that he looked like a hunchback ballerina. His face was a mere inch from the document—and that was not only because his eyesight was fading. If anyone had walked into the reading room at that moment—which would not happen, only three SVR officers possessed the fingerprints to unlock the door—they would have mistaken Rem for a calm yet avid and engrossed reader. Nothing suggested that beneath the surface Rem was stuffed with an anxiety flooding into rage. He sat up for a moment, realizing he had been failed by his sentimentality, and perhaps his greed. He cursed himself. "I should have killed him," Rem murmured, fastening the rubber reading thimble tighter on his thumb, before flicking over to the next page. "I should have killed him."

"An investigation run by Artemis and Sam places everything we are working toward at risk," wrote Dr. B, "but I do believe we have options." Dr. B said Samuel could be shoved out. "He is an emotionally damaged officer stuck at a desk at Headquarters, and will not be missed. But Procter is a different animal." Much of the reasoning here rested on Procter being, as Dr. B described, "a pain in the ass of world-historical proportion, a woman who will not rest until she is satisfied, and who, despite her mistreatment, seems to harbor a slavish devotion to CIA because she has nothing left but her sense of duty. For much of her career this was an asset. Now it is a glaring liability." Dr. B had appended Procter's and Samuel's phone numbers and the physical addresses on file with the Agency's HR and alumni relations departments.

And here, at the end, even Rem had to admire the cold depths of Dr. B's commitment to the cause: the SVR's crown jewel asset was laying out a compelling case that the surest method of safeguarding "the security of our strategic partnership" was to "forcibly silence" an old friend and a recently imprisoned colleague. "Wherever my mission has collided with my friendships," concluded Dr. B, "I have chosen the mission."

THE AMERICANS GLAMORIZED BLACK WORK. THEIR SPY movies, which Rem had consumed compulsively during tours in Rome and London, featured jet-setting assassins in tuxedoes, diabolically clever technology ("Too cutesy," he'd snarl, and Ninel would bop his shoulder and tell him to hush), and beautiful women spilling out of too-tight dresses.

The Americans saw black work this way, Rem thought, because they'd not been forced to shoot dozens of traitors through the neck; their political strongmen had as of yet refrained from poisoning rivals or gunning down dissidents in daylight, broad or otherwise; in America it was uncommon for politicians to fall to their death from balconies. Not that their hands were clean. No, the Americans had spent the decades after 9/11 killing their adversaries in foreign lands, often pulling joysticks, not triggers. At such distances one could afford to glamorize a business.

But in Rem's experience black work was a pudgy former convict in an ill-fitting suit shoving a drugged man from a third-floor window; it was an underpaid civil servant slathering poison in someone's underpants; it was a heroin-addled former gangster from Piter stabbing a journalist to death in her apartment for sums equivalent to a few weeks' pay.

Rem had no appetite for this work. In truth, he considered it beneath him. He was an artist, not a thug. But Rem was not squeamish. He understood that sometimes the solution to a problem was death. And in this case, he believed it necessary because Dr. B was at risk, and Dr. B was worth hundreds of millions of dollars to the Russian Federation. Billions, even, according to the higher-end estimates from the analysts.

He supposed the Americans would also believe that a Russian decision to kill someone would be made by the President, in a wood-paneled room at the Kremlin, in dramatic fashion. This had not once been his experience. More than anything the process was marked by its vagaries, its lack of clarity. You had to discern the deep things of such conversations. You had to scrape the meaning out from under the words.

REM, SEATED IN THE SVR DIRECTOR'S ANTEROOM, RUBBED his fingers; arthritis was acting up that morning, as if anticipating the brittle cold of the coming winter.

The Director's aide put down his phone and said: "Rem Mikhailovich, you may go in now."

Easing up from the tired blue chair, Rem trudged into the Director's office. There had been a time when Rem wondered if he might occupy this space, but long ago he'd realized that the Director's chair required its occupant to forfeit the actual work to play politics, and he could not bring himself to make the sacrifice. You wouldn't have succeeded if you'd tried, Ninel would say. She was right, of course.

The Director's office was situated on a corner of the Forest's executive third floor. Picture windows covered the exterior walls, affording expansive views of the woods sprawling across the campus. The birches had flared to bright orange; many were already stark-naked in preparation for winter, Rem's sixty fourth. He eased into a seat; for some reason the damn cushions at the Director's table were thin as sandpaper, and about as scratchy. The Director took his own chair, tapping his thick fingers on the glossy wood. "Rem"—he cleared his throat, the signal a lecture was coming—"we, you, rather, designed the Special Section to avoid the very situation we now find ourselves in. Our top asset is in danger because of leaks. First Singapore. And now this." Rem saw the Director had a note in his hand, sliding it idly back and forth across the table.

Rem jostled his crotch into a more comfortable position. He'd begun to wonder if the Director—or even the President himself—had accidentally let slip Dr. B's identity in front of Golikov before Singapore. This, though, could not be said aloud, much less investigated. From this opening, Rem could not figure how the meeting the Director had held that morning with the President had gone. Did they want a scapegoat? Or did they want the problem solved?

"I agree with you," Rem said. "And if I could go back and do it again, I would shoot Samuel Joseph. But as it stands, we cannot, which is why I have proposed shooting him and his friend now."

"But you recommend starting with the friend, yes?"

"Yes."

"And why is that?"

"Because she is the only one capable of piecing it all together."

The Director's eyes twinkled with mirth, and he slid the note back and forth once more on the table before shoving it to Rem, who put on his reading glasses. The margins were blank, there was no signature, the few paragraphs that Rem and the Director had penned together were maddeningly unedited.

When he looked up, the Director's hands were folded across his chest. "The President wouldn't mark it up, much less sign it. We had a very general conversation about the rules of the game with our American friends right now, and the aggressive shift this would mark in our posture on their soil. The President is keen to do what is required for Dr. B, he understands the grave risks to our top American asset—his words, Rem, and you know he reads every scrap of intel the good Doctor is providing—but when I pressed the memo into his hands he simply took it, read it, and handed it back to me. He would not say yes. He would not even nod."

Rem grunted, flapped his tie against his shirt, and folded his arms across his own chest, mirroring the Director. "But did he say no?"

24

MOSCOW

REM SLID AN ALKA SELTZER INTO HIS WATER AND WATCHED Gennady patrol the bookshelves. His former protégé was now also a general, head of Directorate S (Illegals), because Rem was of an age where all your old friends and enemies were the ones running the place. Unlike Rem, as Gennady had aged his hair had thinned. His shirts were perpetually untucked, his hair mussed. He'd considered pursuing an academic career prior to the Forest, and still carried the sartorial preferences of a university man. Gennady took his first tentative sips of tea as he wandered along the shelves, scanning the titles with mild amusement. "Your poetry selection is thinning out, Rem," he said, plucking a history of the United States from one of the shelves. "Your library is becoming too . . . practical."

"And I am getting old, Gennady. There is a correlation."

"Aren't we all."

Rem's office was spacious but sparse. His desk had been used by Lenin for a season during the Civil War, but otherwise the furniture was soulless: a circular table, chairs, a tired couch running along the window that he used primarily to store books. The shelves lining the available wall space were groaning with them. He'd long ago hit capacity.

"What are you reading these days, then?" Gennady said, flipping open a memoir written by George Tenet, a former Director of CIA.

Rem shifted in his chair. His arthritis had worsened as the day ground along. He'd felt brittle and achy putting on his suit; now his bones creaked from the mere act of sitting still.

"Your case files," Rem said.

"I see," Gennady said, sliding the book back onto the shelf and joining Rem at the table. He cleared his throat. "Is there a problem?"

"No, no. Nothing like that. I need some black work managed. And I'm looking for a particular profile."

"And you don't want to use the Vympel . . ."

"Oh, you know how it will go," Rem growled, flicking his hand in the air. "It will be echoes of the preparation for Singapore. Bunch of goddamn meetings to figure out who will do it: us or the cousins or, god help us, the bats at the GRU's Aquarium. This time we will lose weeks on ridiculous meetings alone. How long, then, to infiltrate a team into the States that doesn't require us working through mobsters and the cartels? That is time we do not have. And in the end, in any case, we risk such clownish buffoonery as we saw in Salisbury, in Bulgaria, and in the mess with Navalny. I understand that sometimes the warning, the theater is the point, but not here. I don't need poison in someone's Jockeys. I need a problem solved."

"Have you found any of my cases interesting?" Gennady asked.

"MICKEY and MINNIE," Rem said. "Your American volunteers, the patriots we discovered online before cultivating them in the flesh."

"They've never done black work before," Gennady said flatly.

"Their file says otherwise."

"They freelanced," Gennady interjected. "*She* freelanced. We did not ask her to do that."

"Well, in any case," Rem said, "they seem to be eager. The type that might say yes."

Gennady was staring through the bookshelves behind Rem. "And as you doubtless saw in the notes, the case hasn't progressed much because, quite frankly, we're not sure what do with them. Their access is . . . peripheral."

"And the woman is . . ." Rem said.

Gennady looked up, as if the elusive description lurked on the ceiling. When the words came to him, his lips parted into a thin smile. "A budding patriot."

Rem laughed. "The tree of liberty must be refreshed from time to time with the blood of patriots, if I might quote their Jefferson. Eager patriotism is just what we require."

"And tyrants," Gennady said. "Mr. Jefferson also felt their blood was required."

"Well, based on your files, I would wager MICKEY and MINNIE are sufficiently patriotic. There should be no need for such excess. The blood of patriots, that should be enough."

"The security footage in the file, Rem. Did you actually watch it?" Gennady inquired with a thin smile, his gaze returning from the ceiling. His academic sensibilities, Rem thought, sometimes made Gennady appear apprehensive, tentative, passive.

"No, my friend, I merely read the summary," Rem said. "I am an old man. Sleep is difficult enough already."

IT HAD BEEN AT LEAST A DECADE SINCE REM HAD STAYED UP all night planning an operation. On the drive home from Lefortovo he nodded off in the backseat and awoke, head heavy, to the lurch of the driver braking outside his Khamovniki apartment. Ninel was at the kitchen table in her robe, her wet gray hair pinned up in a towel, sipping tea while reading a magazine. The kitchen smelled of burned toast and her shampoo.

Standing, she planted a kiss on his forehead and put on water for tea. Rem flung the suit coat over a couch in the living room and stared for a moment at the obscene number of missed calls on his phone. He powered it off. He required a few hours of rest. He had to be able to think. It was his only advantage. He joined Ninel at the table, where she was steeping his tea. "Some toast, my dear?" she said. "Or *selyodka*? Let me fix you something."

"No, thank you, my love," he said. "Just tea. I am too tired to eat."

They sat for a long while in a companionable silence. "I am proud of you, Rem," she said. "Do you feel proud?"

"I feel exhausted."

"Don't be sarcastic. You are not handsome anymore, so you cannot be sarcastic. Now you must be sweet, gentle, and thoughtful to hold my attentions."

He sipped at his tea with a widening smile. "I'm still quite handsome, I am told."

Ninel arched one of her painted-on brows and snorted, mouth bending into a crooked smile. Taking her teacup in her hands, she fixed him with a stern gaze: "It doesn't suit you to be cocky, Rem. It never has."

He yawned. "My looks are my one indulgence Ninel," he said wryly. "Humor me."

She rolled her eyes and said: "I would, but that rumpled suit says otherwise. What were you doing all night? Should I be jealous, given how allegedly handsome you are?"

He'd found his appetite; he eased up and stood at the counter, where he parachuted bread into the toaster. "All of the young girls helping me plan the operation were ugly dimwits."

Ninel smiled, generously refraining from a reminder that through the years their various infidelities had but one thing in common: whether they had been twenty or fifty, trysts had occurred with lovers their own age. The young were not necessarily to be feared above the old, at least not when it came to the Zhomov marriage bed. Still smiling, Ninel opened her magazine and languidly turned the pages, letting the conversation fizzle out.

Rem ate his breakfast and finished another cup of tea. Ninel leafed through her magazine with a breezy disinterest. With each casual flip of a page Rem could sense that she had things to say but was holding her tongue. "Out with it, love," he said. "Tell me."

The magazine slapped shut. She regarded him thoughtfully for a few significant seconds. "Italy was such fun. And do you know why?"

"The pasta."

"Because it was all in front of us."

"Youth has that quality."

"You are going to be bored when they don't call you away late in the night," she said. "I fear that boredom for you. It will make you even more insufferable. You will become a grumpy, irritable old man who waits by the phone for the youngsters to call and ask for his advice."

"It could be worse," he said. "Imagine if no one wanted to call."

"I look forward to that day," she said.

"I'll find a hobby when they run me out."

She laughed. "Like what?"

"Drinking."

"You haven't had a drink since Pyotr was born. You are not so good at drinking."

"Maybe carpentry, then? I will make you a rocking chair."

"You will cut your fingers off with a saw, Rem. And then I will have to change your diapers. No, no, that will not do. I think it is too late for hobbies." She went back to her magazine. He finished his toast, set the plate in the dishwasher, and as he'd picked up the suit coat from the couch he could sense her presence behind him. He turned to her. She kissed his forehead and took the suit coat from his hands. He lay down for a nap on the couch, setting the alarm for three hours so he could return to the Forest by lunchtime. He drifted off to the sight of Ninel ironing the suit coat. She was whistling a song he did not know.

25

GETTYSBURG, PENNSYLVANIA

PETRA DEVINE'S HOME WAS BURIED IN A PINE FOREST OUTside Gettysburg. Thin reeds of sunlight reached the dirt through the trees. The yard was needles, the drive a minefield of pinecones. The house was one-story and timbered with an American flag hung on a pole stretching from the roof. Procter knocked three times and stepped back. Dogs barked for a while. She knocked again, and now could hear Petra's shouts mixing with the barks. The door opened to a slit, chain lock still in place. Confirming every instinct Procter had about this visit, why she'd put it off for long as she could, Petra met her own half smile with a severe frown that buckled into a look of abject disgust.

"They sent you? For what?"

"To kill you."

The dogs set to barking, though only one of them had the nerve to stick its nose through the door, a little hairy wiener dog yipping away in a nagging tone similar to that of its owner. *Blijf! Blijf!* Petra shushed them in Dutch. *Blijf!* The door was still open a crack, not that the chain would hold if Procter threw her shoulder into the wood.

"I told those clowns on my last day," Petra said, after the dogs finally shut up, "that if they were going to kill me, they should damn well contract a handsome gigolo to do it. Send me to the afterlife satisfied and in style. Instead, they sent you."

"I can rise to the challenge, hon," Procter said. "Don't tempt me." Procter put out a hand toward a dog peering through the crack in the door. Sniffing her, it backed into the house. "And I wouldn't say *they* sent me. This is a shade unofficial. The kind of visit various seniors might be in the dark about."

"I had heard you skipped town," Petra goaded.

"I took my talents to Florida. I'm the chief of operations at a place called Gatorville. Third largest alligator-themed amusement park in Central Florida, if you can believe it."

"They didn't send you? Gus? Theo? Mac? Or maybe Deborah Sweet, *dat pokkenwijf?* You swear it?"

"Shit, Petra, I show up unannounced in biker shorts and a ball cap, and you think they sent me?"

"You always were a nasty little one," she said with a cackle, and flung open the door.

THE DOGS BADGERED THEM FOR AT LEAST TEN MINUTES. Petra would squawk at them in Dutch, Procter would shove them away, but a scrap of peace could not be found until a few squirrels skittered along the pine trunks outside the living room and the dogs focused their energies out the window. Petra made lemonade and laid out a spread of tea cookies on the coffee table and the wiener dogs poached about half before they were swatted and treated to more Dutch profanity, to which they were all quite obviously accustomed, or perhaps deadened.

Pictures of Petra's dead husband and their foreign adventures filled the tables and walls: Helsinki, Amman, Beirut, Paris, London. She'd become a citizen after marrying Chester. The Dutch usually make such nice things, Theo had said once. But Petra? All the goodwill from the flowers and cheese and fancy wooden shoes nullified by the export of one psychotic molehunter.

The woman wore a black vest over a baggy red sweater dress that swung at the ankles. When the dogs had finally settled, she melted into an easy chair and brought her hands to rest on the pouch of her belly. Procter set her lemonade on a doily and ran her tongue along her teeth to dissolve the grains of sugar. We'll have a nice cool drink,

Petra had insisted, but she'd skimped on the water. Procter's mouth was a goddamn sandy beach. Squirrels reappeared outside the window and the two women sipped their drinks for a few minutes listening to the dogs go wild.

"Well?" Petra said, crunching on the sugar, after the dogs had calmed down.

"I need your help," Procter said. "I've been thinking about a few things on Singapore. It still bothers me, for the obvious reasons."

Petra was pulling on her chubby fingers. "Huh," she said. "Trip down darkened memory lane?"

"That's about right. You mind traveling with me?"

"Never liked stories with happy endings. So you go right on ahead."

The sun was about an hour above the horizon. The house was a well of shadows. Procter flicked on a lamp next to the couch. "It took some balls for a Russian team to enter Sam's hotel room. That's off brand right there, and we're not even to the kidnapping, exfil, and prolonged interrogation. I know we had some reports that said it was all a mistake. But why would they go through all that trouble? Take on all that risk? What do you make of it, hand to God?"

"There's no God, Artemis, just the cold black stillness."

"All right, hand to the cold black stillness."

"That Golikov was going to tell us we had a big problem. A penetration. Mole in the CIA. It's a theory, though. Nothing more." Petra stiffened as she spoke. Her gaze, which had been adrift, anchored on Procter's and remained stuck there for a few significant seconds until her attention flitted to the lemonade. Petra had said as much during the briefing for Gosford months earlier, the morning after Singapore, but then there'd been no specifics. Only vague mentions of big problems.

"And it's no more than a theory?"

"That's what I just said, Artemis."

"Your Derm shop make any progress after I got canned?"

"Well, we never did have another briefing with Gosford or *dat pokkenwijf,* Deborah Sweet. They did not want to hear a word about a molehunt, wouldn't even consider the possibility, all those *kankerhoeren* cared about were their own careers. Oh, we had the matrix, all right. Every shred of reporting scoured; every anomaly surfaced. But you know how it goes. Those things are unwieldly and inconclusive. You end up with several theories that fit the facts. Which meant I didn't have the right facts, or close to all of them."

"Did I figure into any of these theories?"

Petra cackled. "Well, you were right at the top of the list. I'd say you've fallen a few spots down since you shat your pants at the Director's table while he was firing you. Maybe a few more after you came here tonight, asking after moles."

"Maybe I'm here to find out what you know before I off you. I did tell you I was here to kill you."

Petra cackled. "No, no, I'm afraid it is unfortunately all too clear that you're not here for that. You hated my guts when we were inside. You wouldn't draw it out, with all this chitchat and lemonade. You would have slid that trusty shotgun of yours into my mouth when I opened the door, painted me across the wall in here. Nice and quick."

"Maybe I'd have used the bat," Procter said. "Once you let me inside."

"Oh, well then the dogs would have killed you," Petra said, and laughed. The lamps cast a warm glow over Petra's flabby face. She'd been pawing at her sculpted hair and it was now tilted, off-center. Maybe a wig, Procter thought.

"Petra, who was on your short list?" Procter asked.

Petra shot her an unkind glare. These were not uncommon, but this one felt different: mirthless, and brutally cold. It said: *You found the line.* They hung in a short, stilted silence.

"If there was a penetration," Petra said, tugging on her lower lip and shutting her eyes to knock the conversation onto a new path, "it would be run out of the SVR's Special Section. Rem Zhomov's shop. That name"—she chuckled—"Rem. R-E-M. I mean, goodness, it's an acronym for the Russian phrase *revolutsky mir.* World revolution. His shop's a home for the true believers, the fanatics. And it's old school, through and through. Though I do wonder how those fanatics are getting on in old age. Could be they've evened out. Maybe their extremism has been eclipsed by a few young turks so it's now quaint and faintly pitiable. Zhomov's only a whisper, of course. A shadow. We know so little."

"The wife had a doozy of a name, too," Procter said, "if memory serves."

"Ninel," Petra said, and a cackle came out. "Lenin spelled backwards."

"Remind me: Where'd we hear about Zhomov? About his group?"

Petra's eyes snapped open. "Oh, well, yes. That traces back to IMPERIAL."

Procter snorted. "Oh for fuck's sake. That degenerate?"

"He is an insufferable rake and a giant pain in the ass, but IMPERIAL did have impeccable access before his defection. For a while he was our taproot sunk deep into the Kremlin."

"Where did he get resettled, anyhow?"

"That most American of towns: Las Vegas. Retiring from both Russia and espionage, IMPERIAL sensibly chose a spot where he might gamble and drink and screw himself to death."

Petra stood and muttered something about feeding the dogs their dinner. When she returned to the living room Procter was patting one on the head. The dog slunk over to Petra's lap with a low growl.

"Zhomov, Zhomov, Zhomov," Procter said, "I seem to remember a file you maintained on the opposition, on the Russians who were trying to wreck our shit, recruit us, penetrate Langley. You've been in the Game so long, so invested in the struggle, that I'd wondered if it might've been something that made the trip out here after retirement. Little memento, I don't know . . ."

"Possession of such material would be illegal, now, wouldn't it?"

"Sure would, hon, but I'd be a pretty unlikely candidate to honeytrap you into a confession, wouldn't I? You think they'd send Artemis out here to wreck you over a box of pure nostalgia?"

"They'd have sent the gigolo for that," she said, her voice firm.

"Now you've got it."

Petra shooed the dog from her lap and heaved up from the couch, wincing as she stood. "Go into the garage and get one of the shovels," she said. "Insect repellant is on the shelf by the door. You'll need it."

THE SPRAY DID NOTHING, BECAUSE PROCTER'S LEGS WERE devoured when they reached the thicket behind the house. The woman led with the flashlight, three wiener dogs slithering behind, Procter trailing the hounds with the shovel on her shoulder, whistling show tunes.

"Stop that," Petra hissed, pushing aside a branch. "It's insufferable."

They soon reached a clearing with a sagging bench and a headstone. Procter squinted at the name in the frayed moonlight.

"Chester's buried out here? Lord almighty."

"Oh, can it. What was I to do? Send poor Chester off to a goddamn cemetery on the edge of town with visiting hours dictated by some dopey rent-a-cop? Pay for a plot when we have land? He agreed. Wanted to be close to me, close to the house. I'm not in the business of looking the other way. Death is all around us, Artemis, why cover it up?"

Procter, caught in a rare speechless moment, paused, looked down at the headstone, then to the shovel. "It's not . . ."

"Don't be absurd, Artemis, I buried them over here." Petra was tapping her foot around in the pine bramble. The bench accepted Petra with a loud creak. She steadied the beam on a brick.

"You're not going to help?" Procter asked.

"You only brought one goddamn shovel."

After a few minutes Procter struck something solid, and a while later, with Petra watching in obvious amusement, she hauled out a Pelican case wrapped in a large bag. Petra shimmied off the bag and clicked open the case to begin sorting. Procter noted classified commendations from past Directors, grainy surveillance photos, a few pieces of hard-copy SIGINT. "My mementos," Petra mumbled, though Procter had not asked. "This one"—she shoved the SIGINT report into Procter's hands—"is a favorite." Putin, she explained, had mentioned Petra by name in a phone call intercepted by the NSA. Procter read the transcript. Mention of Petra: brief, offhand, wildly obscene. The woman let out a riotous laugh and stuffed the report back into the bag. "Russian animals," she said. "As brutal as they are perverse. Ah, here it is . . ."

Petra clutched a folder stuffed with documents, a few photographs peeking haphazardly out. On it was inked: "SVR S.S."

Petra grasped Procter's wrist to stand. Held it tight and didn't let go. "You can read it on three conditions," Petra said. "One, you give me your phone. No pictures, no writing. Two, I'm going to lock you in Chester's study and let you out in the morning. And three, you tell anyone about this little stash and I send someone for you. There are plenty of boys outside Gettysburg who like their meth, and there never is enough money for it. I'm sure they'd be willing to manage your mouth if the money was right."

Procter shook loose her wrist with a half smile and tucked her phone into Petra's vest pocket. Sealed it with a pat.

"No meth heads," Procter said. "I want the sexy gigolo to do me in. Same one you asked for."

BOOKS WERE PILED THROUGHOUT CHESTER'S STUDY: MILItary history, spy novels, academic journals, hard-boiled detective stories. There was also a shelf holding Chester's self-published erotica, of which Procter had heard rumors but never seen. The titles alone made her wish she'd known Chester before he died (*The Ministrations of Herr Doktor Blunderbuss; Dame Rita Knocker*; *Dee Flowers Gets His*).

Procter had flipped a few pages into the *Dee Flowers* book searching for clues as to what was his and how it might have been gotten—she had hunches—but it was getting late. She spread Petra's files under the green glow of the desk lamp, starting with a folder labeled "The Opposition."

Out of what Procter imagined to be a grudging respect—and certain hatred—for the Russian crew attempting to wreck CIA, Petra had shuttled mementos on her tormentors out of the building. There was a profile on Zhomov that she had drafted, with sources running back to the eighties, when he'd joined the KGB. There were incomplete biographies of Zhomov's lieutenants, a roll of grainy photographs of his known associates, a transcript of Petra's debrief with IMPERIAL, with the parts referencing the Special Section highlighted. Procter ticked through a draft roster, compiled by Petra, of the likely composition of the Special Section. The interviews with IMPERIAL stopped around the time of his resettlement in Vegas, two years prior.

After a few hours of reading, with calculated breaks to stand and stretch and patrol the room, Procter had grown as certain as she could be that the study was not wired with cameras. A few hours before dawn, Procter began snapping photos of each document and picture with her prepaid phone, the one she'd not surrendered to Petra.

26

GETTYSBURG

PROCTER AWOKE TO ONE OF THE DOGS LICKING HER BUG bites. She had fallen asleep at the desk. Petra, standing in the doorway, was cursing at the dog, using the same Dutch profanity she'd chosen for Debs the day before. Procter, sitting up to rub sleep from her eyes, noticed the reports had been plucked from the desktop and replaced with the phone she'd turned over the night before. "Rise and shine," Petra said.

Breakfast was cornflakes. Petra sat across from her, one eye shut, the other squinting at a crossword puzzle, pencil tapping on the table. She was sipping coffee from a mug that bore the faded remnants of the seal of the U.S. Embassy, Amman. Chester had been a case officer out there a hundred dim years ago. After ten minutes of silence broken only by occasional bursts of Dutch profanity and the sound of an abused eraser, Procter couldn't take it anymore. "How do you figure IMPERIAL's grasp of the Special Section?"

"Accurate, but incomplete. Man's a degenerate, but he sometimes tells the truth, and he'd received initial briefings from Zhomov when they were standing up the Special Section. Her eyes slatted at Procter, then turned to the crossword. "Five-letter word for the law."

"What does it start with?"

"Maybe an *E*. Or a *G*."

Procter took a spoonful of cereal. "Fuck if I know, hon."

Petra pushed aside the crossword. "IMPERIAL was a nutcase. He'd managed to get a bunch of his money out, so he was rich, too. Felt like he didn't need us. Hard to hold his attention. He was—is—a wild animal. An appetite inhabiting a human body. But he was the only one we had who'd had a look, as it were. He'd met the team running their moles."

"You think Zhomov would've been the one, ultimately, running any penetration?"

Petra was back in the puzzle. "*E-D-I-C-T.* That might work, well, isn't that nice? And yes, to your question. He'd be the top man on the case and he'd have a team in place to manage the details. His prints would be on it, in a way."

"You think you could help me arrange a chat with IMPERIAL? Quiet and casual, no need to involve Vegas Station or, god help us, Langley. Little chat between friends."

Petra sighed, plunked her pencil on the table, said, "It's not a *normal* process to meet with a man such as him. Last time I saw him, in Vegas, out at his place, he got on a roll at the tables and wouldn't come for the meeting."

Procter was pointing her dripping spoon at Petra, who now had a cheery smile on her face. "How'd you manage to pry an Olympian gambler away from a run of cards?"

"Three-letter word for confidence."

Procter crunched on a spoonful of cereal. "*Ego,*" she said.

Petra shut one eye to write. She got up, collected a pencil sharpener from a drawer, and twisted the shavings into the trash.

"We had to lure him from the tables with a girl," Petra said. "He can procure his own, of course, but I thought, what else separates a demented and horny Russian from his gaming? Strange ass, that's what. Moral of the story: two days in Las Vegas, about twenty minutes of cogent discussion, all the next day."

"And what'd he have for you?"

"Well, when we land on the topic of Zhomov and the Special Section, Frankie—that's his new name, of course—well, Frankie says that Zhomov wasn't normal. Zhomov's not one of Putin's Chekists, the shills with the slick suits and cushy apartments suckling off the state.

He was a spartan monk who lived simply, Frankie said, a middle-class worker bee stiff who still referred to the SVR as the First Chief Directorate. His religion was the idea that Russia—in the eighties, Petra said, he would have subbed-in communism—was in a death struggle with the United States. His mission wasn't to steal our secrets, it was to wreck us. He was out to smash America and CIA. To usher in the collapse, Frankie said, as the Sovs and the KGB had collapsed a generation earlier."

"Sounds like a fairy tale," Procter said. "You believe that?"

An unfriendly cackle escaped Petra's lips. "I told you last night: I believe in the cold black stillness. Now, Artemis, finish your cereal. Time to go."

"Wait," Procter said. "One more stroll into the darkness of Singapore. The vague warning we received before Sam went. From REMORA. Mac and Theo's case. You wrote the assessments. And you—"

Petra cut her off: "You're going to ask me what I think about him. That right?"

Procter poured herself another bowl of cereal. "If you'd humor me. It seemed like you thought something was wrong."

Petra had shut her eyes; the lids shivered as if her brain were vibrating inside her skull. She hiccupped. "REMORA passed us some goodies, no doubt. But the quality was uneven, I would say, and I wondered about that. You know how we Derms can be, Artemis, always hunting for an anomaly, and I merely wrote that I would have expected more consistency in production. Bluntly, some of his gruel was thin. And some of it was very specific. I wrote the assessment a few weeks before they fired me, I said—and you know how it is, always with the caveats, like a goddamn analyst—I said, Look here, it could be nothing. Could be he's getting his feet wet with the espionage and doesn't want to give us the goods. Possible? Yes, yes, but still *anomalous*." Said slowly, as if Procter wouldn't understand.

This is why, Procter thought, case officers despise the Derms. Fact was: Derms shut down cases, or shackled them, and you didn't get promoted, didn't get that tingle in your tits, from saying no to cases, from *not recruiting* assets. You got it from hunting and scoring, and if case officers were hunters, the Derms were sniffing at the meat the hunters brought in, concocting reasons to pass on the meal.

"So who yanked you, in the end?" Procter asked, crunching through some cornflakes.

"What was the name," Petra said, so loudly a few of the dogs popped up their heads, "of the goddamn political regime Gosford installed?"

"Reversion."

"Reversion." She cackled. "Those tools. Reversion in Gosford's paradise meant *dat pokkenwijf* Deborah Sweet had her mitts in every cookie jar. Gosford wanted that turkey-necked bitch running things like James Jesus Angleton in his glory. She came to my office one day, not long after you got the ax, and asked after my report on REMORA. His intel was going into reports left and right and *dat nare pokkenwijf* was joining the briefings with Gosford on the backs of that reporting; REMORA's punching her tickets to the Oval. She told me that the Seventh Floor *and* the Russia House Front Office had complaints about my assessment, that now was not the time to question an asset taking *serious risks.* And she said, of all things, why was I even yammering about the safe house expense? I'd sent a few emails on that, you see, nothing in cables, and—"

Procter cut her off. "Safe house expense?"

"Oh, it was stupid, Artemis. There is a farmhouse. Provence, beautiful spot outside Lacoste. Chosen because REMORA could travel there when he visited his wife's family in Barcelona. She's half-Catalan. And the place, as you can imagine, was terribly expensive. Finance threw a fit about it, said why don't we just go through one of the cutouts to rent properties on Airbnb or whatever the hell? Why are we retaining this place? And the answer was always the same: REMORA is one of our top-producing assets, we need a place that is comfortable, that does not change, that is there, always, if he can travel and needs to talk to us. You ever hear of us sitting on a property like that for a single asset?"

"No," Procter said. "No, I have not. What'd you say back to Debs and the boys, hon, you don't mind me asking? About the anomalies?"

"Simple things. REMORA is Deputy in the Fifth? Have him bring us a list of every operation Moscow is running in Europe right now. Have him bring us the names of every SVR case officer working the American target in Europe—whatever he can find. And *dat pokkenwijf* said I was kicking up shit. Deborah Sweet was a washout case officer with an unremarkable and undistinguished record who by dint of proximity to Gosford returned to CIA to run the *Directorate of Operations.* I mean, holy crow, Artemis, she knew zilch, zilch about what we were up to when she walked into Langley for the second time. She needed to find treasure to prove her worth, and REMORA's intel was gold. He'd been tested. He was delivering. Why was I raking shit all over the place, that's what they said, Artemis. Told me to hush up. And I zippered up my cheesepipe like a good girl."

"Who's 'they'?"

"Oh, who knows? All of them, probably. They had their reasons; I was throwing cold water on their case, making Theo's life difficult. Shade on Mac's golden goose. Gus felt that I'd iced a few of the Moscow cases with lousy assessments when he'd been Chief out there, and you damn well know how black his mood was when he came home in the spring. Bad juju, all around. No one likes Derms."

Procter raised her glass with a sick smile.

"In any case," Petra continued, "your Bratva and *dat pokkenwijf* got their mutual wish, though I don't believe they shared motivation. I got knocked off the assessment. They gave it to a more pliant lad, a baby-faced kid with furless balls. Don't remember his name."

"And it was Debs who pushed you out, in the end?"

"Who else? Course, that giraffe wouldn't let me go in peace. The way they pushed me out, I can't even get contract work." Her eyes were bright with anger. "Now, Artemis," Petra said. "Your cereal is mush. And if we talk about this too much longer, I'm going to get so angry that I might kill you just to calm my nerves. Time for you to scram."

THE WOMAN ACCOMPANIED HER TO THE CAR. PROCTER gripped the door handle, Petra her shoulder. Her eyes were a shade wild.

The dogs were yapping again, feeling Petra's energy—there wasn't a squirrel in sight.

Petra spoke to the ground. "If they've been running a high-level penetration and we've lost only a few sources so far, you've got to wonder what the game is, don't you? If Zhomov is playing a different one entirely."

Petra punctuated the sentence by crushing a pinecone beneath her shoe. "I thought I'd be celebrated when I retired. You probably did, too. Gave the place our all, didn't we? Then we got turned out. Not a salute. Not a thank-you. They said they would mail me the Blue Bag with the flag and the medallion and their fucking certificate, and you know what? Never came. Lost in the mail, I'm sure. Lord knows I wasn't looking for a ticker tape parade, but how about some gratitude? A little payout for all the sweat equity. Didn't seem like too much to ask. By the end, after *dat pokkenwijf* and I had said our piece and my head was snuggled under the guillotine, I realized I was done helping that building. If there is a mole digging around in there, I said to myself, Petra, well, you let those ingrates find it. You've done your time. Whole place is just a bunch of limp-dicked managers and woke kids now. Anyone actually spying around here? I thought about that in my last few weeks, dinking around in the cafeteria, not even visiting the vault anymore. Seventh Floor didn't want me there, your Bratva didn't want me there. I would watch the youths walking around, all the contractors and all the managers. What a useless flesh pile Langley had become. They sent a Seventh Floor flunkie, some HR doofus, to speak at my retirement ceremony, and the bastard got my name wrong. Called me Patty. And do you know what I said, Artemis? *Opkankeren.* I said fuck 'em. You might consider that, too. After all you've done. But if you decide not to say that, you should be careful, Artemis. So very careful. You stick your hand down this mole hole, something's going to bite back. Sink its little buck teeth in real nice and deep. You watch yourself. Listen to Petra on this."

Then the woman's grip on Procter's shoulder loosened and she was walking away, dogs plodding at her heels over the carpet of pine needles toward the house.

PART III

FREE RADICALS

27

DALLAS / PUERTO VALLARTA, MEXICO

AROUND THE NEIGHBORHOOD, ON LONG WALKS OR WHEN they played with him in the front yard, Peter and Irene Venable's French bulldog was known as Joseph. Only in their home was he called by his proper name: Stalin. The house was a one-story adobe with a terra-cotta roof fronted by massive palms, snuggled in Dallas's leafy eastern flank, a neighborhood where the deadening flatness of North Texas warps into low rolling hills. They'd purchased the property a few years earlier, after they'd graduated from the University of Texas and moved up from Austin. Peter, slogging through a Zoom call, stared sleepily out the window into the trees. This year the heat had raked its nails across the autumn chalkboard; mid-October, and the mercury would scratch ninety today. He sipped coffee from his home office and daydreamed about snow.

After having contributed nothing during the call, Peter closed out of Zoom, answered three emails from colleagues at Southwest Airlines, where he worked in financial planning and analysis, and opened his personal email. The usual—news, a note from a neighbor planning a poker night, a reminder for the dog's Bordetella shot. What the Venables' unconventional friends would call a lapse in tradecraft had occurred the first time Irene schlepped the dog to the vet: she'd provided his real name, earning, in her telling, not even a sidelong glance or arched eyebrow from the staff, who, like all Americans, were doubtless woefully ignorant of the basic facts of the world, doubly so when the subject was Russian history. The email, which made him smile, announced that Joseph Stalin's appointment was scheduled for the following Tuesday, and included a reminder that, due to a recent spate of biting incidents, Joseph Stalin should be leashed throughout.

He stopped smiling when he saw the subject line of an email that arrived just when he closed out the vet's note.

Subj: Hi from Uncle Stephen

Shit, Peter muttered. Shit. His fingers were frozen to the keyboard.

He opened the note. In an instant he felt that his body had cartwheeled onto a high bookshelf, where he now watched himself sit at the desk.

Hello Peter, I'm sorry it has been such a long while since I wrote to you, but I thought I would tell you about the gardening your aunt and me have been engaged with this past summertime. Golly, such flowers, so many herbs and vegetables and maximum shrubs. It is incredible, we are so so happy. I have included a snapshot your auntie tooken. Tell her how you think, maybe, you and lovely Irene. Mayhaps a visit soon, so you might see the blossoms living in advance of the autumnal fall.

With utmost sincerity, your most favorite uncle Stephen

God, he thought, who wrote that crap? He remembered the simple codes: one before shrubs, one after blossoms. Maximum living.

"Irene, come here," he called to her makeshift desk at the dining room table. Irene ran the social media handles for a rideshare start-up; all morning she'd been posting pictures of local restaurateurs zipping around Dallas in the vehicles.

"One sec, babe, I'm finishing a post."

"Well, when you do, bring the computer."

"Peter? What? Shut up."

THE SPANIARD HAD SUPPLIED THE ASUS LAPTOP TWO months after Oklahoma, the memories of which still made Peter's legs feel like water.

Irene logged in to Instagram and navigated to the handle @maximumliving. There were pictures of jewelry, videos of models hawking outfits, shots of exotic vacation destinations and appetizing meals. Rote influencer fare, doubtless trawled and scraped from other accounts, but Irene cooed that it did boast twenty-one thousand followers and the posts seemed to generate a reasonable level of engagement. Irene had insisted on as much with the Spaniard. Red handbags, he knew, they were looking for red handbags. In mounting frustration, Irene scrolled through a few weeks' worth of posts, then returned to the most recent, and, sure enough, the fourth image in the set boasted a red Hermès bag slung over the shoulder of a waifish blonde. Irene downloaded the image onto the laptop and then dragged it into a folder labeled flowerhappy.exe. Then she punched in a strange twenty-seven key password, written in segments across several pages of a notebook. The picture, dropped into the flowerhappy.exe program on the main computer, was now sent to another program hidden on the hard drive. Irene clicked. Ten percent, twenty, fifty, eighty. Then the computer's hourglass showed up, and she wondered if something was wrong. "Peter? Did you touch something?"

"What? Of course not."

Irene mashed the trackpad with a steady, menacing gaze that seemed to declare her intent to punch it through the desk.

Suddenly: one hundred. Text replaced the hourglass: steganography for the digital age, the art of hiding a message in a picture.

A location, a date, the body language. A note, supposedly from "the highest levels," that their friends were counting on them.

"Peter, like, oh my god," Irene said.

Peter imagined the enfolding winter, the ramparts engulfed in snow; in his mind he reviewed an endless expanse of green-brown rolling hills, took the loam of the black earth into his nostrils. A valve opened to his soul.

TWO DAYS LATER, AND STALIN WAS PACKED AWAY TO THE kennel; they'd held their mail and asked the neighbors to collect the Amazon deliveries. A weekend getaway in Puerto Vallarta to help Irene destress, he told his team. Both had plenty of leave. Indeed, neither company had a formal vacation policy. Work from anywhere! Peter's job at the airline meant the couple flew standby for free. They spent four hours sitting in the Love Field concourse waiting for open seats, three hours on the flight itself, and a few more in the car. By late afternoon they were careening into another round of margarita stress reduction therapy at the resort's deserted beachfront bar, struggling to maintain even a modestly stilted conversation. Irene wore a black bikini and a Texas Rangers ball cap. Peter wore blue trunks and a matching Rangers cap, as the decoded message had instructed.

The burst of gymnastic lovemaking to consecrate their room and the IV drip of alcohol they were wheeling through the day—ding of the button once they'd hit cruising altitude and screwdrivers please, yes, a double would be great—had done little to blunt the edge. He did not know precisely what they wanted from him and Irene, but after Oklahoma he fretted, and in any case he knew for certain that his first sight of the Spaniard would turn up the volume on that memory, and it would be impossible to tune out.

Peter first heard his voice roll down the walkway snaking from the pool to the beach—and fought the instinct to turn his head. The Spanish, bits and pieces of which Peter understood, was silky and assured. He made idle chitchat with an American mounting a lousy, if valiant, effort at the language. Peter sensed the Spaniard taking the scene in, watching, assessing. After a few moments he wound down the conversation with the faceless American and soon Peter heard only his folksy whistle and the smack of his sandals across the planked walkway.

The Spaniard took the seat next to Irene. He wore his usual pleasant smile and slacks and a white linen shirt. The Spaniard, Peter had come to realize, had a way of saying the right things in the right order to arrive, by some form of conversational magic, just where he wanted to be. And he was a gentle guide, willing to zigzag through a discussion not precisely on his chosen path, from baseball to the weather, tequila to the vagaries of the Dallas real estate market.

Like most men, the Spaniard enjoyed the sight of Irene in a swimsuit. But, quite unlike the other resortgoers, the Spaniard made no attempt to mask his interest. He looked her over without shame. For some reason Peter did not find this threatening, as if perhaps the Spaniard were sufficiently professional to appreciate a half-naked, athletic, twenty-eight-year-old body without telegraphing the temptation to screw it. That the Spaniard was at least two decades their senior, that he was working on a second chin without credit of a first, and that Irene had once pronounced him "gross" did not hurt Peter's case: Let him look.

For an hour they drank and made small talk, the Spaniard, Peter could feel, easing them into things. Once he seemed satisfied that it would not appear overly direct or abrupt, the Spaniard suggested they join him for a drink in his villa. His tequila was quite rare, he said, and he had a veranda tickling the beach. For a half mile they shuffled through the trucked-in sand, along the lapping turquoise water, and finally up a meandering boardwalk to the front of a villa the Spaniard claimed was his.

They gathered around the dining room table. The Spaniard looked at them for a few uncomfortable moments, the first of their kind since he'd arrived at the bar: he was constantly pinching his mustache with his thumb and forefinger, tapping the dark wood, and running his fingers over the aquatic engravings running along the table's lip. "We have a big job for you," he said at last.

He slid a black thumb drive and a folded piece of paper to Peter, who opened it.

"This paper has traveled all the way from Moscow," the Spaniard said. "So that you understand the importance of this task. The responsibility we are placing on your shoulders."

He noticed now that Irene had fastened her hand on Peter's knee, squeezing as if she might juice it.

"What do you want us to do?"

The Spaniard laughed, snatched back the paper, and ate it.

LATE THAT NIGHT, BACK IN THEIR ROOM, PETER AND IRENE soaked in a hot bath, rose petals floating lazily across the surface like pink steamboats. They'd not traded a word since leaving the Spaniard's villa. Each time Peter shut his eyes and slid deeper into the bath, he piled up memories: the rich smell of apples floating over Aunt Lidia and

Uncle Alexei's dacha outside Nizhny, that summer so long ago, of the orchards and green hills and the whine of insects; then stronger, searing memories of the spectral Masha, daughter of the neighbors, visionary-eyed girl of seventeen who throughout that summer was stapled to his hip and with whom he would log a decade of bedroom experience in three months' time; and at last he was with Irene in a Russian field hospital outside Rostov on Don, the latest stamp in their passports was from Finland, and they were speaking to a soldier who had lost his legs and a good deal of an arm in a Ukrainian artillery bombardment. "There is a letter from that young man on the thumb drive," the Spaniard had said. "Read it when you get home." The memories dredged from the abyss of Peter's soul an even more dizzying mess: alienation, anger, envy, powerlessness. And, despite his brainpan's emotional clog—to say nothing of the warm water—his thoughts of Masha had made him very hard.

Peter opened his eyes. "We can say no," he blurted out. He eyed the suitcase the Spaniard had left behind. "Throw that thing in the ocean along with the thumb drive, bury it, like, in the jungle, leave it here for the housekeepers."

Irene laughed. "Babe, we've seen the names. We can't do that. And come on: Is that really what you want?"

"No," he said, quickly, to avoid a fight. "It's not." But was he certain? No, he was not.

She slithered across the tub, spreading herself across him to kiss his lips and his neck. She tasted like salt and booze. His fingers slid down the furrow of her spine. His ear went into her mouth for a moment, and he felt her tongue. Then she withdrew ever so slightly and whispered: "This is our chance. They have given us a chance, Peter, and I, like, I think we should take it."

"Why us?" he asked, perhaps more to himself than to her. "They have professionals, for god's sake."

AS THE PLANE DESCENDED INTO DALLAS–FORT WORTH, Peter was thinking of the customs form: Was he carrying more than

$10,000 in cash? There were no paper forms on US-Mexico routes anymore, the flight attendant said, and for some reason that put him at ease. As if his transgressions might still be deniable—future sins considered but not yet committed.

As they crawled through the sweaty line of sun-scorched tourists and screaming children, he thought his heart was going to explode. Irene applied lip balm constantly. He watched the tube disappear and reappear into her pocket, her hands gripping it savagely, as if it might save her, or she might use it to stab an overly inquisitive customs officer.

Finally they were at the front of the line. The customs official called them forward and wordlessly scanned their passports.

He and Irene collected their cases from the carousel and wheeled them past two Customs and Border Protection officers milling by the doors. They strolled through the line for returning U.S. citizens with nothing to declare. The air was oily and metallic and he wondered if this was what it felt like to be alive.

THAT EVENING PETER AND IRENE WERE EXAMINING THE contents of the Spaniard's suitcase, spread open on the floor of their walk-in closet. Irene had already worked open the concealment device with the combination of pressure points and dials the Spaniard had demonstrated not long after he swallowed the paper.

Irene plucked a stack of bills from a pouch and handed it to Peter to count.

"Twenty-five thousand," he muttered.

Irene sniffed. "Excuse me?"

"I said twenty-five. We make this in a month. This is . . . this is chump change. We deserve respect. This does not feel like respect. What is this?"

What was unspoken, and yet so very real that Peter could feel it rattling in his heart, was that money had little or nothing to do with it.

"We do this," Irene said. "We prove ourselves. Then we ask for more."

THAT NIGHT PETER AND IRENE SAT IN THE ENCROACHING dark on green Adirondack chairs, sharing a joint and drinking hard kombucha. Stalin was snuggled on Irene's lap. She'd pulled out her phone and was admiring a few of the rideshare's Instagram posts. "Twice as many likes as last week," she said. "More than double the number of comments." She set down her phone, took a hit of the joint, and handed it to Peter, who was gazing dreamily up at the rising moon.

"Is it a kamikaze mission?" Irene asked, exhaling the smoke. Stalin gave a contented rumble as she dug fingers into his hips.

A head appeared above the back fence. A wave.

"Hi, Venables," came the voice. "How was Mexico?"

"The best," Peter called back. "You guys doing well, Doug?"

"Business is good," Doug said. "So I can't complain." Peter hated when he did that. Talked about business being good. The man was a heart surgeon. "Headed to Breck next week for another break, though. Figured, why the hell not?" He sniffed at the sky and shot Irene a wry look; Doug liked to look at Irene.

"Now, Irene. Young Peter." Fuck you Doug, he thought. "You guys smoking weed?"

"Indeed we are," Irene said. She accepted the joint from Peter and cast a cloud into the air. "This stuff is real sticky, you want a hit?"

Doug laughed. "I'll pass. Hey, mind picking up the mail? Through Thursday."

"All good," said Irene, punctuating her thumbs-up with a stoner smile.

"Cool, thanks, guys. Next time we'll watch Joseph, save you the kennel trouble."

"Deal," Peter said.

"Thanks, Venables, take it easy," Doug said, and disappeared.

Peter took the joint. "Do you want it to be a suicide mission?"

She lay back in the chair and closed her eyes and rubbed Stalin's haunches. "Maybe we see? Maybe we find out together?"

28

LANGLEY / CLARENDON

SINCE PROCTER HAD LEFT TOWN, INFORMATION HAD been running in the wrong direction: Sam was giving it all, with none coming in return, an exceptionally uncomfortable position for any CIA officer. To start, they'd told him the psych and medical reevaluation was routine. A pulse check after the trauma of Moscow. Gus had previewed that it would include a few more "discussions" with Security and the CI debriefers. "Maybe two, three of those," Gus had said, outlining the entire process with a nonchalance that put Sam at ease. He found the reboot odd and inconvenient, but what could he do?

The Security debriefings, spread over two weeks, had been particularly strange. In place of the usual coldness bordering on hostility, the interviewers were, without exception, disinterested, disengaged, bored. At first Sam had taken heart, interpreting this as a signal that the review was in fact a formality, a box-checking exercise to tick and tie any concerns after his captivity, so everyone could just move on.

The calendar invite read "OMS Re-evaluation—Decision and Outbrief" and had been sent by Gus the night before with the Moscow X HR rep cc'd. Sam was half right, then. The process had indeed been a formality. The outcome, though? Well, as Sam walked into Gus's office to a curt nod from the HR rep, he saw that he'd had the outcome ass backwards.

A DECADE EARLIER: SAM JOSEPH'S FIRST TRIP IN FRONT OF A CIA review board.

It had come on the heels of falling in love with his Syrian asset, the kind of pleasurable mistake now rich with layers of joy, regret, nostalgic lust, and self-loathing. In other words: the type of sin you'd gladly commit again. He should have been fired for it, and even now—even knowing the entire story—he marveled that he had not been.

At first he'd gotten the tale in drips. Though she would play a starring role, the Chief, of course, had never said a word about any of it. In fact, for a while after Syria he didn't see her, and she didn't really try to see him. He'd wondered if he should take it personally, but he'd grown to understand the Chief's bizarre weather patterns. Procter, he decided, didn't bear him any ill will. Like everyone else, she'd merely forgotten him.

But during an otherwise innocuous happy hour during the dark early months of that Langley internment, the scars of Syria still fresh on his mind and body, a drunken colleague who also happened to be a Farm classmate pulled him aside and slurred out that his old Chief, Artemis Procter, had come calling during the review board process, had taken him out for a lunch, in fact. "And the thing was," the guy said, "I didn't know her at all. Never talked to the woman, and, lo and behold, I come in one day to find a note from her inviting me to lunch."

"Why'd she do that?" Sam had yelled over the din of the bar.

"She had some excuse, I don't even remember what it was, because after about five minutes she only wanted to talk about you. Sickening, yes?"

"About what?"

"What?" The music had grown louder.

"What did she ask about?"

"Oh. Sappy bullshit. What you were like at the Farm, my impressions of your general character, your honor and good judgment and shit. I said the right things. Lied for you." Big smile, tip of his drink, sloshing over the sides.

"Why did Procter do that?"

The guy didn't answer. Instead, he said that he knew of another Farm classmate who'd received a similar invite for a chat. The Chief had of course been interviewed during the review board process: she'd offered something akin to sworn testimony regarding the cataclysmic events that had marked the last days of his Syrian tour, when he'd wound up in an interrogation room with his asset, who was also his lover, and both had nearly died. He'd returned to Langley not a hero, not a goat, but something far more ambiguous and thus potentially dangerous: a highly capable and wrecked case officer who'd performed heroically and also grievously violated the moral code of the tribe. His old mentor Ed Bradley, then running the Near East Division, had put it simply: The board will weigh the heroism and distinction against your obvious fuckup, and render judgment accordingly. When Sam had asked for odds, Ed said it was better than Vegas. It was a coin flip.

Two months after the review board had flipped the coin and decided he might stay, and one week after he'd learned of Procter's mysterious lunches, Sam drove out to Bradley's farmhouse for beers and a few questions about the Chief's interventions.

"Where is she now?" Sam asked. "She's gone missing. Least to me."

"She's in Florida for a month or so," Ed said. "Family time."

"Chief has a family?"

"I am told," Ed said, with a tone of forced restraint, "that she has family members in Florida, a cousin or something. I don't honestly know what the hell she's doing down there."

Sam opened another beer. "I heard she was doing the rounds with a few of my Farm classmates, asking about me."

"It's normal," Bradley said, "for the board to consider the officer's character in its judgment. Your track record of honor and integrity."

"Is it normal for the subject's former Chief to be the one doing the diligence?"

Bradley looked at him dead-on. "Of course not."

"Well, what's she up to? She won't even return my calls."

"She's not normal Sam, you know that."

"I do. I do know that."

"Let's drop it. What's done is done."

"Where are they going to send her next?"

"Well, with the flak the board shot through her, I don't know. She's not riding a desk yet, but they might put her on ice for a while."

This, from Bradley's lips, was the first Sam had heard of the Chief taking any heat for his decisions in Syria.

"What do you mean?"

"Well, they shoveled some shit on her, Sam. To be honest, she shoveled it on herself."

"Ed, come on, man. Just tell me."

Bradley did not want to talk—Sam had wondered if the board had shoveled some shit his way for the whole thing, too—but he did offer a few clarifying bits. One, that Artemis Procter had, in effect, assumed responsibility for every operational call in those last Syrian days, that she vouched fully and comprehensively for his character—Bradley said Procter had assembled a dossier of approximately twenty testimonials from Sam's colleagues to make this point—and she testified that Sam had come clean about his relationship with the Syrian on his own. He had told the truth, that most precious and essential ethic in a world where, outside the walls of Langley, they were paid to lie and steal. "Why'd she do all of that?" Sam asked.

"I told you. She's not normal."

After three more beers Bradley admitted that she'd lost her next Chief slot. Procter was in Florida licking her wounds, probably on a colossal bender.

It sunk in later, and in pieces: on the drive home from the farmhouse; in his apartment, lying awake; in the endorphin high of the comedown from his evening run; staring through the cable traffic the next morning. The Chief could have walked away, fence-sat, or heaped the blame on him, washing her hands of the ordeal. Instead she ducked into the ring and started swinging.

Two days later, working off a motel address and room number that Bradley had reluctantly provided, Sam was on a flight to Orlando. In those days she did not have the trailer and had taken up at an Econo

Lodge outside Kissimmee. She hadn't been answering her cell phone because it was turned off. She'd apparently gone so far as to call her provider and suspend service for the month. He saw her RAV4 in the parking lot. He walked up to Room 202 and knocked.

"Bad timing, Magda," he heard the Chief growl through the door, along with the slide of the bolt. "I forgot the DO NOT DISTURB"—door swung open—"and anyway, when . . . Oh."

"Hey, Chief."

"I thought you were housekeeping."

"Got that."

"Well, you missed the exit for Disney."

He stole a glance into the room: four feet dangled off the bed's end. A bag of Fritos was scattered across the floor. The smell leaking through the doorway was damp clothes and skunked beer. The Chief met his eyes and then swiveled back to the room to see what was attracting his attention. He thought he caught a flicker of surprise, as if she hadn't quite figured what she might find. "What time is it?" came the pained voice of a man from the bed. "Ugghh . . . shut up," came a girl's.

He poked his head through the door. "Seems like it could be more fun here than at Disney."

"Well, the room is *occupado*," Procter said, and, sliding into sandals, added: "You're driving and paying and going to do most of the talking, Jaggers. Take me to Harmon's."

There is a certain panache to the CIA officer out in the field, but the return stateside can be a bit like the bell tolling midnight on Cinderella, the officer transforming into a pumpkin of humdrum middle-class mediocrity. Artemis Aphrodite Procter, however, was never one for mediocrity. Instead, she had chosen to slide a few rungs lower, into unbridled tropical squalor.

Her sartorial choices in Damascus had been strange—fabrics mismatched to seasons, colors to everything else—but now they veered even further afield: biker shorts, white tank top (no bra), Birkenstocks, Indians hat flocked by grease stains. On the drive to Harmon's she did not ask why'd he come. She seemed to assume no preamble was necessary, no *How are things with you?* small talk to catch up. As was her way, she launched into bantering as if he'd been with her in Florida for weeks: a series of complaints about and praises for the maids at the motel; a run of curses for her cousin, who owned a gator park or something, she was not particularly specific about him, nor her laundry list of grievances.

Harmon's was a bar that also boasted a breakfast buffet stuffed with customers fast-tracking diabetes. The staff all smiled and addressed her by name, and Procter approached the buffet with the certainty of someone getting down to business in their own kitchen. The Chief assembled for herself an overflowing plate—she did not waste a moment debating her selections—and joined him in a quiet booth, where Sam was sipping black coffee and picking at his far more sensible meal: scrambled eggs, sausage links, two pieces of toast.

She shingled four pieces of bacon across a waffle. Atop the bacon went two chicken strips, which she slathered in syrup and a creamy sauce that she sniffed thoughtfully before deciding it passed muster. Four more strips of bacon were draped over top, then a second waffle to complete the masterpiece. Procter took a sip of coffee, then searched around the plate, the table, the booth seat. "Damn thing must've rolled off," she muttered. "One sec." She went to the buffet, where she collected a single strawberry to sit atop the waffle. She picked up her silverware, sighed, and, still staring at her plate, said: "You didn't quit, did you?"

"No."

"Phew," she said, "Fucking phew," before cutting into the waffle to take her first bites, saying she was hungrier these days, lots of time in the gym and I can't seem to get enough calories. "Glad you didn't quit, though. Would've royally pissed me off. What brings you down old Florida way? This a social visit?"

"You haven't been answering my calls."

"Sometimes I don't answer calls."

"Why?"

"I'm in a different zone now, Jaggers, and I don't multitask so good. We're talking now, aren't we? What's up?"

"I spoke with Bradley. And a few old Farm classmates. Heard about how you went to bat for me during the board process. I didn't know. Wanted to say thanks."

"Well, you're welcome," she said, though she was laser-focused on hacking through a piece of chicken. "But you could've said that in a voice mail."

"Felt like something to say in person."

With her fingers she plucked the felled strawberry from her plate and plopped it into her mouth, treating him to a shrug that said: *Whatever, man.*

"I heard that you lost the Chief slot—"

"Oh good grief, not this shit," she said. "Let's talk about something else."

"No. I want to talk about this. I heard you lost the slot in Amman because of me. And I'm—"

"Wrong, all wrong," she said, making a wet noise and picking up her silverware with gusto. "Erroneous! Err—"

"Goddammit," he said. "Shut up for one second. I wanted to say that I am sorry about that. I wanted you to hear that from me."

She was now spearing soggy hunks of chicken and waffle with a manic energy. "Fine, fine, fucking fine. We can do this, Jaggers. You flew down to Florida for the party and I'll deliver, seeing as you're getting all contemplative in your golden years." Monstrous forkful of chicken and waffle, several seconds of chewing. "My tour was *deferred*"—a term she would use with strict consistency in the days to follow—"because of me. Not you. Me. Not always about you, Jaggers, how many times do I have to say it? This was about me. And truth is it's really fucking simple. Seems nowadays Headquarters likes to launder the easy shit into three-dimensional chess or a lubed-up Rubik's Cube or whatever, but sometimes the simple shit is just that: simple. You are a good case officer who fucked up, and this place allows one fuckup, long as you come clean. Which you did. To me." One entire strip of bacon inserted into her mouth, folding over itself like a fleshy piece of chewing gum, and a long pause until she'd gotten it down. "Now, that all being what it is, our friendly spy Service and its doughy overlords sometimes prefer to shove the blame for a disaster on a single intrepid soul before showing them the door. Heap the village's goddamn—" A coughing fit, halted only by the arrival of a waiter with the largest glass of orange juice Sam had ever seen. "Bless you, Sandra, god bless. She's a doll, Jaggers. One of the good ones. Where was I? Ah yes: sins. Sometimes Langley sees fit to heap all the sins onto one goat and slit its throat. I've seen the movie, lord knows I've seen it, and yes, it would've been easier to pile on and let that happen to you, because you fucked up, well and truly. But you know what? I was Chief out there"—she'd shut one eye to refocus on the knifework—"and I was responsible. Responsible for your sorry ass and your sorry-ass decisions. Also, I've been in star-crossed love before and know what that's like, doomed and beautiful all at once. I get it. There is such a thing as honor, among thieves and also friends."

Speech done, her plate ransacked, she said she had to use the ladies' room, and disappeared for what felt like ten minutes.

"Who were you in love with?" Sam asked, after she'd returned.

The Chief's hand flung skyward. "Sandra," she called, "bring this young man the check. And, Jaggers: Fuck off. We are staring down the barrel of a few days of drinking, maybe even a Disney trip if you play your cards right. Plenty of time to cover all that later."

THEY NEVER DID COVER IT, AND HE NEVER THOUGHT IT wise to raise it again, though he'd come to believe it was one of her old friends. And now, a decade on, it was Sam's boss, a member of her Bratva, Gus Raptis, who sat at the table next to the HR rep and solemnly delivered the news: "After reviewing all of this, we think it's best if you resign, Sam. You've had a good run. Tremendous recruitment successes, demonstrated heroism, an illustrious career."

"Then why this?"

"Doctors don't think you'll—"

"Which doctor?"

Gus now spoke clean past him: "Let me finish. Your psych and mental wellness team does not believe you will be able to run ops in a field context again. And I know, from my own extensive review of your performance records, that you are not keen for an endless string of meaningless jobs here in Headquarters. Do I have that right?"

"I don't understand where this is coming from, Gus. What, exactly, did the doctors say?"

"You'll have continued access to the psychologists and counselors," Gus said. "And we're not animals, we're going to pay you for the next six months to sit at home until you find another job. But we're cutting off your access. And it's not like that, I can see it on your face. Not like that. It's merely that I know if I let you stay here, in this vault, with your access preserved, you are going to just keep at it, hope that, as before, rehabilitation is on the horizon and in a year or so you can be out in a Station again."

Up to this point Sam's senses had been numb, as if all of this were theoretical, perhaps a discussion of another unfortunate officer run roughshod by this place. Anger flooded him. He was plummeting into the useless and yet oh so deep abyss of: I gave this place my all and now this? His fist had curled into a ball. He wasn't thinking of his Russian captivity in that moment, but he felt its sting, doubly so because, having been shoved out, it was exceedingly difficult—far more than usual—to make any goddamn sense of what it had all been for. "There any room here for a different call?" He could barely get out the words. "For an appeal?"

"I'm afraid not, Sam," Gus said coldly. "The DDO signed the papers. It's done."

WHEN SAM OPENED THE DOOR TO HIS HOUSE, NATALIE WAS singing in the kitchen. The smells of lamb and za'atar and parsley crashed into him. What was that song? Whatever it was, she was happy. He slapped his bag down in the foyer and ducked back outside to collect the mail. The otherworldly sensation of having been fired from a job—a life, really, a life had ended—crashed into the very embodied experience of Natalie having offered to cook him dinner tonight, a random Tuesday.

From the kitchen, she called in Arabic, the language of their domestic cloister, "*Habibi*, hello?"

He bristled when she called him *habibi*—dear, my love. As of late Sam had invested considerable energy in forcing himself not to think about why it was that he hated the word. Namely, that her feelings for him had clearly outrun his for her. He'd planned to keep things casual and carefree, let the relationship fizzle out when he was inevitably sent overseas, but now? He'd been stripped of the operational cover to avoid her love. "*Habibi?*" she called again, and his jaw involuntarily clenched.

Sam knew he was fiddling around with deep stuff here—he of all people understood the long shadow of desire. In Syria it had also been paired with love. With Natalie it had begun as boredom, and then, after his imprisonment, it had been sustained by shame. Love had yet to show, at least on his end. Natalie had been so goddamn perfect, so lovingly focused on reassimilating him into the human race. He hated himself for wanting to end it. Who was he to cast aside a fiercely loyal, well-adjusted Lebanese American second-grade teacher with a smile that was like light pouring into a room? Said differently: What, really, was wrong with him?

"Hi, *habibti*," he called, careful not to stumble over the word. Walking back into the foyer, he tossed the mail onto a hall table. "It smells amazing in here."

By the time he'd entered the kitchen, kissed her, rolled up his sleeves, and jumped in to help with the lamb and plate the food, he'd managed to convince himself that he would skip over the bit about the firing, enjoy dinner, and then they would retreat to the bedroom, the only place where the relationship was clipping along nicely for him.

When they sat down at the table, the initial shock of the firing had burned to a smoldering anger that reduced his hunger to ashes. The mole was behind the firing; the bullshit from Gus made no sense otherwise. He did not want to speak of it with Natalie. He'd seen that movie when he got home from Russia. She would ask all manner of questions, and the whole thing would remind him that she loved him. Tonight, he burned with too many black emotions to heap shame onto the bonfire.

"How was your day?" she asked. Smiling that big, beautiful smile.

"Fine," he said, picking up a skewer of lamb. "Boring."

AFTER DINNER THEY WENT OUT FOR A WALK, BOUGHT CUPcakes for no reason, and, because he had no shred of self-control—because, as one ex had said, he was a priapic moron—they made love, hopscotching from couch to counter to bed, before settling in for a spree of mindless television and the contemplation of tactics he might use to influence her to leave and to think it had been her idea. On that score, he was not optimistic. He made martinis, which they sipped from the couches amid a languid display of peak gluttony: Netflix rolling, drinks going, greasy cupcake box sprawled on the coffee table alongside the condom wrapper. Natalie wore a robe stenciled with tigers. It parted when she curled toward him, exposing a track of dark hair and offering a fleeting distraction from his anger, which had matured throughout the evening into a silent rage.

He heard his phone ring from the bag in the foyer—the one the Chief called him on. His drink was empty, Natalie's hands had begun exploring the possibility of a second roll in the hay, and this, of all places, was where Sam summoned the moral courage to draw a dull and wobbly line, the best he could manage. He gently set aside her hand. "I should get that," he said, and stood.

"Hey," he said, answering.

"Petra's set us up with Frankie," Procter said.

"Where will the meeting be?"

"Vegas. Apparently Frankie won't travel. He thinks people are trying to kill him, and I'm not sure he's wrong. Vegas work for you?"

"Vegas is fine. It's always fine."

"I've been cautioned that it will not be a linear discussion. Petra's warned us to pack some patience."

"Understood."

"Where should we meet him?"

"Tell him we'll be at the Bellagio."

"When can you get out there?"

He thought about that—he still had to clear out his desk, sign the outbriefing papers. "Thursday night."

"Thursday. What'll Gus think?"

"It'll be fine."

"Okey doke. I'll let Frankie know. I can be at the Bellagio around dinnertime. See you there." She hung up.

He found Natalie at the kitchen sink, filling a glass with water. "The Bellagio? You are going to Las Vegas?"

"Yes."

"Again?"

"This time it's for work."

"What kind of spying happens in Vegas?"

"The fun kind," he said.

29

DALLAS

THE VENABLES' LIVING ROOM BLINDS SLICED THE TWILIGHT into amber bars along the floor. Irene had eaten a THC gummy and was reading a novel. Peter was listening to sauce popping on the stovetop, the bubbles dissolving with the smell of garlic and oil. "I want some before dinner," she said, jamming in the bookmark with a pleasant smile.

Peter looked at Irene. Then the sauce, already thickening. "It could use a few more minutes anyway." In a thunderclap she was done before the beep of the timer for the sauce: heavy breathing, legs trembling, sweat running down his back, the sofa cushions slowly rising from the spots where she'd dug in her fingers. She was laughing; Irene often laughed after they made love. It was a chesty laugh, and kind, as if she were startled by her own good luck.

They ate a quiet dinner in their underpants. A half bottle of white wine disappeared while she sat on the patio scrolling Instagram, Stalin on her lap. Peter popped an Adderall to girdle himself for a batch of crew-planning data he had been ignoring for weeks. Much later, with the chemical blinders subsiding, he pinched the bridge of his nose and looked up from his laptop to find that Irene was beside him on the couch, the television was rolling, and Stalin was asleep at her feet. It was midnight.

"Maybe time for a practice run," she said with her eyes glued to the television. "Low risk, ready the muscles again."

A flash memory of Oklahoma turned his stomach. Irene picked a bottle of nail polish off the coffee table and began working on her toenails. He had always enjoyed watching her do this. The precision and color were enchanting; most of all he liked how she rested her chin on her knee while she worked. He focused on the toenail-painting until the fog of Oklahoma had lifted and his nausea had wilted. She'd chosen an aquamarine-blue. A color he'd not seen before. Peter did not think he liked it.

PETER AND IRENE PURCHASED SKI MASKS AND GLOVES AND boxy sunglasses and booties and loose-fitting sweatshirts and tactical pants on a shopping excursion that concluded with a salad lunch in the cheerful food court at NorthPark Mall. "We are rare," Irene was saying, spearing a tomato on her fork. "We are rare, babe, because we are smart and capable and, more importantly, we are willing."

The next day was Monday, and Peter was in his cubicle deep in the airline's sprawling headquarters outside Love Field. He was finalizing a report on turn-time by station, but his eyes were glazed over. Irene's words echoed through him, and he realized he was struggling to square the Peter Venable in his mind with the man correcting an Excel formula error impacting Cell AB112.

THERE WAS A PANHANDLER WHO SLEPT UNDER AN INTERstate overpass not ten minutes from the Venables' house, but the man might well have been on another planet. The homes nearby were swaybacked and crumbling. Trash fluttered through the streets. The air was choked with urine and diesel and exhaust fed by the unceasing traffic rumbling above. Peter and Irene cased the spot for two nights, and on each found the pattern the same. By midnight he was wrapped in the same ratty sleeping bag. And he was always alone.

On Thursday night, after work, they ate pizza in silence standing over the kitchen island. Irene fed Stalin a morsel of crust, and Peter's mind drifted to morality, a topic that he'd never given much sustained thought. He was a numbers man. And now he ran through the numbers, gathering them, creating order from chaos, and in so doing, quashing the swells of anxiety that had been roiling his conscience all day. How many of these people would die of overdoses or random violence anyhow? How many had any family to mourn them? And this: How many Russians had died in the war? The world was random and senseless anyhow, and this was, let's be honest, small beans. It did not matter. This was a bug squashed in a remote jungle. A baby dies in the womb, in childbirth, a child drowns in a pool, a teenager is killed by a drunk driver, a man's heart gives out, he dies in his bed at ninety, he is stabbed as he sleeps—all the same. He put a whole slice on the floor for Stalin. Irene clicked her tongue, scolding him.

In the closet they changed into tactical pants and loose-fitting sweaters with gloves and ski masks in their pockets. "I will do it," Irene said, reviewing her appearance in the full-length mirror.

"Why?" he said. "I can do it."

The closet safe buzzed, the bolt slid away, and Irene removed the sheathed knife, sliding it into her pants pocket. "Because I want to," she said.

PETER DROVE. A SPOT OF URINE HAD LEAKED INTO HIS pants. His bladder ached, though he had emptied it twice before departing the house.

"I am having trouble breathing," Irene said. He stole a glance at her face, glowing beneath a stoplight. Under the tightness in her chest, he knew, lay excitement: the thrill of finding herself atop a roller coaster creaking toward the plunge. He tried to say something encouraging, but the words would not come out. His throat was constricting from pure terror.

When they reached the overpass, the place was empty. The man's shopping cart and sleeping bag were gone. "Oh for fuck's sake," Irene said, folding her arms across her chest. Peter drove off on the route they had planned, careful to remain under the speed limit. He looked over plaintively at his wife, who seemed to be reading his mind. "It's fine," she said, staring out the window. "We can skip the practice run."

"You're sure?" Peter could breathe again. He was ravenously hungry. He wanted to smile.

"Yes," she said, pouting. "It's fine. It will be just fine."

He stopped at a traffic light and stole another look at Irene. Blood was filling her cheeks, the beginnings of a hangdog look creeping along her face. "What's wrong?" he asked.

"Nothing."

"Irene?"

"Nothing. Just drive."

ON FRIDAY PETER FIRED OFF A FEW FINAL EMAILS AND Irene's day on Zoom ground to an exhausting end. They played a match of doubles tennis with the neighbors, Doug and his wife Lisbeth, freshly returned from Breckenridge. After the good surgeon and his wife made quick work of the hapless Venables, they all went for brisket tacos and Mambo Taxis and listened to Lisbeth slur out a long explanation of their troubles building the second home in Breck: Skyrocketing material prices, slow-motion contractors, workmen who never appear when they should. The problems are endless, guys, endless. She stopped complaining to polish off her Mambo. Peter was acutely aware of their lower position on the social totem pole. Doug was an entrepreneurial doctor with a degree from Stanford Medical School, two Porsches, three practices, and four generations of Dallas blood pumping through him. Lisbeth, a onetime nurse who hadn't worked since Doug finished residency, believed most of all in late-morning spin-bike classes. Her breasts had been expanded and renovated the prior year. Peter gathered it had been far less disruptive than the second home in Breck.

Peter politely agreed with Lisbeth, feigning outrage on her behalf as the woman recounted the difficulty of finding a decent contractor in Breck who knew how to properly apply Venetian plaster. He looked at Doug, smirking into his phone as if he'd dispatched a secretive fart beneath the table. Perhaps it was the alcohol, but in that moment Peter realized that for the first time he felt superior to this man. He knew a great secret Doug did not. He had found a wormhole in the social atmosphere catapulting him and Irene above these two absurd Americans, who were none the wiser.

To betray, you must belong.

I know what I am, he thought. And I'm not one of them.

AS HAD BECOME THEIR RITUAL, THAT NIGHT THE VENABLES streamed Russian state television through a VPN on Peter's laptop.

They watched a lively panel argue over the extent to which the Americans and their NATO pawns controlled the Ukrainian government. Answers ranged from mostly to completely. Later, a jowly man in a shimmering blue tie (an expert on American affairs) explained how the United States was already in a state of civil war, that the front lines were drawn deep inside every American heart, and that Russian purity, perhaps the soil itself, would ensure Moscow's strategic advantage in the generational and spiritual contest with Washington.

Directed to a new Russian blogger by one of the television commentators, Peter and Irene soaked another hour with videos of atrocities committed by the outlaw/Nazi Kyiv regime and margaritas from a mixer purchased that week from Williams Sonoma. There were dozens of clips displaying the bones of Russian victims: skulls, femurs, rib cages showered in dirt.

Over the second round of margaritas, Irene launched into a lecture about her great-grandfather, who had fought and killed Nazis in Russia, in the Ukraine, in Poland, and in Germany. He had seen some of the camps on the march to Berlin. "Nazi expansionism," she said, licking salt from the rim of her glass, "is historically and geographically determined. I say this as a Russian and a Jew." On the floor she crossed her legs; his gaze lingered on the pale skin at the last reaches of her thighs. "What will we tell our children," she said, "when they ask? That we lounged in Texas, playing tennis with Doug and Lisbeth, and did nothing while Nazis killed Russians—again!—on the borders of the motherland? That we did nothing while they dismembered and Nazified the Russian world and killed our boys in their own backyard?"

She wagged a menacing finger at her own question. "Your father is a janitor, Peter. And mine is a monster moonlighting as a mechanical engineer." Here Peter sat upright, because Irene did not like to speak of her father, she'd not seen him in a decade, since fleeing Sheepshead Bay. "But do you know what they have in common? They are cowards. When the going got rough, they fled Russia to play American. And, voilà: Minimum wage, maximum scorn. Your father"—this she sneered, she despised his dad—"with those absurd American flags fluttering from his minivan, and his civics lessons. His land of the free and home of the brave and apple pie shit! After all that, and do you know what? Doug and Lisbeth would need only to hear his ridiculous caricature of an accent, see his ruby alcoholic nose, or smell his bleachy dishwater smell, and they'd pin him as nothing but a low-rent drunken commie. We can do better. They came here for better lives and more money and they have nothing, really. In the end that's all they got. We can do what they would not. We can fight." She stood to address the margarita mixer. "I'm going to have another."

A volley of text messages deluged Peter's work phone, a fire drill on a document for a weekly executive review at Southwest. With Irene glued to the computer, Peter flicked open his work laptop to edit a PowerPoint deck. When he was done, he took a long run to sweat out the tequila, and as he jogged he said hello to a stranger walking a dog, he listened to the rustle of the neighborhood, and he noticed a rising anger at the indifference this world felt to his. He ran faster, down to the winding concrete path along the brown lake, under gnarled oaks. The last quarter mile home he ran in a dead sprint.

He crossed through the bedroom toward the bath, seeing Irene's face glowing pale in the light of the monitor. She'd turned up the sound on another battle video: grunts, screams, harried, exhausted bits of Russian. Another margarita sat full, sweating on the nightstand. Her jaw was locked, a cord of muscle flickering in her neck. She did not look up. He took a long shower and when he returned Irene was unmoved, the margarita still untouched, the sound of gunshots and explosions and screams trickling through the video. For a while he watched alongside her.

"The way we do it," she murmured, "will be, like, super-important. A message in itself."

"What do you mean?" Peter asked. Stalin, who had been curled up at her feet, jumped off the bed and whined by the patio door. Peter let him out.

"Some theater might help," she said. "I mean, it should be impressive, help draw their attention to us as serious soldiers. I'm not kidding, Peter. We can, like, make a splash."

30

LAS VEGAS

AFTERNOON IN VEGAS IS LIKE DAYBREAK AT A BAR: THE glitz and shimmer of the party long gone, replaced by muscular odors and sticky floors. All around the taxi was a living memorial to bad decisions: crumpled nudie flyers carpeted the sidewalks, a bewildered, suited man tripped over a bench at a bus stop; a party of four were face-down, asleep on their table at Denny's. The light flicked green, the cab puttered ahead, and when it turned onto the Strip, Sam felt like he was bumping up his driveway, coming home. For a season before joining CIA he had lived out here to play poker professionally. Vegas was, in fact, where a CIA talent spotter had first laid eyes on him, and it was where he felt most at home outside the Agency. He knew then, in a glorious strike of certainty, that once this work with Procter was done he would break it off with Natalie, spend some time with his family in Minnesota, and then move out here for good. See how it felt a second time. His CIA lives were used up. Time for another run of cards. The cab pulled past the Bellagio fountains, licking skyward into the clear bright desert sun.

HE DUMPED HIS SUITCASE IN HIS ROOM; HE WANTED TO GET his hands, quick as he could, planted on the felt of the Bellagio's poker room.

Sam played for hours, in communion with the cards and the table, enjoying the ballet inside him and the great pleasure of blotting out the noise and distractions of the casino and also his life: Natalie's phone call was answered with a text: "Sorry—can't talk now. Working." (A minute later, sensing he'd been too curt, he sent her a heart emoji before turning off his phone.) Then he was back in the tunnel, only to emerge, briefly, when the table conjured an image of sitting with Golikov in Singapore, and he stood for a stretch and a smoke outside. More cards soon flushed that unhappy memory, and he pressed on, up seventeen grand by the late evening and riding the warm feeling that he could not lose. Money wasn't the goal, it was just a way to keep score. Winning was the idea. And he was winning. For a run of about twenty hands Sam was sorely tempted to melt into Vegas for a few weeks, see how it might feel to put aside justice and revenge and duty and just live, were such a thing even possible.

Around dinnertime the Chief called. "Goddamn airlines. Well, I'm here and I'm hangry," she said. "Those big-ass buffets still a thing around this shithole of a town?"

BUFFETS, SAM WAS LEARNING, WERE VERY ON BRAND FOR the Chief. The Wynn's was in a soaring art deco atrium with bright red awnings covering the stations, green parquet marble floors, and chairs upholstered in silky gold plush. The Chief had arrived first, plopped at a table behind a sad couple bickering over their gambling losses and a gaggle of ladies fretting over a missing bride-to-be. When Sam sat down Procter said, "No offense, Jaggers, I know you're partial to this place, but this town is weird as hell."

"That's a bit harsh coming from a woman whose mailing address is literally in Gatorville."

She gave him a weird wink. "Let's put this buffet to work."

In truth he was not very hungry, but he assembled a thin spread of fish, rice, vegetables, and a lonely strip of prime rib. He slid back into the leather booth with a squeak. Procter returned with a heaping plate that seemed at war with itself: a multiethnic smorgasbord of an American cheeseburger and fries arrayed against Chinese egg rolls, some baklava, and a few scallops on the side caught in a spray of ketchup spattered across the plate like blood.

He took a bite of fish and smiled at one of the women. A redhead. Her smile showed a row of teeth: brilliant white, impossibly crooked.

"Woof," Procter said, turning back to Sam. "Can't un-ring that bell. And those jeans." Procter let out a soft whistle. "Those are the lowest-slung jeans I've seen in my life. Are they getting their vaginas lowered, now? Good grief. How's Natalie, by the way?"

"Same. Good."

"Those," Procter said, with a slice of a scallop, "are not the same thing."

"She's the same, then."

"I'm sorry to hear that. And I'm already on the record here, as you are well aware, but I will say it again, because for some stupid reason I care. Jaggers, just because she's dumb enough to fall in love with you doesn't mean you get to torture the sweet girl for sport. Or to assuage the guiltier regions of your midwestern conscience. Now, I get it. You can't help yourself. Your decision making is both checkered and fiercely dick-centered. But, please, leave the poor girl out of it."

"I don't know why I told you about Natalie," he said.

"Me neither."

The toothy redhead plopped a piece of paper scrawled with a phone number on the table as she sashayed past. Sam took it with a smile. Procter rolled her eyes. "Good grief," she said.

Procter was hacking away at an egg roll with a steak knife when Sam broke the news.

"They fired me."

A twitch of rage shook her face before it went blank. She looked down at her lap, where she kept her eyes for a long time before returning them to Sam. "When?"

"Tuesday."

"Who did it?"

"Gus was the messenger. Might have done it, too, for all I know."

"But you don't know who did it?"

"I don't know. Sweet signed the papers and Gus passed a message. I don't have any other fingerprints."

"And the reason?" Her eyes were wide and still stuck on her lap.

"Some garbage about how the pysch evals ruled out any future fieldwork, and they knew I wouldn't be happy unless I was in the field."

Picking up her knife and fork, Procter tentatively returned to her work on the egg roll. "Hard to figure how they would have made us, given the way we ran the tradecraft outside the building."

"Had to be the REMORA documents," he said. "But if anyone but the mole knew I'd taken those, well, they would have done more than fire me. And if the mole knows we took *those* documents . . ."

Procter pointed a forkful of egg roll at him. "This is good news. This is proof we are on the right path."

"Glad you think the unceremonious end of my career is good news, Chief. Hadn't thought about it that way."

"Well," she said, standing with her plate, "that's because you're the one who just got fired."

The buffet crowd had thinned out: the bordering tables and booths were empty. Across the room sat two old men and a table of college kids glued to their phones, making a racket. Sam refilled his coffee, and when he'd returned the kids had moved along, leaving behind a serene silence that was entirely off brand for this psychotic and beautiful town.

"You're not even going to ask me how I'm doing?" Sam teased. "Pretty insensitive, Chief, after what happened. And here I thought you were a people person."

"I hate people," she said. "Plus: Maybe put on your big boy pants? I'm supposed to inquire about your feelings? That's like asking a guy who's had his leg bit off by a shark, *How are you feeling about all this?* right after you haul him into the boat. You know how he's feeling? Like he lost a goddamn leg, that's how. I'm not a dumbass, Jaggers, I don't ask questions that have too many answers, or, worse, none at all."

He looked down at his plate. Smiled but didn't feel like it.

"But I'm not heartless," she said. "You want a job at Gatorville, you got one."

"Couldn't be worse than paper-pushing at Langley."

"Now you've got it. Say"—she stared off for a moment, her voice dropping to a whisper—"speaking of paper. Who was in the Backroom when you took the REMORA files?"

"The four of them. They were up there for a meeting. They all saw me in one of the bullpens."

"Anyone pay special attention?"

"Not that I noticed."

"But all four of them saw you? Gus, Mac, Theo, Debs? All of them? You're sure of it?"

"I'm sure of it."

They sat for a while in a flung-open silence, watching the ebb and flow of diners, listening to the faint jingle of the slots from the distant floor. The Chief made another strafing run through the rest of the buffet, returning with a lone chocolate muffin. A question had nagged for a few weeks and, unsure of how he might set it up, he simply let it fly: "You were all together that night in Afghanistan, that right?"

Procter, who'd brought the muffin to her lips, set it down without taking a bite. "That's right."

"Would you tell me what happened?"

Procter did not answer. Instead, she picked up the muffin and took a bite while gazing off at the prime rib station. Then she said: "You think you know someone, but you actually don't. There's something, or someone else, in there with your friend. And that other thing has been watching you for years, but you never knew it existed."

"Do you really believe one of them could be a mole?"

"Even now, not really. No."

He frowned at his coffee. "Why are you doing this, then?"

"Because one of them almost certainly is."

31

LAS VEGAS

PROCTER BUSIED HERSELF WITH THE MUFFIN FOR A FEW moments, her mind turning. Sam wanted to ask who she thought the mole might be. But he intuited that, though she doubtless had a front-runner, she would not share it with him, at least not yet. That perhaps the Chief was still reluctant to allow such speculation across her lips.

Instead, she began talking about Afghanistan. About her friends.

"In those days war zone tours were when, not if, kinds of things. And Gus was Base chief in Shkin. He lobbied for us to join him. I was divorced. Theo was divorced for the second time. Loulou was in one of her fugues, fine if Mac left the country for a while so she could sow her oats, which seems to happen about once a decade or so."

"But Sweet and Gosford weren't stationed there?"

"No. They were out for a short visit."

"Why?"

"They were going to see an asset. This was a decade after the Farm. Debs is Gosford's assistant and he's running the Counterterrorism Center at that point. Gosford wants to shake the hand of Shkin Base's best asset, guy who reports on Taliban plans and intentions. Gosford had played some role in recruiting him maybe two years prior, when he'd been in Kabul, though the details are fuzzy to me. So on a whim, really, they come out to our little claptrap frontline Base near the Pak border, our fort peeking into Indian country, hostiles all around. Gosford wanted to see this guy again, and he wanted to visit Shkin, but it wasn't the best meeting to drop in on."

"Why was that?" Sam asked.

"First item on the agenda was paying blood money for a donkey. Wait. Haven't I told you this story?"

"You have not."

She shoved her plate aside and leaned forward with her elbows on the table. "Two or so weeks before Gosford and Debs pop in, we had an engagement party at the Base for one of the case officers. Chick whose future first husband had proposed when she'd gone home for her three weeks of R&R. The aforementioned asset loaned us a camel and a donkey for the party. He'd no idea why we asked but he said yes. Well, the party went as it went, and of course everyone's shitfaced, well beyond the norm. Base had a legendary bar, Christmas lights up year-round, all the hats of the officers who served before us hung up on the wall. I left one of my Chief Wahoos for them. Anyway, we're drinking in the bar, then out in the courtyards, and we're doing camel and donkey rides. Camel bit Theo, if memory serves. Spit on Gus. Chucked Mac clean off his back.

But the donkey was a quiet sufferer. Apparently pretty old, too, because after we'd all had a ride, the bride did one final stroll through the Base on the back of the donkey, waving at all of us, kind of a Palm Sunday vibe, you know, except in this case the crowd's wasted and the rider is trashed and in a trashed wedding dress, and first time she waves to her adoring fans she tips right off the side and into the dust. Donkey goes over next, except he's dead. Keeled over. Killed by the bride-to-be. Right there at the damn party, in the middle of the CIA's Shkin Base."

"Dead, dead?" Sam said.

"As a doornail. Asset's pissed, of course. The donkey is a source of value. And we can't prove it was the old age that killed him. I mean, that played a role, there's no doubt. But so did the proximate factors. Hours of backbreaking work. And the bride wasn't so slim, you know? Point of this being that we had debts to pay. The meeting with the asset's scheduled for the evening of the day when I injected Debs's yogurt with the hot sauce. She's retched by that point, and she's come on back into the bull-pens with Gosford. There's a war party to get to the bottom of things. And Gus says, guys, look, I don't know shit—he said crap, it was Gus, after all—about this yogurt sitch (and that was true) but we've got an espionage business to run here, and a big meet tonight, and—"

"Camel was fine?" Sam interrupted.

"Not a scratch," she said. "Though of course we'd all wished the camel had died, what with the bucking and spitting and biting, and not the poor silent donkey, who'd been a real workhorse through the entire party. But there's no justice this side of eternity, and that's as true for Afghan livestock as it is for all of us. Where was I?"

"The logistics of meeting the guy . . ."

"Right," she said. "Gosford insisted that we all go. Something dumb about numbers making the asset feel warm and celebrated or some non-sense. And the relationship with the asset is fairly casual, which was true. He loaned us the camel and donkey, after all. Place is up in the mountains. Two Hilux pickups, bouncing around. All us old buddies from the Farm, riding silently and joylessly to pay off an Afghan for killing his donkey. Now, it's the Wild West out there in those days, so we're all ready for a gunfight, always and everywhere. Helmets and body armor and M4s and Glocks. Seven-man Afghan security detail. Back of the truck's an armory: single-shot grenade launchers, rifles, pistols, ammo. Debs and me in the backseat. After an hour she leans close, says she knows I did it, that I poisoned her, that she can't prove it but knows it was me. And I said, hon, if I'd done it you wouldn't be walking right now. That made her laugh, a nasty one, and we went back to our hateful silence until we arrived. Big metal gate out front. House is two stories of broken cinder blocks covered in mud. Nice little stand of pomegranate trees in the courtyard. Our security guys fan out. They've been here fifty times and there's a routine. Asset's going to be tickled because there are two people here from Washington. He's a big deal, merit-ing such thoughtful attention on account of his poor deceased donkey. We go inside, sit around a table on the floor on old silky pillows while tea is served. Gosford is talking him up like he's shouldering the load of Afghanistan's flowering Jeffersonian democracy. We're chatting all friendly, but I can feel that something is off with the vibes. I give him the pack with the donkey blood money, he puts his hand to his heart. Then, boom. Explosion outside, in the courtyard. Invades the ears first. I feel it in my teeth. Suicide bomber. One of the source's bodyguards. Blew himself up, along with four of our security guys, out near one of the pickups. Plan, we found out later—much later—was to take us captive. Or as many of us as they could get. But then it's chaos, right? Even now there are portions of my memory with holes blown clean through them; gaps I'll never fill because I can't really talk about it with them. Even Mac and Theo. I imagine a few psychologists and Security types are floating around who could reconstruct it all—just none of the people who actually went through it. For example, I remember a few of the big important set pieces to that night, clear as day. But lots of brain space is clogged with little useless details. Debs wearing a powder-blue hijab, blinking incessantly in the seconds after the blast. Theo flicking at the radio. Gus and Gosford sitting there in a stupor, looking helpless."

And here the Chief stopped for a moment. She ran her finger through a few crumbs on her plate and licked it clean.

"And Mac?" Sam asked.

She shook her head. "Lost him for a spot, there. Theo is shouting into the radio for the reaction force from Shkin, the helos. Twenty-minute ETA. A lifetime. Gus has gathered himself, and so have I. We peek out the kitchen door. The two pickups are mangled. Half the metal gate's been blown right off. Blood and barbecued human are streaked across the walls and the pomegranate trees. Gus takes a step outside, and squish. Still hear it, even now I can hear it. Squish. Like he'd stepped on an overripe orange. Squish. It's a hand. Human hand. Not sure Gus ever saw it, because the first baddie pickup truck is in through the hole in the gate. A round clips off the wall near Gus and he gets a bunch of concrete chips in his face. We turn back, head upstairs for the lay of the land.

"And it's chaos. Remaining three security guys. Me, Mac, Theo, Gosford. Gus—we weren't sure he could see at first because of the concrete in his eyes. Debs straggles up last. All of us, in that room.

Six baddie trucks down in the courtyard, a few of them mounted with Dushkas. They'd like to snag a few of us still breathing—a live CIA officer in Taliban custody, well, there's value there—but they know the air support's coming. These guys like to fight and they are not dumb when it comes to fighting. Some guy gets on a bullhorn and gives us, in pig English, a long message. Essence of which is: it'll go easier if we surrender and please come on downstairs. We check weapons and then radio the response team for an updated ETA. At last, we all sit there in some silent communion making peace with our gods, thinking about loved ones, or whatever one does when you've got a hunch this is the end. And—"

"What are you thinking, then, Chief?"—Sam, with genuine interest.

"I thought it would be a fine way to go. Six stars on the wall. Off to glory." Procter blinked.

And Sam blinked, expecting more, but she just looked at him for a moment before launching back in.

"So anyway, after an eternal three minutes we hear the screech of the bullhorn and the Talib says time's up. Last chance. Through the window one of our security guys gives our answer by lighting up one of their trucks with a grenade launcher, and all hell breaks loose. The Dushkas are rolling. Glass everywhere. Dust from the dissolving concrete hanging real thick. Security guy's legs twisted on the floor; rest of him painted across the walls. First breacher comes in. Gosford points his Glock and fires. Shoots himself in the foot. I see it clear as day. Future Director of the CIA shoots himself in the fucking foot. Mac sees it. No one else. Guy shot himself in the foot for the fucking Intelligence Star."

"Gosford," Sam interjected. He said the name tentatively, not wanting to throw Procter off course, but from an irresistible curiosity. "Just want to make sure I'm getting this right. Gosford not only shot himself in the foot, but he claimed he was shot by the Taliban? He lied about that?"

"Those aren't the same thing. I mean, he did claim later that the Talibs shot him. I don't think he lied, though. Or at least I'm not sure. You trust my recollection of this night, Jaggers, the story you're hearing?"

"Mostly."

"Well, it's rare, in my experience, for one person to have the truth to themselves."

"You got one, too, right?" Sam asked.

"What?"

"The Star."

"Yeah, we all did. Anyhow, Gosford goes down by his own hand. Gus kills the first Talib with his M4. Then the second. Debs is in a corner, screaming. Dushka rolls again, this time Theo goes down. I was sprawled next to him, and he's shouting. There's blood. Another volley, and I get a splinter, piece of the roof I'd bet, in my shoulder. Then things get patchy. Theo's lying on top of me, trying to cover my head. He was like me, at least then: he had no life other than this and his goddamn fish. He was ready to go, fine to sacrifice himself so more of us could live. He didn't save my life, but he tried, and I love him for it. Helos arrive, I can hear the buzz and the first of the explosions. They're lighting up the trucks. Blackout for a minute, two, maybe five seconds, I don't know."

She paused to tie up her hair. "Next I remember, I'm on my knees searching for a weapon and I'm staring at Debs's fancy shoes. Knees pulled into herself. Total shock. Didn't hate her for it then and don't now—it's understandable, isn't it, losing your mind in a moment like that? But it's the kind of thing you carry with you, to your everlasting shame, even if no one else puts that on you. You're gonna drag it along. She hated me. Hated me for the hot sauce, of course. Hated me for passing the Farm when she failed. Hated me for joining Mac and Gus and Theo and leaving her behind. And hated me even more that night for the cold fact that I saw that she'd been a coward. That I *knew*—and she knew—she was a coward. Not that I wouldn't have known even if I hadn't seen her like that. She was the only one unscathed. I mean, you look at a baseball team after a game and say, hey, eight of you guys are covered in dirt and grass and blood, and one of you is clean, did you even play the game? Or did you just ride the bench?

"Gus, though, is on the radio with the reaction force screaming that we're in the main house. Do not light us up. But we can hear a crew of Talibs below and there's an explosion outside the room, in the hallway.

Grenade. This time Theo is yanking me across the floor toward the back window. Didn't know it then, but I had a hunk of metal in my leg. Gus and Mac, I now see, are firing through the door. Gosford grabs Debs and they're moving toward the window. Slowly, mind you, on account of his stillborn foot. I don't hear anything for a minute. I just see moonlight shining through the holes in the roof. A few stars peeking through. Then I can make out the bleats of sheep. We're moving away from the doorway, Theo and me. Following Debs and Gosford."

Then, snatching a glance at her watch, she mumbled: "Shit, I'm rambling." She wiped her hands metronomically across her jeans as if, lacking a cigarette or a drink, they'd nothing better to do. Sam looked at her significantly, wondering what to say and how to say it. He had nothing, so he just asked how she made it out.

Procter said: "Theo got me on the roof. Gus and Mac behind. Gosford and Debs in the lead. We all jumped, in the end. I held hands with Mac and we jumped. The tibia shot out through my leg on the landing. I don't think I saw it happen, though. I just remember the X-rays at the hospital in Germany after the surgery. Because I was in so much pain, Mac was dragging me into one of the sheds. Little stone thing. Just him and I. It was madness. Reaction force was hitting the house after we'd jumped. I heard ringing and felt heat and my body was vibrating, my ribs shaking like someone's jerking on the jail bars. My tibia's jammed through my skin like a loose tent pole and there's a decent-size marble's worth of metal fragments in the leg. Courtyard is an inferno.

"I've got my head on Mac's shoulder and he's shouting into the radio. Talib appears in the doorway, lurching, clutching the frame. Half the face is charred black and looks like rubber. He's got a length of rebar jutting from his chest. He came here to escape the house. And, like me, he's decided it'd be swell to die as long as he takes a few of the opposition with him. So he points a gun at me. One of our Glocks, collected from the house, no doubt. Small detail, but critical. Root of the hatred between Mac and Gosford. Right here, in this moment, little twist of fate that Mac gets shot by one of our weapons, not some ancient Soviet thing or any of the other six hundred varieties of weapon loose in Afghanistan at that time. A Talib shoots Mac with an American Glock. And it gives Gosford air cover for his own claim about the foot. Equivalency. Both guys got shot with American weapons. We're both heroes, Macintosh. Bullshit.

"Anyway, Talib points it at me, and Mac rolls over my body, covering me, and three rounds slap into him. His head goes onto my shoulder, body limp and slack. And we're twisted up together and we roll on the floor. The shooter is slumped over in the doorway. Guy's got a foot of rebar in his stomach. Makes standing tricky. And I held Mac there, waiting to die. Eyes shut. When I opened them and saw we weren't dead I caught sight of the fucking Talib crawling our way. He wants another kill, something to chat about with his virginal mob that night in Paradise. I ease out from under Mac, unholster his Glock, and aim. First two rounds go high because my hand's vibrating like a tuning fork. Third nicks him, fourth sinks clean into his crown. I empty the rest of the mag, for insurance purposes. Big fucking mess."

The Chief wasn't looking at Sam anymore; she was looking down at her emptied plate. A strange thought intruded: He should stand up and give her a hug, or at least say something kind. But there was no precedent for that style of intimacy in their friendship, and, fighting his own good moral sense, he stayed planted in the booth.

"And then I crawl along," she continued—still fixated on the plate. "I scoot alongside Mac, my bum leg's dragging like a bloody windsock, and I held him and said I was sorry; for what, I didn't even know. I told him he was an asshole for not painting anymore. I told him he was an asshole, and so was Theo, for saving me and dying first, that your good friends deserve better, goddammit, don't leave me here, man, just stay with me, I'm going to keep on talking until they find us or kill us or someone rescues us. Hold on. Can you hear me? Goddammit. Your legs and back, man, they are not . . . it'll be fine. I know it. Fine. But you are a selfish prick, Mac, you know that? Jumping in front of me like some moron angel. I can feel your pulse, man, can you hear me? I am going to keep talking. I'm just talking. I've got my forehead on yours and I'm talking. Think about Loulou, think about me, think about that night in

Paris. Man, I hate Paris normally, you know? Sewer of a city, but that night . . . well, I'd go back for that. Maybe soon we go there. You can paint one of your stupid paintings. Maybe a nude of Loulou? We'd all like that. That's two votes yes, me and you, who cares what Loulou says? Mac, are you there? Man, please don't . . . don't go . . . do not leave me here, man. You stay here with my voice, man, it's me, Artemis. If you see light, don't walk into it, just turn around and walk back into the darkness. That's where I am."

32

LAS VEGAS

THE CHIEF'S STORY DID NOT END SO MUCH AS IT TRAILED off. Procter did not discuss the flight back to the Base. Nor did she offer any detail on what Sam knew had been a lengthy and excruciating rehab process in Germany. And she certainly gave no more hints about what had transpired in Paris, or when. But she did share a meaningful glance with him to say, *That's it, Jaggers, all done, forgive me my sins, et cetera*, and he said something meaningless and dumb, thanking her for telling him all that, which was what Dr. Portnoy had told him after he'd first shared about what transpired in Russia.

But it shook him because he'd never seen the Chief like this. Sad. The pain was practically pouring from her face. He was curious *why* she'd shared, though, but Sam knew the Chief well enough to understand that question wasn't going to be answered. She was done, and her face had begun the process of rearranging into its original self, which conveyed that if he asked for more he would be met with scorn, sarcasm, weird noises, and polite suggestions that he go fuck himself.

Procter stood, stretched, looked longingly out toward the casino floor. "Now, we're in Vegas. Let's soak in the tables, shall we? I've got a thirst going, too, and those barmaid chicks wandering around must have some gin in those cups. Let's have a look-see, while the night is young."

NEXT DAY THEY RECONVENED AROUND LUNCHTIME IN the Bellagio Starbucks to prep for the meeting with Frankie. Procter had arrived first, Sam a few minutes later, gingerly nursing a Gatorade. "You want something to eat?" she asked. "I missed you at the breakfast buffet this morning."

The poor guy could only wince and shake his head.

"I'll just go right ahead," Procter said. "You stop me if you're going to hurl or pass out."

He took a sip of Gatorade and offered a slow nod.

"Most defectors are washed-up batshit losers struggling with post-usefulness syndrome, drinking alone at a Red Lobster outside Des Moines, pushing paper in the back office of an insurance brokerage or something equally lame. Typically not a pretty picture. Frankie Potnick, née Fyodor Fyodorovich Trenin, known inside Russia House as IMPERIAL, is indeed batshit, but he managed to smuggle a decent chunk of family money out of Russia when he defected, and he's been putting it to good use here in Vegas ever since. The problem today is going to be focus. Linearity. Conversations with Frankie tend to bounce off in all manner of directions. Our job will be to prevent that. You okay?"

"Fine," he said. "Keep going. Refresh my memory on the case. I wasn't working Russia when he defected."

"Frankie, if memory serves, was recruited in London, then recalled to Moscow to serve as what he called a 'Political Technologist,' in the Kremlin. Whatever the fuck that means. The new access was interesting to us, he'd transitioned from a mid-level Ministry of Foreign Affairs flunkie to a Kremlin official with steady access to the upper rung. He was a risk-taker, an adrenaline junkie. Recruited because he liked the drama of playing spy and his moral compass had been smashed to pieces, if it'd ever existed in the first place. For a while we had a crazy Russian providing hard-copy planning documents and offering color on his interactions with the bosses inside the Kremlin. Frankie-slash-IMPERIAL knew who was up, who was down. He was the source of some primo reporting on Putin's COVID phobias and medical condition because he had firsthand access to people who spoke to the President in those wild years. The cat who spoke to you during your interrogation, Zhomov, well, Frankie bumped into him many years ago. I want to ask him a few questions about that."

Sam checked his watch and stood up. "What time is he picking us up?"

"Eight. Where are you going?"

"To take a nap."

EIGHT P.M.: THE STRIP A SLAB OF LIGHT STRETCHING ALONG the desert floor. The Rolls cruising toward MGM was gunmetal-gray, floors so plush they swallowed Procter's flats, ceiling sparkled with little pin-dot lights like the starry sky. Frankie was in the front seat with the driver, fiddling with a curated EDM playlist so obscure that even Procter did not recognize the tracks. They'd picked Sam and Procter up at the Bellagio and the guy had already swung chaotically between inane chatter and silence. Basic questions ("How's it going, Frankie?") went unanswered or were parried with winding nonsense.

The car turned off the Strip by a Denny's and then onto a darkened service road behind MGM. No signs, only dumpsters and the rusted pipes and boxes of the monstrous HVAC units required to maintain a comfortable seventy degrees in the desert. "I'd like to game tonight, a bit to excess, Charles," Frankie had said, addressing Sam with the throwaway work name Procter had provided. The line he'd taken out at the MGM meant a comped room at the Mansion, the unadvertised property where MGM put up its whales and high rollers and fishermen, the derelicts who wooed their whale friends to Vegas in the first place.

The gate rolled open, swinging the Rolls into a spacious courtyard with a large fountain at its center. No fewer than eight staff members were waiting—bellman, butler, porters, Frankie's smiling casino host in a well-cut pin-striped suit. Frankie stepped out and shook the host's hand and introduced him to Procter as Larry. They walked inside, through rooms decorated with plush furniture and dark wood, into a soaring glass-enclosed courtyard that smelled of grapefruit and bitter orange, gurgling with watercourses, dotted by citrus trees and cypresses and shrubs. It was serene, the chaos of Vegas receding behind them. Even Jaggers, for all his experience in this town, looked impressed by the oasis.

Frankie confirmed his $3 million line with Larry and then asked him to leave. "Bad luck," Frankie said. "Larry not so good for my games. Larry is an icer, holy shit. Villa Eight," he said, pointing as they strolled through the courtyard toward his room. "Tiger Woods sex parties, old times."

Procter had hoped for a few minutes to talk in the room, away from the casino and its cameras, but when the door opened they were greeted by a woman: blond, maybe six feet tall in her heels, wearing the uniform of a French maid, clutching a bottle of champagne.

"Jeepers," said Procter. "Your tits are hanging out."

The woman, her eyes darting from Procter to Sam, landed on Frankie, shooting him a doleful glance while knotting up her top.

"Uh . . ." Sam said, watching the woman, "Frankie? I . . ."

"Frankie, nice as this all is," Procter interjected, "can you have her scram for a while? We need, like, a half hour, as I've said. Not long."

"Sophie is a good-luck charm, she must stay," Frankie said, talking straight past her. They trudged around Sophie deeper into the room, which was far larger than any house Procter had ever, or would ever, own. Sam pulled alongside her and whispered: "I've seen versions of this Vegas story before. It doesn't end with a short conversation."

Sophie poured champagne and handed Frankie a pill, which he swallowed.

"Goddammit," Procter muttered.

They sipped champagne, sauntering down a long hallway lit by Moroccan lanterns, garnished with pots of fresh orchids and lilies. In the cavernous living room Procter noticed that the suite had its own pool, and that three more girls were in there, laughing and drinking champagne from their own bottles, calling for Sam to join them. Jaggers demurred, instead standing with Procter like two idiots in the living room while Frankie changed. He emerged in a gray pin-striped suit and under the lights in the pool room Procter could see that the pinstripes were actually comprised of small letters spelling FUCK YOU, on repeat, across the fabric.

"We game a bit," Frankie said, looking through Procter toward a mousy brunette heaving an exquisite chest from the water. "Then, talk."

LATER, PROCTER WOULD REMEMBER ONLY FRAGMENTS OF the night. Sitting beside Frankie while he played hundred-thousand-dollar baccarat hands in his own room of the private casino, the Russian tugging up his shirt to flash his bare belly at the dealer before jerking Procter into a bear hug with each win. Wondering throughout what pill Sophie had given him: Adderall? Ecstasy? There was Frankie at the cage, asking for thirty grand in cash, then bouncing on his heels in front of her, out through the Mansion atrium, under the art deco glass, through the wall of citrus, past four attendants, into whose palms he crushed wads of hundred-dollar bills, and into another waiting Rolls. They were at a nightclub. XS, it was called. About right. Frankie was twisting cash into the hand of a doorman he called Baby Jesus and then again into the massive paw of the Samoan bouncer at the entrance to their table, which overlooked the dance floor below. The sound inside, even to Procter's EDM-abused ears, was overwhelming to the point where the noise tipped into a ringing silence, as though she'd been hit by a shock wave from a blast. Soon hearing, touch, smell, taste, any attempt to think, all other senses and experiences, any idea that she had a history before she'd plunked onto a couch in this club, it was all gone. The world was the crowd and the crowd was ripping its collective face clean off. She watched Frankie dance on the ledge by their table. She watched Sam dance with an auburn-haired girl. She watched a few people tip off the ledge onto the tables below, where a lunatic was waving around a giant American flag. She remembered the night sky twinkling above her as they cruised back to the Mansion, ears still ringing, girls screaming.

They were walking over a terra-cotta floor, and there was piano music. They marched through the gargantuan atrium, the scent of citrus returning, the world serene except for the tinnitus, and they crossed the path toward Frankie's room and he tripped over a low wall and toppled, buns overhead, a felled log, smack into a koi pond, and Procter remembered that one of the bellmen had said these were sensitive fish, quite old in fact, and that made her wish Theo was here, and Frankie was squirming and shouting in the water. Through the haze came the sound of fins slapping and sloshing, and the Russian stood in the pond, his suit soaked clean through, looking to the glass enclosure above, and he cast a spout of vomit into the night sky, his eyes shut as if in prayer.

33

LAS VEGAS

BY THE TIME PROCTER STUMBLED PAST IN THE LATE morning, the fish pond was drained and there were a few guys in there wearing waders that said: HOUSEKEEPING SERVICES BIOHAZARD TEAM. Procter got a table at the restaurant off the atrium and ordered coffee. In her pocket were the photos lifted from the REMORA files and Petra Devine's unofficial stash—the only documentation she'd brought for this chat. Frankie appeared, alone, an hour later. Sam a few minutes after that, looking awful; perhaps worse than when CIA got him back in Vienna. A night with Frankie had wrecked Jaggers as thoroughly as a hostile Russian interrogation. For a long while they ate a Vegas breakfast: midday, indoors, sunglasses, silence.

"Where's the annual ledger on your gaming after last night, Frankie?" Procter asked on her third cup of coffee.

"Perhaps close to even," Frankie said. "Fuck, who knows?" He sipped his coffee, grimaced, and snapped for a lychee martini. The waiter brought the drink, and Procter clinked her coffee mug to his glass.

"We can do this in Russian if you want," Procter said, in Russian. "But regardless of the language, you need to talk to me, Frankie. Or I am going to murder you."

Frankie did not respond, or even nod. He called to the waiter for steak and eggs.

"I want to talk about the SVR's Special Section," she said, also in Russian. "Few basic questions. I put up with last night's gong show for this."

Frankie paled at another sip of the martini. He pressed his palms into the table; Procter worried he might fall out of his chair.

"This is a friendly chat," Procter said. "Off the record. No recording devices. No cables on the back end. No paper."

He took another sip of his martini. His hands floated low, to the table, while his eyes soared to the glass crown of the atrium. "Does Charles speak Russian?" Frankie jerked a thumb at Sam.

"Not so much," she said.

"English fine," Frankie said, in English. "And, look. I told your people all about Special Section when defect. Three years now, Artemis. Information"—here he paused for a moment to consider the appropriate word—"elderly. And I drink. So much I drink. Erase brain."

"Oh yes," she said. "Fully aware, Frankie. Let's test it, though, eh? Stir that cranium stew for a few minutes, give me a spoonful?"

He licked foam from his lips. "Okay, Artemis and Charles, fine. Fine. Where I start?"

"Beginning," she said. "You start at beginning."

"Okay," Frankie said, with annoyance and a long pause, as if he could barely remember where the beginning might be. "Maybe four years ago SVR reorganize. They lose primo Euro sources. So they do, eh, how do you say, eh . . . gopher hunt."

"They what with gophers?" Procter said.

"A hunt for a gopher," Frankie said, "A gopher hunt."

"What's a gopher hunt?" Sam asked.

"To find spies," said Frankie.

"Ah, you mean a mole hunt," Procter said.

"Right," Frankie said. "Right, right. Mole hunt. Mole hunt. Mole hunt"—his mouth widened with each *o*, as if he might swallow it. "And here they find nothing, but still few poor bastards get shot. Make point. But executive brass say we gotta fix some shit, we gotta plug leaks in departments, and how we gonna do that? When you gotta problem in America, waddya do? More committees. Russia same. So they rip key sources out of Line KR. Out of American Department. Out of Fifth Department. On and on. Give them to old bastard ratfuck named Rem

Zhomov. Clever. Big brain. Old school. He a general but operational. Rare, very rare. But he have SVR Director's ear. He do work because he love, you know? He love the work. And he become proposer of new theory, new idea. He say, look, we want two big things. We wanna know what Americans up to. Basic intel. Plans and intentions, whatever. Two: We want wreck America itself. Active-measures shit, you know, I see in eyes you know, why you come to Las Vegas for this? You know."

Frankie looked toward a gardener pruning a tree inside the atrium. A lime had bounced from a branch to roll along the paving stones.

"This is why we're here, Frankie, keep going," Sam said. "We paid our dues last night, so you keep on rolling."

"Fine, fine, Charlie, fine and dandy"—said with menace. "Well, Zhomov, he huge prick, always looking for the fuck-over, that how you say it? He grab the good cases from the departments and lines and run them from Special Section. He snaggled the best handlers and bring them to Special Section. Honcho budget. And he careful, too. Separate network inside SVR, okay? No mixing. Special Section not appear on documents. This why when I defect they accuse me lying, you see? The Section like ghost. Whispers." He brought a finger to his lips and blew across it.

His food arrived. Procter couldn't make eye contact with the eggs and it didn't look like Sam could, either. Frankie slid the martini away, bracelets and watch jangling over hairy wrists as he unrolled silverware from the napkin. "Russian special services fight like any other place," he said. "That how I came to hear whispers and meet Zhomov and some his guys. SVR pissed at FSB, not new thing, yes, but SVR little shit brother to FSB cousins inside Kremlin. Lost at everything. Potato chip on shoulder, yes, that how you say?"

"Yes," Procter said, "exactly right. Potato chips on the old shoulders. Go on."

A few seconds passed as Frankie chewed his steak, then he said: "SVR crave seat at table. FSB big gorilla, SVR want weapon shoot gorilla, maybe put head on wall, turn foot into garbage pail, fur to rug, all that."

In his past life, Procter remembered from the cables, Frankie had fancied recreational poaching on his African safaris. Sam lifted his coffee to his lips. Then, thinking better of it, set down the untouched mug and just stared at it as Frankie went on.

"Special Section trot down Kremlin to advertise," Frankie continued. "And Zhomov say to us, look, fellas, we got shit in America. The CIA sometimes catch big Russian fish, we get hooks into little guys. Bottom-feeders. Military guys on coke. Douche at thinking tank. Congressional staffer hiding gayness. And, fine, he admitted, no need turn them away, right? We take what we get. But we need group of snipers. Long shots, low chance. But if we getta hit, head explode on impact. Important heads. I speak metaphor. Not wet work. Special Section no murder shop. Special Section chasing big American pelts to recruit. Using best officers. And patience."

Frankie's tone had become respectful, Procter noticed, a reluctant reverence for Zhomov.

"See, Ms. Artemis, common knowledge in Kremlin that half of SVR reports are bullshit. Sorry, no. Like eighty percent. Mostly bullshits. It like this in CIA? Of course. Big organization full of humans. You got humans, you got problems. Tough shit. Special services expected to produce reports. Intelligence." Here he inserted air quotes. "And so SVR officers provide what asked for. Reports. Paper. Quality not priority concern. Priority is numbers. And this disgust Zhomov. He say in his pitch, look, we get two, three sources with real access and there's business. But we gotta be patient. Gotta look for the right prospects. Gotta point at right target. Sniper, not shotgun, he say this, the clever ratfuck." Here Frankie squeezed the trigger on his imaginary rifle, aiming straight through Procter, toward the lime tree.

Frankie pushed aside his half-eaten meal and snapped for another lychee martini. He'd stopped talking to watch a woman walk through the atrium. Another silence descended upon the conversation.

"You said part of the section's work was active measures," Sam said. "How's that different from any other shop at SVR? Everyone thinks about the espionage business that way out in the Forest."

Frankie drank half his martini upon arrival, wagging a no-no finger as he wiped his mouth. "Not that way, different. Different methods. Patience. Zhomov say, look, guys, what rat out Ames and Hanssen? They work for us, our best boys, now they in prison or dead. We give CIA and FBI bread crumbs when we snatch up hard and fast. Americans are decadent but not stupid. Shoota bunch of spies and CIA feels Moscow penetration. They search based on access. Hard to find goph-, I mean moles, but not impossible, and maybe not so hard when we arrest twenty at once. We blow our source. No, Zhomov argue for patience. He say we recruit, we develop. We not be dumbass, go slow. We protect monster sources. He say goal, ultimately, is destruction of CIA. Has to be, Frankie said, and guys, everyone in briefing is nodding, smiling. Destroy CIA? Well, now they eat from Zhomov palm."

"Did Zhomov say," Procter asked, "how they would target the Americans? Or run them?"

Frankie's head was caged in the fingers of his hand; through them he dueled with the idea of finishing breakfast. Scraping up a tentative forkful of jiggling egg, Frankie said that Zhomov had offered little by way of detail, but that he'd emphasized the quirks of running fellow intelligence officers as sources. "Zhomov preach idea that intel guys different cookie jar," Frankie said. "Blackmailed Congress staffer gets website where he types shit. Intel guy's not gonna say yes because he know better. He know about SVR fuckups. Gonna say fuck off on the commo. Zhomov saying this because he trying to steal officers and budget from other departments, and chiefs there fighting his ass bigly. Zhomov say, look, guys, we have some success and handling gonna be different. Gonna take more people. Gonna take more steps. Gonna be slower. Don't push my ass, Zhomov pretty much say, not much nicer. He say you want results, you pay for it. And I gonna give you results. Don't push my ass."

And at this point, Procter, knowing the answer but still compelled to make the journey, asked: "Did Zhomov have any assets inside CIA?"

Frankie drained the martini. Snapped for another. "Ms. Artemis, I spend three months in house by D.C. I talk to hundred you people: job, friends, family, enemies, rumors, Kremlin floor plan, houseplants in Putin office. You think I forget if Zhomov say he had someone? No, waddya think I hiding? No, Zhomov had no one back four years ago. He starting Special Section then. He come for money and show us how he badass. No moles then. Early days."

"Zhomov's crew," Sam said. "You remember them? His guys?"

Frankie, stirring his fork aimlessly through the food, made a wet noise and said: "Same answer, Charles, I told your people the names I knew. All in the reports. They show me stack of pictures and I try my best."

"I'll try again," Procter said. "How do you know if someone is Special Section? There's no org chart, right? No paper trail connecting someone to it?"

"Bingo," he said. "Zhomov tap officers from the lines and departments to work for him. He use guys from all departments, but they not Special Section on papers, just in reality."

"I brought pictures," Procter said, "of a few guys." From her purse she spread a line of five photographs. "Mind humoring me, Frankie? I know your brain is a boozy mush and all, but I'd like you to tell me if any of these handsome gents are fellow travelers with Rem Zhomov."

The martini arrived; he raised it toward the glass ceiling before emptying it in a single pull. Now, as he regarded the line of photos, a shadow seemed to cross his face, perhaps the recognition that he was now on the verge of crossing over from rehashing old background to offering something far more direct and dangerous, and for which, if word were to travel to Moscow, he might find himself in the crosshairs. Frankie put his head down on the table and pretended to snore.

"Or maybe," Procter said, scooting in her chair to speak directly into his ear, "I have your handler-turned-babysitter make a few calls around town. Throw a wrench into your gaming habits. Look at whether you're paying taxes on all those winnings. Or maybe I go into that flop house of a villa and shake a few of those nice ladies awake, see if anyone wants a couple grand to tell a bunch of casino hosts you've been handsy, grabbin' cooches and whatnot. Hell, maybe you've got a problem, Frankie, you're a serial grabber of high-end cooch, and there are just going to be bunches of ladies coming forward with awful stories about this high roller putting sweaty paws on them, and you know what's worse, he says his name is Frankie but he sounds like a Russkie. Sweats like one, too. Smells of onions and beets and vodka. Oh, it'll be gut-wrenching stuff about exploitation and hush money and Russian imperialism and the goddamn patriarchy. Bad for Frankie Potnick, your American alter ego. And bad for the Fyodor inside Frankie's skin. The kind of incident that gets your picture in papers that could find their way to the Kremlin. Putin might take a gander and say: *That snake is in Vegas.* Maybe he gets someone to come out here and wet your shorts with nerve agent or, if they're in a more traditional mood, toss you from one of the Sky Suites over at the Aria. Splatter you like a pizza flung onto the Strip during a rager."

Frankie raised his head, thin smile trickling across his face. He ordered another martini and the waiter's eyebrows fluttered with shock, then sorrow. Head hung, he tramped off to the bar.

"You born wrong place, Ms. Artemis," he said. "Shoulda been Russian."

"*Roditely e Rodinu ne vyberaut,*" Procter said, and shrugged. You don't pick your parents or your motherland.

Frankie stared at the pictures, working up the courage, the skin around his eyes stretching and quivering while he reviewed the lineup. Procter could not tell if one of them had caught his eye but he was unsure, or if the faces drew him back to the nightmare of his defection, or if he knew straightaway and could not decide if he should speak the truth. His fingers wiggled in the air, curling into a fist that he rubbed along the polished table as if working out a stain. For a long while he wrestled with himself in silence.

"Him," he said at last, tapping his finger on one of the photos.

"Know what he did for Zhomov?"

"Old hand in the Fifth, I believe. Odd jobs. Fixer. He close to Zhomov. He and Zhomov boys together in Petersburg."

"How sure are you?"

"Mostly."

"You looked for a good while to be fully sure, if you don't mind me saying, Frankie. Kind of dragged that out."

"I was thinking of lie."

"Couldn't manage one?"

"Brain is mush, as I say. Arrivederci, Ms. Artemis and Mr. Charles. I cover breakfast. Adios." Frankie called the wrong villa number to the waiter and slipped away, out the atrium and toward the pool.

IN PROCTER'S ROOM THE PHOTO FRANKIE HAD SELECTED sat on the desk alongside a clump of hair ties she'd excavated from the bottom of her suitcase. The picture, a headshot, included her short caption at the bottom: *Rodion Vissarionovich Pletkov, Colonel, SVR, Fifth Department (Europe).*

REMORA. An old Zhomov disciple.

Tangles within tangles, she thought, and wondered if she had ever been more tired.

SAM AND PROCTER SAT DOWN IN HER ROOM AND FOR THREE hours they went through it all, front to back. They knew Theo had lied, for instance, about the batting order for the March meeting with REMORA in France, and worried that an innocent explanation was unlikely; they knew that Theo, Mac, and Gus had offered differing versions of the arrival order that also veered off from the cable record; they knew that REMORA was one of Zhomov's men; they knew that Debs had booted Petra Devine from CIA for questioning the REMORA case and kicking up shit about a molehunt; they knew that Mac had not mentioned his stopover visit to New York Station and the briefing with Gus and Debs; they knew Gus had FISA on him after Moscow and might still now; they knew Debs had gotten the White House hooked on the intel and used the addiction to burnish her credentials. Lastly, they knew that the mole was still operating: they could not interpret the Tarrman roll-up and CLAW disappearance any other way.

What they did not have, plainly, was any hard proof. Certainly nothing that two disgraced officers could bring forward in hopes of being taken seriously. "And, to be frank, Jaggers," the Chief said, "I don't think we're going to get it. I think we have reached the limits of these little chats."

And so Procter proposed—and Sam agreed—that they slink to their separate corners. She to Florida, he to Northern Virginia, in a kind of ritual time-out to figure if they might take an alternate, and far riskier, path. That road, they both knew, would shift the trajectory of their investigation: from a series of innocent-seeming discussions—with some thin veneer of operational cover for each—to a real-world interference in CIA operations that would do far worse than just blow exhaust across their faces if it backfired.

Sam also sensed, but did not say, that the Chief had not yet come to terms with the fact that a good friend had betrayed her—betrayed them all. Had the notoriously unsentimental Procter's clarity of vision been blurred by a suspect list made up of her old friends? Perhaps some distance was required before that grim reality could cover the chasm between the Chief's head and heart. Sam had noticed, for one damning example, that throughout their debrief, the Chief refrained from merging the conclusions of her chats in Virginia with the golden nugget gleaned from Frankie: If REMORA was one of Zhomov's men, that made REMORA the likely handler of the mole. The case was inside out.

Sam knew that Procter knew this; in fact, he suspected that she'd had the point nailed before coming to Vegas. But her deflated countenance now suggested that she had gathered here the exact opposite of what she wanted: she had confirmation. "I'm going to piece it through for a spot," she said. "I'm gonna meditate, then scrub the grime of this godforsaken city off my skin so the smell doesn't get me tossed off the plane. You be good and break it off with Natalie. But let her down gently, for god's sake, like you're terminating a swell agent who's been damn good to us. You know the script, plus she deserves better than you. It's a no-brainer. Now get the hell out, I'll be in touch."

34

DALLAS / FORT WORTH / EL PASO / THE BIG BEND COUNTRY

HISTORY TEACHES US, IRENE EXPLAINED, THAT SOLDIERS of Russia must often fight without rations, weapons, or training. We are fortunate to have money, she said, and what of our good food and comfortable shelter? Impossible luxuries to the Russian soldier. And the Venables' inexperience? It would be overcome. Assassination was a trade; they would become master craftsmen. "And we are lucky, Peter, that our fight will not occur in the dead of winter," Irene said, crouching to pull the margarita mixer from a kitchen cabinet.

Around the end of their second round of drinks they settled on a bomb: the preferred weapon of the revolutionary, an act of theater, and a practical means to create distance from the act, so, as Irene put it, "We might live to fight on." Peter had found the tipsy chatter about a bomb thrilling, but the notion of an endless fight overpowered the nervous excitement gifted by the tequila, leaving him merely nervous.

It was slow going at first. The decision to use a bomb was not without complications, but, as Irene had become fond of saying, they had been chosen for this work because they could solve problems, navigate obstacles. "They trust us because we will, like, figure it out, babe." They downloaded a manual drafted by Al Qai'da's branch in Yemen (already translated into English) and perused dark web vendors hawking classified PDF scans of U.S. military bomb tech "lessons learned" from Iraq and Afghanistan. Together they watched dozens of hours of YouTube videos on electrical circuits. They endlessly debated the parameters: delivery device, explosive type, detonators, circuitry.

At work Peter massaged PowerPoint presentations and tweaked Excel models and suffered through hours of pointless meetings. He was bored. But this project had quickly ballooned to devilish complexity, and, much to Peter's surprise, he found it exhilarating, challenging. Because what was this, other than the greatest challenge of their lives?

IN TEXAS, THE ONLY RESOURCE MORE PLENTIFUL THAN land is weapons.

Peter left his cubicle at the airline on a Friday afternoon and by dinnertime he and Irene were strolling among the Fort Worth Gun Show's twelve hundred vendors inside the Will Rogers Center. At the A-Jack Knives table they purchased two Amtac Northman blades. At the Texas Shoots table: two SIG Sauer P320 pistols, a .30-06 Springfield rifle, and several boxes of ammunition. They paid in cash, flashing their driver's licenses for proof of Texas residency, but, because many of the vendors were selling—legally—as unlicensed hobbyists, the Venable name and address would not be connected to the weapons inside any official database. Peter also bought a box of fifty empty .30-06 casings and three pounds of black powder. Because sometimes, he told the vendor, in a speech he had practiced with Irene, he just preferred packing his own ammunition. Big smiles all around. They loaded everything, all purchased legally, into a U-Haul trailer attached to their mud-spattered Mercedes SUV and spent the night at the Fort Worth Sheraton, toasting the day's shopping spree with a nightcap at the Reata bar.

Next morning, a shopping run around Fort Worth. REI. Home Depot. Multiple mom-and-pop hardware stores. AutoZone. Two drugstores. Target, where a generous under-the-table tip to the assistant store manager secured a mannequin wearing mom jeans and a graphic T-shirt decorated with flowers and a message that read: DREAM YOUR LIFE. At every stop they paid cash, wore bulky N95 masks and ball caps, and used hand sanitizer, liberally and theatrically, to complete the picture. At some Peter went inside, at others Irene. Their license plate, as with most of the vehicle, had been caked in mud.

By late afternoon they were heading west. The sun flared blood-red and collapsed into the flattening horizon. Neither had ever been to the Texas west of the Brazos River.

Peter's spirit rose as they crossed into the rolling prairie, the sky opened, and the land began stretching away in every direction. Windmills and cattle dotted the grassy brown pastures, the trees thinned with each passing mile, and the barrenness, the desolate grandeur, overtook him. The motherland made him feel like this, Peter thought, remembering a summer drive east from Nizhny with his uncle. The land was wild and open. They'd driven for hours and all around them was Russia. It had folded him inside of her, cradled him in her womb.

THE EL PASO GUN SHOW IS A TWO-DAY AFFAIR CELEBRATING guns, ammunition, and explosives in the El Maida Shriners complex.

The Venables had come for Tannerite, which Peter had spent dozens of hours researching online. It is a binary explosive: fueled by aluminum powder and titanium; oxidized by ammonium nitrate and perchlorate; popular in target practice. Peter now knew almost everything about it, from chemistry on up to practical application. After mixing the fuel powder with ammonium pellets, and when struck by a high-velocity round, it will explode, producing a bang and a puff of smoke. Peter, adopting the persona of an avid sport-shooter, had called a dozen participating vendors to confirm Tannerite would be for sale on-site.

As Peter and Irene wandered among the stalls—N95 masks and face shields eliciting a mix of irritation, derision, and amusement from the crowd—they came upon a vendor selling explosives: grenades, black powder, and, yes, he said, Tannerite out of the back of one of his box trucks behind the stall. "I'd like to load up," Peter said. "I've got about twenty guys coming to the ranch to shoot here in a few weeks. What's the limit?"

"No limit," the man said, giving Peter an unfriendly stare. "But why are you wearing that face shield, anyway?"

"Wife's going through chemo. Doctor's orders. I know we look like freaks."

The vendor's face sank. "Oh jeez, I'm sorry, man." There were no more questions after that.

That night, in an El Paso Super 8 near the airport, Irene fell asleep in minutes, but Peter churned the sheets, fretting about the gear in the trailer. Next morning, after two large cups of lousy coffee apiece, they began driving south, toward a ranch property they had rented in the Big Bend country.

THE MAIN HOUSE WAS TWO STORIES, A WHITE-PAINTED adobe with a red roof nestled into a grove of pinyon pine and juniper in the northern reaches of the Big Bend. The view from the wraparound porch carried across lowland pasture until it met a rocky ridgeline across the valley. Peter and Irene drank coffee and watched the sunrise. They'd work from the back; there was a large concrete surface for cleaning game, nestled into the trees and boasting a high pavilioned roof. The nearest property was miles away, but the privacy afforded by the foliage was nonetheless comforting. He pulled the car onto the concrete block, opened the trunk, and set up the folding table that would function as his workbench.

Irene gave him a kiss and trekked out to scout the property for test sites. Peter decided to start with the initiator. With frequent references to the classified manuals and YouTube videos, he drilled two small holes in the bottom of an empty .30-06 casing. He checked to ensure the casing was clean and bone-dry. He packed in black powder, crimped the opening, and sealed it with epoxy. He placed it in the sunshine to set.

For a moment he thought about how his Southwest colleagues were spending their weekends: kid's sports, brunches in Uptown and on Lower Greenville, the Financial Planning and Analysis weekly pickup volleyball game, every Sunday at noon, on-site at headquarters in the shade of planes taking off and landing. He looked at the carload of supplies and the initiator and laughed. They were all dumb sheep. Selecting a rock playlist, he cranked up the volume on his phone.

He assembled one of the large cardboard boxes and evaluated the dimensions.

Next, the circuitry. From the bag purchased at a Fort Worth hardware store he removed Gorilla glue, a clock, a two-inch knife pin, a metal hacksaw, and a file. He cut and filed down the knife pin. When the clock struck twelve, the minute hand would kiss the metal of the pin. He glued it to the clock.

Then, cursing himself, he realized he should have tested the initiator without the powder. He drilled two holes in the bottom of another .30-06 casing, then ran two leads through the holes so they jutted into the brass like tines on a fork. He ran those leads to the battery. There was a small, glinting spark inside the casing. Yes, hell, yes.

"Going well?" Irene smiled as she walked up.

"We have a spark," he said, looking up from the table.

She clapped and gave him a kiss. "What can I do?" she said. He pointed to a pile of boxes. Irene began unpacking the magnesium bars from the firestarter kits, the steel balls, and the shanks of nails. The magnesium was pyrophoric. Inside the blast radius, anything flammable would be set alight. An insurance policy, they had decided, to increase the odds of success.

While Irene arranged the magnesium and shrapnel in the box, careful to leave room at center for the bucket of Tannerite, Peter labored over the trembler device. The clock would count down ten, maybe twenty minutes—enough time to clear out—and the minute hand would hit the knife pin, completing the first circuit. When the target moved the box, the trembler device would complete the second circuit. Then the box goes boom.

From a drugstore bag he collected a syringe and cut off the needle, so all that remained was a plastic tube. As he had with the casing, he carefully drilled two small holes in the top, pulled two leads through, then glued them in place. He slipped a steel ball inside the syringe and cut a small wedge of plastic to fill the open end. Then he took two thin strips of wood and glued those to the syringe so it would sit level, like a ship in a bottle. He set up one of the smaller cardboard boxes and taped the syringe to the bottom. He practiced: picking up the box, sliding, dropping. The bearing rolled nicely. He taped it inside the bottom of the larger box.

Now the circuitry. He again watched one of the more helpful YouTube videos and Irene read aloud from a classified manual on the iPad as he worked, laying it out on the concrete like a spaghetti diagram.

When he felt confident in the wiring, he said, "We can do the last bit at the site."

Packing the bomb materials, a hundred-foot length of rope, and the mannequin into the car, they set off for the test site Irene had selected. To his consternation it was flanked by a screen of trees. "Irene, we might start a forest fire," he murmured. "The magnesium."

Irene slipped off her sunglasses and looked around. She bit her lip. "Shit," she said.

They trundled around the property for another hour searching for a suitable spot, finally settling on a patch of treeless valley floor nestled into a rocky crumble at the base of a ridge. Peter filled the bucket with fifty pounds of the Tannerite. He closed the lid and slipped the powder-filled casing inside, through a hole he had drilled, checking to be certain it was snuggled into the explosive and that there was sufficient wire peeking out the back end to close the circuit. The battery went into the box alongside the bucket of Tannerite. Peter wound the rope around the cardboard, securing it with several hastily tied knots. Irene stood the mannequin next to the box.

His hands were shaking while he completed the wiring. Irene's face was rosy when he first looked up at her. Next time he met her gaze her cheeks were flushed, and by the time he was finishing they almost looked bruised. "Focus, baby," she whispered. "Almost there. You are crushing it."

When he was done, he turned the clock hands with his fingers to give them twenty minutes. He slid the clock into the box and for a breathless second took in the stillness, the caw of a distant crow, the rustle of long grass flattening in the wind. Irene set a timer on her phone, and they gathered the rope and hiked up a low rise until they ran out of length and it pulled taut.

They were seventy, eighty feet from the bomb. Was it far enough? Why, he kicked himself, why had he not bought more rope?

Ten minutes left.

Though it was early November, the weather was fair, the sun was high and bright, anxiety was turning them inside out, and they were both soaked in sweat. His phone lit up—he'd not had cell service for most of the morning, but now, on this rise, he did. He mindlessly scrolled through work emails. His boss wanted him to double-check the math on a financial model he'd built. He grimaced, looked to Irene, sweat staining her shirt. "Something wrong, babe?" she asked.

"No." He saw he'd neglected to turn on his out-of-office message. The phone slid into his pocket.

Two minutes. He felt they were maybe too close. Should he say something? One look at Irene and he knew a stony, resolved silence was the answer. None of this is illegal, he reassured himself. You're out here having some fun with your wife.

The phone timer went off. Irene's jaw set, and she twisted her frantic eyes toward the rope, sitting in the dirt.

"Let's do it together," she said.

They knotted their hands together, entwined fingers hovering over the cord. He pulled her in for a kiss. *I love you*, he mouthed to her. *I love you, too*, she said. Then he slid their coupled hands around the rope. They braced themselves like this was tug-of-war. Yanked as one.

The overpressure filled his ears. He ducked, then fell, hearing only a tinny ring. Debris plinked across his back. He looked up.

A fountain of dust had shot into the air above the test site, masking the ridge. Irene's hand covered her mouth. A trace of blood ran from her nostril.

But he could see that she was smiling.

THIRTY MINUTES LATER, WALKING THROUGH A PATCH OF long grass for a tour of the damage, celebratory bottle of tequila in hand, Peter stopped for a pull and peered down at the sound of a crunch. He'd stepped on a charred plastic ball. He bent down for a look. It was the top half of the mannequin's head.

35

KISSIMMEE

IN THE DIM LIGHT OF THE TRAILER, BOGGY AIR RUSHING across the swamp and through windows opened to free the smoke, Artemis Procter sat at her banquette, facing a pile of yellow legal pads and an overworked brass ashtray fashioned into the shape of a gator's snout. An old shoebox sat on the counter above the dishwasher. A haphazard stack of faded photos lay curled beside it. She'd only needed one, from that fateful day in Afghanistan, a shot of them all standing in front of a Hesco barrier at the Base. It was, she believed, the last surviving picture of all five of them. And her scissors were swishing through it.

She'd wanted the pictures because she had to look at their faces for this part, to make it real. A skyline of newly acquired liquor bottles dotted the sill under the bead curtain. Procter had vague memories of chess pieces being used to mount the pictures in the old spy stories, but alcohol was more in line with her present mood. Plus, she could drink the booze, and she fucking hated chess. The occasional whump and flitter of wings floated by the opened window. Procter was so consumed in her work that she did not hear the bump of a fruit bat into the trailer's metal skin, nor the shrieky meows of a pair of coital cats.

Inside the black beating heart of any double-cross operation is an essential and blinding lie, forcing you to reckon with its version of the truth, foisting a set of facts on you that suit perfectly innocent theories, turning you inside out. Tangles within tangles. That afternoon, alone with her thoughts, she'd at last put structure to the dark reality bearing down on her.

All of them had been on the flight from Vienna, when CIA had brought Sam home. Following spy swap tradition, each of her friends had brought something to drink, for the toasts. Jaggers had supplied the details during the all-night debrief when he had first appeared on her doorstep in Florida.

Mac had carried a bottle of Blue Label for the flight from Vienna, Sam had said. But her reptile fund was dwindling so she'd bought Black Label and spruced it up with a blue Sharpie. She taped the cutout picture of his head to the neck of the bottle. Next, Gus. Teetotaling Gus sipped sparkling water on the return—Perrier. Gus's picture was affixed to the bottle. Then Theo, a man whose alcoholism was nothing if not functional, financially reasonable, even. I don't like to break the bank with my bad habits, Artemis, he'd told her once, and she'd held her tongue about the quality of the women he bought. Theo had trucked along a handle of Canadian Club. Onto the bottle squatting on the sill went his picture; she cut out his entire body because in the photo he'd been giving the middle finger salute. Finally, Debs, the brat, brought vodka. What kind of sociopath, Mac had said, brings a bottle of *Russian* vodka to offer a guy who just got sprung from a *Russian* prison? She could have been sensible, brought Grey Goose. Debs had carried along a nice bottle, started with a K, Procter recalled, but she hadn't been able to track it down in Kissimmee and so settled for Stoli. Debs's mug was taped to the neck. Procter looked across their faces, and for the first time forced herself to say it aloud, to speak it into being.

Procter put a finger to Mac's photograph, snug on the Blue-Sharpied bottle of Black Label. Whispered, Rich Man.

As a child, on walks out in the pines, Procter sometimes collected stones and sang a little counting song. At the time she had been unaware of the British version of the rhyme, and its use in the hunt for a fictional mole. As an adult she felt it fitting to put the American version to work in pursuit of a real one.

Then Gus—flash of a wry smile at the memory of his minivan and the family finances. Poor Man.

Theo, and his bottom-shelf Canadian Club: Beggar Man. She spoke louder now, confident, getting the hang of it.

Debs's absurdly expensive Russian vodka: Thief.

Impossible. And yet it must be, because it could not be otherwise; too many facts had gathered.

Skipping Doctor, Lawyer, and Merchant, Procter hoisted her own picture atop a bottle of Sapphire, where it stared down the others.

Chief.

Procter blew a last lungful of smoke outside, shut the window, and killed the lights. The nightcap Slim went into the heap of the ashtray. She sat facing the pictures for a long while, as if in a conclave, or operational powwow—breaking bread, planning, debating, drinking. The emotional bramble here was unbearably thick. She thought of Sam, how he'd suffered, and as she slid into bed she found that made her hate herself. The sensation, unwelcome and foreign, shuddered all thought to a sudden stop, as if a stick had been plunged into the spokes of her brain. She fell asleep.

36

I-10 EAST / I-75 SOUTH / KISSIMMEE

PETER AND IRENE HAD LAST CAST OUT ON A LONG ROAD trip in the first year of their marriage. There'd been so much of Irene bottled up, and one dark piece, quite by happenstance, had spilled out in the first months of matrimony. Peter had the date postmarked in the files of his mind: March 18 of that year. That evening he'd gone out for a casual run, only to halve his usual ten-mile route, which had him back at the house about an hour earlier than anticipated. He saw Irene when he turned into the back alley.

She'd set out the trash cans for the next morning's pickup, and was gazing at something on the ground—she had not even noticed Peter rounding the corner. Irene's face and neck were visibly flushed. You turn red as a fire engine when you're horny, babe, he would say, and she'd coo back: *Well, put out the fire, then.* But that day the arousal he would typically experience at the sight of his wife's flushed face was only horror. He heard something screech and saw a robin, its little legs pinned beneath his wife's Golden Goose tennis shoes, the white ones with the pink stars that he would eventually—and clandestinely—discard. Something pulled taut inside him, made him jerk to a halt. Her shoe was twisting and turning its legs without killing the screeching bird. He had slid back out of the alley, out of sight, when he heard the stomp of a foot. The screeching stopped. Peter turned around and took off running.

An hour later, when he came home, Irene had dinner ready (overcooked burgers, fries out of a bag, salad swimming in vinaigrette—he still remembered that meal, he'd forced it all down) and they'd watched a few hours of television before reading side by side in bed. "You are quiet tonight, babe, what's up?" she'd said, still buried in her book, and he'd fed her something about stress at work. She'd offered sex to calm his nerves, or, in retrospect, perhaps to shut him up. "I love you babe," he'd said, "but can I take a rain check?" He punctuated that with a prudish peck on her forehead that elicited only an eye roll. He'd lain awake that night racked by the sideswiped sensation that accompanies the discovery of infidelity or abject betrayal. Was the savagery in the alley an aberration, or had something very real, and very deep, risen to the surface? What, exactly, had Irene been doing? And worst of all: Who *was* she, really?

Peter had thought a long road trip might create space to answer these questions. He imagined they would spend all those days together in the car, he would coax whatever this thing was right out of her, she would explain everything, show regret, remorse, repentance, whatever, and by the time they'd pulled into their driveway at the end they would be even more in love. That first road trip: Dallas to Nashville to Atlanta to Savannah to Charleston to the Outer Banks to D.C. to Chicago and back home, and when they'd bumped into their driveway he hadn't summoned the courage to ask her one question about the incident with the robin. They'd blazed a trail of tipsy partying and frenetic sightseeing and endless chatter and sensational lovemaking across much of the eastern United States, but by the time they'd arrived home he'd decided that whatever he'd witnessed was keeping a low enough profile that he could just let it be, a benign tumor wrapped around the vital organs of their relationship. Excising it, he sensed, would kill the marriage.

On this current trip, as with the last one, Peter had fantasized about putting all manner of questions and thoughts to his wife. Namely: *When can we stop?* He sustained the fantasy through a short leg in North Texas, on their way to purchase an unmarked Transit van from an Amazon supplier off-loading excess inventory (under the table, of course) that he'd found through a marketplace on the dark web. Once they had loaded up the van, Peter had convinced himself that when they turned east, he would boldly put these questions to his wife. And who knew? He might bring up the robin incident. Or, god help him, Oklahoma. He would get his answers, at last.

Instead, he listened to Irene ramble. Through most of Louisiana she spoke obsessively of Russia, of her visits with her mother and father when she'd been young. She offered these stories unprompted, and he was glad to listen because he was running out of things to say. The drive turned into a kind of confessional; she was plumbing the depths of her father's manias, as she termed it, and then veering off to tell rose-colored stories of her mother's blintzes and cinnamon kugel and a trip from New York to Disney World when she was ten. And then for a long stretch she was quiet, she switched playlists and songs incessantly, veering chaotically between sugary American pop songs and Russian classics: Prokofiev, Rachmaninoff, Tchaikovsky. She spent a good deal of time scrolling through influencer accounts on Instagram. First night they spent in New Orleans. Next day they made for Disney World.

MIDMORNING THE DAY AFTER THE DISNEY EXCURSION, AND the bed still had not disgorged them. Peter woke first, his face smushed into Irene's shoulder, facing the Minnie Mouse print on the back of her T-shirt, mouth dry as cotton. He sat up, rubbed his eyes, and for a moment could not place where he was. On the shuffle to the bathroom he stumbled over the shopping bag they'd filled with souvenirs. He felt his foot crack one of the mugs, next the Mr. Toad Popcorn Bucket, and the bag heaved over with him as he fell, lightsaber igniting and key chains clinking and the rest of the mugs tumbling and Irene's Minnie Mouse–printed handbag spilling across the floor. He caught himself on the footstool. Irene uttered fragments of surprise from the bed. "Oh shit, shit," he said. His foot was throbbing. Reaching down, feeling for his feet in the blackout-shade well of the room, he touched a warm run of blood. He sat up on the footstool. Irene flicked on a light. "Babe, are you okay?"

"I stepped on one of the damn mugs." In the light, he could see a shard of Mickey Mouse's ear stuck in his foot. Wincing, he pried it out.

THEY POPPED THC GUMMIES AND LOUNGED UNTIL LUNCHtime, scrolling their phones until both feared that if they did not move, they would succumb to the tug of afternoon naps. As they packed, Peter felt what he had anticipated: Threads of nausea were climbing his throat. Irene was eating a microwave burrito with gusto, but his was untouched on the nightstand.

"What's wrong babe?" Irene asked, chewing on a bite. She was carefully arranging the Disney mugs in her case, wrapping them in clothes so they would not break.

"I wish we knew if there was a dog."

The pity in her eyes made him hate himself. Heel of her hand brushing his cheek, Irene bit his lower lip and ran her tongue behind his top teeth and said, "Let me show you something, babe. For courage."

On the laptop she navigated to one of their usual Telegram channels; they watched a video of Russian soldiers in a mad dash to clear a home somewhere in Ukraine. The camera, mounted on one soldier's helmet, shook frenetically amid the gunshots and smoke and clamor. The Russian boys, it turned out, were all killed. The camera sizzled static. Irene shut the laptop.

"They walked in like men. No floor plan. They did their duty," she said. "Left their wives and girlfriends back in Moscow or Piter or Novgorod or wherever and marched out from Russia's black soil to defend her, to die in glory and honor." She kissed him again, a feral shadow falling on her face. They gathered up the bags.

THE ADDRESS WAS A SWAMP. NO BUILDINGS WERE VISIBLE on the Google Street View satellite images. The Spaniard had said there was a trailer now, though he did not know where it was parked. Peter pulled the van off the road and they peered into the rustling trees. Nothing. Irene shrugged.

They drove a quarter mile down the road until they came upon a gravel lane that plunged deeper into the bog. He stepped from the car and squinted through the tangle of palm and pine shrouding the drive. The soundtrack was a persistent whine of insects and the distant bark of a dog—though thankfully it did not come from the CIA woman's property.

"We should go in there and see," Irene whispered.

"We don't know if she's home," Peter said, scowling.

"We'll say we got lost. We are Amazon, after all. Wrong turn. We need to see what we're dealing with, Peter."

They crunched slowly down the drive and in about a mile the trees and underbrush thinned and they saw a trailer on a plot of sand overlooking the swamp.

"She's former CIA," he mumbled. "And she lives here."

He kept the van idling at a distance and searched for cameras. He didn't see any. But they had to be there, didn't they? No sign of a dog, but it might be inside. He heard the rustle of a foil package as Irene popped loose a few pieces of spearmint gum and chewed loudly, mouth open, which she did when she was lost in thought, and which he despised. He'd told her so many times. She smacked on the gum fussing with a chipped nail.

"We'll come back at night," he said, and threw it in reverse.

THAT AFTERNOON THEY CHECKED INTO THEIR HOTEL AND drove the fifteen minutes to Gatorville. They wore their N95s, walking through the yawning plaster gator mouth that made up the park's entrance, Peter smacking his hand on one of the teeth, absorbing it all with some measure of wonder and disgust. After saying yes, yes, of course they could pay cash, this wasn't goddamn Disney World, the lady working the ticket booth inquired if they were from San Francisco or New York or maybe Portland, seeing as they still had the ridiculous masks on. Peter delivered the chemo ("Doctor's orders") story and the lady smiled and reached down to rummage inside a cabinet. After a moment she produced two masks stenciled to resemble a gator snout, wide open, teeth bared. "We've got plenty of these left over. You all have fun."

They found the target starring in a wrestling show. The Spaniard had provided several dozen photos from what he had termed "the archives." In truth, it was nearly impossible to miss the wild spray of hair, even if it was tied up under an old Cleveland Indians baseball cap. When they took their seats, she was approaching a gator from behind, finger to her lips, shushing the crowd in what Peter at first took for theater, but upon closer inspection of the woman's countenance he believed instead to be extreme agitation. She paused, bracing herself, then leapt onto its back and fluidly wrapped her hands around its jaw. He was near enough to see that murdering the animal could not have been far from her mind. The gator whipsawed back and forth but the target held on, narrating the experience into a headset mic in a slurred jumble. The specifics were nearly impossible to make out, but the crux of it was simple: she was teeming with rage.

Irene, looking up from Instagram, had lowered her sunglasses for a better look, and her eyes spoke for them both: Moscow cares about her? We have been sent to kill *this*?

37

KISSIMMEE

When Procter pulled her RAV4 alongside her trailer she just sat there for a few minutes and zoned out to the comforting noise of the swamp. The smack of a bug flying into the window broke the reverie, and she went inside. Not caring if she showered—a common feeling since her return from Vegas—she stripped out of her shirt, threw it on the bed, pulled out the ashtray, and fixed herself a smoke at the banquette. She slathered Bengay across her lower back, shoulders, and arms and tried not to look at the bottles across the sill. She often avoided eye contact with the photos of her old friends, but it was typically due to anger or disbelief, not—as it was now—from the temptation for the type of drinking best done alone, without anyone watching.

She knew she should not, but she also couldn't quite come up with any good reasons not to, so she poured herself two fingers of the blue-Sharpied Black Label (Mac: Rich Man) for company, while she did a crossword puzzle. An hour later and she'd sampled the Canadian Club (Theo: Beggar Man) and Stoli (Debs: Thief) and was ready to wave the white flag on the crossword, which, when paired with her drunkenness, had begun to make her very angry. Stubbing out her last Slim of the night, she flicked the picture off the bottle of Perrier (Gus: Poor Man) and took the water into her bedroom, where she promptly fell asleep.

That night the dream slithered back. Unwelcome and uninvited, as always, but not infrequent since Sam had visited with news of a mole.

In the dream she was in Afghanistan with her old friends, and they were all about to die, shuffling through the tick-tock window of silence after the suicide bombing but before the worst of it. They were in the house's upper room together, making peace with their gods or themselves. There was something ordained, even ominous, about former friends, long since dispersed, finding themselves together, years later, on the far side of the world. As if such a thing could not happen without violence or tragedy. She could hear her friends' thoughts, felt their feelings, saw, in pure bright color, their palette of emotions. She was with Gus as he considered his love for Connie and his children, his guilt as he considered death and abandoning them to life, his stoicism in the certainty there'd been no other way; she was with Theo and his desire to live though his life was so miserable, knowing that though he had a daughter, Millie was in that moment absent from his mind; she was with Mac, his thoughts of her and of Loulou, his wonderment that in death he might yet prove a hero to his father, who'd then not yet passed, and who would ultimately offer a cosmically indifferent shrug of the shoulders to his only son though he returned a bona fide Agency legend; she sailed with Debs and her bone-deep fear that all was for naught, that after this there was nothingness; she communed with Gosford, checking his Glock again and again and again, and felt his belief that he would emerge from that night a hero, so foolish, then and now, and yet somehow proven correct. She spoke to Mac as he bled out on the floor of the shed. What was he thinking? Where were her friends?

Procter woke in a pool of chilly sweat. Night was still going; an oppressive, still blanket of darkness. Thunder banged in the distance. She tossed aside the sheets, sat up, and took a few sips of the Perrier. Her room was tilting on its axis, spinning, rotating. She shut her eyes and hoped that she might be spared another dreamworld visit from her friends.

PETER AND IRENE CHANGED INTO THEIR FLEX VESTS IN the back of the Transit van and checked the other duffels: Northman blades, pistols, ammunition. If all went well, the guns and knives would be unnecessary.

The night was moonless. On the way to the swamp a driving rain picked up, whipping water across the windshield in thick drops that were soon falling in sheets. BOGGY CREEK, a sign said, he'd missed that during the scouting run earlier in the day. They turned off the county road and rolled the van down the drive until they reached the trailer. Lightning flared across the edges of the sky. The target's car was there: Irene matched the license plate to the numbers in the files provided by the Spaniard in Mexico. The trailer was dark.

Peter crawled into the back of the van, Irene trailing behind him. The moment—their moment—had arrived. The waiting had left a dreadful weight in his belly, but that stone was now gone, busted to bits by the freakish adrenaline smack of one very simple fact: It was all on the line. Marriage, self-worth, honor. The next half hour on the battlefield would determine what sort of man he was. Peter did not say a word because he knew if he did, he would stammer.

He checked that the ball bearing in the syringe was not kissing the electrical leads.

He turned the minute hand back on the clock—five minutes. They didn't need more than that.

He connected the wires to the battery.

Then he shut the box and ran a line of Amazon tape across the seam.

He flung open the back doors of the van to a crash of thunder. Jumping down, he huffed the box through the rain toward the slab in front of the trailer. Irene held the umbrella in a vain attempt to shield the box from the rain. He left it on the concrete slab. There was an awning overhead, but occasional gusts of wind blew the rain sideways, soaking one side of the box.

He rang the doorbell. Then they ran back to the van.

THE RINGING DROWNED OUT THE EXPLOSIONS; IT PUNCTUated Mac's speech in her dream. She awoke, head floating, to the buzz of the doorbell. Standing, then slumping back onto the bed, then rising again, she tied up her hair and walked through the kitchen. Ping-ponged was more like it—she knocked into everything: dishwasher, banquette, walls. The patter of rain sounded on the roof. She swung open the front door, gripping the frame to keep herself upright.

Procter was looking at a large box, tilting, sliding, spinning. The world a booze-fueled gyroscope. A box. Huh. A whip of lightning brought sudden clarity to Amazon tape across the package. Thunder rolled. She hadn't ordered anything. A gift? The thought made her laugh aloud.

Raindrops were plopping onto the box. Procter looked up into the tilting darkness and a droplet landed square in her eye. Then the volley picked up, the sky finally ready to let loose the worst of the storm.

PETER AND IRENE WATCHED THROUGH SOAKING BINOCULARS from a stand of trees across the swamp. "She's examining," Irene said. "Pondering."

"She's wobbling," Peter said.

"Drunk," whispered Irene. "Good."

There was a crack of lightning, another rumble of thunder in the distance, the rain was crisscrossing the trailer in sheets.

The target put her hands on the box.

Irene put her hands on his arm. "She's going to bring it inside," she said. "She doesn't want it to get soaked."

"FUCKING AMAZON," PROCTER MUTTERED. SHE SLID HER hand across the top and tried to move it. Thing was heavy. She dragged a chair from the kitchen to prop open the door. Rain was really coming down now; the drive had soaked to a sandy muck. Her blood swam with booze. She reached down for the box.

PETER AND IRENE DROPPED TO THE SAND, SHUT THEIR EYES, and braced for the explosion.

There was a boom, a crack. He shuddered.

Then looked up.

Another roll of thunder. He peered through the binoculars. The target had a hand on the box. She was getting into a squat.

"What happened?" Irene hissed.

"The ball in the trembler must not have touched the leads," he said. "She needs to pick it all the way up.

Procter hauled up the box.

ANOTHER FLASH OF LIGHTNING. THEN A BOOM THAT RIPpled into a low drumroll.

Peter watched the target pick up his bomb and carry it inside her trailer. The door swung shut.

"What the hell could be wrong, Peter?" Irene asked.

He felt sick with failure. "I'm a financial analyst, Irene, not a munitions expert." Had he made a mistake wiring the circuit? Was the black powder wet? He didn't know. "We should have used the guns from the get-go."

She smacked him, hard, on the crown of his head.

"You're a soldier," she said. "Act like one."

"She's drunk," he said, standing up and wiping rainwater from his brow. "Let's just shoot her."

Whether wet from pride or merely the rain, Irene's eyes were shining. Then they were in the van, headlamps off, backing from the roadside parking spot to pull onto the main road. Irene was slapping magazines into the pistols, checking the knives in their sheaths.

PROCTER WAS IN THE BANQUETTE, SMOKING, LISTENING to the storm. Her one open eye was stuck on the wet box. Let's have a look-see.

She steadied herself on the cabinets and cooktop to walk through the galley kitchen. Rain was pelting the trailer. She split the tape with a kitchen knife and flipped open the box.

"Lord almighty," Procter said.

THE RAIN HAD WASHED THE TRAILER'S SANDY DRIVE TO soup. Peter kept the van at a slow, steady pace, tires slurping and sliding through the muck. He was hunched over the wheel to peer through the windshield. They could not risk flicking on the lights.

He stopped a few hundred feet from the trailer, before the tree cover thinned and the drive spilled into the clearing, now thick with mud.

"We should use the blades if we can," he said.

They spilled from the van. Hugging the trees along the drive, they padded toward the trailer, knives out, pistols holstered. With each step Peter watched the sheath bounce along his wife's hip.

PROCTER KILLED THE LIGHTS AND PULLED BACK A STRAND of beads and peeked out a front window. She waited, steadying her breathing, her pickled brain straining to focus.

A crack of lightning and the world turned white and she saw the glint of metal in the trees. Movement. A shape. Maybe two or more. Hard to know. She was so very drunk.

She thought for a second—then two, three, four. Deep breath. Shook her head as if that might kick loose a bit of the booze.

Then, on to the bedroom, crouched on the floor, grasping under her bed where she kept the guns. Mossberg twelve-gauge shotgun. A dear friend, but not useful right now. Baseball bat. Same. M4 Carbine. Brought that out.

Her Mk 48 Mod 1, snug in a Pelican case with big latches that gave her drunk hands some trouble. Inside was a belt-fed all-purpose machine gun and a bipod mount. She had some ammo pouches, each with a hundred rounds. She slid one of those on, slung the M4 over her shoulder, and went into the closet. There was a floor hatch for access to the trailer's undercarriage. She pried it off and jumped down. All mud down here; her presence upset whatever the hell had made this home because things were skittering and slithering to the corners. She reached up and slid the hatch shut and took a deep breath and slunk toward an opening covered by thin cross-hatched wood.

AT THE DOOR, PETER FOUND THE KNOB UNLOCKED. HE waited for a rumble of thunder to open it a crack. He peered in, half expecting to be shot, but the trailer was quiet and dark. Where had she passed out? He leveled his pistol and pushed inside, heartbeat in his teeth. His fingers were vibrating and jerking the gun. He stepped over a few boxes and scanned the kitchen. Empty. "You check the bedroom," Irene said, loudly, over the wail of the storm. "I will check out back." Nodding, Peter glided carefully around the bomb and through the kitchen into the bedroom.

From somewhere outside—maybe below?—came the splintering and crackling of wood. An animal rustling under the trailer. Then a banging clap of thunder and Irene was calling but he could not understand her words. He pointed the pistol into the bedroom and squeezed the trigger and the damn safety was on so he clicked that off and began firing, charging forward. When he got there he put rounds into the closet, the bed, the cabinets. It felt like his heart was going to explode.

PROCTER CRAWLED THROUGH THE MUD AND THE BLINDing rain as the gunshots dissolved into the thunder. Then she stood, sprinting into a stand of trees, where she caught her breath. More gunshots rang inside the trailer. A handgun, Procter thought, operated by a moron. She waited for another crash of thunder and then darted across a stretch of mud and dove behind a strip of squatty palms. Dim light poured through the front door, which was swinging on its hinges. Another gunshot. What was that asshat shooting at in there?

The sky was veined with lightning.

A shape appeared from behind the trailer, then it disappeared into the night.

Procter flopped into the mud and pointed the Mk 48 toward the kitchen, where she'd left the box. She extracted the bipod to steady the weapon. Fed in the ammo. Flicked off the safety. A deep breath, then she squeezed the trigger.

PETER HAD TORN AND SHOT THE PLACE APART AND STILL he could not find the CIA woman; he called for Irene, who yelled back from somewhere outside. "She's running!" Irene shouted. "Tracks! Come on, babe!"

He'd just made it into the galley kitchen when he heard a gun roar to life.

THE WEAPON HAD MORE BITE THAN PROCTER REMEMBERED. Then again, she'd never been this drunk while operating the gun, which now swung left, ripping into her bedroom for a couple seconds before she tried to correct, fanning right, a murderous searchlight pouring out twelve rounds per second, punching the trailer's skin into a ragged cheese grater. Her aim tracked through the kitchen, toward the box, and she held it right there, dousing her home with a thick volley of lead until the bomb detonated, everything was noise and light, fire and fragments, and her eyes had barely shut, on instinct from the sudden surge of brightness, when she felt the blast overpressure muscle through her, and then she couldn't tell if her eyes were open, or closed, or had been burned out of her skull.

The world was black, then white, then black again. There was no sky. And the ringing, lordy, the ringing.

PART IV

BARIUM MEAL

38

KISSIMMEE / ORLANDO, FLORIDA

WHEN PROCTER BLINKED AGAIN, HER MOUTH WAS FULL of mud and her nostrils with the scent of burnt hair. She found she could sit up; ears still clanging like church bells but she could see, she had some bloody scratches down her arms but her pieces and parts were still attached. Hair was singed but not aflame, as were most of the bushes and trees and the scattered husk of her trailer, everything soaked from the rain and still burning white. She picked up the M4 that had flown off her back and strolled for a few minutes, dodging the scattered fires and miscellany from her now-exploded life: half the refrigerator door, a mangled forty-pound dumbbell, a twisted scrap of bedframe, a batch of melted VHS tapes bubbling beside a gnarled oak.

In the sand near the swamp she came upon a barbecued human hand short a few fingers; beside a grove of smoldering palms she found a chunk of cranium.

There had been two of them, she'd swear it. She checked both parts again. Did the hand belong to the head? She couldn't tell. It was all blackened char.

Procter took a long look at the twisted metal, the dozen white campfires dotting her land. Had anyone survived? In the distance came the faint wail of approaching sirens. Local cops would be first, then maybe some state officers, and the Bureau would arrive pretty quick.

Briefly she fantasized about running. Dumb. The Russians were clearly hunting her; why add the Bureau to the list? Red and blue lights began painting the drive; the wail of the sirens grew louder. Procter put down the rifle and stretched her hands into the sky.

Damascus, Syria.

Moscow, Russia.

And now, to her list of detention centers, Procter added Orange County, Florida.

The crimes had been different, but the places were pretty much the same. Hard-ass guys would ask you questions, make you feel guilty, though whether you were, well, that was beside the point. They'd put you in a concrete cell reeking of mold and piss. And, if things were tilting spicy, they'd trot in a wacky cellmate who'd prod you to confess or maybe goose you while you slept. Captivity in Orange County wasn't so different from Damascus or Moscow, except that this time she wasn't guilty of anything.

Jittery and severely hungover, she used her one call on Cummings, both to tell him she wouldn't be at work the next day and to ask if she might avail herself of the Gatorville legal team at Carlsberg, Cragg, and Peters over in Kissimmee.

The first night was an exhaustive interrogation with two Feebs from the Orlando Field Office and her mousy legal counsel. Next day a few counterintelligence types showed up from Feeb headquarters for tense chats.

Her cellmate was Barbara, a tweaker who'd been nabbed flashing people out near Lake Eola, but she slept just fine, figured Barbara could show her whatever she liked, long as her eyes were shut.

The end of the second day brought new vibes. When they hustled her back into the white room for a talk with the Feebs, the poor guy's stooped shoulders and lousy posture said it all: This detective had lost a perfectly good suspect to the facts. Which she figured could be that they'd found more fingerprints or footprints or DNA; or that they'd discovered incriminating evidence elsewhere. Explosive residue from the fabrication site, commo to Moscow, a note. Of course, the Feebs would not say.

In any case, by the next morning the walls in the new room were brick and she sat on a green couch and no one was yelling at her anymore. As a rule, Procter was more interested in conversations that featured yelling, but this time she was grateful because she was on a Russian list somewhere, they had decided to reach out and touch people stateside, and being cooped up in jail was making her antsy. And Barbara, she thought, would probably be open to stabbing her to death in exchange for a few kopecks. They returned her personal effects when she'd finished the paperwork. There wasn't much—Indians ball cap, muddy jeans, phone, dozens of voice mails and messages from Mac, Theo, and Gus. The bombing had claimed the burner she had been using for commo with Sam. The guy handling her outprocessing even looked a little sad for her.

PROCTER HAD WALKED OUTSIDE TO START MAKING PHONE calls when she saw Debs. She had wondered who would show, debated if it would tell her anything, provide any hint or clue. The DDO wore a thin-strapped white tank top, white stilettos, and a skintight skirt printed with a yellow rose the size of a basketball. Her face was stern, even angry, but her eyes were smiling.

"Sorry I'm still alive," Procter mumbled.

"Nobody's perfect."

"You here to help, or admire the car wreck of my life?"

"All of your friends wanted to come. Right after we got the news, Mac, Gus, and Theo were booking tickets to check on you. I waved them off. Wanted the first word."

They sat on benches in an interior courtyard. Palms towered overhead, bent like supplicants toward the soiled stone of the building. "Bureau briefed me on the attack," Debs said, smoothing her skirt. "What the fuck?"

"Do they have any leads?" Procter asked.

"The Bureau believes the remains at your trailer were left by one individual, a male, but they haven't been able to ID him yet. DNA hasn't matched to any of their criminal databases, nor any of the military ones they can easily access. And there wasn't enough left of his head to run any facial or dental recognition. They've discovered another set of footprints and an abandoned Amazon van, but, again, no leads. Do *you* have any theories on who tried to kill you?" Debs asked.

"Tough to say," Procter answered. "Lots of folks with motive."

Debs crossed her legs, smoothed her skirt, and tugged at a thread that had come loose near the print of the rose, eyeing it with an air of disgust. "I have three facts," she said. "One: I know you and a nameless friend visited IMPERIAL in Las Vegas last week. I don't know why, nor do I know how you found him, but he complained about the visit to his handler out there, who wrote a cable asking whether Headquarters had gone around him for some reason. So that's one. You saw a twisted Russian in Vegas. Two is that less than a week later someone tried to kill you. And three is that a month ago, in some bizarre fit of nostalgia, you called me out of the blue, and in the grim smokehouse of that karaoke bar put to me a set of extremely strange and provocative questions."

"I need a lawyer?" Procter asked. "I had one inside, I can get him again. Look, you asked me who I think tried to kill me, and my answer is Russians. I don't know why now or who they sent, but they've got their reasons. Last year's covert action work, the unrest in Moscow, and Putin's drained bank account would be at the top of the list. Plenty of others, but those'll do just fine."

"I agree with that," Debs said. "But the timing's wrong."

"The Russians," Procter barked, "don't take their revenge on your timeline. The inner workings of their sadism are mysterious and unfathomable."

"Spare me the lecture," Debs hissed back. "This happened immediately after the IMPERIAL meeting. And what were you trying to kick out of me during our karaoke chat? No, it just smells wrong to me." Debs had uncrossed her legs, and turned to face Procter straight-on. "You're up to something, Artemis. I want to know what it is. So here's what's going to happen. I will give you the chance to keep this in the family for the time being. I have enough to get a FISA warrant on you right now. And there is no way you need that in your life. No way the Bureau needs that, either. Such a headache. Some poor Feeb in the CI Division will have to trek over to AT&T with a pack of lawyers and show them the warrants and hoover up your calls. They'll have to read your emails, follow you across the internet to whatever dark corners you stick your nose or other parts into. And heaven forbid they wire up whatever dump you land in next, seeing as your trailer has been vaporized. All that footage? Why, it'll be fantastically disturbing, don't you think? Not to mention loads of work."

"I don't think you have enough to get a FISA warrant," Procter said. "On what grounds?"

"On whatever grounds I choose. You want to try me? Gosford and the Attorney General were frat brothers. You don't think I can put you in a world of hurt with one phone call? You're a pain in the ass, but you're not stupid."

"What the hell do you want, Debs?" Procter could feel her lips twitching; the siren sound was again ringing through her skull, an angry soundtrack baying in her brainbox. She had to talk to Sam.

"You are coming with me, today. We are going up to the Farm. And there you are going to explain to me exactly what is going on."

39

KISSIMMEE

WHEN IRENE VENABLE WAS FOURTEEN, SHE WROTE A paper for civics class on capital punishment. She'd developed a fascination with one case in particular: a Pakistani national named Mir Aimal Kansi, who in 1993 drove to CIA Headquarters and shot two CIA officers while they waited to turn left into the compound. He fled to Pakistan. Four years later he was nabbed, rendered to the U.S., tried, and convicted of capital murder. He was later executed by lethal injection.

But what was fascinating to young Irene then, as she had poisoned her first stray cats, and what was damn interesting now, on the run, was not the rendering and the eventual execution, it was that Mir Aimal Kansi at first got away with it. Kansi drove to a park after the killings, where he waited for over an hour. He went back to his apartment, hid the rifle, ate at McDonald's—a Big Mac meal, she wrote in the paper, no idea if it was true, just made it up—booked a hotel room for the night, and next morning was on a flight to Pakistan. Scot-free.

From the trailer Irene had sprinted along the edges of the swamp to the van, then drove to the parking lot of a hardware store a ten-minute walk from the hotel. She scanned the back—guns, knives, duffels, disguises, fresh clothes to wear after the attack. Nothing linked to Irene Venable of Dallas, Texas. She slipped on a new pair of Reeboks, khakis, and a sweatshirt.

She'd returned to the hotel and sat on the hotel bed, handgun at her side. For two hours, in shock, she waited for the police. Sirens played in the distance. On the bed she wrestled with her dead husband, some potent mix of grief for his loss and rage for having been left behind. She cried. She fumed at him for fucking up the bomb. She wept sad tears on the scratchy comforter of a dumpy Super 8 in Kissimmee, Florida.

She heard the *whump-whump* of rotors overhead. More sirens. She pointed the gun at the door and resolved to shoot if anyone so much as knocked. But no one came.

Her mind was racing, though, and it was only a matter of time before FBI agents or cops showed up to ask questions at the hotel. The front desk manager had seen Peter.

Where is your husband? they would ask.

She had known all along that she and Peter would be hunted, that there would be a decisive break with their past, that at some juncture they could never again return to their house in Texas. Instead, they would go home. She and Peter had researched how the police and the FBI would use facial and gait recognition algorithms to search for them. How forensics technicians would evaluate the scene. Vehicles leave track marks. License plates would be photographed. There would be deposits of blood or hair or fingerprints or saliva. Were they in any databases readily accessible to the police or FBI? They did not think so. That she'd not already been captured meant one thing: she had time. But not much.

Irene took a shower, packed up, and checked out. She walked two blocks to McDonald's.

She ordered the Mir Aimal Kansi. The precarious nature of her situation hit home about halfway through the Big Mac. Her husband was gone. She had no car. At some point the investigators would connect the remains of her husband to Peter Venable, and her face would be splashed all over the news, right? Or might they get away with it?

For a few moments she considered bolting: fly to Mexico City, walk into the Russian Embassy, perhaps? She set down the burger to research flights until a sickening thought dawned on her: She and Peter had failed. They had failed. *You* failed, Irene, you dumb little bitch. And she was in her aunt's car fleeing her father and Sheepshead Bay, driving south—driving anywhere—and again, for an awful moment, she was young and scared and ashamed. If things are bad, it's probably your fault. To the other McDonald's patrons she appeared to be a quiet woman—slightly out of place, no doubt—enjoying her meal. But inside, Irene Venable was a blast furnace of warring voices, feelings, and memories, her temperature eventually rising until she felt one thing, one feeling, one word slash through her: No.

No, she thought, no. No, no, no, no, no.

He had failed. Peter failed. Then he got himself killed and left me here—his wife!—alone, to sort through the wreckage and soldier on. These are *his* mistakes. Not mine. She took the last bite of her Big Mac.

She needed wheels. But how?

Walk? Too far, too conspicuous.

Hail an Uber?

Rent a car? Then, at the rental counter, pay cash? They would ask for an ID, though. It would be entered into a computer system. She did not like that.

And then, from the corner of her eye, she felt attention on her. Heat. She looked up, and a young man looked sheepishly down, back to scrolling on his phone. Irene Venable's reptilian operating system ran a quick calculation: early twenties, weak eyes, lean and handsome but not strong, clean—no manual labor—likes women, key fob on the table.

She put a fry on her tongue. A salty ball of saliva clung to the back of her throat. She could float beneath the waterline. She had done so before, on the bolt from Sheepshead Bay, and she could muster the cunning and grit to do it again. She could hunt, and be hunted.

Irene smiled, flapped a coy, inviting wave his way. "I'm Steph," she called. She smacked the bench of her booth. "Plenty of room at my table."

40

THE FARM

THE APPROACH TO THE FARM WAS A STOCKADE OF TREES, chain link whipstitched with razor wire, and a gatehouse swimming in sodium light. From the SUV, Procter regarded this with the somber appraisal of an escaped convict being returned to her prison. In part this was because the Farm could be credited with a certain penitentiary atmosphere; but it was also because Procter hated the place for entirely different reasons. The Farm was a reminder that life had once unrolled out before her and now most of it—probably the best fucking parts—was miles behind.

The guards waved the two SUVs through. Procter was in the lead vehicle, the jailhouse vibes reinforced by the two Security officers riding with her. Debs was in the trailing car. They clacked onto the compound, toward a gravel road that led to a few of the houses CIA used for special guests.

The Farm smell, though, was what really got her all bothered. It tackled her, as always, upon opening the door of the rental car: the scent of freshman year. The grounds reeked of river water, the buildings of school lunch and disinfectant, the occupants of sweat and sex. A school bus lumbered around the Base, for god's sake, wending by dorms, gyms, open quads, a chow hall, a bar—the SRB—with darts and ping-pong. The place was lousy with ticks and deer and hornballs, many of whom were also instructors.

Procter's lodging—or cell, depending on perspective—was one of the many homes dotting the expansive Base, nestled along the river. Debs's car idled in the drive; the DDO was probably on a call. The security officers led Procter inside, where she was greeted by a Support officer who informed Procter that her cottage was typically used by VIPs: Seventh Floor leadership, visiting members of Congress, senior members of friendly foreign intelligence services. "You're lucky, Ms. Procter," he said, "that this place is available."

Hale House: A two-story red-brick colonial with a wraparound porch colonnaded by flaking white pillars. The rooms were decorated like a Virginia tidewater plantation: walls were wood-paneled and haphazardly slung with tired antebellum paintings of fox-hunting aristocrats. It was nestled into the woods, set away from the larger neighborhoods on the Base. Easier to keep track of her, she figured.

"Fun fact," the Support officer said, opening the door to her bedroom. "Nosenko stayed here from June of '66 to August of '67." She grunted in recognition—the old defector was a legendary figure in Russia House. The poor bastard had fallen victim to Cold War fever dreams: for three years CIA wasn't sure if he was the real deal or a KGB double, so Angleton locked him up at the Farm and turned the screws to get to the bottom of things. Procter carried with her the firm belief that espionage in those days had been more adventurous and piratical. There'd certainly been lots more leash, even if in the Nosenko case it had been extended only for CIA to mistreat ("torture" showed up in some of the histories, which Procter thought a stretch) a true-blue defector who'd been telling the truth, of all the goddamn things.

"I hadn't realized they preserved the room as it was in his day. That a diktat from the conservation society, or just run-of-the-mill incompetence?" Procter asked, flicking on the lights in a well-worn sitting room stripped of furniture. "Is this where they got him wild on LSD?"

The Support officer shrugged, said to call if she needed anything. Though he did not appear to mean it, and he never did offer a number. Not that she had a phone, anyway. It had been impounded by one of the Security officers. She also had no car; they had whisked her from

Orlando in one of the Air Branch Bombardiers Gosford had loaned to the DDO for domestic travel. Debs's SUV was idling outside.

Procter sank onto the bed in a shadowy limbo. A part of her thought she could wait them out, see what they threw at her, and for how long. The other part remembered the felonies she had committed as of late, namely her participation in the theft of highly classified documents from safes and databases inside CIA Headquarters. She'd run into the sick plot twist of an intelligence Service turned inside out. She could not have run the investigation without breaking the law. And now that law could be turned against her by the mole, the very person most committed to its destruction. Tangles within tangles. Suddenly she felt very tired.

The front door sighed open. "Artemis," Debs called up the stairwell, "let's do this. Come on down."

She found Debs on one of the faded green couches in the living room. Debs gestured for Procter to take a seat. "Our worst nightmare is upon us," Debs said. "We are going to have a nice long chat." Procter plopped down across from her old friend. The doilies on the coffee table reminded her of Petra Devine, which, to her great alarm, she found a strangely comforting memory. Best I've got, she thought, and picked one as her focus object. She'd need it for the segments of this conversation in which she would be sorely tempted to either break things or attack her former friend.

"Let's start with Las Vegas," Debs said flatly. "Your visit to see IMPERIAL. Known as Frankie out there. Tell me why you went. And who was with you? Was it Sam? What exactly did you discuss?"

"It was a stroll down memory lane. Happenstance meeting."

"You met him at the high-limit tables, eh? A typical haunt, I suppose, for an employee of Gatortown."

"Gatorville," Procter mumbled. "Gatortown's the competition."

Debs smiled and shut her eyes and took a deep, meditative breath. When she opened them she said, "Frankie told his babysitter you visited with a friend named Charles. Who is Charles? Is Charles in fact Sam?"

"Charles is Charles."

"Artemis, is Charles Sam Joseph?"

"How could Charles be Sam? Charles is Charles."

"Oh fuck you, Artemis. If it was a happenstance meeting, why did Frankie tell his handler that you called him before you went out there? Why did he complain?"

"Frankie won big that night," Procter said. "And I'm fairly certain he screwed no fewer than three very attractive women. I can't imagine what he had to complain about."

"What exactly are you up to?" Debs repeated. She was speaking quietly, as if she did not trust herself to raise the volume above a whisper. She crossed her long legs. After a few seconds of exchanging dumb stares, Debs said, "Let me set the table for you, Artemis. There is a general malaise in Russia House and the CIA writ large upon Finn Gosford's arrival. He's a former officer who sold out, they say, he's unconventional, he's a maverick, a—"

"*Unconventional maverick*," Procter said, "is a nice turn of phrase for his directorship. Bravo. You have a future in PR after the Agency."

"Oh shut up," Debs sputtered. "You get the point. The Agency rejected him. And the Reversion idea. No one wanted us sticking our noses into their cookie jars, questioning things. Interfering. Finn and I receive a general cold shoulder upon touchdown. And I rile and rankle my old friends in the Russia House Bratva all the more because I'm demanding to be kept in the loop. And who hates transparency more than CIA's Russia hands?"

"Probably just the actual Russians," Procter said.

"Clever. Finn's entire mandate is to keep CIA out of the news. No fuckups, that was literally what POTUS told him when he was sworn in. In the Oval, those words. And then week one on the job Singapore happens. It's your brainchild, and it's a disaster. You call the Director a cunt, in a meeting. And of course we needed a scapegoat, and you'll do just fine because you're both responsible for the disaster and also insubordinate. So you're fired."

"I said he was acting cunty, remember? Procter clarified. "Not that he was one."

"You're such a prick, Artemis. A pain in the ass. And everywhere else. Point is, Langley was primed for rebellion. And you know what I think? That you are searching for material to use against Finn and me. I do not know what it is, but you're pushing at something. And I think that something just shoved you back."

"As we have discussed," Procter said, "the Russians have long-standing reasons to target me."

"That is true," Debs said. "But this most recent shove happened right after you met with a Russian defector. And it follows you dredging up the Russian-tinted past with all your old chums. It leaves a girl wondering, Artemis, doesn't it? Like, what the hell is going on?"

"Russkies blew up my trailer, Debs," Procter said, eyes boring a hole through the doily. "What the hell are you insinuating? You're going to full-court-press a former officer who almost got her shit kicked in by a Russian bomb? Even that's a tricky spin for the Gosford regime's propaganda department. And, honestly, you know what? Fuck you. You ran me out of CIA, you poisoned me, cut my team, put me in the basement, hid a bunch of dirty pictures around my office, got the OEEO on my ass, you—"

"Hold on. I denied your promotion, and yes, I gutted Moscow X. But I didn't put any pictures in your office, that's for sure. Why would I? And I sure didn't get anyone in Equal Employment Opportunity involved. Why bother? I'm the goddamn Deputy Director for Operations and I don't need a reason to sunset senior officers, only a story."

The fight had burned through its fuel: a silence settled between them.

"There were a number of ethics complaints," Procter mumbled, "in those months."

"I'm sure there were, knowing what I do of your morals and management style. But am I to understand, Artemis, that you are just going to stonewall? That you will not answer any of my questions?"

"Well, it depends on what they are."

"How about this one: Why did you ask to meet with me a month ago?"

"Stroll down memory lane, as I said."

"Ah yes. Lots of memory strolling for Artemis Procter. With me, your old friends, Frankie."

"What can I say, my midlife crisis has made me a sucker for nostalgia."

"It's interesting, Artemis. After our weird little conversation last month I put out feelers to a few friends who are up to their eyeballs in the contracting world. They then asked a few of their friends at DynCoTel, who said you'd never applied for a job there, much less come in for an interview."

"Huh," Procter said. "Well, DynCoTel is a big shop. Information sharing's a problem, too. Worse than the Agency. If your sources are in the wrong division, they'd never have heard of me."

"That so?"

"That's so."

"What division did you say you were interviewing in?"

"Insider Threat," Procter said, her eyes finding the doily on the table.

"Now, that's fascinating, because that is *precisely* where my friend's sources work. How about that? And Insider Threat has never heard of you."

"It's a big shop," Procter said, staring through the doily into nothingness.

Debs looked right at the doily, too, sporting a wide, wicked smile. "A team of Security debriefers and polygraphers will be out here first thing tomorrow. Good luck."

IN HALE HOUSE THAT AFTERNOON PROCTER TRIED IN VAIN to take a nap, only to twist and turn in the scratchy sheets. After a while she padded downstairs and flicked on the TV. A memory seeped through her mindless stupor. It was twenty-five years earlier and she was driving away from the Farm.

Their class had straddled Christmas, so she'd gone to join her then-future-ex-husband Tom and his family for the holiday. No one there knew what her job was, really. Except Tom. And by this point she knew that she loved the work, that nearly all of her could not wait to be done with the family, get back to the Farm, pronto. But the other part of her, the part she increasingly hated, had to spend a few days suffering in a thick cowl-neck Christmas sweater in wintry southern Ohio, gold wedding ring snug on her finger, Carpenters Christmas album blaring, everyone gathered in the kitchen like a goddamn Norman Rockwell painting, Tom chattering on an endless loop about applying for Ph.D. programs—all in the U.S. He didn't want her going overseas, was the bottom line. He'd prattled on about how maybe they could get a loan from his parents—they'd be happy to do it, thrilled, they wanted to help—so she could quit the Agency and they might rent a place in Boston or Palo Alto depending on the program he chose. And maybe also, he said plaintively, maybe Artemis could find it in her heart to go to Crate & Barrel over the holiday, for a spot of girls' time with his mom and the older sister who lived down in Houston with four kids and a peppy smile and a husband who did something with mortgages.

And Procter, who was then Artemis Jackson, having finally caved to the pressure and changed her name, was in the kitchen and said, hey, give me a job, something to help with, and Tom's mom had her start carving up one of the turkeys. More than twenty people were in the house that day. Whole extended Jackson family jammed in there together—Merry Fucking Christmas!—and that included four nieces and three nephews under the age of six, and she was pretty agitated while she sliced the bird, a smidge distracted, she'd say later. In the moment the looming Crate & Barrel outing was certainly a thundercloud on the horizon, but deeper still was the growing sense that she was on a collision course, the various trains hauling Artemis Aphrodite Procter's life were going to slam into each other and it was going to suck.

She saw the turkey breast turn bright red even before she felt the searing pain in her finger. And she let it fly, called the bird a fucking cocksucker and about a dozen iterations of that same sentiment. The adults were earmuffing the kids with their hands, bystanders had taken a sudden interest in their shoes, there were many sad shakes of the head all around. Her mother-in-law said, Artemis, please, the children, and she said, I'm sorry, I'm sorry, it just hurts like a bitch, can someone hand me a fucking towel. What?

Later, she and Tom were snug in their sexless bed, staring at the ceiling, her finger bandaged up with tape and gauze because she hadn't wanted to further demolish the family dinner by making Tom drive her to urgent care, though she probably did need stitches. Finally, Tom said, Where did that come from? And she wanted to ask what, but she knew what he was talking about. She had said, I'm sorry, okay? It hurt like hell and I'm sorry. Then they had one of those long pauses where the tension was unbearable but maybe also someone might just fall asleep. And even now she wished one of them had. Because Tom finally said, I don't like what the job is doing to you. It's twisting you up. Changing you into something else. And I sometimes don't recognize the woman I married.

That night, she thought, was the first time he'd really seen what she was, even just that little bit peering above the waterline. He had hated it. And she said, Look Tom, I love my job. I can't do anything else. Another long pause. Then Tom rolled over, pulled the chain to kill the lamp, and went to sleep.

PROCTER SHUT OFF THE TELEVISION. TOM HAD THREE KIDS now, she knew from a Google search she'd done a few years back. Photographs suggested he hadn't gotten fat, which was a shame. He ran marathons with his wife, who looked about ten years younger and was a babe. The man had written six books and had tenure, she gleaned from his Wikipedia page. She'd chosen the job over Tom to save herself. But maybe she'd also been saving him.

Procter absentmindedly twisted and folded the doily in her fingers; for a long while thoughts clanked uselessly through the can of her head, until she was up, strolling through the fading afternoon light into the bathroom, where she hiked up her shirt and looked at the nine stars tattooed in a line across her lats, the words IN HONOR inked above. One star for each of the fallen officers she had avenged. A personal memorial wall on her skin. She looked hard at those stars in the mirror. There was a world where she just stopped, let it go. CIA had tossed her out. The building doesn't love you back, after all. What could she possibly owe to a place that had released her from her vows? And yet . . .

Procter went to the bedroom and searched through her purse. Not finding what she wanted, she padded downstairs and pulled off the couch cushions. A Lifesaver. Two pennies. Crumbs. There—a quarter.

Sitting on the couch, she held the coin up to the light and told herself how it was going to be, in either case. Her fate in the hands of the intelligence gods.

She flipped the coin, caught it in her palm, and slapped it onto the back of her hand. She sneaked a peek.

George Washington.

"Goddammit," she said, and flung the quarter across the room.

SHE PACKED HER BAG AND WALKED TO THE MAIN GATE, FIGuring she would just call a cab to pick her up out front. It was hard to get into the Farm, not out. Upon seeing her, the guard said he had to make a call.

"No," she said. "Open the gate."

"Ms. Procter, I have instructions."

"Who are you calling?"

"DDO's office."

"It's pretty late, man, and Debs was just here. Said I could leave, so I'm leaving. Open the gate."

The guard, hand on his carbine, said: "Why don't you wait until morning to leave?"

"I'd like to leave now."

Procter pointed at the lowered boom. The guard gave a weary smile, looked down, and tapped a palm on his carbine, the gesture more of a tic, she thought, than a threat. "Just got to be after I speak with the DDO."

Procter stood there, reviewing the lowered boom. She told the guard to call Debs in the morning and was about to storm away when she stopped and said, "SRB still open?"

The guard gave her a barely perceptible smile and nodded.

THE STUDENT RECREATION BUILDING, THE SRB, HOUSES the Farm's primary drinking establishment. Set in a common building surrounded by dorms, the SRB is the beating heart of the Base. Procter could recall Farm classmates whose labors here had netted spouses and exes, one-night stands and loving relationships, tradecraft acumen and chlamydia, sometimes one and the same.

Procter, in general a fan of drinking establishments, was not, however, fond of the SRB. Most of her memories involved pacing the sidewalks outside, burning through her phone's minutes in tense conversations with Tom while her classmates inside drank and played darts and strutted around trying to bang each other.

In the bar fresh-faced trainees were playing pool and lobbing darts, drinking and laughing and telling each other lies. Procter spotted a bartender she recognized from her own Farm days—a rheumy-eyed woman with tremors who spilled a lot and doubled as one of the cafeteria lunch ladies. She'd been old back then and now she was a raisin. Procter ordered a beer and focused on a herd of paunchy graybeards. The instructors.

The classes required instructors who most nights would sidle up at the SRB to toss back a few beers and indoctrinate the trainees into the DO brotherhood (and it was a brotherhood). The communal drinking and raucous nighttime banter were encouraged by the instructors who, in addition to drilling the trainees on their tradecraft, paid close attention to how they handled their liquor and their tongues and bodies while under its influence. Now, beers in hand, sinking into tired green armchairs, the graybeards watched a trainee's rump bend and wiggle while lining up her pool shot.

Procter approached the oldsters, said it had been a hot minute since she'd been to the Farm, and did the instructors permanently stationed here still get the houses down near the river? She was curious, is all. Had thought it seemed like a first cabin opportunity and was considering putting her name in the hat for a PCS job out here. One of the graybeards smiled.

"Of course," he said. "I've been here fifteen months. Got one of the white bungalows near Dock A."

Procter whistled and took a seat on an armrest. Two instructors tilted their heads to see around her. She twisted her neck to catch a glimpse of the trainee chick's cleavage spread on the felt for another tricky shot. Procter turned back to the white bungalow guy.

"Let me guess," she said. "You put the overtime and danger pay from a few war zone tours toward a sweet boat."

He smiled; one of his comrades shook his head in knowing frustration, his face seeming to say: *Not this damn story again.*

"A twenty-seven-foot Albemarle." The first instructor beamed.

"Twenty-seven-footer? No shit?" Procter said. "Set you back a pretty penny?"

"Put it this way. Its less expensive and more fun than a new wife," said the man. "And the old wife, too. The lease is even less than the alimony."

THE FARM IS A SECURE INSTALLATION DEFENDED BY fifteen-foot fencing, razor wire, guards, pole cameras, and an army of unseen infrared cameras and sensors. But inside the Base almost no one locks houses or cars. Keys are left in the open. Bikes are strewn about.

Procter walked down toward the long row of primo Farm real estate overlooking the river. It was dark and, from the road, through the tree cover, she could not quite make out the color and design of each home, nor the presence of a trailer in the drive. Four times she hiked up driveways to find no trailer, no white bungalow.

On the fifth she found it. "Holy hell," Procter muttered, and just looked up at it for a moment, her brain firing off in all directions under the assault of the memories. The guy lived in Ganston's old house. She imagined herself up there with her friends, looking down at herself two decades later, a long cord drawn through the years. A gust of cold wind kicked up and the siren that announced her victories and her failures—Damascus, Dushanbe, a black farm outside Petersburg, Afghanistan—began to bay from deep in her brainbox, and she could feel the truth, the awful truth that the whole Service had been turned inside out by one of her friends, Langley's collective butt had been pulled through its mouth like a tongue and its tongue from its butthole like a tail, and if she did not do her part, then everything strung on that cord from then to now would be for naught.

The boat was hitched to a black King Ranch pickup. The car doors were unlocked but she could not find the keys inside. She peered into the darkened house. Rang the doorbell. No answer. Like everything else, the front door was unlocked. A wooden bowl sat on a table in the foyer. Papers, pens, cigarettes, a lighter. Ford keys. She punched the unlock button and headlamps flicked on in the drive. Rifling through the papers, she found another key ring with a plastic chain on it that read: *Dove Marina and Watersports.*

On a whim she stopped halfway out the door. Turning around, she marched upstairs and into the master bedroom. She opened the cabinet under the sink and felt around the bottom of the basin. Her fingers met tape, then paper. She plied back the tape, then, kneeling, she worked off the nub of glue she'd applied to the photo in that long-ago November. Apparently, a plumber had not visited this sink during the intervening quarter century. She tugged it out, blew off the dust, and stared at it for a moment: yellowed and fraying and faded. She'd thought the photo scandalous then, could recall nudging Debs's shoulder for a laugh while she'd been cutting it out. But now? Hell, twenty-five years later, and she'd done the stuff in the photo herself. More than once, in fact. She tucked the picture in her pocket and hustled downstairs.

She tossed her duffel into the pickup and drove to Dock A, backing the trailer down into the launch. Two trainees, necking on the dock, did not bother asking why Procter might be putting a boat into the river alone, and well past dark. In the pickup she scribbled a note that read: *I'll leave the boat near the Point. Sorry about this.* She set it on the dash and left the keys in the center console.

Tossing her duffel into the boat, Procter brought the engine to life and eased out into the glassy, moonlit water of the river.

41

I-95 NORTH / CRYSTAL CITY

AT THE POINT, PROCTER HAD TIED UP THE BOAT AND walked to a bar. Using the bar's phone, she called Sam on the burner number she'd memorized, then a cab that ferried her to the bus station, where she paid cash for a ticket on the last northbound Greyhound, now grinding through inexplicable late-night traffic on I-95. It had been stop-and-go for a while, but Procter hardly noticed; she was thinking about what she might set in motion, racking her brain to remember every detail of the REMORA case from back in the mists of time, before this sordid affair had become a blood-soaked journey into the pit of her soul. Brake lights ahead glowed orange. The bus stopped again, and another collective groan went up. Procter's head slumped into the window. Up to this point Procter didn't think she'd see the inside of a prison cell for her crimes. Now, though? Well, after flipping that coin, she wasn't so sure.

THE AIR IN THE CRYSTAL CITY SAFE HOUSE WAS STALE WHEN Procter flung open the door and waved Sam inside. Place was trashed, whether from neglect or the Chief's few hours here alone, Sam could not know. A trail of ants was running up one of the counters toward a lime the color of sack paper. She'd brewed a pot of coffee and, judging by the smell, had vaporized maybe a half pack of cigarettes, fumigating the place while she waited for him to show. Sam lugged in a bag of groceries. She shut the door behind him.

"Don't give me any goddamn sympathy about the bombing," she said. "I can't handle any of the mushy stuff from you. Let's just eat. Yeah, you can put it over there."

He did the steaks on the cooktop, then arranged the table with a loaf of sourdough, a wedge of blue cheese, and two glasses, each of which he filled with a sensible finger of whiskey. With about six ounces to go in his steak, Sam said, "Does Sweet know I was in Vegas with you?"

"She knows somebody was with me. Not necessarily that it was you, though she has her suspicions. Frankie's description of you was apparently not so detailed."

Sam spread cheese across a hunk of bread. "The other three would probably guess it was me. The mole certainly would."

"The mole knows you're involved already," Procter said.

"Why'd they try to kill you, then?"

"They could be coming for you next, who knows? You break it off with Natalie yet? You've got an even better reason now. Her safety."

"Not yet," he mumbled. "There's been a lot going on."

"You're a dumbass. You mind if I smoke, by the way?"

"I think you've earned it."

"Bless you." Procter eased back from the table and reached into her pocket for her lighter. Her lips pursed into a knowing smile while she was fishing around in her jeans. She emptied her pocket on the table. Setting aside the lighter, she unfolded a single picture. At first she was amused, grinning—it was weird, he thought, she seemed almost happy—but her face shed its humor the longer she stared. The grin melted into a thin, rueful smile that soon liquefied entirely, leaving the Chief looking merely sad. She folded up the photo and flicked angrily to light her cigarette. The cheap lighter gave her some trouble.

"Can I see it?" He extended a hand across the table.

She smacked it into his palm with a smirk. He unfolded it. Stared. Blinked.

"Jeez," he said. "This real? Doesn't seem possible."

"Oh, it's possible," she said, casting a cloud of smoke over her shoulder. "Believe me."

"You carting it around like some twisted security blanket?"

"Found it at the Farm. Little souvenir."

"Is it . . ."

"It is. An original. Turned out the guy I stole the boat from lives in Ganston's old house. I went in for a look-see." She laughed and took a long drag on the cigarette.

"Who hid this one?"

"Who do you think? None of those other clowns would've been able to find a spot so secure that it'd still be there twenty-five years later. I might not have been the top dog, but I was the scrappiest. You can take that to the bank." Her laugh this time was more melancholic. "True at the Farm, true again in Afghanistan, and now . . ."

She trailed off, and for a moment of companionable silence he went back to his steak and she to her cigarette until she was ready to go on.

"I've got a theory I'd like to test with you," she said. "I'd wager that you're with me on most of it already, but I think it's time to say it aloud, figure out where we might go from here."

Kicked back in her chair, slowly burning through a Slim, she began: "The Russians have recruited a senior CIA officer. But instead of a turn-and-burn to wreck our Moscow stable, roll up twenty sources overnight, Zhomov plays it slow and creative, possibly because he understands the nature of the clay he's molding here. He's got a big fish on his hook, a guy or gal who understands that what happened to Ames and Hanssen was in part because their reporting got assets killed or jailed, and the Derms wove together their matrices, and then a hunt was on. Zhomov sees this mole as a potential agent of influence, maybe someone who could be Deputy Director or even Director someday. Someone that might hand the Agency, effectively, over to Russian control. Zhomov's patient with his burrowing mole. Sticks-and-bricks commo plan, infrequent meets, maybe annually, maybe twice if they can find the cover. The mole's in it for money, sure, but also for some hidden fanaticism that I cannot, as of yet, truly see or understand. I'd submit the first time the mole peeks its head aboveground is to rat on the outreach from Golikov and your meeting in Singapore. The mole was surprised by Golikov—hell, if what that Russian told you is true, the Special Section sprang a leak somewhere, and the whole promise of Zhomov's shop is that it doesn't leak. I'd also wager that poor BUCCANEER's recall from Greece, and maybe CLAW's roll-up, were overreaches, mistakes, or the result of bureaucratic shenanigans or dysfunction in Moscow. SVR doesn't always play so nice with the FSB cousins, and vice versa. I could see the FSB jonesing for arrests."

Sam had so far maintained a steady gaze in the direction of the living room wall, sometimes folding his napkin in his fingers, or drumming them nervously across the table. "How would the mole have known what Golikov was going to share with me?"

"I think it was an educated guess. Golikov's message wasn't specific, but it was very urgent. Very serious. And he had primo access inside the Kremlin. My theory—again, Jaggers, theory—has it that the mole thought, based on Golikov's position, that he might be trying to sell the mole's identity to us. And in that case, something had to be done. Action had to be taken."

"And the timing works," he said. "Even if we assume the commo plan is sticks-and-bricks."

"Just barely," she acknowledged. "But it works. In this theory, Zhomov's principal deception is the asset known as REMORA, an SVR colonel, and now arguably Russia House's crown jewel, whose information"—she was watching him closely to see its impact—"has been critical in three major events of the past year. One, he signaled for a crash meet just as you and I were planning for Singapore, and at this meeting told Mac, Theo, and Debs that the Russians were looking to target Americans in Asia. Two: REMORA supplied an innocent rationale for your imprisonment, and, in a wild twist, helped CIA target the SVR officer that we would eventually swap for you. And three: it was REMORA who again flew the signal just as you and I were ramping up this investigation, before the bombing at my trailer perpetrated by freaks doubtless in Kremlin employ. Three emergency signals precede meetings in France significant to Golikov, your imprisonment, and the attempt on my life. Those are verifiable facts. Now, REMORA has given us some good shit, Jaggers. It's a primo case. The haul has catapulted careers inside Russia House. It's the kind of case ops officers make their bones on. And seen in one light, that's all it is."

"And in the other?" he asked.

"It's a drip to screw with us, influence us, and to provide operational cover for the mole to meet with Russians to sell our secrets. The facts are consistent with a theory that what we have seen is a pattern of Russian attempts—quarterbacked, sure as sugar, by Rem Zhomov—to protect their mole. To safeguard their access and investment."

"And there is no proof," he said. "After all of it, there is no proof yet."

"Right. This really won't wash anywhere," she said. "There's the pattern in the finished intel: the wheat to get us hooked, then the chaff so they don't give away the farm. There's the firing of Petra Devine after she started poking around. There's Frankie's recollection that REMORA is one of Zhomov's men. There's grist for motive among our little bestiary of suspects. There are garden-variety lies and deceptions, particularly about who was at the REMORA meeting on the cusp of Singapore, in what order, and when. But I do not believe, Jaggers, that a desktop exercise will untangle this web. It takes a mole to catch a mole. No Derm matrix is going to give us the answer, but it's narrowed the field, and—"

"If," he interrupted, his tone becoming muscular, "it's narrowed the field, *if* we accept the premise that"—insistent tap of a finger against the table—"the REMORA stream is inside out. If we buy Frankie's claim about REMORA's history with Zhomov, and assume that they're still teamed up. That REMORA works with, or for, Zhomov."

"Fair, fair," she said. "Fucking fair. If you accept all that, I've got suspects and an idea that could lure our mole aboveground."

"Which is what, precisely?"

"You ever hear of a barium meal, Jaggers?"

"That some lingo from the Cold War glory days?"

"Means we feed something into the system and see where it comes out on the other end. Or who it comes out of."

Sam made a face. "That implies we need to see it at both ends."

"Oh, it doesn't imply that. That's what it is. We feed the meal into a few mouths and position ourselves for a good look at the butts." She paused. Then said, "Look, man, it'll be hard to do it without you. But even I'm not sure. I made up my mind, but I'm not sure."

"Why's your mind made up?" he asked.

"I was fifty-fifty, so I flipped a coin at the Farm. Let the intelligence gods decide. Heads, I keep at it. Tails, I disappear. It was heads. So I bounced from the Farm, then I called you."

42

FAIRFAX, VIRGINIA / CRYSTAL CITY

PAUL PORTNOY, A PSYCHOLOGIST ON CONTRACT WITH CIA, was a former case officer of no repute who'd quit the Service three decades prior, deciding he'd attempt to treat mental illness rather than encourage it in the form of coaxing foreigners to commit treason. Portnoy had at first sworn off any entanglements with CIA, but by the mid-aughts his private practice had stagnated and the Agency had generous coin to throw his way. Those days were peak War on Terror, and there were plenty of officers returning from the war zones with problems to work through. At any given time, about half of Portnoy's patient load came from his contract with CIA, which paid its bills on time and had even set him up with a counseling room and office that were graded as commercial sensitive compartmented information facilities, SCIFs. Under the terms of his master contract with CIA, Portnoy was required to write up cables following each session. Many of the officers were dealing with issues—Post Traumatic Stress, burnout, on and on—and their Langley components wanted to know if they might again be trusted in the field. Portnoy's sign-off was critical to reestablishing that trust.

And now one of his patients, Sam Joseph, a recently terminated case officer, was sitting on the floor outside his office, waving, as Portnoy rounded the corner from the elevator bank. Joseph's hair was mussed, and he had a frantic energy rolling off him. Up to this point the patient had functioned pretty well given the circumstances, but as

Portnoy approached, he had the distinct impression Sam was strung out on something.

"Doc! Dr. Portnoy!" Sam called out as he stood up. "We gotta talk. Have a chat."

"Sam, our appointment is not until next week," Portnoy said.

"Need to do it today." Sam slurred back. Definitely on drugs, Portnoy thought, steeling himself for what would certainly be an unpleasant start to his morning.

Sam offered Portnoy his hand, and when he took it Portnoy caught the stench of whiskey wafting toward him. He looked the patient up and down for a beat. "You on drugs, Sam?"

"No, Doctor."

"No?"

"Nothing illegal. Just a little tipsy."

Portnoy did not need this. He had an hour and a half until his first appointment at ten, but that was reserved for charting and bookkeeping. Then he had a full roster of appointments.

"Are you having suicidal thoughts?" Portnoy said, scowling. "If you're considering self-harm, I will escort you to the ER."

"Gotta be in your SCIF room," Sam said, talking past him. "Gotta be right now. I'm working through something."

Portnoy sighed. What this smelled like, other than booze, was a lost morning. A wasted hour babysitting a lunatic. A session that, though he could bill CIA, would not be worth the squeeze, given the quantity of frustrating cables he would be forced to draft in its wake. He could call the police, but that would definitely ruin the entire morning.

"How drunk are you?" Portnoy was scowling.

"Not enough. Look."

Standing, Sam walked heel to toe in a passably straight line. Then he said, "Z, Y, X, W . . ."

"Enough!" Portnoy shouted. "Let's make this quick."

PORTNOY OPENED THE VAULT AND SAT DOWN AT HIS DESK. He flicked on the microphones and collected a notebook and pen. The harsh overhead lights buzzed; above them a wall clock ticked away. Sam flopped into one of the tired green easy chairs.

"What is going on? What could not wait?" Portnoy asked flatly.

"I've been thinking more about the time before they got me. The few minutes when I was talking with him."

"They? Who is they? And who is him?" Portnoy said, exasperated.

"They is the Russians," Sam said. "And him is Golikov. When I got home I spent a few weeks at Langley running through what I told the Russians in Moscow, and what I heard from Golikov before he disappeared. And, here's the thing, Doctor, I've been foggy and the memories roll back unevenly, in waves, and I was talking to Natalie"—*Natalie Karam*, Portnoy would write in the cable, *REF C/O's significant other*—"this morning and I said that I'd been playing more poker, maybe too much, kind of a problem because impulse control's a challenge after the unpleasantness"—here Portnoy snatched a glance at Sam's face, remembering what had been done to him in Russia, and how the guy had looked when he'd finally told the story—"and I mentioned how a few weeks back I went out to Vegas for a little gambling and I was at a table chatting up a dealer and I was suddenly, like, I don't know, transported to Singapore, and I was remembering the few words Golikov shared with me before he went upstairs, and if I'm remembering them correctly it's pretty damn important."

In the throes of a PTSD collapse, Portnoy scribbled illegibly into his notebook. As Sam prattled on, his voice rose and fell at random, his feet bounced so wildly he was probably shaking loose the ceiling spackling downstairs, sending it down like rain on the good folks at Labcorp. "What was so important?" Portnoy asked.

"In Singapore," Sam replied, "Golikov said SVR had someone inside CIA."

At this, Portnoy swiveled his head to face Sam's directly, his naturally sweaty skin suddenly cold and dry. "Hey," he said. "Hey, now. Easy, Sam. What?"

"Golikov said SVR had someone inside CIA. Run by the Special Section. Some other clues I can't remember. But I will, or I think I will."

"Look," Portnoy said again, "you're drunk. Let's just be honest about that. Maybe we call it here, I don't write this up, and you come back tomorrow and we see where we are?"

"Dr. Portnoy," Sam said, staring through him with no small amount of menace, "I remember it clear as day now. This is important."

"Fine. Is that exactly what this Golikov said?" Portnoy asked, beginning to write. "Give me the chain of the information, if you remember it?"

"Golikov said he'd gotten it from someone on . . . the Russian Security Council. Don't remember the name, but he said it, I'll remember it. He said, and I quote, 'SVR has someone inside CIA, an asset run by the Special Section.' That's what he was in Singapore to trade. From there it's fog. Smoke in the brain. Write that down, Doctor, I've gotta set the record straight, we've gotta fix this."

AFTER HE HAD LEFT PORTNOY'S OFFICE, SAM MADE THE call from the Crystal City safe house with a new burner, purchased in cash, and loaded with an Ultra Mobile international SIM card he picked up at an electronics shop run by Serbians. As expected, Rami Kassab did not answer. And why would he? He did not recognize the number. But Sam left a short voice mail, saying he would be in Paris for a few days and was keen to see the brothers. He rang off by suggesting he'd love to go out for some *barazek*, a Syrian sweet biscuit covered with sesame seeds and crushed pistachios. And while Sam did love *barazek*, he had no illusions that there would be any waiting for him in Paris. It was a brevity word, from their Damascus days; the brothers had mentioned *barazek* in time-sensitive communications to signal freedom from hostile control. He called Natalie and said he'd be traveling for a few days. Back soon, *habibti*, he made himself say, and when he'd hung up Procter smacked him on the back of the head, said she wasn't angry with him, just disappointed. "Chief," Sam replied, "give it a rest. Why do both of our homes need to explode at the same time?"

Procter and Sam purchased their tickets in true name—a risk, but what could be done? There was so little time. They rolled through a mad-dash shopping spree for any equipment they could acquire stateside and pile into their carry-ons. Commercially available surveillance cameras were now so small, flexible, and cheap that it was straightforward to quickly acquire an adequate supply.

Rami Kassab returned Sam's call before they left for the airport. He and Sam made plans for breakfast upon arrival in Paris. When Rami asked after the purpose of his trip, Sam said business, and let it sit there for a few silent seconds. He could hear Rami breathing through the speaker, his lips clicking together, thinking. The Kassabs had no clue Sam and Procter were no longer with CIA. We shouldn't burden those poor boys with more complexity, Procter had urged. Let's keep it simple for them.

"How are we going to pay them?" Sam asked after he'd hung up.

"We? You're the card shark, Jaggers, you'll figure it out."

43

MOSCOW

ACCORDING TO THE CIA PROFILE DR. B HAD PASSED ALONG, the Americans believed Rem to be a chess champion. The document stated that he'd been fond of the game since youth, and assessed that he brought *hard-won lessons in strategic thinking, patience, and tactics to the recruitment and running of spies.* The faulty analysis amused and flattered Rem. It was not so terrible for the opposition to paint you as a modern-day Karla, cunning and competent, always one step ahead. He rearranged his donut pillow; hemorrhoids had been flaring up as of late, an awful distraction from his arthritic knees and hips.

In truth, Rem did not play much chess, and he'd certainly not excelled at the game as a boy. He found it boring: the low stakes, the snobby ritualism, the pieces as preprogrammed automatons. Rem did not think about his world as a chessboard, he did not use such analogies to order his moves. Now, despite the feverish complexity of the war he was fighting, he thought only of how Dr. B might be preserved to continue reporting. How the threats facing the doctor might be eliminated. And here, even if chess had been his bailiwick, Rem would have vainly struggled for any comparison to a board game in which two opponents sit politely in seats and flick plastic pieces across a board in a make-believe war.

The photos of MICKEY and MINNIE's disastrous performance, first of all, put paid any notion of a stuffy conflict pitched across a wooden battlefield. He slid the printouts onto the table, cupped his hands around his nose, and looked straight at Gennady. "A bomb?" Gennady looked down. "What did your Spaniard tell them?"

"He did not tell them to build a bomb. And they did not tell him they were building a bomb," Gennady said.

"They live in a country with more guns than people, and they chose to build a bomb?"

"Apparently not a good one."

Rem nudged his chin at the pictures; the one on top was a close-up of a charred head. Such things made Rem think of Afghanistan. Even now he did not like to think of Afghanistan. "The body is MICKEY's?"

"Right."

"And MINNIE is asking for guidance?" Rem asked.

"Correct. She has sent a message through the usual channel asking for instructions."

"She will certainly be taken into custody soon, yes? Don't you think?"

"I would assume so. We should assume so."

"Put her on ice. No contact. Nothing. Not after this fiasco. She's cut off. Now, I do not like to do this, but get me Laskin. And do it now."

REM LIKED LASKIN EVEN LESS THAN HE LIKED THINKING about Afghanistan. In fact, when he had to make use of Laskin he typically did so through intermediaries, usually the Director, whom Laskin would heed without question. The questions. With Laskin there were always so many questions, and all were volleyed in a tone so brusque it often drifted into outright hostility.

"And what, exactly, is happening at this French farmhouse?" This was Laskin's fourth question, and by a wide margin his most hostile. He gestured toward the map on the table. A blue sticker had been placed at the farmhouse's location.

They were in Rem's office sitting around the corner table, which was set into the windows facing the forest. When Rem had walked outside that morning he'd found the air crisp, announcing a winter that had mercifully not yet fully arrived. The Moscow sky was bright blue.

He'd traded a joke or two with his neighbor and inquired about his son's swimming exploits. He'd passed a silent and contented breakfast with Ninel and she'd laid out his clothes and he'd gotten dressed without any expectation of arriving at the office to pictures of a muffed assassination attempt and an emergency signal from Dr. B. Strange times to be a Russian bureaucrat.

"Doesn't matter what's happening at the house," Rem growled. "It only matters who is there."

Laskin turned imploringly to Gennady. Finding no moral support there, he swung to the windows, as if the trees might back him. "And you have permission for this, Rem? This is approved?"

Rem wagged his finger, each jerk of the hand seeming to bring Laskin nearer to punching him. An aide knocked to bring in tea. "Go away," Rem shouted. They listened to footsteps padding off.

"Before I ask for permission," Rem said, "I need to know what resources will be required. And we both know, Colonel Laskin, just how tentative these approvals can be. This is all in the spirit of building the package. We have hours, not days. This is Singapore all over again."

The mention of Singapore elicited from Laskin a weak grunt, and then a shine in his eyes that made Rem want to throw him into oncoming traffic. "I'm brought in to shovel your shit," he said. "As usual. I don't know what exactly you are protecting, Rem, but it's making me jumpy. Isn't this shop supposed to be boring? Knife-and-fork business, right? Yakking up Americans at cocktail parties, that kind of thing? Buckets of blood have been spilled as of late. Hardly the calling card of a jet-setting alumnus of the First Chief Directorate. It's not a good sign, when you hoist old Laskin up from the basement for a chat about source protection. When I get involved, the source isn't being protected. By definition."

"Colonel," Rem said dryly, "sometimes it is best to keep your mouth shut."

Gennady began unfurling maps across the table.

Laskin had said his piece, the hands up, *Fine, fine*, retreat was entirely predictable for the man, who now stood for a more expansive view of the detailed maps depicting the Provençal village of Lacoste and its immediate environs. The SVR had produced high-quality maps of the area after Dr. B had been recruited.

Rem tapped his finger on the sticker marking the farmhouse. Gennady shoved a binder of photos at Laskin. "Landscapes and terrain. There's a thumb drive in there with a handful of videos."

"Two hours, Laskin," Rem said. "You have two hours to tell me how many people you need to maintain overwatch on this property and intervene if necessary. And how many you can slip into France on zero notice."

"That is not enough time," Laskin said, in a lawyerly voice, still hunched over the map.

"Two hours," Rem snapped, "is what you've fucking got, Colonel."

THIS TIME THE SVR DIRECTOR ASKED REM TO ACCOMPANY him to meet the President. Rem found himself in a four-car convoy of armored Land Cruisers, blue sirens wailing, flying down the reserved center lane where the roads had them. His knee pain was worsening as the day went on, he was famished from the day's sprint, and worn down by the drip of arguments with Laskin, which, as had been the case with Singapore, had stretched exhaustingly into the afternoon, the insufferable bastard. Laskin was the type of subordinate that made you fantasize about a return to Stalinism, if only to end the argument by putting a bullet in his neck.

The car swaddled Rem: dim, plush, and warm, womblike excepting the pleasurable smell of smoke and an overmatched citrus that made him think of Rome. The ride was smooth as marble and the gentle hum of the car tugged at his eyelids. The Director was reading a briefing book in silence. He also seemed to loll forward in fits; when the Director shot up straight he would press fingers into the corner of his eyes and blink feverishly for a reboot. Rem, surrendering, clutched his documents and nodded off.

He woke to the driver's voice: "Director? Comrade Director?" The tone was insistent, layered by the obvious worry that they were both dead. It was very clearly not his first attempt to wake them.

The Director mopped spittle from the corner of his mouth and heaved himself out of the car. "Let's hope we can make this quick," the Director said. "I need to eat something so I can take my back pills."

THE OFFICE'S ANTEROOM WAS BROWN: DARK MAHOGANY walls, carved paneled ceiling, clock engraved with the imperial double eagle, brown leather chairs and sofa, bookshelf groaning with brown-jacketed books, a collection of encyclopedias, by the look of it. They'd submitted to the COVID PCR test, completed the medical questionnaires, and, an hour earlier, had been green-lighted for their face-to-face with the President.

Now they waited. There was no food, no tea. Rem was alone and hungry on a brown sea. The chairs were thinly cushioned, razors on his ass. The troubling absence of the President's security detail made Rem wonder if this meeting would be canceled. Out of precaution for any leaks inside the President's staff, the topic had been submitted as "*Director's Brief*"—there had of course been no mention of Dr. B—and Rem now wondered if that had been a mistake, a signal this meeting could be skipped or perhaps attended by an uncleared aide. The slanted amber light of a November afternoon poured through the window and made his limbs feel numb. To fight sleep Rem rehearsed what he might say to any number of specific questions raised about the France operation, MICKEY and MINNIE, or Dr. B.

Two hours later. An aide beckoned them into the President's office. Putin sat behind a desk with the size and clutter of an emptied flatbed truck. He was reading a thin stack of papers that Rem was certain bore no relation to this meeting. He did not greet them, nor acknowledge their presence. Both men sat at a long pine table at least five meters downrange, waiting to be addressed.

"Small gathering for a budget meeting," the President said.

"What?" the Director called back. "No. That's next week. This is about the good Doctor. Our American source."

"Ah. Yes?"

"Dr. B is in some trouble," the Director said, palm sliding across the table. "We think—"

An aide flung open the door, stomped to the President's side, and whispered something in his ear, the impact of which made his eyes roll. "Tell them I will speak to him first," the President muttered to the aide, perhaps at a higher volume than intended. The aide scurried out, the door—which, Rem now saw, had to be at least six meters high—sighed shut, and they were all staring at each other.

"When *is* the budget discussion?" the President asked.

The Director thought about that one. For longer than he should have, Rem thought. "Next Tuesday, I believe."

Putin sniffed, nodded, grunted for the Director to continue.

"Dr. B is in a bit of trouble," the Director went on. "We need to have a chat in France. And that's normal, but there's been some heat as of late, reasons to wonder if the Doctor might arrive at the meeting with coverage. And if that's the case we need more eyes and ears on the ground. Make sure we own the turf. We're bringing this to your attention because I am suggesting that we may be required to eliminate problems as they might arise." The Director punctuated the subtle request with a cough.

"Didn't this happen some time ago?"—the President, interest rising.

"Yes. In Singapore. There was a leak. We patched it before the Americans learned anything of value, but it was messy, as you recall."

"It was sloppy."

"This will not be a mess."

"I recall that promise from last time. Someone said that. Maybe even you, Rem Mikhailovich." He tilted to face Rem.

The aide reappeared. This time his stomps toward the desk were harder, his whispers softer. When he was done speaking, the President jerked his head toward the aide with the universal expression of *Are you kidding me?* and flicked his hand in a curt dismissal. The President had now leaned forward in his seat—though it was not visible, Rem believed that his hand was snug on his crotch—where he picked up one of the phones and made a call while Rem and the Director sat twiddling their thumbs. When he was done, the President stood, shrugged on his suit jacket, and looked at the Director: "Dr. B's intelligence is invaluable. Let's be sure you don't lose it."

ON THE RIDE BACK TO THE FOREST, REM AND THE DIRECTOR did not sleep. Instead they reconstructed the discussion word for word, moment by moment, divining the President's fluid wishes from his words, glances, body language, and silences. Rem was no fool. He did not speak his mind; he waited for the Director to do so. By the time they'd eased out of the car to walk inside Headquarters, Rem felt certain of two things: neither he nor the Director had a clue as to what the President wanted, and it would fall to him to make the call. SVR was a hierarchical system, and that meant shit rolled downhill. The slogging and fighting—the work—drizzled down to guys such as Rem, who clung to this business like the abusive spouse it was. Ninel would remind him of his impending retirement. Tell him to back off and let someone else handle it. But how could he? He knew exactly what to do. He'd known since the information had arrived that morning but had been forced to suffer through this circus for the ass covering and, let's face it, the pomp. Because what good is a big bureaucracy and a Russian chief executive if you don't use the machinery? The bills had to be justified somehow. They had reached the building. "I've got confidence in you, Rem," the Director said, taking his shoulder into a chummy grip. "You'll manage. It's what you do."

44

PARIS

THEY TRAVELED ON SEPARATE ITINERARIES. PROCTER caught a flight to Brussels and then hired a car for the drive to Paris. Sam flew to London and then rode the Eurostar through the Chunnel. By the time they reunited outside the Gare du Nord, Procter had conceded that she would contribute to the common fund. By the time they were in the taxi, driving through the suburbs toward a café in the 3rd, they'd agreed to split the Kassabs' fee, should the topic of money come up. Though she was praying that they would not charge when they eventually found out the stakes—and that the U.S. government was not footing this bill. Family and friends discount, she hoped, they'll be thrilled just to be back in the Game. Jet-lagged and early, they bought watery machine coffees at a boulangerie and scouted the area around the café. An odor rose from the Saint-Paul Metro station that to Procter mingled burnt paper and blocked drains and piss: the smell of Paris. They watched an old man's dog defecate at the top of the station stairs.

The café had a bright red awning and the gray stone was bearded with ivy. A window for takeaway sandwiches swung open. A waiter was setting out tables, chairs, and heaters. Like all Parisian waiters, he excelled at avoiding eye contact, particularly with two foreigners lugging suitcases. "I'm going to take a walk," she said.

"I'll come with you," Sam offered.

"Alone."

The neighborhood had been hers once. First tour, one year after the

Farm, Tom reluctantly in tow. She strolled along the narrow cobblestone streets, under the black mansard roofs and hanging lanterns flickering off in the gray morning light. She passed the cornflower-blue shop front; a café, top-shelf duck, she remembered. In a few blocks she came to the little boulangerie run by the angry couple. Procter peeked inside, saw a familiar woman jabbering in rapid-fire French at her husband, whose back Procter made out. The woman looked old now. But unlike Procter, she was still married.

Sunlight had begun to splinter through the clouds, but the cold was still biting, and Procter huddled into her tweed blazer as she walked on. She'd left her heavier jacket in her suitcase with Jaggers at the café.

After a few blocks, she came upon the old apartment. The door was still green; the paint still peeling but now bubbled with age. She looked up. Second story, window sharing a wall with a bank. Empty flower pots on the sill. Red curtains. Not much had changed.

The *tabac* did not have Slims, so she had to settle for smoking a Gauloise outside her old building, a place where she'd loved, cooked, fucked, cried, argued, made up, argued some more, and, at last, shed her old skin to become who she'd always been. Tom had gone home after six terrible months; she would see him once more after that, when she paid a visit to their D.C. apartment for a duffel bag of clothes. On the walk back to the café, she tripped over an upturned cobblestone, just managing to catch herself on a parked scooter. She dusted herself off, righted the handlebars, and spat into the road.

"City of Light, my ass," Procter said.

BANDITO HAD BEEN THE AGENCY CRYPTONYM FOR THE Kassab triplets: Elias, Yusuf, and Rami. They were former CIA support assets—the type who can acquire cars, apartments, equipment, or conduct surveillance. The Kassabs were Syrian American dual citizens hailing from a wealthy Christian family that had once owned car dealerships throughout Syria and Lebanon. The collapse of both countries had led many in the Levantine middle and upper classes to flee for safer harbors: London, Dubai, Paris. Sam had recruited the brothers, years earlier, in Istanbul. They'd helped on a few of the thornier operations during Procter's tour in Damascus. But somewhere between the shuttering of the family business and the permanent move to Paris they'd ended the relationship with CIA. No bad blood, Procter remembered. Agents stopped working all the time. Not much you could do to persuade them otherwise. It was insane to work for CIA in the first place. You had to have a screw loose somewhere, Procter figured. And, hell, she of all people could appreciate that. She had her own wobbly rivets to manage.

When Procter returned to the café, the brothers were sitting with Jaggers at a quiet table in the back, laughing. Yusuf's smile disintegrated as she approached.

"Relax, Yusuf," she said.

Rami and Elias spun around to see her, then back to Sam, with a look that said: *Not this lady.*

Procter shoved into the booth alongside Yusuf. She kissed his cheeks, then leaned across and did the same for Rami and Elias. She hailed a waiter and in butchered French ordered a black coffee and an omelet and a bottle of champagne. The waiter asked what type of champagne and Procter, channeling Gus perhaps, said, "the cheapest one you've got." There was no bread, so she called for that, had a quick little spat with the garçon on account of the bread baskets traditionally coming out around the lunch hour, but then, as usually happened, they had some sticky eye contact for a few seconds and he knew it would not end until there was bread, so he scurried off and returned with a few slices of a sourdough boule and a small cup of salted butter. Procter was famished. She thickly buttered a slice, took a bite, and then realized no one was talking.

Elias was looking at the door. Contemplating evac, thought Procter, maybe not the worst move for these three right now. "Well, it's good to see you boys again," she said. "How's the family? How's life in this shithole of a town?"

THEY BROKE BREAD FOR AN HOUR. THE CHAMPAGNE RAN out, so Rami ordered another bottle. A goddamn expensive one. They drained that, too. There was no mention of Syria, of CIA. That would have been uncouth this early in the dance. As they spoke, and the BANDITOs' initial shock and disbelief subsided, the rickety hamster wheel inside Procter's head that assessed, developed, and recruited human beings creaked into gear. Time to move this along. As discussed with Jaggers, she turned over her fork and tapped a finger on the tines.

When Yusuf had finished describing his girlfriend's interest in working for an art studio, Sam gently turned to Rami. "This is part social call, part business, as I said on the phone. There's a job, and Artemis and I could use some help."

"A job?" Rami said. His face brightened. Good, Procter thought, we can work with that. So did Elias's. Yusuf, not so much.

"There is a farmhouse down south," Sam said, "outside Lacoste. Russians are meeting someone there. We want to know who it is."

The brothers were all looking at each other, some unspoken energy passing between them. They all had the same tics, but didn't look much like brothers. Rami was squatty, and had gotten squattier; Yusuf, long and lean; Elias had always been right down the middle, and remained so.

"Russians," Elias said, "don't love jobs involving Russians."

"Right?" Procter said. "Sheesh. But it's the hand we've been dealt. We live in a world with Russians, maybe in the next life we won't have to deal with them, but for now? All jammed up. Look, we need your help, guys. We need to case the place, wire it for audio and video, and see what goes down. Need to start now."

"You're talking about today?" Rami said. He shot Yusuf a bemused look.

"Short notice," Sam said.

"That's called no notice," Elias retorted, frowning. "You guys have equipment?"

"Some," Sam said. "We may need your help with a few things."

"How much does it pay?" Yusuf asked.

"We pay in honor and gratitude," Procter said, with heart.

"CIA pays in honor and gratitude these days?" Elias said.

"You might say it's a tad unofficial," Sam offered.

The brothers' eyes flitted around again. Rami coughed.

Procter sighed. "Goddammit."

45

LACOSTE, FRANCE

IN THE SPY FLICKS PROCTER HAD ENJOYED AS A TEENAGER, the breaking-and-entering (B&E) operations were typically conducted by teams of busty and/or burly operatives with elaborate gadgets and hard attitudes. The crews were usually small; they took few precautions to cover their tracks; they did not use layers of countersurveillance as protection; they hid cameras and microphones in locations professionals would uncover in minutes. Also, nothing randomly awful happened, as when Procter had been running a B&E op in Amman and they knocked over the target's terrarium and there was a pet scorpion in there and it jabbed one of her guys in the arm and he nearly died in a dusty Jordanian hospital.

After, in the movies, the surveillants would sit watching the feeds and sometimes things would get sweaty on account of the sexy crew, butt cheek to butt cheek, in a teensy van.

The vans were the only accurate bit. A good van was critical, and the BANDITOs had found one, a weather-beaten Mercedes Sprinter, from a dealer in one of the Paris suburbs. But now Procter was faced with a conundrum: she had an under-funded, under-peopled, under-prepped B&E op on her hands—just like in the movies—but instead of the silent drills and the sexy surveillant partners, she was trundling down a rutted dirt road with three out-of-practice Syrians and a fellow disgraced CIA retiree in a smelly van groaning with tape, wire, and ladders, hoping to catch sight of a fully clothed CIA traitor.

It was Monday morning: Procter was struggling with bone-deep fatigue from the one-two-three punch of sleepless nights, a frenetic pace of work, and near-constant surges of anxiety. Last night when she had tried to sleep, her heart had been beating so quickly she could hear it in her ears, feel it thudding against the sheets. They were three days removed from Sam's discussion with Portnoy and the cable that, if they were correct, would have triggered another meeting with REMORA. Saturday, after the pitch to the BANDITOs, had been a frenzied shopping run. On Sunday they'd secured the van, and by the afternoon they'd all split off again. The BANDITOs drove the van down to Provence, taking shifts through the night. Sam and Procter had rented separate cars, avoiding trains and the risk of bumping into whichever of her friends was on their way here to meet with REMORA. They had reunited with the BANDITOs at a threadbare home the brothers had rented outside the village of Lumières, where, that morning, they made final preparations before setting out for the farmhouse.

The clock was ticking, and fast: REMORA's commo plan stipulated that, once the emergency signal was flown, a meeting should occur at the farmhouse in three days' time. Which could happen as early as that evening. And based on the message Sam had passed to CIA through Portnoy, well, their mole would have to be asleep at the wheel not to signal for a crash meet.

On the final approach to the farmhouse Sam and Procter again argued over the wisdom of running a shoestring countersurveillance operation. Procter wore him down, insisting no, no, if they beat us here they've already won. We won't see it. Not with the time and the people we've got. No offense, man. That's a comment on number, not quality. Though they did complete a long loop around the hillside switchbacks above the farmhouse to map sight lines and assess the risk of neighborly snooping. It was low, they decided, not zero but low. And that had no doubt figured into the use of this property for CIA business. Much of the house and drive were walled off by towers of cypress. Clean views into the house itself would require hiking off the road, down the hill, and up another, to a forested stretch just above the swell of a vineyard.

They opened the unlocked iron gate and crunched up the drive, stopping out front of the farmhouse. One story, stone, ancient oak door, a dry and flaking fountain decorated by cherubs. Theirs was just another dented white van. Could be a delivery truck or plumbing van—except that the people emerging from it were dressed more like crime scene technicians than tradesmen. The entire team wore N95 masks, nitrile gloves, booties, and hairnets. Procter's curly mane required two, which she hid under a ball cap.

The front door's lock gave quickly at Procter's handiwork, and then they were inside, Sam and Yusuf snapping photos and rolling video so they could be sure they left the home in its virginal state. Happily, they discovered there was not much furniture, and the rooms were spartan and uncluttered. There would be little to move.

Normally, they would have swept for countermeasures and run a radio frequency survey to see if the TV, say, or the microwave hummed with extra energy. But they had no RF analyzer, and little time. They saw that there were no extra wires trailing from the appliances or climbing the walls outside. Nothing sticky on the door, no double-sided tape with hair on it. The REMORA cables, too, had noted that the house was not wired. Nothing to do but knock on wood and press on.

They did have two advantages over a traditional B&E op. One: Their equipment only had to function for a few hours—not days, weeks, or months. That meant they did not need to rip up baseboards and crown molding and run wires from a power source through the floors and walls to, say, the back of a stereo system, with the pinhole cameras snuggled inside. Though larger and more expensive than Procter would have liked, the cameras that Sam pulled out of his case ran on batteries with a durable life measured in days. More than enough time.

Two: Their targets had not been in the home in months—and they did not live there. Normally a B&E team is disrupting a target's home or office; in this case the visitors were unlikely to notice crooked picture frames or out-of-place knickknacks.

Procter checked all sixteen feeds from a laptop as Sam and the BANDITOs placed the cameras and mics in track lights, chandeliers, cupboards, the ceiling, wall outlets. A desperate feeling began gnawing at her guts. This is a waste, it said, you are a lunatic for even trying. Pale sunlight faded as they worked. Though the windows were shuttered, the breeze found its way inside, bringing with it an earthy scent that tweaked Procter's already fraying nerves.

46

LOURMARIN, FRANCE / LACOSTE

INSIDE A CONCRETE-BLOCK BUILDING IN THE SHADOW OF a crumbling winery twenty kilometers south, near Lourmarin, a herd of Russians unpacked surveillance equipment and a collection of weapons smuggled through a roundabout journey originating in eastern Libya before terminating in a cache SVR maintained outside Avignon. The members of the Russian team had traveled to France in alias and on tourist passports—many of them German—by way of complex itineraries that, in the most extreme cases, had required more than a day of constant travel, across no less than two countries and three modes of transport. All had crossed the French border by car or train, and all had paid cash for their tickets. The French security services would have been quite interested in putting questions to more than a few of them—Laskin foremost—if only they'd been aware any were in-country.

Had the team been less unwieldy—comprised, as it was, of Laskin's trigger-pullers and the legs of the operation, the counter-surveillants who had arrived first—or had the gears of bureaucracy in Moscow cranked at the same speed as Artemis Procter's shoestring operation, they might have arrived in time to disrupt the breaking and entering work her team had completed that afternoon. Instead, hunched over maps, Laskin and his men marked out the coverage, unaware of the grave threat posed by a tattered van parked in a shady lot several hundred meters down the road from the farmhouse.

Over the next six hours, the Russian surveillance teams fanned out across the area, establishing positions at the main arteries leading to the farmhouse. One team drove south, toward Aix-en-Provence, where they would pick up Dr. B's tail, trailing the agent to the farmhouse to check for surveillance.

In two rented Renault sedans, Laskin took four of his men north to Bonnieux before elbowing west toward Lacoste. They drove under the watch of imperial cypresses, through vineyards now shed of their grapes and greens, past low stone walls dotted by moss. The cars zigzagged up the rise. They stopped at an overlook. Gathering up the packs, they hopped a stone wall, tramping through the dry, crackling leaves until the vines became pockets of gnarled olive trees and he could make out the house in the stretch of the valley below.

Laskin studied the area with his binoculars for a long while. It was a gray, cold afternoon, and the paths and yards were empty. He did not catch sight of any lights or movement inside the two neighboring homes. He took note of each vehicle within range of the house: two cars parked at each of the neighboring homes, three in the lot of a winery, and a van up the road, outside a café, tucked into a strand of trees.

FROM THE FLOOR OF THE SPRINTER VAN, PROCTER SAT alongside Sam watching the feeds from the house on four computer screens. The BANDITOs were piled behind them. Sam was smacking on some gum. Procter handed him an emptied sandwich wrapper. "Stop that."

The green dials of Sam's watch illuminated his face in the darkness of the van. He slid the gum from his mouth and crinkled it across the wrapper. "Everyone's late," he said.

LASKIN MET COLONEL PLETKOV IN THE MAKESHIFT COMmand center near Lourmarin. He understood from Zhomov that CIA knew Pletkov as REMORA, and Laskin could not help but find the name amusing, largely because he had considered the man to be a parasite long before the CIA had bestowed the cryptonym on him. Pletkov was seated in a chipped wooden chair, feet bouncing, reviewing his notes. A few of the surveillants were buried in their laptops; one was murmuring something into his encrypted radio. Pletkov had not looked up at Laskin. "Are we in the clear?" the man said. "I really should be going. The window will be short tonight."

"We have not seen anything," Laskin replied.

"That doesn't mean we're clear." Pletkov languidly flipped the page. Had Laskin caught the beginnings of a yawn stretching across the man's face? If Laskin had to maim or kill someone tonight, over and above anyone the Americans might throw at him, he would have chosen Pletkov.

"We have not seen anything," Laskin repeated.

SOON A BLUE RENAULT CLIPPED BY THE THICKET SHROUDing the surveillance van, slowed, and pulled into the farmhouse drive. Procter turned to the screens and saw, from the feed in the foyer, the door opening. One man stepped inside the house. Here, in the flesh, was REMORA. He flicked on lights, plunked his satchel bag down on a sofa, then made a pass through each room, taking a mental inventory of the place. REMORA moved through the farmhouse with confidence, like a man who knew what he was doing, inspecting a familiar place to see how it might have changed in the intervening months. Procter caught his eyes darting here and there, neck swiveling, nostrils flaring like a rabbit taking stock of the unseen deep things that signal danger. He appeared wary but not anxious, alert but unbothered. When he'd completed his review, REMORA unloaded from the cabinets a bottle of scotch, two glasses, and a pack of cigarettes, spreading it across the coffee table in the living room.

He lit his cigarette and smoked with carefree luxury: long, deep pulls, clouds billowing into the ceiling before cascading around him. He looked comfortable waiting.

Zhomov, Procter figured, would have scouted for that.

IF SPYING IS MOSTLY WRITING, A GOOD DEAL OF THE remainder is waiting. Sam was back into the gum, but Procter no longer had the energy to fight him on it. Elias was picking at some leftover bread; Rami and Yusuf sat stupefied in the glow of the screens. Procter watched the Russian finish his third cigarette and crack open the scotch and she thought: What if we have it wrong? She prayed, in fact, that she was wrong. That in a few hours they'd pack it all up and say big mistake, thank god. We got tangled up. Had it backwards, in the end.

IN THE FADING LILAC LIGHT OF THE OVERLOOK, THE MAJOR, one of Laskin's men, worried he'd flooded the Vespa's engine. He turned the key to a stutter and wheeze. Another attempt coaxed a sadder wheeze and a mechanical cough. He waited for a moment. From behind came the tick of an engine. Soon headlamps were spread across the road and a silver Peugeot sedan sped past, winding down into the valley. He recognized the make, model, and the license number from the surveillance reports earlier that day. The major had no idea who was in the car, other than that its occupant was an asset of the SVR. And a hugely valuable one at that, to merit such manpower for a simple meeting in southern France.

He tried again, and this time the engine coughed to life. The major zigzagged down the hillside until he reached the straight track of the road that halved the valley floor. He clipped past an unlit home, then the farmhouse.

Nearing the shuttered café, he nudged the headlamp slightly left, drifting the scooter briefly into the left lane. He glimpsed wheel-furrowed gravel tracking directly back to the van's parking spot in the trees. He had not noticed the tracks earlier in the day, when the team had initially canvassed the area. He radioed Laskin with the news.

"We will have a look, then," Laskin said. "A casual one. Come back here and a few of us will go." The radio crackled off.

The major had not participated in the Singapore operation, but he had heard rumors of what had been done to protect Zhomov's prized source. Laskin didn't care if the van's occupants were just gypsies in need of a nap, or star-crossed farmworkers in need of privacy and a flat surface. It would not end well for them.

47

LACOSTE

IN THE PASSENGER SEAT OF ONE OF THE RENAULT SEDANS, Laskin checked and rechecked his Beretta M12. They'd cleaned and prepped every weapon in Lourmarin, but the thing had been stuffed in a warehouse outside Avignon for several years and, before that, had seen service in the Libyan civil war. Who knew what the damn Libyans had done to it? Finally satisfied, he slid the gun to the floor. Darkened vineyards passed by the window as the four Russians went down, down, down into the valley.

"Let's practice your French again," Laskin said to the major. "Tell me how you'll introduce yourself to the people in the van."

48

LACOSTE

THE CAR ARRIVED FROM THE DIRECTION OF BONNIEUX. A silver Peugeot, running at a sensibly fast clip. When it turned into the drive, Procter felt her lung catch on a rib. No matter how many times she tried, tying and untying the band holding a flop of her curly hair did squat to calm her wrecked nerves. Had she made a wrong turn along the way? Was she now as lost as she'd been from the start, perhaps even more so? Then arrived the sudden, almost irrepressible urge to sleep, to find oblivion through the gentle ministrations of all the drinks, to wreck each piece of equipment in the van in a violent rage. Each thought she entertained, however briefly, before succumbing to utter paralysis and, in the end, sitting in a slack-jawed stupor to watch, praying something might happen, something that—and she still had hope for this—would convince her, fully, that she had it all wrong.

49

LACOSTE

THROUGH THE SCREEN OF THE LAPTOP PROCTER watched REMORA ease up from the couch at the sight of headlamps in the drive. The video resolution was so clear she could see the scotch jostling in his glass as he shuffled to the door. REMORA's face was impassive; he might have been responding to a gentle knock from the mailman.

Her friend walked inside, shut the door. Embraced REMORA.

And Procter still clung to the delusion that she had it all wrong.

REMORA offered the opening catechism, as if it were his meeting: "How much time do you have?"

"An hour until company arrives."

And still. Later, even here, Procter would remember savoring the thought: This proves nothing.

"Scotch?" REMORA asked.

"A double," Mac said. Then: "Your people missed her."

"The bastard," Sam whispered, then made a noise that might have been words, she did not know.

Procter swung open the van's back panel doors. Cold air rushed in. The moment was stuffed so full she could absorb only useless details: the moonlit sheen of the graffiti on the café, the reflections of the screens playing across the walls of the van. Her afternoon coffee barreled up into her throat. She swallowed, took a few long slow breaths, and let the air fill her lungs. She jammed one of the pistols in the waistband of her jeans. Sam did the same. They jumped out of the van and ran across the lot. Sprinting through the cover of the trees and thickets bordering the road, Procter and Sam set out for the house.

50

LACOSTE

THE RUN TO THE FARMHOUSE WAS A BLUR, AN AWFUL dream broken by the occasional jab of branches and the crunch of leaves and the huff of Sam's heavy breaths. For all the twists of the past month, Procter's instinct was now frighteningly simple: she was running through the Provençal woods on the compulsion that Mac had to feel pain, and that she and Sam had to be the ones to make him feel it. For a few glorious moments, before the Feebs commandeered the investigation, Procter and Sam would break things: his nose, jaw, fingers, ribs. The point wasn't to gloat over winning, and it sure as shit wasn't to ask any more questions. The point was that Mac should suffer. Traitors are eventually seen as pathetic, laundered into a brand of white-collar criminal, but here was a brief moment to deal with Mac as she now saw him: a monster. Procter tripped over a rock and stumbled into the leaves. Standing, she saw streaks of blood across her hands. The branches had cut her up pretty badly. She ran on.

51

LACOSTE

THE GUNFIRE BEGAN WITH A FEW TENTATIVE CRACKS before exploding into the low, sustained growl of a snare drum. It came from behind, in the direction of the van. Procter stopped, ducked, hustled back into the undergrowth. Another long burst crackled through the crisp air. When it was done, she heard a lone desperate cry, then the report of a single gunshot, a handgun, tore through the night. She heard two subsequent shots, and those might well have ripped through her soul, because she did not hear the volley that followed. She did not hear the van doors slam shut. She did not hear its engine kick to life. She just ran.

But now she ran the other way.

Sprinting through the trees, back toward the darkened lot and the van, Sam on her heels, shoving aside branches, stumbling over unseen rocks and roots, her guts in her throat. A few more sticks punctured the skin of her hands and face, but she was feeling too much else to let pain into the mix. With each stride the black vine stretched deeper inside her, and by the time she'd reached the edge of the gravel lot, it had knotted into the dreadful knowledge that yet more blood had been spilled. That more friends had been hurt. That it was her fault. That she'd been outfoxed. A frenzy of fresh tire tracks scarred the gravel. The van was gone.

52

LACOSTE / LUMIÈRES

PROCTER STOPPED TWICE TO DRY-HEAVE ON THE FORTY-five-minute run back to the safe house. She hadn't slept in four days. She'd barely eaten in two. One of her dear friends had twice tried to have her killed and three other friends had instead punched their ticket to the afterlife. All she could feel was the red-raw friction, the pain from scraping the last drops out of her body and mind and spirit. She tripped once and slid into the dirt, and if it hadn't been for Sam she'd have just lain there until someone found her and took her away.

Procter and Sam went into the safe house they had shared with the BANDITOs half wondering if Russians might jump out to bag them or shoot them, and she was a bit disappointed they did not, because at present a bullet in the neck would be inked in the ledger as a mercy. She didn't tell Jaggers any of this. They were so tweaked they'd said almost nothing since the van had disappeared. Get off the X—that was all this was. Get away. Regroup. They grabbed the bags and reviewed the maps to see how they might shake loose of the Luberon without running into whatever team had killed the BANDITOs. They checked flight schedules. Her nose was running; she wiped and plugged it with toilet paper but it would not stop.

"I'll drive to Marseille," Procter said, running her sleeve across her face. "First flight to London. Then Dulles."

"I'll do Nice to Paris," Sam said. "Then Dulles. The Kassabs are dead, aren't they?" He was scratching his nose as if he wanted to feed the cartilage to his nails.

"I heard a bunch of gunshots," Procter said.

"We've got nothing, Chief," Sam said, tossing a bag into the trunk of his rental. "It was all in that van."

"We've got Mac's name and our word," Procter said.

"His against ours."

"You see another way?"

He just scratched his nose.

"I'll meet you outside customs at Dulles." She tossed her duffel into her rental and slammed shut the trunk. "The nightmare rolls on."

PART V

THE CHIEF

53

LANGLEY

PROCTER AND SAM LANDED SEPARATELY AT DULLES THE next afternoon. They met at baggage claim and she drove them straight to Langley. Lacking badges, they waited for an hour at the front gate until the Security Protective Officers, the SPOs, finally got through to Debs's office, and relayed that the DDO wanted to know what the fuck Procter was doing here and where she'd crawled after fleeing the Farm, and other such pleasantries, though of course it was all delivered by the SPO with a cold civility, and in far less hostile language.

"You tell her it's about REMORA," Procter replied. "You tell her I was there, in France, I was watching the fucking meeting, and I have something very fucking important to say. You tell her that word for word, and whatever she says back, whatever bullshit excuse she offers for why she cannot talk to me right now, well, you tell her to think about why on earth I would be here unless I brought with me end-of-the-world-is-nigh kind of shit. The DDO hates my guts and I hate hers and I wouldn't be here unless it was critical. This is the last place I want to be, matter of fact. I'd find a recreational lobotomy preferable to a meeting with Deborah fucking Sweet right now." The SPO took a half step away from the car and stooped down for a look at Sam, in the passenger seat, who said, "What she said." Two more SPOs had gathered around the vehicle; they had brought out a dog to sniff the undercarriage of her RAV4. One of the officers looked pretty keen to shoot them.

"Have you been drinking, Ms. Procter?"

"Surprisingly, no. You tell the DDO that, too, when you talk to her. You mention that."

An hour later, and Sam and Procter had red ESCORT REQUIRED visitor badges clipped to their lapels. They sat in the Director's bustling anteroom with a babysitter support officer, Rudy, an old man with a face like a catcher's mitt and a voice that seemed ripe for a tracheotomy. As she had requested, Gus and Theo appeared, standing beside them to wait because there were no more chairs. Sam, seated on the couch, tapped his foot with such force it was whipping up a tide in Rudy's water glass. Each man's face creased in confusion at Sam, who hadn't even looked up to acknowledge their presence. In the span of a few seconds a dozen or more questions seemed to briefly flash through their eyes before disappearing like falling stars, but Theo whispered only one: "What the fuck is going on, Artemis?"

"I'll tell you when we're in there. I . . . Hey, Sam, stop it." She put a hand on his knee. "You gotta work out some wiggles, go out there and walk down the hall. Rudy, maybe you take him for a stroll?"

"I'm good," Sam said. "All good."

"Mac's not here right now," Gus offered.

"I know. He's in France," Procter said. "And I didn't ask for him to join."

Theo and Gus swapped yet more confused glances but said nothing.

"You been drinking, Artemis?" Theo asked.

"Surprisingly, no," she said. "Not even on the plane."

"The plane from . . . ?" Gus asked.

"France," she answered.

Theo, in a nice summary, mumbled: "What the fuck . . ."

"Artemis," Gus hissed, "you tell me what this is about right now."

"Not till we get in there, Gus. I can only go through it once."

Finally one of the EAs, said yes, yes, yes into a phone, set it down, and waved to them: "You can go in now."

The last time she had been in this office she'd retched on the floor and soiled her pants, and she'd thought it would be impossible for any return visit to be worse, but this one was definitely going to be, and by a wide margin. Gosford and Debs sat at the table, and no one was smiling.

Debs wore a canary-yellow dress with ruffled sleeves so large they could have been flotation devices in case the meeting ended in a water landing. The dress was a study in contrast with her eyes, which were—there was no other word—murderous. Procter briefly wondered if Debs had taken a shot at siccing the Feebs on her, only to come up short. They all sat around Gosford's table. This time she did not even think of the Intelligence Star on the wall, much less look at it. All of that was dim now.

"You have five minutes," Gosford said. "We've accommodated this bizarre request, brought Gus and Theo here as you asked. I have zero patience remaining. Go."

"Mac is working for the Russians," she started in, jerking her head toward Sam. "We heard—"

"And saw," Sam cut in.

"And saw," she said. "We heard and saw him discussing the attempted bombing on my trailer with REMORA. His line was: 'Your people missed her.' Mac signaled for the meeting after the cable from Sam's shrink, Portnoy. He did not recruit REMORA. REMORA recruited him. The Russians have been using the case as a conduit to pass information they want us to have, and to provide operational cover for Mac to meet them. It's all inside out. Mac's a traitor."

Gosford put a hand to his mouth and tugged on his lower lip. The noise that sprang from Theo recalled someone working to clear a bone from their throat. Gus could only slam the heels of his hands into his temple and look at her in a stunned silence. Theo did manage to scrape out fragments of a word, veering toward the incomprehensible but bearing some resemblance to, simply: 'What?' Debs stiffened and stared her down, face impassive and cold. She said nothing.

Gosford, taking stock of the room, stopped tugging at his lips and instead brushed knuckles across them. Turning to Procter, he said, "Keep going."

And they were off. By minute five Gosford said she could have ten more. By minute fifteen no one again mentioned the time. She went through it all, front to back, save for the document theft. Confession there brought no upside.

Two hours passed. No one said she was lying, and no one said they believed her, either. It was, frankly, too enormous a thing to consume in one sitting, and she knew that. Gus and Debs pondered how REMORA could have been inside out for so long; Gosford posed reasonable questions regarding the reliability and mental wherewithal of IMPERIAL (aka Frankie Potnick); same for Sam's memory of his brief chat in Singapore with Golikov, which, in Theo's words, could have been an attempt to chum the Langley waters with a chaotically bloody hunk of disinformation. What was harder to argue was that *something* had tried to kill Procter; that Procter and Sam had appeared with an eyewitness account of Mac's misdeeds; that REMORA's emergency signal mapped eerily to a string of recent disasters. In one light REMORA was helping CIA cope with these disasters, but in another, he and his compatriots were their cause. "I'm either insane or telling the truth," Procter concluded, and Debs shot back that insanity was the baseline case when it came to Artemis Procter and, further, the options were not mutually exclusive.

But they did listen. Whether Procter was cashing in on the last drops of mercy and grace from her busted-up friendship with Debs, or whether Theo or Gus had ever suspected Mac, she did not ask. Gosford and Debs both wiped their afternoon calendars. At Procter's urging, two sets of facts were checked. One, the timeline on the most recent REMORA meeting: the receipt of the emergency signal in relation to the cable from Portnoy. And two, a chronology of the REMORA reporting, seen through the light of the case being inside out. Here, Gosford's mind would screech to a halt.

"Now, this part, this I still cannot really grasp," he said. "There is no solid proof, am I hearing you correctly? Nothing crunchy."

"I saw it with my own eyes." For perhaps the fifth time that afternoon, she repeated Mac's lines, verbatim.

"You mean you heard it," Gus said, "through a microphone."

"And it's not a silver bullet for the Feebs," Debs said. "Hard to bank that."

"They can bank my testimony," Procter said.

"You realize that you're admitting to interfering in a CIA operation?" Debs said. "You unofficially wired up a safe house. You haven't said it, but surely one of you found a way to scuttle documents out of Headquarters."

Procter didn't respond to that, and Debs, well, Procter never thought she'd say this, but God bless her, Debs didn't press the matter. Debs was a bunch of things, not many of them good anymore, but she wasn't a traitor.

Gosford had steepled his hands in front of his face, leaning forward with his elbows on the table. He'd consumed five cups of coffee during the meeting and was now idly sliding his emptied mug around the tabletop. Procter braced herself for a professorial lecture, but instead Gosford stood and excused himself for the bathroom. They all sat in a pure and awful silence, waiting for him to return. No one could even look at her, and she could barely look at them. Something had died when she'd walked out of Langley earlier that year, and something was dying again here. Gosford came back, sat, and again steepled his damp hands. "What would you recommend I do?"

Procter had rehearsed this answer on her drive to Marseille, after she'd put in an anonymous tip to the French police about the shoot-out at the van. She'd gone through it again with Jaggers on the drive from Dulles. Anything else, they had agreed, would have been irresponsible, risked Mac leaking more information, and further reduced the already slim odds they would ever recover the BANDITOs, dead or alive.

Procter said: "Have the Feebs get FISA rolling on Mac. Force him out immediately, like today. There is no use keeping him close, because you won't catch him, and the longer he's inside, the more damage he'll do. Bring back Petra Devine and her Derms on a special project to run through everything and see what they can dig up. Cut REMORA off, end the case, retract everything he's reported so far. And put out feelers to the French about the Kassabs, drop a few bread crumbs to kick-start a criminal investigation."

"A long list," Debs said. "And a hard one."

"Talking to the French about the Kassabs is not hard," Sam said.

"Pushing Mac Mason out of CIA is hard," Gosford said. "Slapping our tails between our legs and marching downtown to explain why the REMORA stream is bogus, well, that's hard. Wouldn't you say?"

"Those are awkward," Debs offered, "not hard. At least not technically."

"Well, you can go talk to POTUS and the National Security Adviser, then," Gosford said, and laughed. "Mac's a hero. Afghanistan, of course. And then he helped bring Sam home. He's one of our most decorated officers."

"So are you," Procter said, nudging her chin toward the Star on the wall, succeeding in not quite looking at it.

A cold and hostile silence descended over the room. "Seems to me," Debs said, "that unless we resurrect the Derm shop—"

"Which you fucking should," Procter said. "That one's easy as pie. It's—"

"Let me finish," Debs barked. "That unless we resurrect the Derm shop and they sniff out a smoking gun, or unless Mac makes a mistake, the prosecution's case will rest on your testimony alone. Your recollection of what Mac said in France. Espionage Act cases are hard slogs. The bar is very high. You know this. And, well, given your past here, and their reliance on your word, well, that is, it's, how to, uh . . ."

"Out with it Deborah," Gosford said. But he was staring at Procter.

"Well, it's common knowledge, isn't it?" Debs said. "Artemis was in love with Mac back in Afghanistan. They were on the edge of the world, she was freshly divorced, and Loulou was off screwing painters far more successful than Mac. There were plenty of stories—why am I getting these looks? we all heard them, this is not *news*—there were the stories about the two of them and there were even sordid rumors about a trip to Paris with Loulou in the mix. Heard it ended, like most of Artemis's business, well . . . how to put this one now?" Debs paused, unfolding that blank mask of a face with its smiling eyes. "Weirdly. There it is. The end was weird, as everything seems to be with her."

"And?" Procter said. "Your fucking point?" The siren was playing through her skull, bringing with it a medieval slideshow that was borderline orgasmic: tipping Debs into a boiling vat, jerking out those perfectly done fingernails, turning a crank to stretch her across the rack.

"You know my fucking point," Debs said.

"It's been almost fifteen years. It's irrelevant."

"It is not. It risks discrediting you. Discrediting your version of events."

"Have Sam talk to the Feebs, then," Procter said—perhaps too loudly, she was speaking over the skull-siren. "He never banged Mac. Or Loulou. Far as I know."

"Enough," Gosford said. "Quite enough." He crossed his arms, sat back, glanced at Debs. He stared up at the ceiling and rifled a long breath through his nostrils. It was a long moment, the one on which it all turned. Looking at the floor, Procter realized that she'd sat down in the same spot where she'd tossed her cookies during the firing. Full fucking circle.

Gosford scanned each set of eyes across the table before settling them, at last, on Sam, and finally Procter. "We will take all of this into consideration. And you will both need good lawyers. Of that, I am quite certain." Removing from his pocket the notecard bearing his schedule, Gosford slid on reading glasses and heaved out another long sigh. "Dismissed."

54

LANGLEY / CRYSTAL CITY

IN A SILENT PACK THEY MARCHED DIRECTLY FROM THE Seventh Floor to the cafeteria. Procter and Sam sat at a table with a window facing the courtyard and a clean view of the cryptographic sculpture, Gus and Theo across. The late lunch set was a trickle, but the afternoon coffee crowd was thickening: the Dunkin' Donuts line was at least twenty people deep. The chemical-coffee smell on the air was making her sick. One friendship had already been flung off the cliff and she worried two more might jump with it. The familiar squeaky sound of the halls and the sight of strangers she recognized, and many she knew, was making her even more unbearably sad.

"What have you fucking done, Artemis?" The rare, jarring sound of a Gus Raptis curse might as well have been a slap, and it brightened her sadness to anger.

"A fucking national service," Procter said, "that's what. You're fucking welcome Gus, by the way."

"Why bring us into that meeting?" Gus seethed. "Now we're involved, we're—"

"You know damn well why, Gus," Theo snapped. "She tells Gosford and Debs, who knows what happens? They might just sit on it. But bring us in? Well, once you've got a rumor like that out there . . ."

"The only possible outcome of the stunt you just pulled is to force Mac out, nothing more," Gus answered. "You understand that, right?"

"I have no idea what Gosford will do," she said. "There are lots of ways this goes. I couldn't sit on it. Not after what I saw."

"Well, Gosford's not going to don the hair shirt over Mac," Gus said. "He's not going to drag CIA through the mud over this. We know that much."

"Mac's on fuck-you time," Theo said, pondering the soaring cafeteria ceiling. "What is he, fifty-three? -Four? With twenty in the bank and plenty more than five overseas. Pension's his. He was older than us when he joined because of the art detour. Anyway, doesn't matter. Point is that Gosford's got wiggle room to shove him aside, regardless of what was said upstairs. Gosford might even want to. Mac's kind of a rival. I'd bet Gosford's keen for a reason to get rid of him."

"Gus," Procter said, "do you believe me?"

Gus stood, looked out the window. "I've got no clue what to believe. You just dumped a load of shit on us, Artemis." He walked out into the hallway, turned the corner, and marched out of sight.

Theo looked at Sam and then off at the Dunkin' Donuts line. "You must have taken a bunch of documents. And the stunt with the support assets? Guys, holy shit . . ."

Through the window, Procter made eye contact with a guy lighting the bowl of a pipe on a bench in the courtyard, and he literally spun away, turning his back to Procter. Powerful impulse, she thought, to just look away. Not the worst idea when you can't make any sense of what you see. She watched smoke drift off and looked over to Theo, who was easing up from the table. Hand on his arm, she stood to face him.

"What do you believe, Theo? Tell me. Just talk."

Theo fixed her with a grave stare, then jerked her into a friendly bear hug. "I believe most of all in fish," he said, and laughed.

THAT NIGHT SAM AND PROCTER SAT IN THE CRYSTAL CITY safe house. There were other options, of course, other paths, and they discussed them with the detached air of a corporate planning meeting.

There were potentially receptive Feebs that might be contacted. Hill staffers and Intel Committee members could be tipped off. Plenty of journalists who might be offered a scoop. In all paths, they slammed into dead ends when debating the odds of a prosecution. All roads led to their word against Mac's—he'd been meeting with REMORA on official Agency business, after all—and all equally risked tarring and feathering CIA for nothing. When they'd exhausted their options, and when Procter at last ate a few sleep gummies, hopeful that tonight they might help her find some rest, Sam's face tightened and he became pensive and sad. She felt the same. Here they were, at the end. It was, she supposed, the way that most adventures end: as big fucking let-downs.

"What will you do now?" Sam asked.

"Trawl the American West," she said. "Walk the earth, that kind of thing. See who I meet. See what happens. Never seen the damn Grand Canyon, can you believe it? So I'll have a peek. We've spent so much time talking about the past that I feel like I've got bits and pieces of it stuck to me, and I don't care for that. A few months behind the wheel will even me out."

"Funny," he said, "when I drive, I don't think of much other than the past."

"That's because your brain's not so strong," she said. "That's why you showed up on my boardwalk in Florida in the first place."

He smiled, then his grin faded and his face grew serious. "The Kassabs are dead, aren't they?"

"I don't see how it could be otherwise."

"We got them—"

"Stop you right there," Procter said. "*He* killed them. Mac and his Russian friends. Not us. No use thinking about it any other way."

"You really believe that?"

"I must. The alternative is too fucking awful. I can't give any more headspace to the darkness. I've rented out so much as it is."

"Do you think they're going to hunt us?"

"At this point I can't imagine why they would care. After what happened in France, there is no way the Russians keep the case going.

There's too much hair on it. No matter what happens, Moscow will cut Mac loose. What's the point of killing us now? Also, there's the fact that we're nobodies."

"Speak for yourself."

"I speak," she said, "for both of us. Now: What are you going to do? Gambling junket in Vegas with Natalie? Garden-variety bender? Spend time with the fam? Maybe stalk the fields and farms for Minnesotan ass, jiggling like the Jell-O that made it? Maybe the sample platter, bit of everything?"

"You know, Chief," he said, "we've been friends for a long time, and when people ask, I still struggle to explain what exactly is wrong with you."

"Let me know if you ever do figure it out," she said. "Color me curious."

"I'm going to break it off with Natalie. Get my head straight. I might go home for a while. But I do have one more question about all of this." He looked up at the ceiling. "Then, no more."

She looked at him.

"Did you suspect Mac from the start?" Sam asked.

Procter craned her neck at the ceiling, then tilted it toward Sam. "No," she said. "Never."

"Even after we narrowed down the list?"

"Look at me, Jaggers."

"What?"

"Look at me."

"I'm looking."

"What are we, you and I?"

"Friends."

"Right. I'm looking at you right now and I feel the same feelings I felt for him: Chums, fellow travelers, members of the same tribe, whatever the fuck. We did life together for so long. And he saved mine, to boot: I'd be dead if he hadn't slid in front of me in Afghanistan. Like dead, dead."

"Is it true, what Sweet said earlier today?" Sam asked. "That you loved him once?"

"Love," she said, with a sad laugh and a wipe of her nose. "We drank and laughed together and he always had my back. Twenty-five years of having my back. Long history. How could I have thought it was him? Or any of them? That one of my best friends is—"

And Artemis Aphrodite Procter suddenly sniffled, then choked, and finally let out a short cry. A few tears traced down her cheeks before she could stopper them, but she did catch herself before things got out of hand. She turned away to dry her face. "Little malfunction there. Sorry about that."

"I'll add it to the list for the docs, the ones who might tell us what's wrong with you."

"I think it'll still be pretty unclear," she said.

"Even so," Sam said. "Even so."

55

ON THE RUN

IRENE SLID BACK INTO HER AMERICAN SKIN. SHE WAS AN everywoman, a wanderlust darkening the distant corners of her native and forsaken land. In front of cracked hotel mirrors, she perfected a big friendly smile. On stained hotel desks she scribbled out her legend, her backstory, reciting it to herself when she was behind the wheel. At night, lying in bed, she rehearsed conversations with men, hinting that the favors she sought might be repaid with her body, but they never would be. As she moved, she acquired: documents, references, cash, car. And this most of all: A vision of a new home. A place far from these grubby motels, poisonous food, and soulless people. A hope that soon she would not feel the sting of abandonment, nor the rockslide through her chest at the sight of an idling police car or the blare of a siren.

Years later, breastfeeding her five-month-old son from her favorite chair, the one in her bedroom facing the windows out into the woods, with her husband asleep on the bed and her daughter in a bedroom down the hall, Irene will think, as she often does, of a night in a motel in Jacksonville, Florida.

Thousands of miles and a few years removed from that rathole, and the memory will resurface of the mildewy smell of the room, the wet crunch of a belly-up roach beneath her feet, the taste of pure terror in her throat, and the sight of the lifeless eyes of the dead boy as she stowed him in the trunk of his own car before she stole it. She plunked down her duffel, sat on the bed, and checked for messages from the Spaniard's people. There weren't any, there hadn't been any the day before, and she knew then there wouldn't be any ever again. They were cutting her off. After the disaster at the trailer, after their failure—she was a liability. There would be nothing from Moscow or the Spaniard. On a pad of paper, she scribbled the relevant bits of information—addresses, phone numbers, full names—committed it to memory, and thought about what she might do. Turn herself in, kill herself, hide, press on with the fight; that night she weighed each one with great care. By dawn, she knew.

The Marble Spring Motel: birthplace of her new life.

She went to Texas to torch their old one. She cried once on that trip and it was for her dog, Stalin, dropped in a box outside a shelter on her way out of town. She visited a dozen other states, searching, wandering. Three months on, and she had not seen her face on television, on the FBI's website, or anywhere. Six months on, and the only stubborn connection to her dead self was Peter's parents, who often emailed him—sad, angry, confused, or some combination—and who could not comprehend how she had so thoroughly brainwashed their perfect son to the point where he would not speak to them.

And in that new home, far away, her baby suckling from her breast, she would sometimes wonder if Peter would hate her for what she had done. Or if, like a true soldier, he would have understood that she'd been forced to sacrifice everything. The price for her future was their old life, and with it his honor.

By summertime a bell was jangling on a door, and she was walking inside, that glowing smile planted on her face. She was driving a car with Iowa plates. Her purse boasted an Iowa driver's license with her picture and someone else's name. She had three months' rent in cash, and pocket money to cover her bills. She was looking for work, she said. She carried two reference letters, both impeccable: One from a restaurant in Old Town Alexandria. Another from a bar in Orlando. "I'm a wanderer," she offered, as she had rehearsed, when the owner asked how she'd found her way here. "Hard time sitting still, I guess you could say." Flash of that smile. In those days, visions of her future—the home yet to be seen, the daughter and son yet to be born, the husband yet to be met—propelled her onward. These gave Irene hope in a coming metamorphosis, that soon she would writhe free of the American heartland. That she would, at last, be wrapped in her true skin.

56

LANGLEY / MOSCOW

MAC MASON WAS PUT OUT TO PASTURE WITH A STILTED formal ceremony in the first floor CIA Awards Suite, spread catered by Corner Bakery, plaque presented by the Deputy Director because, though Finn Gosford was doubtless thrilled by the departure of a potential rival, he was otherwise occupied and unable to attend. In truth it was unimaginable that he might speak generously of Mac in public for any sustained period of time. Others would be forced to do so in his stead. Theo, drearily sober, offered a grindingly formulaic speech, vaguely recounting a buffet of Mac's adventures and contributions to CIA. Gus was more glowing, even by the stiff standards of a Langley awards ceremony: he spoke of Mac's valor in Afghanistan, his feats to earn the Intelligence Star; their long friendship and Mac's decades of public service.

After, in the windowless din of the Awards Suite, a crowd of two hundred—the Russia House faithful, old colleagues from the Farm, long-lost friends from the salad days in Afghanistan and the Counterterrorism Center—waited patiently in a proper breadline for rubbery sandwiches and a mess of a pastry spread. Everywhere Mac was mobbed. Every word was kind, respectful, awe-filled.

That afternoon, surrounded by well-wishers and friends, Macintosh Mason completed his walk-out ceremony. Loulou at his side, he handed his badge to the SPO on duty in the marble-floored lobby of the CIA's Original Headquarters Building. Mac was full of cheer and nostalgia; a few tears, plenty of smiles. Stopping three times for official photos,

Mac walked across the marble seal and out the door of CIA, Loulou on his arm.

Many pondered the abruptness of the departure. Mac had grumbled, as had all of them, about the new regime; about the weakening of CIA's influence in the world; about the youngsters mucking up a perfectly decent espionage outfit. He had more money than they did, a fat reptile fund courtesy of Loulou's family, on which they could spend a splendid retirement, and that surely helped. What Mac Mason's dearest friends, Gus Raptis and Theo Monk, thought of the departure, no one could quite figure. When pressed by a few Russia House hands in the run-up to the ceremonies, both men had demurred. And, oddly, neither had materialized for the post-ceremony festivities at the Vienna Inn. This was most unusual, given their long-standing friendship and, for Theo at least, the cold fact of an open bar. Come to think of it, one Russia House hand mused, watching the Masons' Porsche putter out of the parking lot, neither Theo nor Gus had even been present in the lobby when Mac had walked out of CIA for the last time.

THAT SAME WEEK, IN MOSCOW, REM ZHOMOV'S ILLUSTRIOUS career fizzled to a similarly whimpering end. With Dr. B's ominous retirement message, the Director had pounced, said it was, at last, time to go. Rem had no clue what would happen to his Special Section, but, at the Director's explicit direction, he'd focused his last energies, as he supposed all old men must, on making himself irrelevant. He spent his final days digging his own grave.

The Dr. B case had given Rem purpose in his final years in the Forest. Here had been a shot that he would not fade into irrelevance but might manage, like almost none before him, to go out with a bang. What would become of Dr. B? What improvements in security might Russia see from his work? What gains might be reaped from the trade of his material to the Chinese? Rem would not be around to answer these questions: he would be gone.

Rem spent five days washing Dr. B's material, retaining its fundamental essence while obscuring its true origin. Any shred of intelligence that might link SVR to the good Doctor was carted off to the incinerators.

Rem himself ventured downstairs while they burned the compendium of hard-copy operational notes. He took the privilege of rereading the first letter passed from Macintosh Mason to Rodion Vissarionovich Pletkov, eventually known to CIA as REMORA, during their time in Paris. The note, quite short, explained Mac's desire to meet with Pletkov *away from my friends*. It had been the first true line Macintosh had crossed. Rem read it in a solemn silence. You had to be delusional to betray your country and your service, he thought. But to betray your friends? Well, that happened every goddamn day. He set the note on the stack. The clerk pressed the button. The papers slid into the flames.

THE FORMALITIES COMMENCED IN THE SVR BANQUET HALL where, for two hours, colleagues, friends, and enemies alike trotted onstage to laud Rem's accomplishments and victories. There were stories from his service in Afghanistan, from his first days in London, from the tour in Rome. The Director pinned on his left breast the ruby cross of the Order of Alexander Nevsky, awarded to recognize those who have "achieved personal merit in nation-building" following at least twenty years in the civil service. Well, then, maybe I should have received two, Rem thought, watching the Director fumble with the pin. Rem lost count of the toasts. His friends and colleagues put back vodka like water, and by nightfall the celebration had crawled to one of the events dachas on the Forest campus, accessible by a walking path curling deep into the pine and ash.

Pletkov sidled up to Rem while he refreshed his sparkling water. Even Rem had begun to think of the man by his CIA cryptonym: REMORA. "A fine send-off," he said, and clinked his vodka to Rem's glass. "What's next?"

"You'll have to ask Ninel."

Pletkov gave him a wan smile. "I don't envy you."

"You shouldn't. I'm going to be bored."

"But you have Ninel. You shouldn't get bored. Shame on you if you do."

Rem flicked his hand through the air. "Still."

"I'm looking forward to retirement," Pletkov said. "Travel, fishing, reading. A younger mistress, perhaps. I have a decade left and it is already calling me. But you, Rem? That freedom quite literally starts tomorrow and you don't have a plan?"

"I'll figure it out, Rodion Vissarionovich."

"Think of it this way, Rem Mikhailovich: What would you do, if you could do anything?"

Rem clapped Pletkov on the shoulder, raised his glass to a passing well-wisher, and took a long drink. "I would work."

57

SHERMANS CORNER, MINNESOTA
MONTHS LATER

SAM JOSEPH SLID INTO HIS REGULAR BOOTH. FROM THE waitress he ordered black coffee, scrambled eggs, and toast. He worked through two newspapers over his meal and the first half of a novel over three refills of coffee. The breakfast crowd drifted into lunch. He ordered a fourth cup of coffee, plugging away at the book. Such was his discomfort with the actual world that he'd averaged around a novel a day for going on three months; Sam felt that a reckoning with reality might pull the life right out of him. Reading kindled hopes that there would be something else. That other worlds existed.

A plate bearing a roast beef sandwich and fries—his usual—clanked onto the table; he looked up. He'd not ordered it. The waitress was smiling. "On the house today," she said. "You seem to have a lot on your mind."

"Thanks. You sure?"

"Totally sure."

The waitress had foolish brown eyes and jet-black hair and he did not remember once seeing her smile. He'd never asked her name and felt bad about that now; he'd been a regular for months, since he'd come to spend time with his parents. "Sam, by the way," he said, and offered his hand.

"Melissa," she said. "Everyone calls me Mel."

Her hand was soft and dry; he noticed the heat of her skin when they shook. She treated him to another broad smile, smoothed her apron, dawdled for a half moment, and said: "So. Whatcha reading, Sam?"

"A book."

She rolled her eyes and shook her head and laughed; a hearty, chesty one that threw its arms around him. "I figured you'd be a dick," she said, voice tinged with play. "Now I've got proof. Enjoy your sandwich, Sam." She turned for the counter, and he stole a glance at her ringless left hand. He also took note of what could possibly be curves, cloistered under her sensible slacks and the black long-sleeved shirt required of the waitstaff.

"Mel," he called. "When does your shift end?"

She turned around and looked up at the clock hung above Sam's booth. "Fifteen minutes."

"Have lunch with me?"

"I don't like eating here."

"Why not?"

"Company's bad. Food's worse. You suggest somewhere else and you stand a chance at a yes." She was smiling again. She righted a tipped-over saltshaker on one of the neighboring tables.

"But I've already got my sandwich."

FIFTEEN MINUTES LATER THE SANDWICH WAS IN A TO-GO box in the backseat of his car and the engine was running. Mel emerged from the diner, walking toward her own car. He called to her across the lot. "I can drive," he said.

She laughed. "I'm not getting in the car with you," she said. "How do I know you're not a serial killer? Or a perv?"

There was a knot in his belly, pulled taut at the thought of Mel. First time in months he was excited about someone's company.

STONEHOUSE COFFEE WAS A TIMBERED STOREFRONT TEN miles north, off Highway 53 on the approaches to Orr and Pelican Lake. She took her coffee black, like him. Mel enjoyed electronica and had done something in marketing for an uncle's wilderness excursion business until it went under. Her husband had died in Iraq, in 2006. They'd married young. She did not keep pictures, she said; she did not think the past should be granted such power. She possessed a thoughtful intelligence that seemed to float above something scrappier, harder. He wondered if someone, somewhere, had beaten her.

After a few hours he told her about CIA. Nothing specific, of course, but he was out now—what was the point in the charade? Mel at first did not seem to believe him, but he insisted it was no joke, and soon she was asking all manner of questions. And not the ridiculous, cartoonish, awful ones (*Have you ever killed someone? Did you carry a gun? Are you like James Bond?*) that would have made him want to get up and leave, to say nothing of answering. No, Mel asked the questions that he asked himself. The ones that he pondered in the clockless hours. It struck him that maybe he and Mel had been pulled from the same depths. Heated in the same kiln. Over the table he knotted his hand in hers. She feathered her fingers around his. She spoke openly and casually of her doubts and mistakes, in the way only a stranger can. After a while she inquired after his.

"What do you regret?" she asked, bringing her other hand onto the table so he might take it, which he did. "Or do you regret anything?"

He thought about that. "There was a woman, once," he said. "We were in love. There were good reasons we shouldn't have been, but we were. And it didn't work. It's hard to explain, but the CIA wouldn't—couldn't—allow it. I don't know what's happened to her. She was one of those beautiful things you lose along the way."

"Which do you regret?" she said, brushing his fingers. "Falling in love in the first place, or not making it work in the end?"

"Both."

"Do you resent CIA for interfering in your love? For forbidding it?"

"No. If it hadn't been for CIA, I'd never have met her."

"What do you think of the place?"

"CIA?"

"Yes."

"Tough question. Complicated."

"You worked there for a long time," she said. "Then they threw you out. You're living at home and picking up the pieces and whiling away the days reading at a diner. Of course you're thinking big thoughts. Tell me."

"I stole secrets for a living," he said. "And what you are asking is a mystery. Not a secret. Not my department. I haven't considered it once. Might as well ask what I think of planet Earth. I could give you ten answers. They'd all be true. And they'd all be lies."

"Well, let me put it this way," she said. "In the end, were you a good guy or a bad guy?"

"That one's easy," he said. "Good guy. And not only at the end."

It was well after closing, and the manager had to ask them to leave. They had refilled their cups four times; they had ordered dinner; they had been talking at the table for nearly ten hours. The moon was bright over the lake and the skyline of pines on its banks. He took her hand in his, and they shuffled into the parking lot. At her car, he drew Mel to him and kissed her. At first she did not kiss him back—shock? guilt?—but soon she was reciprocating, kissing him long and deep. When he pulled back, Mel's eyes were already open and listless, as if she were asleep behind them. And, really, after all they had talked through and shared, he could make no sense of that.

"Spend the night with me," he said.

58

ON THE ROAD

MOVE, PROCTER THOUGHT, JUST MOVE.

By summer she had carved up much of the American West. Trailing in her slipstream were lovers jilted and relieved and terrified, a quantity of empty liquor bottles sufficient to fill a commercial dumpster, and a shockingly sparse quantity of photographic or forensic evidence. She spoke frequently with Sam and her cousin, Cummings. A few times, Theo checked in. She called Gus once, and spent a few minutes making small talk before she lost reception in a stretch of western Nebraska. Highlights had been the Big Bend country and the parks in Utah. The Grand Canyon she had found mostly underwhelming.

When, as sometimes happened, her mind veered in agitating, senseless directions—in other words, to the past—Procter would stare gravely through the windshield and slam on the gas and imagine those thoughts on foot, vainly chasing the car, hands up, waving, shrieking like an unwanted child that has been left behind. Straight ahead and onward, she thought. There's a good girl. Move.

PROCTER WAS SUNK DEEP INTO A BURGER AT A BREWERY outside Denver. Her phone shivered on the table. Unknown number. She ignored it.

When she'd moved on to a bar seat and a beer, the unknown number called again. This time she answered. It was Debs.

"Well, holy hell," Procter said. "This a butt-dial?"

"That would be impossible. I've deleted your number from all my phones."

"Well, if you're calling to apologize for everything, let me just say I humbly and readily accept. You, Deborah Fraser Sweet, are hereby forgiven."

"Where are you, Artemis?"

"That," Procter said, with a long swig of her beer, "is super-classified."

"It's super-loud in the background, is what it is."

"I am out with the general public, for a change. They make my skin crawl, and I'm working on that. I can hear you, though. Loud and clear."

Debs said, "Hey, Artemis, this call didn't happen. Okay?"

"Course."

"The Feebs have stopped the FISA surveillance on you. Investigation's done. Same for Sam."

"Are they looking at Mac anymore?"

"You found the line, Artemis."

"I always do."

A dog barked in the background. "Tell her Artemis says hello," Procter said, taking a few sips of beer because the barking carried on for a while. When it stopped, because she was so far from Langley, or perhaps it was the altitude, Procter said: "Was it ipecac in the muffin, Debs? I've wondered."

There was a pause. "I have no idea what you're talking about."

Then Debs laughed, and Procter laughed, and she looked around the bar, and an old guy drinking a dark beer raised his glass to her and smiled. She put back a good bit of beer, until Debs had stopped laughing.

"Thanks for letting me know, Debs. And it was good to hear your voice. For once."

"You, too, Artemis. Be good."

"I won't." Then she hung up.

PROCTER UNPLUGGED AND DISAPPEARED INTO THE ROCKies. A week later, on a Tuesday morning, she trudged out of the wilderness, and by nightfall the headlamps of her RAV4 were painting the slats of her rented cabin.

Much later, Procter would come to believe that she had felt it then, the moment she stepped out of her car. There was a new dent in her universe, and darkness filled her like a can of oil.

In the moment Procter chalked it up to paranoia from her smokes and a couple mushroom experiments out in the mountains, and maybe also fatigue: she'd been on the move since dawn. Her back ached from her rucksack, her legs were stiff from sitting immobile behind the wheel. Too tired to heat anything in the microwave, for dinner she picked at surviving bags of trail mix and beef jerky. Collecting her phone from the closet to briefly reconnect with the world, she sat on the edge of the bed. It went berserk soon as it powered up, a cacophony of dings and beeps and a notification that her voice mail was full.

There are moments that, even while living through them, you understand to be dividing lines: End of an era, beginning of another. From here on out, there will be a before and an after, marked by this slash of time. Afghanistan had been one such day. And this night, for Artemis Aphrodite Procter, would be another.

The first sensations were oddly dull, arriving at the ten-second mark of a long voice mail from Theo, like rocks shaking around in the jar of her head. Then pure agony came. At first it felt painfully concentrated, like the tip of a glowing needle jammed into her neck—a shock, searing and immobilizing. With each word the hot needle twisted and jerked, dialing up her temperature, fraying the edges of her vision, and shivering the skin around her eyes, which were now blinking frantically.

Procter retained sufficient command of her faculties that, by the time the message was done, the phone had not been flung through a window, smashed against a wall, or pulverized in her grip. Instead it was gently returned to its shelf in the closet. She stood there in the darkness for some time—how much of it, she was not sure. She moved only because it became unbearably hot: her skin was scorching, though not a drop of sweat had seeped through her pores.

Procter wandered into the living room. The world beyond the immediate searchlight of her eyes had slipped into a dreamy haze. There were a few glorious moments in which, while languidly twirling fingers through the curls of her hair, she wondered if this might be a dream, and she desperately tried to soak in the relief that comes upon waking. That fantasy was cut to ribbons with the shrieking pain that arrived when she punched a hole clean through the drywall and into the unforgiving pine of a stud beam.

The paroxysm of anger and despair and guilt would run, end to end, for nearly an hour, and it would consume much of the cabin. Drywall was pockmarked by knees and elbows and feet and her operable hand. Mantels and desks were swept of knickknacks, which were then loaded up as ammunition into the cannons of her rage and fired off in all directions, against glassware and windows, appliances and walls.

Lulls—breathless, ragged, desperate—were quickly drowned by swells of panic and anger that only sowed more destruction. This was the kind of unnatural fire that could only be doused with alcohol. The type of drinking only possible when no one was watching. She drank. In a quantity shocking for even Artemis Aphrodite Procter, she drank.

WHEN PROCTER WOKE, THE SUN WAS HIGH AND SHE WAS sprawled on a bed of pine needles. A painting lay in tatters next to her on the forest floor. The microwave, flung through a window, had come to rest at the foot of a fir tree. A faint sound of music floated through the open front door of the cabin. Procter tried to sit up but found she could not. A squirrel bolted across the lawn. She began to cry.

59

THE ROAD HOME

IRENE SLID FROM THE SHEETS AND PULLED FRESH CLOTHES from her backpack and changed and left Sam sprawled in bed, a few hours before first light. By dawn she was deep into Iowa. On the backseat floor of her Kia was a backpack. Inside was the precious little box, the tapes, a knife, and half the cash in neat stacks. The remainder she'd hidden around in her car. Next to the backpack was a duffel: a few changes of clothes, her .38 Special handgun, boxes of ammunition, and the laptop. She wore diapers to limit her stops, popped caffeine pills and Adderall to ward off sleep.

Through her windshield America unrolled like a nightmare she was at last escaping. In Kansas City the buildings were scarred with graffiti. In Tulsa they crumbled like dry cakes. In Austin a litter of children mewled and stomped for Slurpees at a gas station while obese parents scrolled on their phones. Approaching San Antonio, she watched a deranged man hurl obscenities at passerby, all of whom looked away. The light flicked green. She drove on.

This was the last days of an empire, its decline marked not by some great battle but by the slow and gouty death of decadence. She was hurtling through a tunnel on the verge of collapse. But she would not perish. She was a soldier on the march.

THE SVR'S MEXICO CITY *REZIDENT* CLANKED OPEN THE DOOR of the consular interview room and returned to his seat in front of the American woman, who had insisted on addressing him in broken Russian. "The names," he said, sliding her pen and paper. "Write them for me once more. From memory. And in English. No more attempts at Cyrillic." She did, returning the paper with a shove and an air of haughty indifference. The *rezident* was not so much bothered as intrigued. Who was she? He fixed himself a smoke and offered her one.

"No, thank you. You have what you need." Her chin nudged at the paper. "You make your calls."

The presumptuousness took him aback, but he did have calls to make, so, after a few more questions—all unequivocally dodged—about her journey here, and the pack she was clutching but would not relinquish, and the laptop she insisted that "representatives of your intelligence service examine" (though he'd not told her he was SVR), he rode the elevator to the sixth floor *rezidentura* and placed a call on the secure line to Moscow. After a few minutes he was patched through.

"Gennady Arkadyavich," he said at the sound of his old friend's voice, and they exchanged greetings. "I have a walk-in here, an American, who claims to be working for us. She has written down the name of one of ours as her bona fides . . . Yes . . . Yes . . . Dominguez, precisely. She claims he handled her in the States, and I was wondering . . . I see. Yes. Okay." He listened to Gennady for a few minutes, then hung up.

The *rezident*'s men sent the photos and video of her interview to Moscow. Were he in charge, he would have opted to quietly shoot her, but, alas, he was not. Gennady's department sent over the woman's file. The *rezident* reviewed the documents while he smoked. A cursory review made him even more certain that his approach was the sensible one: they should shoot her.

That evening the *rezident* returned to the interview room and sat across from the woman. He introduced himself as the senior officer of the Russian SVR in Mexico, noted that he understood she had been of service to the state, and inquired whether she had information for him, or perhaps a request. He said that he had placed calls to Moscow. Her bona fides were not in question. She should speak freely.

"My work is done," she said. "I was given a job and I've done what I can." She thrust the backpack across the table, nodded, said: "Go ahead. Open it. I mean what I say."

The *rezident* unzippered the bag and looked at a brick of American dollars. "A few thousand of that came from your man, the Spaniard," she said. "I am sure somewhere you can match the serial numbers. But there is much more than that in there because what he provided was not sufficient. In the end I had to buy several cars and alias documents." He let them sit in silence, until she nodded at the small cardboard box. "That one. Open that one."

He opened it: small tapes from a recorder.

"Those," she said, "are backups."

"In case of what?"

"In case you don't have his fingerprints."

"I don't follow."

She leaned over the table to slide the last container his way. It looked to him like a modestly sized jewelry box. It was shrouded in cling wrap and entombed in a Ziploc bag. The *rezident* did not want to open it.

"You looked so different in the files," he said. "Quite the transformation."

"I've made adjustments to survive," she replied. "Open it, please. I want them to know that I am done. This was all I could manage. I pray that it will be enough."

The *rezident* opened the Ziploc bag. He sloughed off the plastic wrap. He popped the top off the box. There was another bag inside. He tugged at a corner for a look. He was not surprised by the sight of mangled flesh and dried blood congealing inside—only by the quantity. Like a pile of stubby sodden carrots. The faint trace of rot that reached his nostrils curdled instantly into nausea. He zippered the bag up, placed it back in the box. He lit himself another cigarette to smoke out the smell. "What do we have here?"

"Fingers," she said.

"They all belong to Samuel Joseph?"

"They do."

"When the papers covered the murder, they did not mention any missing fingers."

"And why would they?"

"I understand from my colleagues in Moscow that there were two targets."

A hangdog look contorted the woman's face. She is ashamed, he thought, she thinks she is a bad girl. She went back to her stilted Russian: "I could not find her. I looked, believe me, I did. In Florida. In Washington. I had Sam's parents' address from the commo. It was sent to me before your people stopped responding. Before—"

He cut her off, in English: "You have come a long way. So tell me: Why you are here? What do you want, Irene?

"Irina."

"Irina," he said, and conceded to her Russian with a sigh. "What do you want, Irina?"

"I want to go home."

60

PARIS
MONTHS LATER

MAC MASON WAS PAINTING AGAIN. THE MUSCLES HAD been slow to revive, the initial attempts as exhausting as they were embarrassing. He'd begun by treating it as a casual hobby, a way to burn a lovely afternoon in Paris. A landscape at the Luxembourg Gardens, Loulou at his side reading a novel or picnicking, or in the 3rd near Place des Vosges, brushing out a dramatic red door set under stone arches. The results were disappointing. No energy, no life. He heard the voice of his father while he worked.

But Paris, ah, Paris, the City of Light: Mac was anonymous, unburdened, free. He and Loulou had acquired an old gallery in the Marais, and by summer the long-atrophied muscles, unused since youth, began to strengthen and grow. He and Loulou visited the south on a painting holiday: Arles, Saint-Saturnin, Collioure near Spain, along the sea. The daily ten-milers soon shed fifteen pounds of flab. His desire for Loulou was rekindled. His hands were on her, always and everywhere.

Their gallery, christened LoulouMac, sat on a sidestreet in the Marais a few blocks north of the Place des Vosges. To the left was a green-awninged café, his first stop every morning.

During the pleasant springtime months, the surveillant noted, Mac Mason had become a creature of habit: an unwise decision for a man of his profession. A stop at the café in the morning—same route—out for lunch—typically at one of three cafés, all within walking distance—

then out for painting, location variable here, no pattern, then back to the studio and home for aperitifs and intercourse by the dinner hour, like a good Parisian. Though in Mac's case, the logs noted, he made love only to Loulou. He did not spot the surveillance.

Operationally unawares, she wrote. Hazards of old age.

ON A BRIGHT SPRING MORNING, CAFÉ AU LAIT AND BRIOCHE in hand, Mac turned the key in the lock and pushed in the door to LouLouMac, heading straight for the studio in back. Loulou was down south with her mother for a run of shopping, leaving him with quality time to put the finishing touches on his current project: a reimagination of a cubist work he'd pursued before joining the Agency. He clicked open the studio door and turned on the lights.

The café au lait splattered onto the concrete, the brioche not far behind.

ARTEMIS APHRODITE PROCTER STOOD IN THE MIDDLE OF the studio. She wore a jacket, sweatshirt, jeans, and a beanie—all black. Her wild spray of hair was jammed in a hairnet. She wore gloves and booties over her shoes. She was pointing a Mossberg twelve-gauge semiautomatic shotgun at his head. A suppressor the size of a coffee can sat on the barrel.

She jerked the gun away from the door. "Two steps in, Macintosh. There's a good boy."

He was standing in front of a canvas that stretched from the floor to the ceiling. Bunch of red and black squares. She'd had to look at that damn thing all night, waiting in here. She fucking hated it.

"What are you doing?" he asked. "What do you want?" His eyes were flitting around, searching.

"Gonna make something clear up front, Mac," she said. "If you try to run, if you try to fight, I am going to kill you, and then—and I don't want to do this, Mac, god help me, I do not—but if you make me I am going to head to your apartment, wait for two days, and I'm going to kill Loulou when she returns from Avignon."

"Don't hurt Loulou," Mac said.

"Don't give me a reason."

"What do you want, Artemis?"

"You're going to confess to me, right now. In return, I spare Loulou, who's in on this, of course."

"You've got no proof of anything, Artemis," he said. "This is dumb. Don't be dumb."

"But I know," she said. "I fucking know. You were a double. I know it, and you know it. And you also know that I'm a woman of my word. I've walked this one to the end, which is why I'm here in your studio with a gun. You think that I won't skip over to your apartment and wait for Loulou to get back? You think I'll be merciful? Well, I've tossed restraint out the window since your freaks finally scored a direct hit and killed Sam. Loulou is your coconspirator here, as in all things. This I also know. She is fair game."

"She doesn't know anything."

A quick step forward, and Procter thrust the shotgun barrel into his stomach; he let out a sad grunt, fell to his knees, then curled into himself on the floor.

Procter wagged the gun, said: "Get up. Now."

He wiped his coffee-wet hands on his pants and stood slowly, clutching his stomach.

"I am going to try a theory on you," Procter said, "and you're going to answer me, truthfully and in the King's fucking English, because you're speaking for Loulou's life. Understand?"

The mask of his face offered a slow, reluctant nod.

"REMORA was never recruited," she said. "You and Theo were developing him in Paris, and he was developing you. He recruited you sometime at the tail end of that period, but ultimately you're being handled by a cat in Moscow named Zhomov. That right?"

Something shone in his eyes, but he looked away, and did not answer.

She leveled the gun at his foot. "That was a question. I don't get an answer, I give that foot the Finn Gosford special."

"Zhomov is a genius," Mac said.

"Groovy. So Zhomov's got Macintosh Mason, hotshot recruiter of Russians, on the line and his star is rising. You're the Chief of Ops in Russia House. I mean, the Russkies have *never* had someone so high up. And this is where, frankly, you and Zhomov blow my fucking mind, Macintosh. The patience. Restraining yourself from burning the entire Russia House stable. Sticks-and-bricks commo, I'd wager. No devices. Have that right?"

"Yes."

"And the Singapore debacle, when Sam was taken. Try on this version. You hear about Golikov from Gus. He calls you with the news on vacation, right? And immediately you're worried about what Golikov could be primed to share, so you leave Lou in the Adirondacks and hustle down to New York Station, where Gus is prepping Debs. You want to see with your own eyes what's come in. And it spooks the hell out of you. So you send a crash signal to Zhomov that results in REMORA asking for a meet, creating operational cover so you can get to France to talk it all through. But you've got a problem: Theo is coming to France, and lo and behold so is Debs. Debs you can kick to the end of the meeting, she doesn't want to do the work anyway. But Theo? Well, officially he's REMORA's handler now. But you need him away for a bit so you can speak freely with REMORA. What did you put in Theo's way to distract him, make him late to the meet and unwilling to tell me why? A Russian girl?"

"What else?" Mac said. "Budapest playbook. Zhomov took the initiative. Dropped a girl at a bar Theo frequents near Avignon and let his libido do the rest. Zhomov thought it would be helpful to have Theo in our debt." Mac's tone was cool and even; he was reciting dry facts from a history text.

"Whose idea was it to fuck with me in the months before I got fired?

You put those pictures in my office, didn't you? Ran a whisper campaign to rustle up all those ethics complaints? Were those your ideas or Zhomov's? Did you convince Debs to fire me?"

"Don't you think she was going to fire you anyway, Artemis? Come on."

"Who did it?"

Mac looked away from her, looked down.

She continued: "Was it Zhomov's idea to elevate you through the swap for Sam? Did he tap some goat officer in Vienna as bait for us, once the Russians had sweated Sam sufficiently and thought he didn't know squat? You designed the op, led the charge on the trade. You're a fucking hero. Zhomov's put you in prime position for a Seventh Floor slot in the next few years. Long game, as I said. How am I doing?"

"You're doing pretty well for a drunk, Artemis," he said. "Bravo."

Her laugh was a sad blend of hatred and genuine amusement. She went on, "So let's go through it, shall we, the destruction you wrought? You gave up two Russian assets, yes? BUCCANEER is dead. Leaves behind a young daughter. CLAW is missing, probably dead. Our Moscow officer's cats were butchered, and his wife, her name's Molly by the way, has PTSD. There's Golikov, of course: dismembered and carted home in a box. And then, when Sam and I started nipping at your heels, you called down their freaks on us. They tried to blow me to bits. The three dead former Support assets in France, well, that was the price you and your friends made us pay for confirming your treason. And now they've killed Sam, you fuck. You've killed him."

He clammed up at this part, looking down at the spilled coffee to avoid her eyes. He was wearing leather driving shoes, too-tight jeans rolled up at the hem, and a red sport coat over a white T-shirt with a matching white silk square peeking from the breast pocket. At first she hadn't noticed the stupid fucking getup. Now she couldn't look away.

"I helped get him back, didn't I?" Mac blurted out. "I sure as hell didn't kill him, Artemis. I didn't kill any of them."

Careful to keep the shotgun level, she removed an envelope from her other jacket pocket, dropped it on the floor, and kicked it his way.

"You are going to look at those pictures. Every one of them is someone you betrayed. You are going to study the photos like they are the fucking Gospels."

Reluctantly, he opened the folder. She had most of the pictures from Theo, though he did not know why she had wanted them. The stack began with BUCCANEER, CLAW, Golikov, and CIA headshots of the Kassab triplets. Mostly expressionless for those, she thought, Mac had made his peace with it, dangerous business and all, but he paused at Procter's blown-apart trailer, and stopped entirely at the first documenting Sam's murder, one of him sprawled across a blood-soaked bed. "She did it with a knife," Procter said.

"Enough," he said. "I didn't ask anyone to kill anybody."

She raised the gun. "Not enough. There are more. Keep going."

He leafed through more pictures, face settling into that blank mask.

And it sent a long ache running through Procter like a blade. There are two of him, she thought; someone else is in there with my old friend. Mac's thoughts had often been known to her. Not now. She had no clue what he was thinking.

"Feebs have pieced together that the freaks are Peter and Irene Venable, of Dallas, Texas, of all fucking places. Peter got himself killed at my trailer. Theo tells me Irene's got a few medals, a dacha, and a boyfriend with bushy Slavic brows. High on the hog, ensconced in the dark Russian woods. And this was *you*, Mac. The chain starts with you."

"I didn't do this." He let the pictures fall to the floor. A few fluttered into the coffee spill. His face darkened. "Why are you doing this for them, carrying their water, Artemis? After all they've done to you. Finn fucking Gosford pitched himself as a hero after Afghanistan. He's a fraud. A huckster mercenary cashing in on our sacrifices. And he fired you, Artemis. He and Debs sacrificed you for their glory."

Procter spat onto the floor. "We were friends, Macintosh, you and I."

"Yes," he said. "We are."

Eye contact was beginning to disgust her; she had to look up, toward the wall above him. "What's it been," she said, "four years since your old man died? Timing works, I'd say. Couldn't deal with the brute this side of eternity, could you? You never got his approval and you never told him to fuck off, either. So you had to tell him to fuck off after he was gone. How much did the Russians pay you, Macintosh?"

His nose wrinkled. He said nothing.

"You are going to do two things for me," she said. "Right now. You are going to write a note about what you've done. Short, punchy. To the point. I'll supervise, offer suggestions. And you are going to tell me where you hid the money. Or the diamonds. Or gold. However they paid. Start with the note." She jerked the gun toward a desk. "Go on, get."

He stood there, jaw set. He folded his arms across his chest. A whitish paste was forming at the corners of his mouth.

"Do it for Lou," she said. "You can still save Lou."

Mac shuffled to the desk. He wrote. Procter thought the second draft was good enough. "Leave it," she said, rumpling the first draft into her coat pocket. "Get up, there you go. Back to the wall. Now the money."

It took him a few moments to answer, and when he'd finished she said: "You will add a postscript to the note. Right fucking now."

"I don't know it all by heart Artemis."

"Bullshit. Gambling with Lou's life over blood money you don't need? Not so smart."

His look was now one of pure hate. He stomped back to the desk, scribbled down the information. Sweat was running down his face. He wiped it from his upper lip and hairline, twisting damp palms against his shirt while he wrote. Procter reviewed it, made him repeat it back to her a few times so she could watch his face. But would she have even the slightest hint if he was lying?

"You feel good about the trade?" she asked.

"I didn't do it for the money, Artemis. Please." His tone sharpened; his eyes darkened; his face contorted awfully. Then Mac started rambling out a convoluted fucking jumble of justifications: the mess with his dad, a frozen memory of his old man dangling him by his leg until he pissed himself; the failed paintings and Loulou—again he tried to sell the lie that she had no idea. He had turned to explain the cube painting thing behind him, waving his hands, spewing gobbledygook about how as a young man he'd believed art offered hope to the world, but in truth it could only make a statement about destruction. And he was just going on and fucking on, parading in front of his weird painting, and she wasn't sure how much more of this she could take; it was making her sick to look at him, to hear his voice, to smell him in her nostrils. "Shut up," she said. "Shut. The. Fuck. Up."

His attention twisted between her and the painting. He wiped his shining forehead. "You don't want to know why I did it?" he asked. "You don't care?"

"No," she said, "I don't."

Procter muttered something to herself, like an incantation. "In honor," she said. Then she squeezed the trigger.

The top half of Mac Mason's head sprayed across the canvas, the last strokes of his masterpiece painted by Artemis Aphrodite Procter in his own blood and brain.

61

LANGLEY / GENEVA FREEPORT MONTHS LATER

PROCTER WAS SPLAYED FACEDOWN ON THE BED, HER EARS filled with the sound of the tattoo gun buzzing. On the backside of her shut eyelids danced their faces and the places they'd died and the people she'd killed to avenge them.

The gun went silent. The tattooist ran a disinfectant wipe over the fresh ink; she heard the crinkle of a bandage wrapper opening. "You want to see?" he said.

Easing herself up, pointing her back to the mirror, Procter looked at the fresh black star and its five bloody points. It joined the other nine in a trail stretching from clavicle to clavicle.

She spoke to Sam through the star, all the things she never did say.

TEN PEOPLE, NINE MEN AND ONE WOMAN, STOOD BEFORE A vault door inside a nondescript warehouse on the grounds of the Geneva Freeport. The fountain on the lake outside was shooting blue water into an even bluer summer sky, but inside the Freeport the world managed only variations on black and gray. Doors, suits, carpets, curtains, floors: though these buildings housed billions of dollars' worth of colorful paintings, fine wines, glittering jewelry, and artifacts from antiquity, Lambert hadn't seen a color since they'd passed under the Swiss flag flying outside. What would have been the largest art gallery or wine cellar in the world was instead shrouded in the secrecy of gray.

Deborah Sweet, Lambert's boss and the only woman in this motley group, stood behind the gray-suited Freeport managing director in a long hallway lined by banks of double-locked gray doors, each leading to a separate vault. Behind Lambert huddled a pile of Swiss officials, and behind them was a crop of Feebs from Washington and Bern and Geneva, who were not as well dressed as the Swiss but had admirably managed to color-coordinate the gray. Only he and Sweet, the CIA contingent, stood out. Lambert for his navy-blue suit and red tie, she for her form-fitting sleeveless red dress and the chunky blue costume pearls coiled around her neck.

The CIA delegation had been so rushed this morning that Lambert had snatched only a few sips of coffee on the drive to the Freeport from Geneva Base. They'd made him surrender his cup to a trash bin upstairs in the customs offices before visiting the vaults downstairs, and Lambert was now craving a caffeine hit. He had slept so little in the month since the call from Paris had arrived. There had been a time when he'd comfortably managed to drink less than five cups of coffee each day. That world had vanished with the arrival of Mac Mason's suicide note. Lambert stifled a yawn.

The Freeport director punched his fingerprint onto the pad and swung open a set of doors. The group shuffled into a vault the size of a racquetball court, with shelves from floor to ceiling. They followed the Freeport director to the far end of the room, where he halted in front of a gray metallic box with the numbers 6.24.2 stenciled above a keypad. Lambert recognized the numbers from the transcribed suicide note and the search warrant they had served to the Swiss. The clank of the bolt sliding open carried through the room like a gunshot.

Two boxes were removed from the safe and slid onto a table in the room's center. The Freeport director opened the first box. Lambert, jostling here and there for a clean view, stole a peek inside. The box was felt-lined and dotted by perhaps two or three dozen shallow pits. Each was filled with diamonds. For a moment no one spoke. Later, Lambert would remember the tomblike silence and the feeling of nausea coiling in his throat.

"My god," he heard Sweet whisper. "I thought it was a prank."

ONE OF THE STRANGER REVERBERATIONS OF THE MASON affair concerned a woman Lambert had known only by reputation—and it was a colorful one. The most recent entry filed in his mind was that she'd vomited at the Director's table amid her involuntary retirement. Maybe a week after the trip to the Freeport, Sweet had asked him to contact the woman, a former case officer by the name of Artemis Procter, to invite her to Langley for a meeting. Normally one of his aides would have arranged the logistics, but on Sweet's explicit instruction, Lambert made the call himself. He began by explaining that the DDO wished to speak with Procter about "the Mason suicide." Sweet had insisted that he use those exact words when describing the meeting's purpose. The conversation that followed had been so singularly bizarre that he would later be able to replay it all, word for word:

"Put Debs on the line, then," Procter said.

"No, no. She wants to speak to you in person. Here at Langley."

"Just put her on the goddamn line."

"I . . . I can't. It's not that type of conversation."

"Well, now, that sounds awful."

"Uh . . . so, could you come up here on Thursday? For a one p.m.?"

"This a practical joke?"

"It is not."

"Thursday I got work. I'm covering the afternoon Jumparoos and I'm in the doghouse with my cousin-boss as it is."

"We would be happy to contact your employer and let them know that your presence is requested by the CIA's Deputy Director for Operations. Obviously, we will cover your travel."

"Look . . . uh . . . what's your name again?"

"Lambert."

"Did we know each other when I was on the inside, Lambert?"

"No. I'm afraid our paths never crossed."

"Well, look. I have history with Debs and also with Gosford, and it's mostly variations on a dumpster fire. But if Debs is sincere and wants me to come up to Langley, she will send down one of the Air Branch birds the Seventh Floor groupies use when flying in the States. I am willing to trek up to Orlando International Airport to meet the thing. Willing but not happy about it. That's my concession. A drive to Orlando. You—"

"Ms. Procter," Lambert interjected, "we will reimburse you for all expenses. I cannot—"

"Shut—"

"I cannot—"

"Shut up for—"

"Ms. Procter! I cannot. I—"

"Lambert. Lambert. Lambert . . ." She just repeated his name until he stopped trying to talk over her. The line went silent for a few moments. He heard the tinkle of ice into a glass.

"Phew," she piped in. "Where was I? Yes, the plane. You will tell your master Deborah Sweet that I will not kowtow to Langley unless you send the plane. And this is not about first cabin accommodation and pampering, understand? I'm no prima donna. I'm barely five feet tall, so I don't give a shit about leg room. And with you allegedly reimbursing my commercial travel, I also do not give a shit about the in-flight liquor charges. No, this is about my firm belief that it is well within the realm of possibility that I will fly to Washington, there will be no meeting, and I will be shafted with the bill. So, there you have it."

"I would be happy to book the tickets so that you do not incur any personal expenses."

"Go talk to Debs and call me back when the answer on the plane is yes."

When Lambert relayed her demand, the DDO's mouth twitched into an icy smile. Sweet's grim nod of approval signaled to Lambert that this was the sort of relationship in which minor concessions were extracted only through brutal warfare. Two days later the Bombardier duly collected the Procter woman from Orlando, and that afternoon she was sitting with Lambert outside Sweet's office. She was indeed short, but it was her hair that struck him. Jet-black, it was the curliest hair he had ever seen. Like a cartoon character who'd been plugged into an electrical socket. Inside the office, the only thing she'd said to Lambert was, "No chocolate muffins, huh?"

Before he could ask her what she meant, Sweet opened the door. He watched the two of them shake hands and stare each other down with some weird blend of disdain and amusement, as if they might stab each other to death and have a ball doing it. The DDO told Lambert to sit this one out. The woman went inside and Sweet shut the door.

The meeting had been scheduled for thirty minutes but went on for more than ninety. Lambert, whose office sat immediately across from Sweet's, heard yelling and shouting on two, maybe three occasions. Muffled voices were raised with some frequency. There were brief patches of laughter. At one point he swore he heard the clink of a glass. After the Procter woman had left, Lambert shuffled in to ask the DDO what, if anything, had come from the meeting. Were there to be follow-ups? Taskings to distribute? A hint of vodka floated on the air, and the empty table was decorated by two tiny paper parasols protruding from drained glasses standing proudly in rings of their own condensation. The DDO was seated at her desk scribbling in a notebook.

Lambert, who'd grown accustomed to his boss's moods and facial grammar, believed the meeting had left her both wildly agitated and thoroughly entertained. The corner of her left eyelid was twitching, a clear relic of her anger. But she was also smiling. It was a genuine, happy smile, and he had the impression that she did not even know she was doing it. He knew she could show both emotions, but he'd never seen her manage both at once. She waved him off. "I've got it," she said.

Less than six months in the DDO's office, and Lambert was already something of a meeting connoisseur: long and short, large and small, tense and happy, vapid and productive, he had seen it all. Though he knew little of the meeting's content beyond the DDO's vague subject line, its apparent chaos and the strange light now pouring from Sweet's face left him with the singular impression that something weighty had been turned over, and that Sweet and Procter had done the lifting together. He also knew that they had made decisions requiring Sweet to take action. After all, she was jotting down notes in her green notebook, the one she did not share with him.

Lambert saw Procter again about a month later. It was a flyby in the hallway, and he noticed her only because of her spray of hair. She now wore the blue badge of a full-time CIA employee, the lanyard of the China Mission Center, and a look of casual menace. They passed without acknowledgment.

His second sighting came months later during an intramural baseball game, when he was standing in at second base for the Screwdrivers of the Seventh Floor. Procter was playing center field for the Cold Warriors. That game, she hit an infield single in which she nearly bowled over the first basemen while sprinting it out down the line, and Lambert swore that when she slid into second on a hustle double in the bottom of the fifth, she'd gone in spikes up. He'd let the rage pass, remembering the conversation about the plane and the look in Sweet's eyes after their meeting. In the dugout, though, he had asked why she was playing with Raptis and Monk and the Russia House Cold Warriors, not the Dragons of the China Mission Center.

"I wouldn't press it," a guy named Tobin had called out from down the bench.

"Why's that?"

"Eh . . . I'd just leave her well alone."

The third Procter sighting was at the annual Memorial Ceremony in the spring. Only one star went up that year, and to the public the recipient was anonymous. Lambert, though, knew that it was for a former case officer named Sam Joseph, who'd been killed by the Russians in the Mason affair. Lambert had followed every detail of the investigation, but the part about the Russians murdering someone on U.S. soil had been so thoroughly compartmentalized that even he'd been left off the distro. Lambert only had Joseph's name and that flash of context because Sweet had overshared once, while planning for the event, grumbling that Artemis Procter had pointedly declined to speak at the closed, classified version of the ceremony for Sam. "What the hell is wrong with her, exactly?" Sweet had asked. "Twenty-five fucking years with her, and

I still don't know the answer." And Lambert hadn't known, either, nor was he read in on Sam Joseph, so he merely shrugged and they moved on to other business.

The Memorial Ceremony was a brisk affair, complete with the usual speeches at the Memorial Wall by Director Gosford and DDO Sweet. Lambert caught the spray of curly black hair out in the crowd, a few rows in front of him, legs crossed, face impassive when he managed to score a quick glance. She was sitting with Raptis and Monk from Russia House. She listened, expressionless, and left quickly after the ceremony.

Later, when the DDO was meeting with Sam's family, he asked one of the SAs about Procter.

"Oh sure," the SA said, still facing his computer screen. "Chief of Moscow X once upon a time, right? She's done a bunch of spooky stuff against the Russians. She was Chief in Damascus back in the day. Few other places."

"I heard," Lambert said, "that the Russians tried to blackmail her. Put some rather revealing pictures on the web. They say she nearly killed the Russian pitching her."

"Sounds made up," the SA said, and paused. "But they do call her the Angel of Death, you know."

"You're kidding."

"There are stories," the SA whispered, now turning to face Lambert. "From Afghanistan. From Syria. You kill one of ours, she kills you. She has the stars tattooed on her back. One for each officer avenged. But, I mean, come on. Those are probably just rumors, right?"

THAT EVENING LAMBERT RODE THE ELEVATOR DOWN FROM the Seventh Floor for a smoke in the courtyard, tracing a meandering path that took him through the hallway near the lobby. He saw the curly hair peeking out from behind a column as he approached. She was facing the Memorial Wall, and, from his vantage, seemed very close to it, along the far end with the newest stars. Lambert considered stopping for a look, but he did not have anything to say to her, and he did not want to risk being spotted. Walking by, he looked down the steps and snatched one brief, clean glance of Artemis Aphrodite Procter through the columns. She had a hand extended to touch the newly etched star. He thought her lips were moving, but he could not be certain. A column had broken his view, and she was gone.

ACKNOWLEDGMENTS

THE THIRD ONE CAME A LITTLE EASIER THAN THE SECond. But not by much. As with the first two novels, this book only exists because it had so many friends helping the story (and its author) along the way.

Spy fiction aficionados will note that *The Seventh Floor* tips its hat on occasion to John le Carré's exceptional novel *Tinker Tailor Soldier Spy.* Like Le Carré, the essential double-cross at the heart of my story draws on the success seen by the British secret services during World War II, when its famed "Double-Cross System" managed to flip the entirety of the German spy network in Britain for the purposes of feeding disinformation to the Nazi High Command. For intrepid readers looking for more, I recommend the interesting—but admittedly dense—*Double Cross System*, written by, J. C. Masterman, one of its chief strategists. Hundreds of additional books and articles were consulted while writing this novel, too many to name here, but suffice it to say that aspiring Dermatologists seeking an education in the dark arts of mole-hunting should find no shortage of material. One need only search the name of a famous, or infamous, traitor, and you're off to the races.

I am supremely grateful to my agent, Lisa Erbach Vance, who sagely shepherded the novel through the perilous and uncertain journey from unruly Word document to finished book.

Tremendous thanks to my editor at Norton, Star Lawrence, who continues to bet on me and who sharpens my writing and storytelling with each novel.

I am indebted to the team at Norton: Nneoma Amadi-obi, who expertly wrangles it all; Dave Cole for his keen eye on the manuscript; Kyle Radler and Steve Colca for getting the word out.

To Mark Richards, Diana Broccardo, the indomitable Lisa Shakespeare, and Rachel Nobilo at Swift Press, for launching my books and spreading the word across the Atlantic, and for several exceptional bottles of Domaine de Bargylus whilst in London: thank you. Tremendous thanks also to Caspian Dennis, who makes it all happen across the pond.

Bill and Lorenzo served as field guides to Las Vegas, the habits and habitat of the high roller, and also generously shared many of the stories that comprise Frankie, Sam, and Procter's wild night out on the town. Here in the real world, more than a year on from that Vegas visit, and I have barely recovered from the whirlwind tour.

Dave Michael again submerged the writing in a world of pain, and the story is so much better for it. Thank you, Dave.

Former CIA comrades graciously contributed time and insight to this novel: Glenn Chafetz, John Sipher, and Mark Pascale helped this unreformed analyst navigate the world of modern-day tradecraft and counterespionage. Don Hepburn again advised on all manner of CIA tradecraft, Marc Polymeropoulos offered a groaning portfolio of Agency prank stories and his war zone experiences. Charles Finfrock had extremely useful insight on the brave new(ish) world of ubiquitous technical surveillance. Steve Slick, Lizzy M., Anna Connolly, and Christina Hillsberg generously read early drafts and provided invaluable comments and insight. Several other former colleagues and friends, nameless here, shared their insights and experiences and read early drafts. As always, all lapses in operational wisdom and tradecraft are my own.

Jan Neumann, a former FSB officer, yet again helped me ensure I didn't mess up Moscow, the Russian, or the secret services too badly.

Frank Montoya read several versions of the manuscript, offered wise counsel on all things Feeb, and saved me from numerous forensic errors.

Jenny Green called a spade a spade and told me plainly what needed fixing. I am grateful for a frank conversation in a Galveston kitchen that helped put the story on the right path.

Mike Green again served as the book's resident doctor—thank you for your counsel on all manner of calamities and illnesses, from the strain of a rough interrogation to hemorrhoids.

Thanks are also due to Joe L. for his help designing Peter and Irene's choice of weaponry, and to Gordon Corera for his insights on Russian illegals.

Several other dear friends read versions of this novel and offered help along the way. Kent Woodyard, Erin Yerger, Becky Friedman, Jaclyn Edwards, Alex Blackwell: all took the time to read and offer helpful feedback and encouragement.

As always I must give my love to my children, Miles, Leo, and Mabel, who, to this author's tremendous relief, are not yet interested in books without pictures.

Finally, and most importantly, my deepest love and gratitude goes to my wife, Abby. She is my first reader, greatest champion, fiercest (and most loving) critic, and most wonderfully prescient muse. The book simply would not exist without her.